Penelope Fitzgerald is the
author, most recently, of *The Blue Flower*,
a national best-seller in its Mariner edition.
Her first novel, *The Golden Child*, was
published in 1977, and of the
eight that have followed, three have been
shortlisted for the Booker Prize —
The Bookshop, The Beginning of Spring, and
The Gate of Angels. She won the prize
in 1979 for *Offshore*.

"The finest British writer alive."

— *Los Angeles Times Book Review*

"Fitzgerald writes with a mysterious clarity nobody else approaches."
— A. S. BYATT

"Where some writers like to build effects slowly, Fitzgerald prefers a quicksilver economy. Vivid . . . elegant . . . astonishing."
— *Washington Post Book World*

"The compression of her characterization is extraordinary; she can sum people up in a single sentence that begs as many questions as it answers but is worth pages of analysis."
— VICTORIA GLENDINNING

"[Her] dry, shrewd, sympathetic, and sharply economical books are almost disreputably enjoyable . . . Fugitive scraps of insight and information — like single brushstrokes of vivid and true colors — convey more reality than any amount of impasto description and research. In Mrs. Fitzgerald's novels you can breathe the air and taste the water."
— *New York Times Book Review*

The Bookshop

Books by Penelope Fitzgerald

Fiction

THE GOLDEN CHILD

THE BOOKSHOP

OFFSHORE

HUMAN VOICES

AT FREDDIE'S

INNOCENCE

THE BEGINNING OF SPRING

THE GATE OF ANGELS

THE BLUE FLOWER

Nonfiction

EDWARD BURNE-JONES

THE KNOX BROTHERS

CHARLOTTE MEW
AND HER FRIENDS

Penelope Fitzgerald

The Bookshop

A MARINER ORIGINAL
HOUGHTON MIFFLIN COMPANY
BOSTON • NEW YORK

FIRST U.S. EDITION
September 1997

First published in Great Britain in 1978
by Gerald Duckworth & Co. Ltd.

Published by arrangement with Flamingo,
an imprint of HarperCollins Publishers

For information about permission to reproduce
selections from this book, write to Permissions,
Houghton Mifflin Company, 215 Park
Avenue South, New York, New York 10003.

Library of Congress Cataloging-in-Publication Data

Fitzgerald, Penelope.
The bookshop / Penelope Fitzgerald.
— 1st U.S. ed.
p. cm.
"A Mariner original."
ISBN 0-395-86946-3
I. Title.
PR6056.I86B66 1997
823'.914 — dc21   97-25389 CIP

Printed in the United States of America

QUM 10 9 8 7 6 5

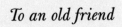

To an old friend

The Bookshop

1

In 1959 Florence Green occasionally passed a night when she was not absolutely sure whether she had slept or not. This was because of her worries as to whether to purchase a small property, the Old House, with its own warehouse on the foreshore, and to open the only bookshop in Hardborough. The uncertainty probably kept her awake. She had once seen a heron flying across the estuary and trying, while it was on the wing, to swallow an eel which it had caught. The eel, in turn, was struggling to escape from the gullet of the heron and appeared a quarter, a half, or occasionally three-quarters of the way out. The indecision expressed by both creatures was pitiable. They had taken on too much. Florence felt that if she hadn't slept at all – and people often say this when they mean nothing of the kind – she must have been kept awake by thinking of the heron.

She had a kind heart, though that is not of much use when it comes to the matter of self-preservation. For more than eight years of half a lifetime she had lived at Hardborough on the very small amount of money her late husband had left her and had recently come to wonder whether she hadn't a duty to make it clear to herself, and possibly to others, that she existed in her own right. Survival was often considered all that could be asked in the cold and clear East Anglian air. Kill or cure, the inhabitants thought – either a long old age, or immediate consignment to the salty turf of the churchyard.

She was in appearance small, wispy and wiry, somewhat insignificant from the front view, and totally so from the back. She was not much talked about, not even in Hardborough, where everyone could be seen coming over the wide distances and everything seen was discussed. She made small seasonal changes in what she wore. Everybody knew her winter coat, which was the kind that might just be made to last another year.

In 1959, when there was no fish and chips in Hardborough, no launderette, no cinema except on alternate Saturday nights, the need of all these things was felt, but no one had considered, certainly had not thought of Mrs Green as considering, the opening of a bookshop.

'Of course I can't make any definite commitment on behalf of the bank at the moment – the decision is not in my hands – but I think I may say that there will be no objection in principle to a loan. The Government's word up to now has been restraint in credit to the private borrower, but there are distinct signs of relaxation – I'm not giving away any state secrets there. Of course, you'll have little or no competition – a few novels, I'm told, lent out at the Busy Bee wool shop, nothing significant. You assure me that you've had considerable experience of the trade.'

Florence, preparing to explain for the third time what she meant by this, saw herself and her friend, their hair in Eugene waves, chained pencils round their necks, young assistants of twenty-five years ago at Müller's in Wigmore Street. It was the stocktaking she remembered best, when Mr Müller, after calling for silence, read out with calculated delay the list of young ladies and their partners, drawn by lot, for the day's checking over. There were by no means enough fellows to go round, and she had been lucky to be paired, in 1934, with Charlie Green, the poetry buyer.

'I learned the business very thoroughly when I was a girl,' she said. 'I don't think it's changed in essentials since then.'

'But you've never been in a managerial position. Well,

8

there are one or two things that might be worth saying. Call them words of advice, if you will.'

There were very few new enterprises in Hardborough, and the notion of one, like a breath of sea air far inland, faintly stirred the sluggish atmosphere of the bank.

'I mustn't take up your time, Mr Keble.'

'Oh, you must allow me to be judge of that. I think I might put it in this way. You must ask yourself, when you envisage yourself opening a bookshop, what your objective really is. That is the first question needful to a business of any kind. Do you hope to give our little town a service that it needs? Do you hope for sizeable profits? Or are you, perhaps, Mrs Green, a jogger along, with little understanding of the vastly different world which the 1960s may have in store for us? I've often thought that it's a pity that there isn't some accepted course of study for the small business man or woman . . .'

Evidently there was an accepted course for bank managers. Launched on the familiar current, Mr Keble's voice gathered pace, with the burden of many waters. He spoke of the necessity of professional book-keeping, systems of loan repayment, and opportunity costs.

'. . . I would like to put a point, Mrs Green, which in all probability has not occurred to you, and yet which is so plain to those of us who are in a position to take the broader view. My point is this. *If over any given period of time the cash inflow cannot meet the cash outflow, it is safe to predict that money difficulties are not far away.*'

Florence had known this ever since her first payday, when, at the age of sixteen, she had become self-supporting. She prevented herself from making a sharp reply. What had become of her resolve, as she crossed the market place to the bank building, whose solid red brick defied the prevailing wind, to be sensible and tactful?

'As to the stock, Mr Keble, you know that I've been given

the opportunity of buying most of what I need from Müller's, now that they're closing down.' She managed to say this resolutely, although she had felt the closure as a personal attack on her memories. 'I've had no estimate for that as yet. And as to the premises, you agreed that £3,500 was a fair price for the freehold of the Old House and the oyster shed.'

To her surprise, the manager hestitated.

'The property has been standing empty for a long time now. That is, of course, a matter for your house agent and your solicitor – Thornton, isn't it?' This was an artistic flourish, a kind of weakness, since there were only two solicitors in Hardborough. 'But I should have thought the price might have come down further . . . The house won't walk away if you decide to wait a little . . . deterioration . . . damp . . .'

'The bank is the only building in Hardborough which isn't damp,' Florence replied. 'Working here all day may perhaps have made you too demanding.'

'. . . and then I've heard it suggested – I'm in a position where I can say that I understand it may have been suggested – that there are other uses to which the house might be put – though of course there is always the possibility of a re-sale.'

'Naturally I want to reduce expenses to a minimum.' The manager prepared to smile understandingly, but spared himself the trouble when Florence added sharply 'But I've no intention of re-selling. It's a peculiar thing to take a step forward in middle age, but having done it I don't intend to retreat. What else do people think the Old House could be used for? Why haven't they done anything about it in the past seven years? There were jackdaws nesting in it, half the tiles were off, it stank of rats. Wouldn't it be better as a place where people could stand and look at books?'

'Are you talking about culture?' the manager said, in a voice half way between pity and respect.

10

'Culture is for amateurs. I can't run my shop at a loss. Shakespeare was a professional!'

It took less than it should have done to fluster Florence, but at least she had the good fortune to care deeply about something. The manager replied soothingly that reading took up a great deal of time. 'I only wish I had more time at my disposal. People have quite wrong ideas, you know, about the bank's closing hours. Speaking personally, I enjoy very little leisure in the evenings. But don't misunderstand me, I find a good book at my bedside of incalculable value. When I eventually retire I've no sooner read a few pages than I'm overwhelmed with sleep.'

She reflected that at this rate one good book would last the manager for more than a year. The average price of a book was twelve shillings and sixpence. She sighed.

She did not know Mr Keble at all well. Few people in Hardborough did. Although they were constantly told, by press and radio, that these were prosperous years for Britain, most of Hardborough still felt the pinch, and avoided the bank manager on principle. The herring catch had dwindled, naval recruitment was down, and there were many retired persons living on a fixed income. These did not return Mr Keble's smile or his wave out of the hastily wound-down window of his Austin Cambridge. Perhaps this was why he went on talking for so long to Florence, although the discussion was scarcely businesslike. Indeed it had reached, in his view, an unacceptably personal level.

Florence Green, like Mr Keble, might be accounted a lonely figure, but this did not make them exceptional in Hardborough, where many were lonely. The local naturalists, the reedcutter, the postman, Mr Raven the marshman, bicycled off one by one, leaning against the wind, the observed of all observers, who could reckon the time by their reappearance over the horizon. Not all of these solitaries even went out.

Mr Brundish, a descendant of one of the most ancient Suffolk families, lived as closely in his house as a badger in its sett. If he emerged in summer, wearing tweeds between dark green and grey, he appeared a moving gorse-bush against the gorse, or earth against the silt. In autumn he went to ground. His rudeness was resented only in the same way as the weather, brilliant in the morning, clouding over later, however much it had promised.

The town itself was an island between sea and river, muttering and drawing into itself as soon as it felt the cold. Every fifty years or so it had lost, as though careless or indifferent to such things, another means of communication. By 1850 the Laze had ceased to be navigable and the wharfs and ferries rotted away. In 1910 the swing bridge fell in, and since then all traffic had to go ten miles round by Saxford in order to cross the river. In 1920 the old railway was closed. The children of Hardborough, waders and divers all, had most of them never been in a train. They looked at the deserted LNER station with superstitious reverence. Rusty tin strips, advertising Fry's Cocoa and Iron Jelloids, hung there in the wind.

The great floods of 1953 caught the sea wall and caved it in, so that the harbour mouth was dangerous to cross, except at very low tide. A rowing-boat was now the only way to get across the Laze. The ferryman chalked up his times for the day on the door of his shed, but this was on the far shore, so that no one in Hardborough could ever be quite certain when they were.

After her interview with the bank, and resigned to the fact that everyone in the town knew that she had been there, Florence went for a walk. She crossed the wooden planks across the dykes, preceded as she tramped by a rustling and splashing as small creatures, she didn't know of what kind, took to the water. Overhead the gulls and rooks sailed confidently on the tides of the air. The wind had shifted and was blowing inshore.

Above the marshes came the rubbish tip, and then the rough fields began, just good enough for the farmers to fence. She heard her name called, or rather she saw it, since the words were blown away instantly. The marshman was summoning her.

'Good morning, Mr Raven.' That couldn't be heard either.

Raven acted, when no other help was at hand, as a kind of supernumerary vet. He was in the Council field, where the grazing was let out at five shillings a week to whoever would take it, and at the extreme opposite end stood an old chestnut gelding, a Suffolk Punch, its ears turning delicately like pegs on its round poll in the direction of the human beings in its territory. It held its ground suspiciously, with stiffened legs, against the fence.

When she got within five yards of Raven, she understood that he was asking for the loan of her raincoat. His own clothes were rigid, layer upon layer, and not removable on demand.

Raven never asked for anything unless it was absolutely necessary. He accepted that coat with a nod, and while she stood keeping as warm as she could in the lee of the thorn hedge, he walked quietly across the field to the intensely watching old beast. It followed every movement with flaring nostrils, satisfied that Raven was not carrying a halter, and refusing to stretch its comprehension any further. At last it had to decide whether to understand or not, and a deep shiver, accompanied by a sigh, ran through it from nose to tail. Then its head drooped, and Raven put one of the sleeves of the raincoat round its neck. With a last gesture of independence, it turned its head aside and pretended to look for new grass in the damp patch under the fence. There was none, and it followed the marshman awkwardly down the field, away from the indifferent cattle, towards Florence.

13

'What's wrong with him, Mr Raven?'

'He eats, but he's not getting any good out of the grass. His teeth are blunted, that's the reason. He tears up the grass, but that doesn't get masticated.'

'What can we do, then?' she asked with ready sympathy.

'I can fare to file them,' the marshman replied. He took a halter out of his pocket and handed back the raincoat. She turned into the wind to button herself into her property. Raven led the old horse forward.

'Now, Mrs Green, if you'd catch hold of the tongue. I wouldn't ask everybody, but I know you don't frighten.'

'*How* do you know?' she asked.

'They're saying that you're about to open a bookshop. That shows you're ready to chance some unlikely things.'

He slipped his finger under the loose skin, hideously wrinkled, above the horse's jawbone and the mouth gradually opened in an extravagant yawn. Towering yellow teeth stood exposed. Florence seized with both hands the large slippery dark tongue, smooth above, rough beneath, and, like an old-time whaler, hung gamely on to it to lift it clear of the teeth. The horse now stood sweating quietly, waiting for the end. Only its ears twitched to signal a protest at what life had allowed to happen to it. Raven began to rasp away with a large file at the crowns of the side teeth.

'Hang on, Mrs Green. Don't you relax your efforts. That's slippery as sin I know.'

The tongue writhed like a separate being. The horse stamped with one foot after another, as though doubting whether they all still touched the ground.

'He can't kick forwards, can he, Mr Raven?'

'He can if he likes.' She remembered that a Suffolk Punch can do anything, except gallop.

'Why do you think a bookshop is unlikely?' she shouted into the wind. 'Don't people want to buy books in Hardborough?'

14

'They've lost the wish for anything of a rarity,' said Raven, rasping away. 'There's many more kippers sold, for example, than bloaters that are half-smoked and have a more delicate flavour. Now you'll tell me, I dare say, that books oughtn't to be a rarity.'

Once released, the horse sighed cavernously and stared at them as though utterly disillusioned. From the depths of its noble belly came a brazen note, more like a trumpet than a horn, dying away to a snicker. Clouds of dust rose from its body, as though from a beaten mat. Then, dismissing the whole matter, it trotted to a safe distance and put down its head to graze. A moment later it caught sight of a patch of bright green angelica and began to eat like a maniac.

Raven declared that the old animal would not know itself, and would feel better. Florence could not honestly say the same of herself, but she had been trusted, and that was not an everyday experience in Hardborough.

2

The property which Florence had determined to buy had not been given its name for nothing. Although scarcely any of the houses, until you got out to the half-built council estate to the north-west, were new, and many dated from the eighteenth and nineteenth centuries, none of them compared with the Old House, and only Holt House, Mr Brundish's place, was older. Built five hundred years ago out of earth, straw, sticks and oak beams, the Old House owed its survival to a flood cellar down a flight of stone steps. In 1953 the cellar had carried seven foot of seawater until the last of the floods had subsided. On the other hand, some of the seawater was still there.

Inside was the large front room, the backhouse kitchen, and upstairs a bedroom under a sloping ceiling. Not adjoining, but two streets away on the foreshore, stood the oyster shed which went with the property and which she had hoped to use as a warehouse for the reserve stock. But it turned out that the plaster had been mixed, for convenience sake, with sand from the beach, and sea sand never dries out. Any books left there would be wrinkled with damp in a few days. Her disappointment, however, endeared her to the shop-keepers of Hardborough. They had all known better, and could have told her so. They felt a shift in the balance of intellectual power, and began to wish her well.

Those who had lived in Hardborough for some time also knew that her freehold was haunted. The subject was not avoided, it was a familiar one. The figure of a woman, for example, could sometimes be seen down at the landing-stage

16

of the ferry, about twilight, waiting for her son to come back, although he had been drowned over a hundred years ago. But the Old House was not haunted in a touching manner. It was infested by a poltergeist which, together with the damp and an unsolved question about the drains, partly accounted for the difficulty in selling the property. The house agent was in no way legally bound to mention the poltergeist, though he perhaps alluded to it in the phrase *unusual period atmosphere*.

Poltergeists, in Hardborough, were called rappers. They might go on for years, then suddenly stop, but no one who had heard the noise, with its suggestion of furious physical frustration, as though whatever was behind it could not get out, was ever likely to mistake it for anything else. 'Your rapper's been at my adjustable spanners,' said the plumber, without rancour, when she came to see how the work was going forward. His tool bag had been upended and scattered; pale blue tiles with a nice design of waterlilies had been flung broadside about the upstairs passage. The bathroom, with its water supply half connected, had the alert air of having witnessed something. When the well-disposed plumber had gone to his tea, she shut the bathroom door, waited a few moments, and then looked sharply in again. Anyone watching her, she reflected, might have thought she was mad. The word in Hardborough for 'mad' was 'not quite right', just as 'very ill' was 'moderate'. 'Perhaps I'll end up not quite right if this goes on,' she told the plumber, wishing he wouldn't call it 'your rapper'. The plumber, Mr Wilkins, thought that she would weather it.

It was on occasions like this that she particularly missed the good friends of her early days at Müller's. When she had come in and taken off her suede glove to show her engagement ring, a diamond chip, there had been a heteningly long list of names on the subscription list for her present, and it was almost the same list when Charlie had died of pneumonia in an improvised reception camp at the beginning of the war. Nearly all the girls in Mailing, Despatch and Counter Staff had lost touch; and even when she had their addresses, she found herself unwilling to admit that they had grown as old as she had.

It was not that she was short of acquaintances in Hardborough. At Rhoda's Dressmaker's, for example, she was well liked. But her confidence was hardly respected. Rhoda – that is to say, Jessie Welford – who had been asked to make her up a new dress, did not hesitate to speak about it freely, and even to show the material.

'It's for General and Mrs Gamart's party at The Stead. I don't know that I'd've chosen red myself. They've guests coming down from London.'

Florence, although she knew Mrs Gamart to nod to, and to be smiled at by, after various collections for charity, had never expected to be invited to The Stead. She took it, even though none of her stock had arrived as yet from London, as a compliment to the power of books themselves.

As soon as Sam Wilkins had fixed the bath to his own satisfaction, and the tiles were re-pegged on the roof, Florence Green moved out of her flat and boldly took up residence, with her few things, at the Old House. Even with the waterlily tiles firmly hung, it was not an altogether reassuring place to live. The curious sounds associated with the haunting continued at night, long after the ill-connected water pipes had fallen silent. But courage and endurance are useless if they are never tested. She only hoped that there would be no interruption when Jessie Welford brought the new dress in for a fitting. But this particular ordeal never arose. A message came, asking her to try on at Rhoda's, next door.

'I think perhaps it's not my colour after all. Would you call it ruby?' It was a comfort when Jessie said that it was more like a garnet, or a deep rust. But there was something unsatisfactory in the red, or rust, reflexion which seemed to move unwillingly in the looking-glass.

'It doesn't seem to fit at all at the back. Perhaps if I try to stand against the wall most of the time . . .'

'It'll come to you as you wear it,' the dressmaker replied firmly. 'You need a bit of costume jewellery as a focus.'

'Are you sure?' asked Florence. The fitting seemed to be turning into a conspiracy to prevent anyone noticing her new dress at all.

'I dare say, when all's said and done, I'm more used to dressing up and going out in the evening than you are,' said Miss Welford. 'I'm a bridge player, you know. Not much doing here – I go over to Flintmarket twice a week. A penny a hundred in the mornings, and twopence a hundred in the evenings. We wear long skirts then, of course.'

She walked backwards a couple of steps, throwing a shadow over the glass, then returned to pin and adjust. No change, Florence knew, would make her look anything but small.

'I wish I wasn't going to this party,' she said.

'Well, I wouldn't mind taking your place. It's a pity Mrs Gamart sees fit to order everything from London, but it will be properly done – no need to stand and count the sandwiches. And when you get there, you won't have to bother about how you look. Nobody will mind you, and anyway you'll find you know everyone in the room.'

Florence had felt sure she would not, and she did not. The Stead, in any case, was not the kind of place where hats and coats were left about in the hall so that you could guess, before committing yourself to an entrance, who was already there. The hall, boarded with polished elm, breathed the deep warmth of a house that has never been cold. She caught a glimpse of herself in a glass much more brilliant than Rhoda's, and wished that she had not worn red.

Through the door ahead unfamiliar voices could be heard from a beautiful room, painted in the pale green which at that time the Georgian Society still recommended. Silver photograph frames on the piano and on small tables permitted a glimpse of the network of family relations which gave Violet Gamart an access to power far beyond Hardborough itself. Her husband, the General, was opening drawers and cupboards with the object of not finding anything, to give him an excuse to wander from room to room. In the 1950s there were many plays on the London stage where the characters made frequent entrances and exits out of various doors and were seen again in the second act, three hours later. The General would have fitted well into such a play. He hovered, alert and experimentally smiling, among the refreshments, hoping that he would soon be needed, even if only for a few moments, since opening champagne is not woman's work.

There was no bank manager there, no Vicar, not even Mr Thornton, Florence's solicitor, or Mr Drury, the solicitor who was not her solicitor. She recognized the back of the rural dean, and that was all. It was a party for the county, and for visitors from London. She correctly guessed that she would find out in time why she herself had been asked.

The General, relieved to see a smallish woman who did not appear to be intimidating or a relation of his wife's, gave her a large glass of champagne from one of the dozen he had opened. If she was not a relation of his wife's there were no elementary blunders to be made, but although he felt certain he had seen her somewhere before, God knew who she was exactly. She followed his thoughts, which, indeed, were transparent in their dogged progress from one difficulty to another, and told him that she was the person who was going to open a bookshop.

'That's it, of course. Got it in one. You're thinking of opening a bookshop. Violet was interested in it. She wanted to have one or two of those words of hers with you about it. I expect she'll have a chance later.'

Since Mrs Gamart was the hostess, she could have had this chance at any time, but Florence did not deceive herself about her own importance. She drank some of the champagne, and the smaller worries of the day seemed to stream upwards as tiny pinpricks through the golden mouthfuls and to break harmlessly and vanish.

She had expected the General to feel that his duty was discharged, but he lingered.

'What kind of stuff are you going to have in your shop?' he asked.

She scarcely knew how to answer him.

'They don't have many books of poetry these days, do they?' he persisted. 'I don't see many of them about.'

'I shall have some poetry, of course. It doesn't sell quite as well as some other things. But it will take time to get to know all the stock.'

The General looked surprised. It had never taken him a long time, as a subaltern, to get to know all his men.

'"It is easy to be dead. Say only this, they are dead." Do you know who wrote that?'

She would dearly have liked to have been able to say yes, but couldn't. The faltering light of expectancy in the General's eyes died down. Clearly he had tried to make this point before, perhaps many times. In a voice so low that against the noise of the party that sipped and clattered round them she could only just hear it, he went on:

'Charles Sorley . . .'

She realized at once that Sorley must be dead.

'How old was he?'

'Sorley? He was twenty. He was in the Swedebashers – the Suffolks, you know – 9th Battalion, B Company. He was killed in the battle of Loos, in 1915. He'd have been sixty-four years old if he'd lived. I'm sixty-four myself. That makes me think of poor Sorley.'

The General shuffled away into the mounting racket. Florence was alone, surrounded by people who spoke to each other familiarly, and some of whom could be seen in replica in the silver frames. Who were they all? She didn't mind; for, after all, they would have felt lost in their turn if they had found their way into the Mailing Department at Müller's. A mild young man's voice said from just behind her, 'I know who you are. You must be Mrs Green.'

He wouldn't say that, she thought, unless he was sure of being recognized himself, and she did recognize him. Everybody in Hardborough could have told you who he was, in a sense proudly, because he was known to drive up to London to work, and to be something in TV. He was Milo North, from Nelson Cottage, on the corner of Back Lane. Exactly what he did was uncertain, but Hardborough was used to not being quite certain what people did in London.

Milo North was tall, and went through life with singularly little effort. To say 'I know who you are, you must be Mrs Green' represented an unaccustomed output of energy. What seemed delicacy in him was usually a way of avoiding trouble; what seemed like sympathy was the instinct to prevent trouble before it started. It was hard to see what growing older would mean to such a person. His emotions, from lack of exercise, had disappeared almost altogether. Adaptability and curiosity, he had found, did just as well.

'I know who you are, of course, Mr North,' she said, 'but I've never had an invitation to The Stead before. I expect you come here often.'

'I'm asked here often,' said Milo. He gave her another glass of champagne, and having expected to be left indefinitely by herself after the retreat of the General, she was grateful.

22

'You're very kind.'

'Not very,' said Milo, who rarely said anything that was not true. Gentleness is not kindness. His fluid personality tested and stole into the weak places of others until it found it could settle down to its own advantage. 'You live by yourself, don't you? You've just moved into the Old House all by yourself? Haven't you ever thought of marrying again?'

Florence felt confused. It seemed to her that she was becalmed with this young man in some backwater, while louder voices grew more incoherent beyond. Time seemed to move faster there. Plates that had been full of sandwiches and crowned with parsley when she came in now held nothing but crumbs.

'I was very happily married, since you ask,' she said. 'My husband used to work in the same place as I did. Then he went into the old Board of Trade, before it became a Ministry. He used to tell me about his work when he came home in the evenings.'

'And you were happy?'

'I loved him, and I tried to understand his work. It sometimes strikes me that men and women aren't quite the right people for each other. Something must be, of course.'

Milo looked at her more closely.

'Are you sure you're well advised to undertake the running of a business?' he asked.

'I've never met you before, Mr North, but I've felt that because of your work you might welcome a bookshop in Hardborough. You must meet writers at the BBC, and thinkers, and so forth. I expect they come down here sometimes to see you, and to get some fresh air.'

'If they did I shouldn't quite know what to do with them. Writers will go anywhere, I'm not sure about thinkers. Kattie would look after them, I expect, though.'

Kattie must certainly be the dark girl in red stockings – or perhaps they were tights, which were now obtainable in

23

Lowestoft and Flintmarket, though not in Hardborough –
who lived with Milo North. They were the only unmarried
couple living together in the town. But Kattie, who was also
known to work for the BBC, only came down three nights a
week, on Mondays, Wednesdays, and Fridays, which was
thought to make it a little more respectable.

'It's a pity that Kattie couldn't be here tonight.'

'But it's Wednesday!' Mrs Green exclaimed, in spite of
herself.

'I didn't say she wasn't down here, only that it was a pity
that she couldn't come. She couldn't come because I didn't
bring her. I thought it might cause more trouble than it was
worth.'

Mrs Green thought that he ought to have had the courage
of his convictions. Her notion was of a young couple defying
the world. She herself was older, and had the right to anxiety.

'At any rate, you must come to my shop,' she said. 'I shall
rely on you.'

'On no account,' Milo replied.

He took her by both elbows, the lightest possible touch,
and shook her by way of emphasis.

'Why are you wearing red this evening?' he asked.

'It isn't red! It's garnet, or deep rust!'

Mrs Violet Gamart, the natural patroness of all public
activities in Hardborough, came towards them. Although
her back had been turned, she had noticed the shake but felt
that it was suggestive of the freedom of the arts and therefore
not out of place in her drawing-room. The moment, however,
had come for her to have a few words with Mrs Green. She
explained that she had been attempting to do this all evening,
but had been repeatedly spirited away. So many people
seemed to have come, but most of them she could see at any
time. What she really wanted to say was how grateful
everyone must feel about this new venture, such foresight
and enterprise.

24

Mrs Gamart spoke with a kind of generous urgency. She had dark bright eyes which appeared to be kept open, as though by some mechanism, to their widest extent.

'Bruno! Have you been introduced to my husband? Come and tell Mrs – Mrs – how delighted we all are.'

Florence felt a muddled sense of vocation, as though she would willingly devote her life to the service of Mrs Gamart.

'Bruno!'

The General had been trying to call attention to an abrasion on his hand, caused by the twisted wire on one of the champagne corks. He went up to every group of guests in turn, hoping to raise a smile by referring to himself as walking wounded.

'We've all been praying for a good bookshop in Hardborough, haven't we, Bruno?'

Glad to be summoned, he halted towards her.

'Of course, my dear, no harm in praying. Probably be a good thing if we all did more of it.'

'There's only one point, Mrs Green, a small one in a way – you haven't actually moved into the Old House yet, have you?'

'Yes, I've been there for more than a week.'

'Oh, but there's no water.'

'Sam Wilkins connected the pipes for me.'

'Don't forget, Violet,' the General said anxiously, 'that you've been up in London a good deal lately, and haven't been able to keep an eye on everything.'

'Why shouldn't I have moved in?' Florence asked, as lightly as she could manage.

'You mustn't laugh at me, but I'm fortunate enough to have a kind of gift, or perhaps it's an instinct, of fitting people and places together. For instance, only just recently – only I'm afraid it wouldn't mean very much to you if you don't know the two houses I'm talking about – '

'Perhaps you could tell me which ones you're thinking of,'

25

said the General, 'and then I could explain it all slowly to Mrs Green.'

'Anyway, to return to the Old House – that's exactly the sort of thing I mean. I believe I might be able to save you a great deal of disappointment, and even perhaps a certain amount of expense. In fact, I want to help you, and that's my excuse for saying all this.'

'I am sure no excuse is needed,' said Florence.

'There are so many more suitable premises in Hardborough, so much more convenient in every way for a bookshop. Did you know, for example, that Deben is closing down?'

Certainly she knew that Deben's wet fish shop was about to close. Everybody in the town knew when there were likely to be vacant premises, who was in financial straits, who would need larger family accommodation in nine months, and who was about to die.

'We've been so used, I'm afraid, to the Old House standing empty that we've delayed from year to year – you've quite put us to shame by being in such a hurry, Mrs Green – but the fact is that we're rather upset by the sudden transformation of our Old House into a shop – so many of us have the idea of converting it into some kind of centre – I mean an arts centre – for Hardborough.'

The General was listening with strained attention.

'Might pray for that too, you know, Violet.'

'. . . chamber music in summer – we can't leave it all to Aldeburgh – lecturers in winter . . .'

'We have lectures already,' said Florence. 'The Vicar's series on Picturesque Suffolk only comes round again every three years.' They were delightful evenings, for there was no need to listen closely, and in front of the slumberous rows the coloured slides followed each other in no sort of order, disobedient to the Vicar's voice.

'We should have to be a good deal more ambitious, particularly with the summer visitors who may come from

26

some distance away. And there is simply no other old house that would give the right ambience. Do, won't you, think it over?'

'I've been negotiating this sale for more than six months, and I can't believe that everyone in Hardborough didn't know about it. In fact, I'm sure they did.' She looked for confirmation to the General, who stared fixedly away at the empty sandwich plates.

'And of course,' Mrs Gamart went on, with even more marked emphasis, 'one great advantage, which it seems almost wrong to throw away, is that now we have exactly the right person to take charge. I mean to take charge of the centre, and put us all right about books and pictures and music, and encourage things, and get things off the ground, and keep things going, and see they're on the right lines.'

She gave Mrs Green a smile of unmistakable meaning and radiance. The moment of confusing intimacy had returned, even though Mrs Gamart, in the course of her last sentence, had withdrawn, with encouraging nods and gestures, into her protective horde of guests.

Florence, left quite alone, went out to the small room off the hall to begin the search for her coat. While she looked methodically through the piles, she reflected that, after all, she was not too old to do two jobs, perhaps get a manager for the bookshop, while she herself would have to take some sort of course in art history and music appreciation – music was always appreciated, whereas art had a history – that, she supposed, would mean journeys over to Cambridge.

Outside it was a clear night and she could see across the marshes to the Laze, marked by the riding lights of the fishing boats, waiting for the low tide. But it was cold, and the air stung her face.

'It was very good of them to ask me,' she thought. 'I daresay they found me a bit awkward to talk to.'

As soon as she had gone, the groups of guests re-formed

themselves, as the cattle had done when Raven took the old horse aside. Now they were all of the same kind, facing one way, grazing together. Between themselves they could arrange many matters, though what they arranged was quite often a matter of chance. As the time drew on for thinking about going home, Mrs Gamart was still a little disturbed as what seemed a check in her scheme for the Old House. This Mrs Green, though unobtrusive enough, had not quite agreed to everything on the spot. It was not of much importance. But a little more champagne, given her by Milo, caused her mind to revolve in its giddy uppermost circle, and to her cousin's second husband, who was something to do with the Arts Council, and to her own cousin once removed, who was soon going to be high up in the Directorate of Planning, and to her brilliant nephew who sat for the Longwash Division of West Suffolk and had already made his name as the persevering secretary of the Society for Providing Public Access to Places of Interest and Beauty, and to Lord Gosfield who had ventured over from his stagnant castle in the Fens because if foot-and-mouth broke out again he wouldn't be able to come for months, she spoke of the Hardborough Centre for Music and the Arts. And in the minds of her brilliant nephew, cousin, and so on, a faint resolution formed that something might have to be done, or Violet might become rather a nuisance. Even Lord Gosfield was touched, though he had said nothing all evening, and had in fact driven the hundred odd miles expressly to say nothing in the company of his old friend Bruno. They were all kind to their hostess, because it made life easier.

It was time to be gone. They were not sure where they or their wives had put the car keys. They lingered at the front door saying that they must not let in the cold air, while the General's old dog, which lived in single-minded expectation of the door opening, thumped its tail feebly on the shining floor; then their cars would not start and the prospect of

28

some of them returning to stay the night grew perilously close; then the last spark ignited and they roared away, calling and waving, and the marsh wind could be heard again in the silence that followed.

3

The next morning Florence prepared herself a herring – there was not much point in living in East Suffolk if one didn't know how to do this – two slices of bread and butter, and a pot of tea. Her cooker was in the backhouse. This was the most companionable room in the Old House, white-washed, with not much noise beyond the sighing of the old bricked-up well in the floor. Previous residents had counted themselves lucky that they did not have to go outdoors to pump, luckier still when the great buff-glazed sink, deep as a sarcophagus, was installed. A brass tap, proudly flared, discharged ice-cold water from a great height.

At eight o'clock she unplugged her electric kettle and plugged in her radio set, which immediately began to speak of trouble in Cyprus and Nyasaland and then told her, with a slight change of intonation, that the expectation of life was now 68.1 years for males and 73.9 years for females, as opposed to 45.8 for males and 52.4 for females at the beginning of the century. She tried to feel that this was encouraging. But the Warning To Shipping – North Sea, wind cyclonic variable strong becoming NE strong or gale sea rough or very rough – moved her to shame. She was ashamed of sitting in her backhouse and of her herring from the deep, and of the uselessness of feeling ashamed. Through her east-facing window she could see the storm warning hauled up over the Coastguards against a sky that was pale yellowish green.

By mid-day it was clear. The sky brightened from one horizon to the other, and the high white cloud was reflected in mile after mile of shining dyke water, so that the marshes seemed to stand between cloud and cloud. After her morning errands she took a short-cut back across the common. The Primary School were having their second play out. Boys separated from girls, except for the top class, coming up to their eleven plus, who circled round each other. Entirely alone, a small child stood howling. It had been well sent out, with a scarf crossed over the chest and secured behind with a safety-pin, and woollen gloves fastened to a length of elastic passed round under the coat collar. Patently it was a Mixed Infant, unqualified to mingle with either boys or girls. She attempted to calm it.

'You're from the Infants, you oughtn't to be playing out now. Are you lost? What's your name?'

'Melody Gipping.'

Florence took out a clean handkerchief and blew Melody's nose. A waif-like figure, with hair as fine as dry grass, detached itself from the Girls.

'That's all right, miss. I'm Christine Gipping, I'll take her. We've got Kleenex at ours – they're more hygienic.'

The two of them strayed back together. The Boys were shooting each other dead, the Girls bounced old tennis balls, forming a wide ring, and sang.

> One, two, Pepsi-Cola,
> Three, four, Casanova,
> Five, six, hair in rollers,
> Seven, eight, roll her over,
> Nine, ten, do it again.

Florence looked southwards, where the horizon was bounded by a dark stretch of pine woods. That was the Heronry, but in 1953, when the sea had drowned the woodlands in salt, the herons had flown away and no longer nested there.

At the kissing-gate which led off the common, she saw

31

approaching her, stalking her almost, with the sideways look
of the failed tradesman, Mr Deben from the wet fish shop.
He must have followed her up there, indeed he as good as
admitted it.

'It's about my place, Mrs Green. It's going up for auction,
but that won't be till April, or it might be later still. I'd very
much prefer to come to terms privately before that. Now, as
you've expressed an interest in the property – ' He did not
pause long enough for her to say that she had done nothing
of the kind, but hurried on: 'If you're not going to remain at
the Old House, and if you're not leaving the district
altogether – you'll appreciate I'm too busy to pay attention
to all the rumours I hear – well then, it stands to reason
you'll have to make an offer for another place.'

He must be distracted by his business worries, she
thought. He had come straight out of his shop with his
fishmonger's straw hat still on his head, and a dreadful old
suit of overalls. Meanwhile his sly and muddled discourse
had brought an idea to her mind, sudden but not strange,
for she recognized it immediately as the truth. It was the
truth in the form of a warning, for which she must be
thankful.

'There has been a misunderstanding, Mr Deben. But that
doesn't matter in the least, and I should like to help you.
Mrs Gamart was kind enough to tell me about her scheme
for an arts centre – which would, I'm sure, benefit every one
of us here in Hardborough. She is, I believe, looking about
for premises, and what could be better than a vacant wet
fish shop?'

Without giving herself time for reflection, she left the
common by the kissing-gate, which stuck awkwardly, as
usual, while she and Deben exchanged politenesses, crossed
the High Street, turned right by the Corn and Seed Merchant's, and right again for Nelson Cottage. Milo North

could be seen through the downstairs window, sitting at a table with a patchwork cloth, and doing absolutely nothing.

'Why aren't you up in London?' she asked, rapping on the pane. She felt mildly irritated by the unpredictability of his daily life.

'I've sent Kattie to work this morning. Do come in.'

Milo opened the tiny front door. He was much too tall for the house, which was tarred and painted black, like the fishermen's huts.

'Perhaps you'd like some Nescafé?'

'I have never had any,' she said. 'I have heard of it. I'm told it's not prepared with boiling water.' She sat down in a delicate bentwood rocking-chair. 'These things are all much too small for you,' she said.

'I know, I know. I'm glad you came this morning. Nobody else ever makes me face the truth.'

'That's fortunate, because I came to ask you a question. When Mrs Gamart was talking at her party about the ideal person to run an arts centre, it was you, of course, wasn't it, that she had in mind?'

'Violet's party?'

'She expected me to move out – probably, in fact, to move somewhere else altogether – with the understanding that you would come to the Old House to manage everything?'

Milo gazed at her with limpid grey eyes. 'If she meant me, I don't think she could have used the word "manage".'

Florence accused herself of vanity, self-deception, and wilful misconstruction. She was a tradeswoman: why should anyone expect her to have anything to do with the arts? Curiously enough, for the next few days she was on the verge of offering to leave the Old House. The suspicion that she was clinging on simply because her vanity had been wounded was unbearable. – Of course, Mrs Gamart, whom I shall never speak of or refer to as Violet, it was Milo North you had in mind. Instal him immediately. My little book business can be fitted in anywhere. I only ask you not to allow the conventions to be defied too rapidly – East Suffolk isn't used to it. Kattie will have to live, for the first few years at least, in the oyster warehouse.

In calmer moments she reflected that if Mrs Gamart and her supporters could extract some kind of Government grant and could afford to pay her price for the freehold, plus moving expenses and a fair profit, she would be open to new opportunities, perhaps not in Suffolk, or even in England, and with that precious sense of beginning again which she could not expect too often at her age. No doubt it was absurd to imagine that she was being driven out, and that the hand of privilege was impelling her to Deben's wet fish shop.

She blinded herself, in short, by pretending for a while that human beings are not divided into exterminators and exterminatees, with the former, at any given moment, pre-dominating. Will-power is useless without a sense of direc-tion. Hers was at such a low ebb that it no longer gave her the instructions for survival.

It revived, however, without any effort on her part, and within the space of ten minutes on a Tuesday morning at the end of March. The weather was curious, and reminded her of the day she saw the flying heron trying to swallow the eel. While the washing on the lines was blowing to the west with the inshore breeze, the pumping mill on the marshes had caught the land breeze and was turning east. The rooks circled in the warring currents of the air. She left her little car in the garage next to the Coastguards, which was as near as she could manage to the Old House, and took the short lane or passageway from the foreshore which led to her backhouse door.

The passage was very narrow, and in a hard blow the little brick-and-tile houses seemed to cling to each other, as the saying went, like a sailor's child. Her back door had to

34

be opened carefully, or the draught blew out the pilot light in the cooker. She turned the key in the mortice lock, but the door would not open.

She wasted only a moment's thought on stiff hinges, warped wood, and so on. The hostile force, pushing against her push, came and went, always a little ahead of her, with the shrewdness of the insane. The quivering door waited for her to try again. From inside the backhouse came a burst of tapping. It did not sound like one thing hitting another, more like a series of tiny explosions. Then, as she leaned against her door, trying to recover her breath, it suddenly collapsed violently, swinging to and fro, like a hand clapping a comic spectacle, as she fell inwards on to the brick floor on her knees.

Everyone in Score Lane must have seen her pitch head foremost into her own kitchen. But stronger than the embarrassment, fear and pain was the sense of injustice. The rapper was a familiar of the bathroom and the upstairs passage. In the backhouse she had never heard or seen any signs of malignancy. There are unspoken agreements even with the metaphysical, and the rapper had overstepped them. Her will-power, which she felt as indignation, rose to meet the injury. The Unseen, as the girls had always called it at Müller's, could mind its own business no better than the Seen. Neither of them would prevent her from opening a bookshop.

In consequence, Mr Thornton was instructed to finalize the business as soon as possible, which meant that he proceeded at the same pace as before. Thornton & Co had been established for many years. The court work might be largely left to Drury, the solicitor who wasn't Thornton, but Thornton was reliable through and through. He had heard, of course, that his client had been seen falling about the street, holding a horse's head for that old scoundrel Raven, and calling on Milo North, of whom Thornton disapproved.

35

On the other hand, she had been asked to a party at The Stead, where he himself had never been invited, although he still hoped that the Gamarts would see sense one day and transfer their affairs from Drury, who was simply not up to handling important family business. Well, so Mrs Green knew the Gamarts. But even about that, he believed, there were reservations.

Taking out his file on the Old House, he explained that there was some little difficulty about the oyster warehouse. It could be upheld that the fishing community, by right immemorial, were entitled to walk straight through it on their way to the shore, and possibly to dry their sails in the loft.

'You don't get to the shore if you walk through the warehouse,' she pointed out. 'You get to the gas-manager's office. Nothing can be dried there anyway – the walls are running with condensation. The loft has fallen to pieces, and none of the longshore fishermen go out under sail. Surely that question won't take long to settle.'

The solicitor explained that rights were in no way affected by the impossibility of putting them into practice. Conveyancing, he added, was not as simple as the general public imagined. 'I'm pleased that you called in today, as a matter of fact, Mrs Green. Something that I heard, quite by chance, made me wonder whether you were thinking better of the whole transaction.' He appeared to be trembling with curiosity.

'By thinking better you mean thinking worse, of course,' she said.

'Having second thoughts, dear lady. It's always sad to think of losing a member of a small community like Hardborough, but if there are greater opportunities elsewhere, one can only applaud and understand.'

'You mean you thought I might want to change my mind and go somewhere else?' She wished that she could grow much taller, if only for half an hour, so that she could look down, rather than up, during interviews like these. 'You mean you thought I wanted to get out of the Old House – which, by the way, is my only home – while you're still dithering about the fishermen's right of way?'

'There are many other empty properties in Hardborough, and, as it happens, I have a list of some other ones farther afield – Flintmarket, and even Ipswich. I don't know whether you've considered . . .'

It was May, and flocks of terns had arrived, rising and falling with every wingbeat, and settling by the hundred on the sandy patches towards the shore. The stock from Müller's came down in two Carter Paterson vans, followed a week later by orders from the book wholesalers. For the rest, for the new titles, she would have to wait for the salesmen, if they would venture so far across the marshes to a completely unknown point of sale. Since the warehouse had proved unusable, everything had to be piled into the spacious cupboard under the stairs while Florence pondered the arrangement.

She drove back one morning from Flintmarket to find the premises full of twelve- and thirteen-year-old boys in blue jerseys. They were Sea Scouts, they told her.

'How did you get in?'

'Mr Raven got the key from the plumber,' said one of the children, square and reliable as a straw-bale.

'He's not your skipper, is he?'

'No, but he told us to come over to yours. What do you want doing?'

'I want all the shelves put up,' she said, with equal directness. 'Can you do that?'

'How many hand-drills can you get us, miss?'

She went out and bought hand-drills, and screws by the pound. The scouts worked for two hours, went home for

37

their dinners, and then knocked on again. By the time the shelves were up, the whole floor, and most of the books, were covered with a quarter-inch layer of sawdust.

'We could make it good later, and clear up this lot,' Wally said.

'I shall clear up myself,' she said. She felt overwhelmed with love for them. 'I'd like to give you something for your headquarters.' Scout Headquarters was the wreck of an old three-masted schooner, beached on the estuary.

'Have you got any morse codes, or *Pears Medical Dictionary*?'

'I'm afraid not.' They were both at a loss. 'I tell you what, Wally. I want you to take these hand-drills. They're no use to me, I don't know how to use them properly. If I want a hole made in anything, I shall have to send you a signal.'

'Thank you. I daresay we could make use of those,' said Wally, 'but with every job we undertake we're obliged to contribute the value of twelve bricks to the new Baden-Powell House that they're building up in South Kensington.'

She gave him five pounds, and he saluted.

'South Kensington's an area of London,' he explained.

The scouts, over whom Raven exerted a mysterious but direct influence, returned to do the white-painting, and then she was free, refusing any further offers, to arrange the stock herself.

New books came in sets of eighteen, wrapped in thin brown paper. As she sorted them out, they fell into their own social hierarchy. The heavy luxurious country-house books, the books about Suffolk churches, the memoirs of statesmen in several volumes, took the place that was theirs by right of birth in the front window. Others, indispensable, but not aristocratic, would occupy the middle shelves. That was the place for the Books of the Car – from Austin to Wolseley – technical works on pebble-polishing, sailing, pony clubs, wild flowers and birds, local maps and guide books. Among these the popular war reminiscences, in jackets of khaki and blood-red, faced each other as rivals with bristling hostility. Back in the shadows went the Stickers, largely philosophy and poetry, which she had little hope of ever seeing the last of. The Stayers – dictionaries, reference books and so forth – would go straight to the back, with the Bibles and reward books which, it was hoped, Mrs Traill of the Primary would present to successful pupils. Last of all came the crates of Müller's shabby remainders. A few were even second-hand. Although she had been trained never to look inside the books while at work, she opened one or two of them – old Everyman editions in faded olive boards stamped with gold. There was the elaborate endpaper which she had puzzled over when she was a little girl. *A good book is the precious life-blood of a master spirit, embalmed and treasured up on purpose to a life beyond life.* After some hesitation, she put it between Religion and Home Medicine.

The right-hand wall she kept for paperbacks. At 1s. 6d. each, cheerfully coloured, brightly democratic, they crowded the shelves in well-disciplined ranks. They would have a rapid turnover and she had to approve of them; yet she could remember a world where only foreigners had been content to have their books bound in paper. The Everymans, in their shabby dignity, seemed to confront them with a look of reproach.

In the backhouse kitchen, since there was absolutely no room for them in the shop itself, were two deep drawers set apart for the Books of the Books – the Ledger, Repeat Orders, Purchases, Sales Returns, Petty Cash. Still blank, with untouched double columns, these unloved books menaced the silent commonwealth on the shelves next door. Not much of a hand at accounts, Florence would have preferred them to remain without readers. This was weakness, and she asked Jessie Welford's sharp niece, who worked with a firm of accountants in Lowestoft, to come over once a month for a check. 'A little Trial Balance now and then,' said Ivy

Welford condescendingly, as though it were a tonic for the feeble-minded. Her worldly wisdom, in a girl of twenty-one, was alarming, and she would need paying, of course; but both Mr Thornton and the bank manager seemed relieved when they heard that Ivy had been arranged for. Her head was well screwed-on, they said.

4

The Old House Bookshop was to open next morning, but Florence did not have it in mind to hold any kind of celebration, because she was uncertain who should be asked. The frame of mind, however, is everything. Given that, one can have a very satisfactory party all by oneself. She was thinking this when the street door opened and Raven came in.

'You're often alone,' he remarked.

He apologized for wearing his waders, and looked round to see what kind of a job the scouts had made of the shelving.

'An eighth of an inch out over there by the cupboard.'

But she would have no fault found. Besides, now that the books were in place, well to the front (she couldn't bear them to slide back as though defeated), any irregularities could scarcely be noticed. Like the red dress, the shelving would come to her as she wore it.

'And that plastering looks unsightly,' Raven went on. 'You can point that out, next time you see them.'

She did not feel confident that she would recognize any of the scouts out of uniform; but she was wrong, for Wally appeared, dressed in his school blazer and a serviceable pair of trousers from the Agricultural Outfitters, and she knew him at once.

He had a message, he said, for Mrs Green.

'Who gave it you?' Raven asked.

'Mr Brundish did, Mr Raven.'

'What? He came out of Holt House and gave it to you?'

'No, he just leaned a bit against the window and clicked.'

41

'With his tongue?'

'No, with his fingers.'

'Then you couldn't hear it through the window?'

'No, it was more like I was aware of it.'

'How did he look, then? Palish?'

Wally seemed doubtful. 'Palish and darkish. You can't really say how he looks. His head's a bit sunk down between his shoulders.'

'Were you scared?'

'I felt I'd have to jump to it.'

'A Sea Scout should always jump to it,' Raven replied automatically. 'I don't reckon to have seen him for more than a month, in spite of the fine weather, and I haven't heard him speak for much longer. He didn't say anything to you, did he?'

'Oh yes, he cleared his throat a bit, and told me to give this to Mrs Green.'

Wally had in his hand a white envelope bordered with black. Although she had been staring at it all this time, she took it almost with disbelief. She had never spoken to Mr Brundish. Even at the party at The Stead she had had no expectation of meeting him. It was well known that Mrs Gamart, as patroness of all that was of value in Hardborough, would have liked to count him as a friend, but since she had been at The Stead for only fifteen years and was not of Suffolk origin, her wishes had been in vain. Perhaps her presence had not been drawn to Mr Brundish's attention. And then, of recent years he had been so much confined to his home that it was a matter of astonishment that he should know her name.

'I don't see how this can be for me.'

It did not occur to either Raven or Wally to go away until she had opened it.

'Don't you worry about the black edges,' Raven said. 'He had those envelopes done it must have been in 1919, when they all came back from the first war, and I was still a nipper, and Mrs Brundish died.'

'What did she die of?'

'That was an odd thing, Mrs Green. She was drowned crossing the marshes.'

Inside the envelope was one sheet of paper, also black-bordered.

Dear Madam,

I should like to wish you well. In my great-grandfather's time there was a bookseller in the High Street who, I believe, knocked down one of the customers with a folio when he grew too quarrelsome. There had been some delay in the arrival of the latest instalment of a new novel – I think, *Dombey and Son*. From that day to this, no one has been courageous enough to sell books in Hardborough. You are doing us an honour. I should certainly visit your shop if I ever went out, but nowadays I make a point of not doing so; however, I shall be very willing to subscribe to your circulating library.

Yours obediently,

Edmund Brundish.

A library! She hadn't contemplated it, and there was nothing like enough room.

'He's evidently not satisfied with the Mobile,' said Raven.

The public library van came over from Flintmarket once a month. The books, from much use, had acquired a peculiar fragrance. All who cared for reading in Hardborough had read them several times.

She accompanied Wally, who nodded acknowledgment to her thanks, to the street door. He appeared to be a general messenger. His bike was loaded with shopping, and from the handlebars, which he had screwed on upside down to look more like a racer, hung a wicker basket containing a hen.

'She's broody, Mrs Green. I'm taking her round from ours to my cousin's half-sister's. She wants to rear chicks.'

Florence put her hand lightly on the slumbering mass of feathers. The old fowl was sunk into a soft tawny heap, scarcely opening her slit-like eyes. Her whole energy was absorbed in producing warmth. The basket itself throbbed with a slow and purposeful rhythm.

'Thank you for bringing the note, Wally. I can see you've got plenty to do.' She had brought her bag, and subscribed quietly to another brick.

Raven did not leave at once. He explained that he had come in the first instance to suggest that she needed a bright youngster to give her a hand, perhaps after school.

'Were you thinking of Wally?'

'No, not him. He won't be at home with books. It's maths that attracts him. If he'd been much of a reader, he'd have taken a look at your letter on the way over here, and you could see he hadn't done that.'

Raven was thinking of one of the Gipping girls. He didn't say how many of them there were, or appear to think that it mattered which one. The reputation for competence was shed upon them by their mother, Mrs Gipping. The family lived in that house between the church and the old railway station, with a fair piece of ground. Mr Gipping was a plasterer but could be glimpsed often from the rear staking peas or earthing up his potatoes. Mrs Gipping went out to work a little. She favoured Milo, on the days when Kattie was up in London, and she went regularly to Mr Brundish.

'I'll speak to her,' Raven said. 'She can send one of her lot down after school. That finishes at twenty-five past three.'

He took his leave. The wet footprints of his waders looked like the track of some friendly amphibian across the floor-boards, polished more than once for tomorrow's opening. The sensation of having something organized for her was

44

agreeable. Left to herself, she would not have had the confidence to call at Mrs Gipping's populous house.

Her mind went back reluctantly to the problem of the lending library. It would be a nuisance, and might even be a failure. Could Mrs Gamart, for instance, reasonably be expected to subscribe to it? Nothing more had been heard from The Stead, but Deben had given a half-reproachful, half-knowing glance as he laid out the sprats on his marble slab, which had shown her that the controversy was still alive. The more modestly she ran her business, for the first year at least, the better. But after reading Mr Brundish's letter through again, she said aloud, 'I will see what I can do about a library.'

If she had thought that the poltergeist would relax its efforts after the shop had opened, she was wrong. At various times in the night, behind every screw which the scouts had driven in, there would be a delicate sharp tap, as though they were being numbered for future reference. The customers, during the day, would remark that it was very noisy at Rhoda's next door, and that they had never heard a sewing-machine make a noise like that before. Florence would reply, conscious of telling the exact truth, that you could never tell with these old houses. She installed a cash register with a bell, a sound that will distract the attention from almost anything else.

Her opening day had drawn only mild attention in Hardborough. There was no curiosity about the Old House itself. It had stood empty so long, with broken windows and unlocked doors, that every child in the district had played there. The turnover for the first week had been between £70 and £80. Mrs Traill from the Primary had made a clearance of *Daily Life in Ancient Britain*, Mr Thornton bought a birdwatching book and the bank manager, rather unexpectedly, one on physical fitness. Mr Drury, the solicitor who was not Mr Thornton, and one of the doctors from Surgery,

45

both bought books by former SAS men, who had been parachuted into Europe and greatly influenced the course of the war; they also placed orders for books by Allied commanders who poured scorn on the SAS men, and questioned their credentials. That was on Tuesday. On Wednesday, when rain set in, the local girls' boarding school, out for a walk, had taken refuge in the shop, which was entirely filled, like a sheep-pen, with damp bodies closely pressed together and gently steaming. The girls turned over the greeting-cards, which had been grudgingly given a space next to the paperbacks, and bought three. Envelopes had to be found, and the till stuck when it was called upon to add 9½d., 6½d., and 3½d. On Thursday – which was early closing, but Florence decided to make her first week an exception – Deben appeared, to show that there were no hard feelings, and poked round, running his scrubbed hands over the fitments. He asked for a vocal score of the *Messiah*.

'Do you want me to put that on order?' she asked, trying for a friendly tone.

'How long will that take to come?'

'It's rather hard to give a date. The publishers don't like sending just one thing at a time. I have to wait to order until I've twelve titles or so from the same publisher.'

'I'd have thought you would have had a thing like that in stock. Handel's *Messiah* is sung every Christmas, you know, both in Norwich and at the Albert Hall, in London.'

'It's rather hard to keep everybody's interests in mind when you only have room for a small stock.'

'It's not as though you had to depend on the day's catch, though,' said Deben. 'There's nothing here to deteriorate.' He was still unable to find a purchaser for his shop.

In the evenings she put up the shutters, got the orders away, cleared the correspondence on her old typewriter and read *The Bookseller* and *Smith's Trade News*. Completely tired out by the time she went to bed, she no longer dreamed of the heron and the eel, or, so far as she knew, of anything else.

Perhaps her battle to establish herself in the Old House was over, or perhaps she had been wrong in thinking that one had taken place, or would ever take place. But if she was not sure which of these alternatives she meant, the battle could hardly have been decisive.

When the bookshop had been open for three weeks, General Gamart came in unobtrusively. With a sudden pang, she feared he was going to ask for the poems of Charles Sorley; but he, too, wanted the reminiscences of the former SAS man.

'I've often felt like writing down something myself, now that I've got a certain amount of spare time. From the point of view of the infantry, you know – the chap who just walks forward and gets shot.'

She wrapped his purchase carefully. She would have liked to have been instrumental in passing some law which would entail that he would never be unhappy again. But perhaps he ought not really to have been in the shop at all. He was there, at the very least, on sufferance. He glanced about him as though on parole, and retreated with his parcel.

Jessie Welford's sharp niece was somewhat surprised when she drove over for the first time to lend a hand with the books. The turnover was higher than she'd anticipated. There must have been quite a lot of interest in the new venture.

'Shall we just have a look at the transactions?' she asked, clicking her silver Eversharp, and using the tone which brought her employers to heel. 'Three accounts have been opened – the Primary School and the two medical men. Where is your provision for bad debts?'

'I don't know that I've made any,' said Mrs Green.

'It ought to be 5% of what is due to you on the ledger. Then, the depreciation – that should be shown as a debit *here*, and as a credit in the property account. Every debit must have its credit. It is essential that you should be able to see at a glance, at any given time, exactly what you owe and what is owing to you. That is the object of properly kept books. You do want to know that, don't you?'

She guiltily wished she did. It often seemed to her that if she knew exactly what her financial position was down to the last three farthings, as Ivy Welford impressed upon her that she should, she would not have the courage to carry on for another day. She hardly liked to mention that she was thinking of opening a lending library.

The weather had broadened into early summer. 'There's a delivery for you!' Wally sang out from his bike, one foot resting on the pavement. 'He asked the way twice, once at the gasworks, and once at the vicarage. Now he's in trouble turning. He's trying to reverse round in one go, do he'll go straight through your backhouse.'

In time to come this particular van, elegant in its red and cream paint, was to become one of the most familiar in Hardborough. It was from Brompton's, the London store which offered a library service to provincial booksellers, no matter how remote. Summoned by Florence, it brought her first volumes and required her to sign an undertaking and to read the conditions laid down by Brompton's.

These were suggestive of a moral philosophy, or the laws of an ideal state, rather than a business transaction. The books available on loan were divided into classes A, B, and C. A were much in demand, B acceptable, and C frankly old and unwanted. For every A she borrowed, she must take three Bs and a large number of Cs for her subscribers. If she paid more, she could get more As, but also, a mounting pile of Bs and the repellent Cs, and nothing new would be sent until the last consignment was returned.

Brompton's did not offer any suggestions as to how the

48

subscribers were to be induced to take out the right book. Perhaps, in Knightsbridge, they had their own methods.

When the opening of the lending library was announced, simply by a hand-written notice in the window, thirty of the inhabitants of Hardborough signed up on the first day. Mr Brundish could be considered a certainty. But while he had given no indication at all of what he would like to read, the other thirty were perfectly sure. Comfortably retired or prosperously in business, fond of looking at images of royalty, praisers of things past, they all wanted to have the recent *Life of Queen Mary*. This was in spite of the fact that most of them seemed to possess inner knowledge of the court – more, indeed, than the biographer. Mrs Drury said that the Queen Mother had not done all those embroideries herself, the difficult bits had been filled in for her by her ladies-in-waiting. Mr Keble said that we should not look upon her like again.

Queen Mary was, of course, an A book. In point of time, Mrs Thornton had been the first to put it on her list; and Florence, confident in the justice of her method, placed the Thornton ticket in it. Every subscriber had a pink ticket, and the books were ranged alphabetically, waiting for collection. This was a grave weakness of the system. Everybody knew at a glance what everybody else had got. They should not have been poking about and turning things over in the painfully small space which had been cleared for the library, but they were unused to discipline.

'I think there has been some mistake. I thought I made my choice quite clear. This appears to be a detective story, and not by any means a recent one.' Mrs Keble added that she would be back in half-an-hour. She always thought that things would take about half-an-hour. 'I am not interested in *The History of Chinese Thought* either,' she said.

The library was to open from two to three on Mondays. This was normally the slack time. Mrs Keble really had no business to come so early, but on the point of two o'clock several subscribers came in at once, and the atmosphere, in the cramped back of the shop, at once began to resemble the great historic runs on the Bank of England. During the '45, Mrs Green remembered, the Bank had been forced to hold the customers at bay, to melt down the ink-wells to make bullets and to pay out in sixpences. If only Mrs Thornton would come to take her *Queen Mary* away – but satisfied, perhaps, by her incontestable acquisition of right, she failed, though expected every time the street door opened, to appear. Everyone could see her ticket, 'which, I suppose, means that she is to be allowed to have *Queen Mary* first. I happen to have been told that she is a particularly slow reader, but that isn't really my point.'

'Mrs Thornton asked for the book first. That's the only thing I take into account.'

'Allow me to say, Mrs Green, that if you had a little more experience of committee work you would realize how rash it is to come to a decision as the result of one consideration only. A pity.'

'In a small town we cannot help knowing something of each other. Some of us may be more attached than others to the concept of royalty. Some may feel that they have the *right* to read first about the late Queen Mother. It may have been a loyal devotion of long standing.'

'Mrs Thornton was quite definite about it.' The air of the summer afternoon grew uncomfortably warm. Two more subscribers crowded in, and one of them told Florence, in confidence, that Mrs Thornton was known to have voted Liberal in the last election. Both the backhouse and the street door were now cut off by ladies. At four o'clock – for office hours were short in Hardborough – their husbands joined them.

'I shouldn't have thought it was possible to misunderstand my list. Look, it's written perfectly clearly. It looks like a failure in simple office routine. If everyone wanted this *Life of Queen Mary*, why were not more copies ordered?'

The Old House Bookshop lending library temporarily closed, to reopen in a month, by which time the proprietor hoped to have more assistance. This was an admission of weakness. Wally took a formal note round to Mr Brundish to explain the situation. He hadn't been able to see the old gentleman anywhere; so he gave the note to the milkman, who had left it with the milk under the sacking on the potato clamp, which was where Mr Brundish, whose letter-box had long been rusted up, received his correspondence.

5

I need help – Florence thought – it was folly to think that I
could manage all this by myself. She put through a call to
the offices of the *Flintmarket, Kingsgrave and Hardborough Times*.

'Can you get it as quickly as possible, Janet?' she asked.
She had seen Janet's one-stroke motor-bicycle outside the
telephone exchange, and knew she would be in safe hands.

'Are you trying the small ads, Mrs Green?'

'Yes. It's the same number.'

'That won't be worth the money, if you want to advertise
for an assistant. One of the Gippings is going to come round
to yours after school.'

'A possibility, Janet, but not a certainty.'

'Raven spoke to them about a week ago. He'd have liked
to get you the eldest, but she'd have to stay home when Mrs
Gipping went to the pea-picking. Or then there's the second
one, or the third one.'

She reminded Janet that there might be other subscribers
waiting for calls to be put through, but was told that there
weren't any.

'The private lines have mostly gone over to Aldeburgh for
that music, and the others are at the new fish-and-chip
parlour. That opens for the first time tonight.'

'Well, Janet, it might very well catch fire. I believe they
use cooking oil. We ought to clear the line for emergencies.
Is Mr Deben running it?'

'Oh, no, Deben reckons it'll be the death-blow to his trade.
He's attempting to get the Vicar on to his side, saying the
odour of frying might waft into the church at Evensong. But

the Vicar doesn't like to be drawn into these arguments, he told Deben.'

She wondered what the telephone operators said when they discussed her bookshop.

At teatime next day a little girl of ten years old, very pale, very thin and remarkably fair, presented herself at the Old House. She wore a pair of jeans and a pink cardigan worked in a fancy stitch. Florence recognized her as the child she had seen on the Common.

'You're Christine Gipping, aren't you? I had rather thought that your elder sister . . .'

Christine replied that now the evenings were getting longer her elder sister would be up in the bracken with Charlie Cutts. In fact, she'd just seen their bikes stashed under the bracken by the crossroads.

'You won't have to worry about anything like that with me,' she added. 'I shan't turn eleven till next April. Mine haven't come on yet.'

'What about your other sister?'

'She likes to stay at home and mind Margaret and Peter – that's the little ones. That was a waste giving them those names, it never came to anything between him and the Princess.'

'Please don't get the idea that I don't want to consider you for the job. It's just that you don't really look old enough or strong enough.'

'You can't tell from looking. You look old, but you don't look strong. It won't make much difference, as long as you get someone from ours. We're all of us handy.'

Her skin was almost transparent. Her silky hair seemed to have no substance, ruffling away from her forehead in the slightest draught. When Florence, still anxious not to hurt her feelings, smiled encouragingly, she smiled back, showing two broken front teeth.

53

They had been broken during the previous winter in rather a strange manner, when the washing on the line froze hard, and she was caught a blow in the face with an icy vest. Like all the Hardborough children, she had learned to endure. Running like tightrope walkers across the narrow handrails of the marsh bridges, they fell and were fractured or half drowned. They pelted each other with stones or with beets from the furrows. A half-witted boy was told that the maggots used as bait would be good for him and make him less dull, and he had eaten a whole jar full. Christine herself looked perilously thin, although Mrs Gipping was known as a good provider.

'I'll come and see your mother tomorrow, Christine, and talk things over.'

'If you want. She'll say I'm to come down every day after school, and Saturdays all day, and you're not to give me less than twelve and six a week.'

'And what about your homework?'

'I'll fare to do that after tea, when I'm at home.'

Christine showed signs of impatience, evidently having decided to start work at once. She deposited her pink cardigan in the backhouse.

'Did you knit that yourself? It looks very difficult.'

'That was in *Woman's Own*,' Christine said, 'but the instructions were for short sleeves.' She frowned, unwilling to admit that she had put on her best to make an impression at the first interview. 'You haven't any children, Mrs Green?'

'No. I should have liked to.'

'Life passed you by in that respect, then.'

Without waiting for explanations she bustled round the shop, opening drawers and finding fault with the arrangements, her faint hair flying. Not enough cards were on display, she declared – she'd see about sorting out some more. And indeed there were large packets of samples still in

54

their wrappers, because Mrs Green hated them, at the back of the drawers.

At first the child's methods were eccentric. With a talent for organization which had long been suppressed by her position as third daughter in the family, she tried the cards first one way, then another. Ignoring the messages, she sorted them largely by colour, so that roses and sunsets were put with a card representing a bright red lobster wearing a Scottish bonnet and raising a glass to its lips with the words '*Just a wee doch an doris afore we gang awa!*' This, certainly, must have been a sample.

'They really ought to be divided into Romantic and Humorous,' said Florence. These, indeed, were the only two attitudes to the stages of life's journey envisaged by the manufacturers of the cards. The lobster took a humorous view of parting. The sunset card was overprinted with a sad message.

'What do "o'er" and "neath" mean?' asked Christine sharply. This first admission that there was something she didn't know encouraged her employer a little. Christine saw immediately that she had lost ground. 'There's a whole lot more you've never even unpacked,' she said reprovingly. They looked together at a brand-new set, naked men and women interlaced, with the caption *Another thing we didn't forget to do today*. 'We'll throw these away,' said Florence firmly. 'Some of the reps have little or no idea of what's suitable.' Christine was doubled up with laughter and said that there were quite a few in Hardborough who wouldn't mind having them through the letter-box. She was well prepared, Florence thought. She would be invaluable when the lending library reopened.

There hardly seemed anything to discuss that evening with Mrs Gipping, who stood tolerantly at her half-open gate when Florence accompanied Christine home.

Little Peter was planting rows of clothes pegs between the rows of early French beans. 'Why's Christine late?' he asked.

'She's been working for this lady.'

'What for?'

'She's got a shop full of books for people to read.'

'What for?'

Now vans and estate cars began to appear in increased numbers over the brilliant horizon of the marshes, sometimes getting bogged down at the crossings and always if they tried to turn round on the foreshore, bringing the publishers' salesmen. Even in summer, it was a hard journey. Those who made it were somewhat unwilling to part with their Fragrant Moments and engagement books, which were what Florence really wanted, unless she would also take a pile of novels which had the air, in their slightly worn jackets, of women on whom no one had ever made any demand. Her fellow-feeling, both for the salesmen and for the ageing books, made her an injudicious buyer. They had come so far, too, that they ought to have tea made for them in the backhouse. There, in the hope that it would be long before they returned to this godforsaken hole, they stirred their sugar and relaxed a little. 'One thing, the competition's not keen. There isn't another point of sale between here and Flintmarket.'

Their hearts sank when they realized that there was no rail-service at all and that all future orders would have to come down by road. By the time they felt that they had to be moving on, the wind had got up, and their vans, without the load which had kept them stable, went weaving to and fro, unable to hold the road. The young bullocks, most inquisitive of all animals, came stepping across the tussocks of grass to stare mildly at them.

'I don't know why I bought these,' Florence reflected after one of these visits. 'Why did I take them? No one used force. No one advised me.' She was looking at 200 Chinese book-markers, handpainted on silk. The stork for longevity, the

plum-blossom for happiness. Her weakness for beauty had
betrayed her. It was inconceivable that anyone else in
Hardborough should want them. But Christine was consoling: the visitors would buy them – come the summer, they
didn't know what to spend their money on.

In July, the postman brought a letter postmarked from Bury
St Edmund's, but too long, as could easily be seen from the
thickness of the envelope, to be an order.

> Dear Madam,
>   It may be of interest, and perhaps of entertainment
> to you, to know how it was that I came to hear of
> your establishment. A cousin of my late wife's (I
> should, perhaps, call him a cousin once removed) is
> connected, through a second marriage, with that
> coming young man, the Member of Parliament for
> the Longwash Division, who mentioned to me that at
> a gathering of his aunt's (Mrs Violet Gamart, who is
> personally unknown to me) it had been remarked in
> passing that Hardborough was at last to have a
> bookshop.

She wondered in what possible way this could be considered entertaining. But she must not be uncharitable.

> It may increase your amusement to learn that I am
> not writing to you on the subject of books at all!

There were several pages of thin writing paper, from
which it emerged that the writer was called Theodore Gill,
that he lived somewhere near Yarmouth, and that he was a
painter in watercolours who saw no reason to abandon the
pleasant style of the turn of the century, and that he would
like to organize, or better, have organized for him, a little
exhibition of his work at the Old House. The name of Mrs

Gamart and of her brilliant nephew would, he was sure, be sufficient recommendation.

Florence looked round at her shelving, behind which scarcely a square foot of wall space could be seen. There was always the oyster warehouse, but even now, in the height of summer, it was damp. She put the letter away in a drawer which already contained several others of the same kind. Later middle age, for the upper middle-class in East Suffolk, marked a crisis, after which the majority became water-colourists, and painted landscapes. It would not have mattered so much if they had painted badly, but they all did it quite well. All their pictures looked much the same. Framed, they hung in sitting-rooms, while outside the windows the empty, washed-out, unarranged landscape stretched away to the transparent sky.

The desire to exhibit somewhere more ambitious than the parish hall accompanied this crisis, and Florence related it to the letters which she also received from 'local authors'. The paintings were called 'Sunset Across the Laze', the books were called 'On Foot Across the Marshes' or 'Awheel Across East Anglia', for what else can be done with flatlands but to cross them? She had no idea, none at all, where she would put the local authors if they came, as they suggested, to sign copies of their books for eager purchasers. Perhaps a table underneath the staircase, if some of the stock could be moved. She vividly imagined their disillusionment, wedged behind the table with books and a pen in front of them, while the hours emptied away and no one came. 'Tuesday is always a very quiet day in Hardborough, Mr ——, particularly if it is fine. I didn't suggest Monday, because that would have been quieter still. Wednesdays are quiet too, except for the market, and Thursday is early closing. The customers will come in and ask for your book soon – of course they will, they have heard of you, you are a local author. Of course they will want your signature, they will come across the

58

marshes, afoot and awheel.' The thought of so much suffering and embarrassment was hard to bear, but at least she was in a position to see that it never took place. She consigned Mr Gill's letter to the drawer.

She had been almost too busy to realize that the holiday season had arrived. Now she noticed that bathing towels hung and flapped at every window of the seafront houses. The ferry crossed the Laze several times every day, the fish-and-chip parlour extended its premises with pieces of corrugated iron transferred from the disused airfield. Wally appeared to ask if Christine would like to come camping, and she wondered if he was not hanging round rather often, and in a marked manner. Christine, however, rejected his invitation with a dignity imitated from her elder sisters. 'That Wally's after your washboard for his skiffle group. I've seen him eyeing it in your backhouse.' 'Then he'd better have it,' Florence said. 'I've never known what to do with it. He can have the mangle too, if he likes.'

She ought to go down to the beach. It was Thursday, early closing, and it seemed ungrateful to live so close to the sea and never to look at it for weeks on end. In fact she preferred the winter beach; but, reproving herself, she had a bathe and then stood in the sun at the end of the long swale of multi-coloured pebbles. Children crouched down to decide which of these pebbles they would put into their buckets; grown men selected others to throw into the sea. The newspapers they brought with them to read had been torn away from them by the wind. The mothers had retreated from the cutting air into the beach huts, which were drawn up in a friendly encampment as far as possible from the coldly encroaching North Sea. Farther to the north unacceptable things had been washed up. Bones were mixed with the fringe of jetsam at high tide. The rotting remains of a seal had been stranded there.

The Hardborough locals mingled fearlessly with the visitors. Florence saw the bank manager, unfamiliar in striped bathing-trunks, with his wife and the chief cashier. He called out, and was understood, in snatches, to say that all work and no play made Jack a dull boy, and that it was the first time he had been able to set foot on the beach this year. No reply was needed. Another voice, from inland, shouted that it had held up bright. Raven was running in his new van. Next week he was going to run some of the sea scouts up to London for their annual day out. They were going to check the progress of Baden-Powell House, and after that they had voted unanimously to go to Liverpool Street Station, and watch the trains go out.

Walking further up the beach was more like plunging at every step. The wet sand and shingle sank as though unwilling to bear her slight weight, and then oozed up again, filling her footprints with glittering water. To leave a mark of any kind was exhilarating. Past the dead seal, past the stretch of pebbles where, eighty years ago, a man had found a piece of amber as big as his head – but no one had ever found amber since then – she reached a desolate tract where the holiday-makers did not venture. A rough path led up and back to the common. Human figures, singly and in pairs, were exercising their dogs. She was surprised to find how many of them were known to her by now as occasional customers. They waved from a distance and then, because the land was so flat and approach was slow, had to wave again as they drew nearer, reserving their smiles until the last moment. With the smiles, most of the exercisers, glad to pause for a moment, said much the same thing: When would the lending library be open again? They had been looking forward to it so much. The dogs, stiff with indignation, dragged sideways at their leads. Florence heard herself making many promises. She felt at a disadvantage without

60

her shoes and wished she had put them on again before leaving the beach for the common.

On wet afternoons, when the heavy weather blew up, the Old House was full of straggling disconsolate holiday parties. Christine, who said that they brought sand into the shop, was severe, pressing them to decide what they wanted. 'Browsing is part of the tradition of a bookshop,' Florence told her. 'You must let them stand and turn things over.' Christine asked what Deben would do if everyone turned over his wet fish. There were finger-marks on some of her cards, too.

Ivy Welford called in to have a look at the books somewhat before her visit was due. Her inquisitiveness was a measure of the shop's success and its reputation outside Hardborough.

'Where are the returns outward?'

'There aren't any,' Florence replied. 'The publishers won't take anything back. They don't like sale or return arrangements.'

'But you've got returns inwards. How is that?'

'Sometimes the customers don't like the books when they've bought them. They're shocked, or say they've detected a distinct tinge of socialism.'

'In that case the price should be credited to your personal account and debited under returns.' It was an accusation of weakness. 'Now, the purchases book. 150 Chinese silk book markers at five shillings each – can that be right?'

'There was a different bird or butterfly on each one. Some of them were rice birds. They were beautiful. That was why I bought them.'

'I'm not questioning that. It's not my concern to ask you how the business is run. My worry is that they're posted in the sales book as having been sold at fivepence each. How do you account for that?'

'It was a mistake on Christine's part. She thought they

were made of paper and misread the price. You can't expect a child of ten to appreciate an Oriental art that has been handed down through the centuries.'

'Perhaps not, but you've failed to show the loss of 4s. 7d. on each article. How am I supposed to prepare a Trial Balance?'

'Couldn't we put it down to petty cash?' pleaded Florence.

'The petty cash should be kept for very small sums. I was just going to ask you about that. What is this disbursement of 12s. 11d.?'

'I daresay it's for milk.'

'You're absolutely certain? Do you keep a cat?'

By September the holiday-makers, with the migrant sea birds, showed the restlessness of coming departure. The Primary School had reopened, and Florence was on her own in the shop for most of the day.

Milo came in and said he would like to buy a birthday present for Kattie. He chose a colouring book of Bible Lands, which Florence considered a mere affectation.

'So Violet isn't going to get her own way,' he said. 'Has she been in here yet?'

'We haven't been open very long.'

'Six months. But she will come. She has far too much self-respect not to.'

Florence felt relieved, and yet obscurely insulted.

'I'm hoping to reopen my lending library quite soon,' she said. 'Perhaps Mrs Gamart – '

'Are you making any money?' Milo asked. There were only two or three other people in the shop, and one of those was a Sea Scout who came every day after school to read another chapter of *I Flew for the Führer*. He marked the place with a piece of string weighted down with a boiled sweet.

'You really need something like this,' Milo said, not at all urgently. Under his arm he had a thinnish book, covered with the leaf-green paper of the Olympia Press. 'This is volume one.'

'Is there a volume two?'

'Yes, but I've lent it to someone, or left it somewhere.'

'You should keep them together as a set,' said Florence firmly. She looked at the title, *Lolita*. 'I only stock good novels, you know. They don't move very fast. Is this good?'

'It'll make your fortune, Florence.'

'But is it good?'

'Yes.'

'Thank you for suggesting it. I feel the need of advice sometimes. You're very kind.'

'You're always making that mistake,' Milo replied.

The truth was that Florence Green had not been brought up to understand natures such as Milo's. Just as she still thought of gravity as a force that pulled things towards it, not simply as a matter of least resistance, so she felt sure that character was a struggle between good and bad intentions. It was too difficult for her to believe that he simply lapsed into whatever he did next only if it seemed to him less trouble than anything else.

She took a note of the title *Lolita*, and the author's name, Nabokov. It sounded foreign – Russian, perhaps, she thought.

6

Christine liked to do the locking up. At the age of ten and a half she knew, for perhaps the last time in her life, exactly how everything should be done. This would be her last year at the Primary. The shadow of her eleven plus, at the end of the next summer, was already felt. Perhaps, indeed, she ought to give up her job and concentrate on her studies, but Florence, for fear of being misunderstood, could not suggest to her assistant that it might be time for her to leave. The two of them, during the past months, had not been without their effect on one another. If Florence was more resilient, Christine had grown more sensitive.

On the first evening of September that could truthfully be called cold they sat, after the shutters were up, in the front room, in the two comfortable chairs, like ladies. Then the child went to put on the kettle in the backhouse, and Florence listened to the drumming of tap water, followed by a metallic note as the red Coronation tin containing biscuits was banged down on the dresser.

'We've got a blue one at ours. It's Westminster Abbey the same, but the procession goes all the way round the tin.'

'I'll light the heater,' said Florence, unused to idleness.

'My mam doesn't think those paraffin heaters are safe.'

'There's no danger as long as you're careful to clean them properly and don't allow a draught from two different sides at once,' Florence replied, screwing the cap of the container hard down. She must be allowed to be in the right sometimes.

The heater did not seem to be quite itself that evening. There was no draught, as far as that could ever be said in

64

Hardborough; and yet the blue flame shot up for a moment, as though reaching for something, and sank back lower than before. It went by the perhaps extravagant brand name of Nevercold. She had only just managed to get it adjusted when Christine came in seriously with the tea-things, arranged on a large black and gold tray.

'I like this old tray,' she said. 'You can put that down for me in your will.'

'I don't know that I want to think about my will yet, Christine. I'm a business woman in middle life.'

'Did that come from Japan?'

The tray represented two old men, fishing peaceably by moonlight.

'No, it's Chinese lacquer. My grandfather brought it back from Nanking. He was a great traveller. I'm not sure that they know how to make lacquer like this in China any more.'

By now the Nevercold was burning rather more steadily. The teapot basked in front of it, the room grew close, and the difference in age between Christine and Florence seemed less, as though they were no more than two stages of the same woman's life. In Hardborough an evening like this, when the sea could only just be heard, counted as silence. They had, therefore, warmth and quiet; and yet gradually Christine, who had been sitting back, as totally at ease as a rag doll, began to stiffen and fidget. Of course, a child of her age could hardly be expected to sit still for long.

After a while she got up and went into the backhouse – to make sure of the back door, she said. Florence had an impulse to stop her going out of the room, which was proved to be ridiculous when she came back almost immediately. A faint whispering, scratching and tapping could now be heard from the upstairs passage, and something appeared to be dragged hither and thither, like a heavy kitten's toy on a string. Florence did not pretend to herself, any more than she had ever done, that nothing was wrong.

'You're quite comfortable, aren't you, Christine?'

The little girl replied that she was. Unaccountably, she used her 'best' voice, the one urged by her class teacher on those who had to play Florence Nightingale, or the Virgin Mary. She was listening painfully, as though her ears were stretched or pricked.

'I've been wondering if I could help you at all with your eleven plus,' said Florence conversationally. 'Something towards it – I mean, we might read something together.'

'There's no reading to do. They give you some pictures, and you have to say which is the odd one out. Or they give you numbers, like 8, 5, 12, 9, 22, 16 and you have to say which number comes next.'

Just as she had failed to understand Milo, so Florence was unable to tell which number came next. She had been born too long ago. In spite of the Nevercold, the temperature seemed to have dropped perceptibly. She turned the heater up to its highest register.

'You're not cold, are you?'

'I'm always pale,' Christine replied loftily. 'There is no need to turn that thing up for me.' She was trembling. 'My little brother is pale as well. He and I are supposed to be quite alike.'

Neither of them was prepared to say that they wished to protect the other. That would have been to admit fear into the room. Fear would have seemed more natural if the place had been dark, but the bright shop lighting shone into every corner. The muffled din upstairs grew into a turmoil.

'That's coming on loud, Mrs Green.'

Christine had given up her Florence Nightingale voice. Mrs Green took her left hand, which was the nearest. A light current semed to be passing through it, transmitting a cold pulse, as though electricity could become ice.

'Are you sure you're all right?'

The hand lay in hers, weightless and motionless. Perhaps

it was dangerous to press the child, and yet Florence overwhelmingly felt that she must make her speak and that something must be admitted between them.

'That's going down my arm like a finger walking,' said Christine slowly. 'That stops at the top of my head. I can feel the hairs standing up properly there.'

It was an admission of sorts. Half rigid, half drowsy, she rocked herself to and fro on the chair in a curious position. The noise upstairs stopped for a moment and then broke out again, this time downstairs and apparently just outside the window, which shook violently. It seemed to be on the point of bursting inwards. Their teacups shook and spun in the saucers. There was a wild rattling as though handful after handful of gravel or shingle was being thrown by an idiot against the glass.

'That's the rapper. My mam knows there's a rapper in this old place. She reckoned that wouldn't start with me, because mine haven't come on yet.'

The battering at the window died to a hiss; then gathered itself together and rose to a long animal scream, again and again.

'Don't mind it, Christine,' Florence called out with sudden energy. 'We know what it can't do.'

'That doesn't want us to go,' Christine muttered. 'That wants us to stay and be tormented.'

They were besieged. The siege lasted for just over ten minutes, during which time the cold was so intense that Florence could not feel the girl's hand lying in hers, or even her own fingertips. After ten minutes, Christine fell asleep.

Florence did not expect her assistant to return; but she came back the very next afternoon, with the suggestion that if they had any more trouble they could both of them kneel down and say the Lord's prayer. Her mother had advised that it would be a waste of time consulting the Vicar. The Gippings were chapel and did not attend St Edmund's, but the minister would be of no use either, as though ghosts could be read down or prayed out, rappers could not. Meanwhile, it must surely be time to wash the dusters.

Florence regretted what seemed a slight on the gracious church whose tower protected the marshes, and whose famous south porch, between its angle buttresses, had been laid in flint checkerwork, silver grey and dark grey, by some ancestor of Mr Brundish. She wished that, when she spoke to the Vicar, the subject did not have to be money. She had been glad to give some of her stock to the harvest festival, although wondering a little how *Every Man His Own Mechanic*, and a pile of novels, could be considered as fruits of the earth and sea. It must be a burden – she realized that only too well – for the Canon to have to devote so much time to fund-raising. She wished she could see him for a moment simply to ask him: Was William Blake right when he said that everything possible to be believed in was an image of Truth. Supposing it was something not possible to be believed in? Did he believe in rappers? Meanwhile she went to the early service at St Edmund's, noticing, on the way out, that it was her turn to do the flowers next week. The list stared at her from the porch: Mrs Drury, Mrs Green, Mrs Thornton, Mrs Gamart for two weeks, as having a larger garden.

Mrs Gipping, whose house was between the old railway station and the church, was pegging up. Seeing Christine's employer walking down from early service, she signalled to her to come into the backhouse. Gipping, glimpsed between rows of green leaves, was tending the early celery, which would stand fit until Christmas.

In the damp warmth of the washday kitchen, Mrs Gipping was reassuring. She had been told about the rapper's visit-ation; but in her opinion there were disadvantages in every job. 'You'd like a drink, I expect, before you open up your business.' Florence was expecting some Nescafé, to which she had grown accustomed, but was directed to a large vegetable marrow hung over the sink. A wooden spigot had been driven into the rotund and glistening sides of the marrow. It was boldly striped in ripe green and yellow. Cups and glasses were ranged beneath it, and at a turn of the spigot a cloudy liquid oozed out drop by drop and fell heavily into the nearest cup. Mrs Gipping explained that it hadn't been up for long and wasn't at all heady, but that she'd seen a strong man come in and take a drink from a four-week marrow and fall straight down on to the stone floor, so that there was blood everywhere.

'Perhaps you'll give me the recipe,' said Florence politely, but Mrs Gipping replied that she never did, or the Women's Institute, against which she appeared to have some grudge, would go and put it in their collection of Old Country Lore.

Opening the shop gave her, every morning, the same feeling of promise and opportunity. The books stood as neatly ranged as Gipping's vegetables, ready for all comers.

Milo came in at lunch-time. 'Well, are you going to order *Lolita*?'

'I haven't decided yet. I've ordered an inspection copy. I'm confused by what the American papers said about it. One of the reviewers said that it was bad news for the trade and bad news for the public, because it was dull, pretentious, florid and repulsive, but on the other hand there was an article by Graham Greene which said that it was a masterpiece.'

'You haven't asked me what I think about it.'

'What would be the use? You have lost the second volume, or left it somewhere. Did you ever finish reading it?'

'I can't remember. Don't you trust your own judgment, my dear?'

Florence considered. 'I trust my moral judgment, yes. But I'm a retailer, and I haven't been trained to understand the arts and I don't know whether a book is a masterpiece or not.'

'What does your moral judgment tell you about me?'

'That's not difficult,' said Florence. 'It tells me that you should marry Kattie, think less about yourself, and work harder.'

'But you're not sure about *Lolita*? Are you afraid that the little Gipping girl might read it?'

'Christine? Not in the least. In any case, she never reads the books. She's an ideal assistant in that way. She only reads *Bunty*.'

'Or that the Gamarts mightn't like it? Violet still hasn't been here, has she?'

Milo added that the General had told him, when their cars were both waiting at the Flintmarket level crossing, that his wife didn't expect *Lolita* would ever be sold in a dear, sleepy little place like Hardborough.

'I don't want to take any of these things into account. If *Lolita* is a good book, I want to sell it in my shop.'

'It would make money, you know, if the worst came to the worst.'

'That isn't the point,' Florence replied, and really it was not. She wondered why this matter of the worst coming to the worst seemed to recur. Only a few days ago, down on the marshes, Raven had shown her a patch of green succulent weeds which, he said, were considered a delicacy in London and would fetch a high price if they were sent up there. 'That might help you, Mrs Green, if things don't work out.'

'We're doing quite respectably at the moment,' she told Milo. 'I shall take good advice about *Lolita* when the time comes.'

Milo seemed vaguely dissatisfied. 'I should like to read *Bunty*,' he said. Florence told him that there was a large pile of *Bunty*s in the backhouse, but she couldn't part with any of them without Christine's permission, and school wasn't out until half-past three.

After six months of trading Florence calculated that she had £2,500 worth of stock in hand, was owed about £80 on outstanding accounts and had a current bank balance with Mr Keble of just over £400 – a working capital of £3,000. She lived largely on tea, biscuits, and herrings and had spent almost nothing on advertising, except, for she couldn't disoblige the Vicar, in the parish magazine. Her wages bill was still twelve and sixpence a week, thirty shillings during the holidays. She didn't allow discount, except to the Primary School. Despatch was not at all the same as it had been at Müller's. The inhabitants were all used to dropping things in as they passed by. Everyone on two or four wheels, not only the obliging Wally, was a potential carrier. She herself was going to take the ferry across the Laze, as it was early-closing day, to deliver thirty Complete Wild Flower Recognition Handbooks to the Women's Institute. Remembering this, she took the top book off the crisp pile and looked through the illustrations for the green marsh plant which Raven had shown to her. It was not mentioned.

7

Eventually Mrs Gamart did come to the Old House Book-shop. It was a fortnight after the library reopened, this time at a much calmer tempo, as though the subscribers had re-strained themselves and the atmosphere had mellowed with the advancing year.

Christine had grasped the system rapidly and had made short work of learning the names of subscribers she did not know, that is, those who lived outside Hardborough. She classified them by attributes – Mrs Birthmark, Major Wheezer, and so forth – just as Raven did to tell the cattle apart; otherwise he'd never know the strays. Their correct names followed, and in remembering what books they had asked for, and what in fact they were going to get, the child was unerring. Impartiality made her severe. The library did not open now until school was out, and under her régime no one was allowed so much as to look at anyone else's selection.

The late autumn weather made the little expedition to the library just about the right length for the retired, both for those who drove and walked and for those who pottered. They seemed to be prepared to accept the B books, and even the Cs, without much complaint.

Mrs Gamart opened the street door on an afternoon at the end of October. The sun had gone round, and her shadow preceded her down the steps. She wore a three-quarter length Jaeger camel coat. Florence recognized the moment as a crisis in her fortunes. She had been too busy lately to think about the pressure that had been put upon her, six months earlier, to leave the Old House – or rather, to be honest, she kept herself busy so that the thought would not be uppermost in her mind. It was uppermost now. The shop had been transformed into a silent battleground in a nominal state of truce. She was in authority, on her own ground, and with some kind of support, since Christine had arrived and was depositing her Wellingtons and cardigan in the backhouse. On the other hand, Mrs Gamart, as a customer, must be deferred to; and as a patroness she was in the unassailable position of having forgiven all. She had made a request in the name of the Arts, and it had been refused; the Old House was still a shop, and yet she continued to behave with smiling dignity.

The library section was full of mildly loitering subscribers. There were customers in the front of the shop as well.

'I can see you're very busy. Please don't put yourself out. I really came to have a look at your library, just to see how it works. I've been meaning to do it for so long.'

Christine, by arrangement, looked after the issues and library tickets, particularly if several people were waiting. Glad to be indispensable, she was combing out her pale hair, tugging at the knots, and energetically ready to take over. Then, more or less tidy, she sprang out of the backhouse with the enthusiasm of a terrier empowered, for the afternoon, to act as a sheepdog. With rapid fingers she began to flick through the pink tickets. 'Just a tick, Mrs Keble. I'll fare to look after all of you in turn.' This would not quite do for Mrs Gamart's first visit, and Florence left the cash desk to escort her and to explain the system personally. At that moment she felt herself grasped forcibly by the elbow. Something with a sharp edge caught her in the small of the back.

It was the corner of a picture frame. She was held back by an urgent hand, and addressed by a man, not young, in a corduroy jacket, smiling as a toad does, because it has no other expression. The smile was, perhaps, 'not quite right'.

He had been manhandling a large canvas down the steps. Other smaller canvases were under his arm.

'You remember my letter. Theodore Gill, painter in water-colours, very much at your service. The possibility of an exhibition . . . a small selection of my work – poor things, madam, but mine own.'

'I didn't answer your letter.'

There were frames and sketches everywhere. How could they have invaded the shop so quickly?

'But silence means consent. Not as much room as I anticipated, but I can arrange for the loan of some screens from a very good friend, himself a watercolourist of note.'

'He doesn't want to exhibit too, I hope?'

'Later – you are very quick to understand me – but later.'

'Mr Gill, this isn't the best time to discuss your pictures. My shop is open to everyone, but I'm busy at the moment, and now that you've seen the Old House you'll realize that I've no room at all for your exhibition or anyone else's.'

'Sunset Viewed from Hardborough Common Across the Laze,' Mr Gill interrupted, raising his voice. 'Of local interest! Westward, look, the land is bright!'

All this time, beyond the scope of her immediate attention, a murmur of unease, even something like a shout, was rising from the back of the room. As she attempted, in an undignified scuffle, to prevent Mr Gill from tacking up his sunset, she became aware, for the first time, of a breaking up and surging forward of ranks. Mrs Gamart, very red in the face, one hand oddly clasped in the other, and possessed by some strong emotion, passed rapidly throught the shop and left without a word.

'What is it? What happened?'

Christine followed, redder still. Indeed her cheeks were red as fire and beginning to be streaked with tears.

'Mrs Gamart from The Stead, she wouldn't wait her turn, she picked up other people's books and looked at them. Do they were hers she wasn't allowed to do that, and she's muddled my pink tickets!'

'What did you do, Christine?'

'You wanted me to do it orderly! I gave her a good rap over the knuckles.'

She was still holding her school ruler, ornamented with a series of Donald Ducks. In the flow and counterflow of indignation, Mr Gill succeeded in hanging several more of his little sketches. The subscribers clamoured against the poor judgment shown. They had always known it was folly to entrust so much to a child of ten. Look, she was in tears. Mrs Gamart had suffered actual physical violence, and one of the customers tried to make off with a card and envelope. He said he had despaired of getting proper attention. Florence charged him 6¾d. and rang it up on the till; and that was her sole profit for the afternoon.

If she had gone out immediately into the High Street and apologized, the situation might have been retrieved. But she judged that the most important thing was to console Christine. Of course the subscribers had been right, the girl had been given too much authority, a poison, like any other excess. The only remedy, however, in this case was to give her more.

'I don't want you to think any more about it.' But, Christine blubbered, they had gone off with their pink tickets, and without their books. She mourned the destruction of a system.

'But there's still this one for Mr Brundish. He'll be waiting. I'm relying on you to take it round to him as usual.'

Christine put on her cardigan and anorak.

'I'll leave it for him where I always do, by the milk bottles. What are you going to do with all those old pictures?'

Mr Gill had gone to seek, as he put it, a cup of tea, which he wouldn't find any nearer than the Ferry Café. That, too, might well be shut in October. He might be grievously disappointed, possibly after a lifetime of disappointments. Florence would have to find time to mind about that, and indeed about a number of things; but all she wanted at the moment was to think of something which would give more dignity to Christine's errand.

'Wait a moment. There's a letter I want you to take as well, a letter to Mr Brundish. It won't take me long to write it.'

That morning the post had brought the inspection copy of *Lolita*. She took off the jacket and looked at the black cover, stamped in silver.

Dear Mr Brundish,
   Your letter to me when I first opened this shop was a great encouragement, and I am venturing now to ask for your advice. Your family, after all, has been living in Hardborough a great deal longer than anyone else's. I don't know if you have heard of the novel which Christine Gipping is bringing with this note – *Lolita*, by Vladimir Nabokov. Some critics say that it is pretentious, dull, florid and repulsive; others call it a masterpiece. Would you be good enough to read it and to let me know whether you think I should be doing right in ordering it and recommending it to my customers?

                    Yours sincerely,
                    Florence Green.

'Will there be an answer, then?' asked Christine doubtfully.

'Not today. But in a few days, a week or so perhaps, I'm sure there will.'

The lending library did not close the next week, but continued business in a hushed and decorous fashion. Theodore Gill, with his seemingly endless reserves of watercolours, had been evacuated. This was a bold stroke. Rhoda's

76

Dressmaker's, next door, was certainly not an old house, and it was perhaps a pity that it had been refaced with pebble-dash and the window-frames painted mauve, but it had an excellent, well-lighted showroom.

'You've got such nice clear walls, Jessie,' Florence began diplomatically. 'I don't know whether you've ever felt the need of a few pictures?'

'A semi-permanent exhibition,' put in Mr Gill, who was wandering about as usual. He would ruin everything.

'No, just a few watercolours for the time being. Perhaps one or two each side of your Silent Memories Calendar,' said Florence, who had supplied the calendar at cost price.

Jessie Welford did not answer directly, but turned to the artist himself. 'I never really think a wall needs anything, but I'm prepared to oblige if you're in a difficulty.'

He was hammering and banging all afternoon; the noise was almost as irritating as the poltergeist. Jessie's deprecatory laugh could also be heard. A card advertising the exhibition was placed in Rhoda's window. Jessie continued to laugh, and said that she had never had anything to do with an artist before, but that there had to be a first time for everything.

Florence had not considered how the answer to her note might come. She had certainly not expected it to be conveyed by Mrs Gipping. But Christine's mother, standing in front of her next day at the grocer's, told her suddenly and quite frankly that she was buying a pound of mixed fruit because Mr Brundish had told her to leave a cake for him on Sunday. He'd made up his mind, and she might as well pass this on now and save trouble, to ask Florence to tea on that day. In this way what was presumably a device to gain a measure of privacy became known to the whole of Hardborough. It was so improbable as to be almost frightening. Nobody, except an occasional mysterious old friend from Cambridge or London, ever received such an invitation. This, no doubt, was why Mrs Gipping had not wanted to waste her news on a smaller public.

To go there would be to increase the misunderstanding with Mrs Gamart, still unacknowledged at Holt House. Perhaps this was vanity. What could it matter where she went? An instinct, perhaps a shopkeeper's instinct, told her that it would matter. She hesitated. But an oddly-expressed reply from Mr Brundish, conveyed by Wally, and mentioning honour, convenience, and a-quarter-to-five exactly on Sunday afternoon, decided her. He told her that he had given careful consideration to what she had asked him, and hoped she would be satisfied with his answer.

The beginning of November was one of the very few times of the year when there was no wind. On the evening of the 5th a large bonfire was lit on the hard, near the moorings on the estuary. The pile of fuel had stood there for days, like a giant heron's nest. It was a joint undertaking about which every parent in Hardborough was prepared to give advice. Diesel fuel, although it was said to have burnt someone's eyebrows off last year, and they had never grown again, was used to start it. Then the sticks caught. Gathered up and down the shore, coated with sea-salt, they exploded into a bright blue flame. The otters and water-rats fled away up the dykes; the children came nearer, gathering from every quarter of the common. Potatoes were baked for them in the fire, coming out thick with ashes. The potatoes also tasted of diesel fuel. The organizers of the bonfire, once it had got going, stood back from the cavernous glow and discussed the affairs of the day. Even the headmaster of the Technical, who kept an eye on the blaze in a semi-official capacity, even Mrs Traill from the Primary, even the dejected-looking Mrs Deben, knew where Florence was going to tea on the Sunday.

* * *

She was not even sure how to get into Holt House. There was an iron bell-pull on the right of the front door, she told herself, as she set out. She had noticed it often. It was ornamental and massive and looked as though it might pull away leaving a length of chain in the visitor's hand. What a fool one would look then.

But the front door, when she got there, was not locked. It opened on to a hall lit dimly from a cupola, two floors above. The light struck the sluggish glass of a large Venetian mirror on the dark red wallpaper, patterned with darker red. Just inside the door stood a bronze statue of a fox-terrier, rather larger than life size, sitting up and begging, with a lead in its mouth. The lead was of real leather. On the hall chest there were porcelain jars, balls of string, and a bowl of yellowing visiting cards. The strong scent of camphor came perhaps from this chest, which stood against the left-hand wall. 'It formerly contained a croquet set,' said a voice in the gloom, 'but there is not much opportunity to play nowadays.'

Mr Brundish came forwards, looking critically round the hall, as though it were an outlying province of his territory which he rarely visited. His head turned gradually and suspiciously from side to side on his short neck. A clean white shirt was all that could properly be made out in the gloom. The collar seemed like the entrance to a burrow into which his dark face retreated, while his dark eyes watched anxiously.

'Come into the dining-room.'

The dining-room was straight through, with French windows closed on the garden. The view outside was blocked by a beech hedge, still hanging with brown leaves, heavy in the November damp. A mahogany table stretched from end to end of the room. Florence felt sad to think of anyone eating alone at such a table. It was laid, evidently for the occasion, with an assortment of huge blue-and-white earthenware dishes, looking like prizes at a fairground. Lost among them was a fruit-cake, a bottle of milk and an unpleasantly pink ham, still in its tin.

'We should have a cloth,' said Mr Brundish, taking the starched white linen out of a drawer, and trying to sweep the giant crockery aside. This Florence prevented by sitting down herself. Her host immediately took his place, huddling into a wing chair, spreading his large neat hairy hands on each side of his plate. Shabby, hardly presentable, he was not the sort of figure who could ever lose dignity. He was waiting, with a certain humility, for her to pour out. The silver teapot was the size of a small font, awkward to lift, and almost stone cold. Round the crest ran a motto: *Not to succeed in one thing is to fail in all.*

Fortunately, since there was only one knife on the table and the forks had been forgotten, Mr Brundish made no attempt to press the cake or the ham on his guest. Nor did he drink his cooling tea. Florence wondered whether, as a general rule, he had any regular meals at all. He wanted to welcome her but was more used to threatening, and the change of attitude was difficult for him. She felt the appeal of this. After a period of absolute silence which was not embarrassing because he was evidently so used to it, Mr Brundish said:

'You asked me a question.'

'Yes, I did. It was about a new novel.'

'You paid me the compliment of asking me a serious question,' Mr Brundish repeated heavily. 'You believed that I would be impartial. Doubtless you thought that I was quite alone in the world. That, as it happens, is not so. Otherwise I should be an interesting test case to establish whether there is such a thing as an action which harms no one but oneself. Such problems interested me in younger days. But, as I say, I am not alone. I am a widower, but I had brothers, and one sister. I still have relations and direct descendants, although they are scattered over the face of the globe. Of course, one can have enough of that sort of thing. Perhaps it strikes you that this tea is not quite hot.'

Florence sipped gallantly. 'You must miss your grand-children.'

Mr Brundish considered this carefully. 'Am I fond of children?' he asked.

She realized that the question was simply the result of lack of practice. He talked so seldom to people that he had forgotten the accepted forms of doing so.

'I shouldn't have thought so,' she said, 'but *I* am.'

'One of the Gipping girls, the third one, helps you in your shop, I believe. And that is all the assistance you get.'

'I have a book-keeper who comes in from time to time, and then there is my solicitor.'

'Tom Thornton. You won't get much out of him. In twenty-five years of practice I've never heard of his taking a case to counsel, or even to court. He always settles. Never settle!'

'There's no question of any legal proceedings. That wasn't at all what I wanted to ask you about.'

'I daresay Thornton would refuse to come to your place in any case. It's haunted, and he wouldn't care for that. Perhaps, by the way, you would have liked a wash. There is a lavatory on the right side of the hall with several basins. In my father's day it was particularly useful for shooting parties.'

Florence leant forward. 'You know, Mr Brundish, there is a certain responsibility about trying to run a bookshop.'

'I believe so, yes. Not everybody approves of it, you know. There are certain people, I think, who don't. I am referring to Violet Gamart. She had other plans for the Old House, and now it seems that she has been affronted in some way.'

'I'm sure she knows that was an accident.' It was difficult to speak anything other than the truth in Holt House, but Florence added, 'I'm sure that she means well.'

'Means well! Think again!' He tapped on the table with a weighty teaspoon. 'She wants an Arts Centre. How can the arts have a centre? But she thinks they have, and she wishes to dislodge you.'

'Even if she did,' said Florence, 'it wouldn't have the slightest effect on me.'

'It appears to me that you may be confusing force and power. Mrs Gamart, because of her connections and acquaintances, is a powerful woman. Does that alarm you?'

'No.'

Mr Brundish ignored, or perhaps had never been taught, the polite convention of not staring. He did stare. He looked fixedly at Florence, as though surprised at her being there at all, and yet she felt encouraged by his single-minded concentration.

'May I go back to my first question? I am thinking of making a first order of two hundred and fifty copies of *Lolita*, a considerable risk; but of course I'm not consulting you in a business sense – that would be quite wrong. All I should like to know, before I put in the order, is whether you think it is a good book, and whether it is right for me to sell it in Hardborough.'

'I don't attach as much importance as you do, I dare say, to the notions of right and wrong. I have read *Lolita*, as you requested. It is a good book, and therefore you should try to sell it to the inhabitants of Hardborough. They won't understand it, but that is all to the good. Understanding makes the mind lazy.'

Florence sighed with relief at a decision in which she had had no part. Then, to reassure herself of her independence, she took the single knife, cut two pieces of cake, and offered one to Mr Brundish. Deeply preoccupied, he put the slice on his plate as gently as if he were replacing a lid. He had something to say, something closer to his intentions in asking her to his house than anything that had gone before.

'Well, I have given you my opinion. Why should you think that a man would be a better judge of these things than a woman?'

At these words a different element entered the conversation, as perceptible as a shift in wind. Mr Brundish made no attempt to check this, on the contrary he seemed to be relieved that some prearranged point had been reached.

'I don't know that men are better judges than women,' said Florence, 'but they spend much less time regretting their decisions.'

'I have had plenty of time to make mine. But I have never found it difficult to come to conclusions. Let me tell you what I admire in human beings. I value most the one virtue which they share with gods and animals, and which need not therefore be referred to as a virtue. I refer to courage. You, Mrs Green, possess that quality in abundance.'

She knew perfectly well, sitting in the dull afternoon light, with the ludicrous array of slop basins and tureens in front of her, that loneliness was speaking to loneliness, and that he was appealing to her directly. The words had come out slowly, as though between each one she was being given the opportunity of a response. But while the moment hung in the balance and she struggled to put some kind of order into what she felt or half guessed, Mr Brundish sighed deeply. Perhaps he had found her wanting in some respect. His direct gaze turned gradually away from her, and he looked down at his plate. The necessity to make conversation returned.

'This cake would have been poison to my sister,' he observed.

Not long after, and not daring to make any suggestions about washing up, Florence took her leave. Mr Brundish accompanied her back across the hall. It was quite dark, and she wondered whether he would sit alone in the dark, or whether he would soon turn on the lights. He wished her good fortune, as he had done before, with her enterprise.

'I mustn't let myself worry,' she said. 'While there's life, there's hope.'

'What a terrifying thought that is,' muttered Mr Brundish.

British Railways delivered the copies of *Lolita* from Flint-market station, twenty-five miles away. When the carrier van arrived it drew, as usual, a ragged cheer from the bystanders. Something new was coming to Hardborough. Outside every public house there were parcels waiting to go out, and Raven, to save petrol, wanted a lift to the upper marshes.

Christine was aghast at the large numbers ordered. They hadn't sold so many of any one thing, not even *Build Your Own Racing Dinghy*. And it was long – four hundred pages. Yet she admired her employer's integrity and seeming excess. Florence told her that the book was already famous. 'Everyone will have heard of it. They may not expect to be able to buy it here in Hardborough.'

'They won't expect to find two hundred and fifty copies. You've lost your head properly over this.'

They closed earlier than usual so that they could re-dress the window. Behind the shutters they arranged the *Lolita*s in pyramids, like the tins in the grocer's. All the old Sellers were put in with the Stayers, and the dignified Illustrateds and flat books were shifted and disturbed without respect. 'What's all this cash in the till?' Christine asked. 'You've got a float of nearly fifty pounds in here.' But Florence had drawn it specially, being pretty sure that she would need it all. The cashier looked up at her with suspended animation, waiting until she had left the bank to see what Mr Keble thought about it.

8

December 4 1959

Dear Mrs Green,

I am in recept of a letter from John Drury & Co, representing their client Mrs Violet Gamart of The Stead, to the effect that your current window display is attracting so much undesirable attention from potential and actual customers that it is providing a temporary obstruction unreasonable in quantum and duration to the use of the highway, and that his client intends to establish a particular injury to herself in that it is necesary that she, as a Justice of the Peace and Chairwoman of numerous committees (list enclosed herewith), has to carry out her shopping expeditiously. In addition, the regular users of your lending library, who, you must remember, are legally in the position of invitees, have found themselves inconvenienced and in some cases been crowded or jostled and in other instances referred to by strangers to the district as old dears, old timers, old hens, and even old boilers. The civil action, which remains independent of course of any future police action to abate the said nuisance, might result in the award of considerable damages against us.

Yours faithfully,

Thomas Thornton,

Solicitor and Commissioner for Oaths.

December 5 1959

Dear Mr Thornton,

You have been my solicitor now for a number of years, and I understand 'acting for me' to mean 'acting energetically on my behalf'. Have you been to see the window display for yourself? We are very busy indeed on the sales side at the moment, but if you could manage the 200 yards down the road you might call into the shop and tell me what you think of it.

> Yours sincerely,
> Florence Green.

December 5 1959

Dear Mrs Green,

In reply to your letter of 5 December, which rather surprised me by its tone, I have endeavoured on two separate occasions to approach your front window, but found it impossible. Customers appear to be coming from as far away as Flintmarket. I think that we shall have to grant that the obstruction is unreasonable, at least as regards quantum. As to your other remarks, I would advise that it would be as well for you, as well as for myself, to keep a careful record of what has passed between us.

> Yours faithfully,
> Thomas Thornton,
> Solicitor and Commissioner for Oaths.

December 6 1959

Dear Mr Thornton,
What do you advise, then?
> Yours sincerely,
> Florence Green.

December 8 1959

Dear Mrs Green,

In reply to your letter of 6 December, I think we ought to abate the obstruction, by which I mean stopping the general public from assembling in the narrowest part of the High Street, before any question of an indictment arises, and I also think we should cease to offer for sale the complained-of and unduly sensational novel by V. Nabokov. We cannot cite Herring v. Metropolitan Board of Works 1863 in this instance as the crowd has not assembled as the result of famine or of a shortage of necessary commodities.

> Yours faithfully,
> Thomas Thornton,
> Solicitor and Commissioner for Oaths.

December 9 1959

Dear Mr Thornton,

A good book is the precious life-blood of a master-spirit, embalmed and treasured up on purpose to a life beyond life, and as such it must surely be a necessary commodity.

> Yours sincerely,
> Florence Green.

December 10 1959

To: Mrs Florence Green

Dear Madam,

I can only repeat my former advice, and I may add that in my opinion, although this is a personal matter

and therefore outside my terms of reference, you
would do well to make a formal apology to Mrs
Gamart.

Yours faithfully,
Thomas Thornton,
Solicitor and Commissioner for Oaths.

December 11 1959

Dear Mr Thornton,
Coward!

Yours sincerely,
Florence Green.

If Florence was courageous, it was in quite a different way
from, for example, General Gamart, who had behaved
exactly the same when he was under fire as when he wasn't,
or from Mr Brundish, who defied the world by refusing to
admit it to his earth. Her courage, after all, was only a
determination to survive. The police, however, did not
prosecute, or even consider doing so, and after Drury had
advised Mrs Gamart that there was nothing like enough
evidence to proceed on, the complaint was dropped. The
crowd grew manageable, the shop made £82 10s. 6d. profit
in the first week of December on *Lolita* alone, and the new
customers came back to buy the Christmas orders and the
calendars. For the first time in her life, Florence had the
alarming sensation of prosperity.

She might have felt less secure if she had reviewed the
state of her alliances. Jessie Welford and the watercolour
artist, who by now was a permanent lodger at Rhoda's, were
hostile. Christine's comment, that she'd as soon go to bed
with a toad as with that Mr Gill, and she was surprised he
didn't give Miss Welford warts, was quite irrelevant; the fact

was that the two made front together. Not one of the throng in the High Street had come into the dressmaker's, still less bought a watercolour. Nor had they looked at the wet fish offered by Mr Deben. All the tradespeople were now either slightly or emphatically hostile to the Old House Bookshop. It was decided not to ask her to join the Inner Wheel of the Hardborough and District Rotary Club.

As Christmas approached, she grew reckless. She took her affairs out of Mr Thornton's wavering hands and entrusted them to a firm of solicitors in Flintmarket. Through the new firm she contracted with Wilkins, who undertook building as well as plumbing, to pull down the damp oyster warehouse – work, it must be admitted, which went ahead rather slowly. She could decide later what to do with the site. Then, to make room for the new stock, she turned out, on an impulse, the mouldering piles of display material left by the publishers' salesmen. A life-size cardboard Stalin and Roosevelt and an even larger Winston Churchill, an advancing Nazi tank to be assembled in three pieces and glued lightly on the dotted line, Stan Matthews and his football to be suspended from the ceiling with the string provided, six-foot cards of footsteps stained with blood, a horse with moving eyeballs jumping a fence, easily worked with a torch battery, menacing photographs of Somerset Maugham and Wilfred Pickles. All out, all to be given to Christine, who wanted them for the Christmas Fancy Dress Parade.

This was an event organized by local charities. 'I'm obliged to you for these, Mrs Green,' Christine said. 'Otherwise I'd have fared to go attired as an Omo packet.' The detergent firms were prepared to send quantities of free material, as were the *Daily Herald* and the *Daily Mirror*. But everyone in Hardborough was sick of these disguises. Florence wondered why the young girl didn't want to go dressed as something pretty, perhaps as a Pierrette. Out of the unpromising materials, however, Christine sewed and glued together an odd but striking costume – Good-bye, 1959. One of the *Lolita* jackets provided a last touch, and Florence, whose feet were almost as small as her assistant's, lent a pair of shoes. They were crocodile courts, the buckles also covered with crocodile. Christine, who had never seen them before, although she had had a good poke round upstairs, wondered if they were by Christian Dior.

'You know that Dior met a gipsy who told him he'd have ten years of good fortune and then meet his death,' she said. Florence felt she could hardly afford to speak lightly of the supernatural.

'That'd be a French gipsy, of course,' said Christine consolingly, slopping about in the crocodile courts.

The patroness of the Fancy Dress Parade was Mrs Gamart, from The Stead. The judge, in deference to his connection with the BBC, and therefore with the Arts, was Milo North, who protested amiably that he should never have been asked, as he tried to avoid definite judgments on every occasion. His remarks were greeted with roars of laughter. The Parade was held in the Coronation Hall, never quite completed as Hardborough had intended, so that the roof was still of corrugated iron. The rain pounded down, only quietening as it turned to drizzle or sleet. Christine Gipping, wheeling Melody in a pram decorated with barbed wire, which had been sent down to publicize *Escape or Die*, was an easy winner of the most original costume. Discussion on the point was hardly possible.

The Nativity Play, which followed a week later, was on a Saturday afternoon, when the shop was too busy with the Christmas trade for Florence to take time off. She heard about the performance, however, from Wally and Raven, who dropped in, and Mrs Traill, who had come to see about her orders for next term.

The critical reception of the play had been mixed. Too much realism, perhaps, had been attempted when Raven

90

had brought a small flock of sheep off the marshes on to the stage. On the other hand, no one had forgotten their parts, and Christine's dancing had been the success of the evening. As a result of her success in the Fancy Dress she had been awarded the coveted part of Salome, which meant that she was entitled to appear in her eldest sister's bikini.

'She had to dance, to get the head of John the Baptist,' Wally explained.

'What music did you have?' asked Florence.

'That was a Lonnie Donegan recording, "Putting on the Agony, Putting on the Style." I don't know that you cared for it very much, Mrs Traill.'

Mrs Traill replied that after many years at the Primary she had become accustomed to everything. 'Mrs Gamart, I'm afraid, didn't look as though she approved.'

'If she didn't, there was nothing she could do about it,' Raven said. 'She was powerless.' He exuded a warm glow of well-being, having had one or two at the Anchor on the way over.

Florence was still anxious about Christine's prospects in the eleven plus. 'She is such a good little assistant, I can't help feeling that after she's been through grammar school she might make it her career. She has the ability to classify, and that can't be taught.'

The glance that flashed through Mrs Traill's spectacles suggested that everything could be taught. Nevertheless, a sense of responsibility weighed on Florence. She felt she ought to have done more. Granted that the child didn't like reading, with the exception of *Bunty*, or being read to, mightn't there be other opportunities? She kept Wally back after the others had gone and said that she had been interested to hear about the play, but had he or his friends or Christine ever been to a real theatre? They might go over to the Maddermarket, at Norwich, if something good came on.

'We've none of us ever been there,' Wally replied doubt-fully, 'but we did go over from the school to Flintmarket last year, to see a travelling company. That was quite interesting, to see how they fixed up the amplification.'

'What play did they put on?' asked Florence.

'The day we went it was *Hansel and Gretel*. There's singing in it. They didn't do it all – they did the bit where the boy and girl lie down and get fresh together, and the angels come in and cover them with leaves.'

'You didn't understand the play, Wally. Hansel and Gretel are brother and sister.'

'That doesn't make it any different, Mrs Green.'

January, as always, brought its one day when people said that it felt like spring. The sky was a patched and ragged blue, and the marsh, with its thousand weeds and grasses, breathed a faint odour of resurrection.

Florence went for her walk in a direction she usually avoided, perhaps not deliberately, but certainly she had not been that way for a long time. Turning her back on the estuary of the Laze, she walked over the headland, north-wards. A notice on a wired-up gate read PRIVATE: FARM LAND. She knew that the path was a right of way, climbed over, and went on. Presently it took a sharp turn to the sea, which idled on its stony beach, forty feet below. The turf was as springy as fine green hair. Running to the cliff's edge could be seen the ghost of an old service road, and on each side of it were ruins, ruins of bungalows and more ambitious small villas. A whole estate had been built there five years ago without any calculation of the sea's erosion. Before anyone had come to live there the sandy cliff had given way and the houses had begun to totter and slide. Some of the FOR SALE FREEHOLD notices were still in place. One of the smaller villas was left right on the verge. Half the foundations and the front wall were gone, while the sitting-room, exposed to all the birds of the air, flapped its last shreds of wallpaper over the void.

For ten minutes or so – since it felt like spring – Florence sat on an abandoned front doorstep, laid with ornamental tiles. The North Sea emitted a brutal salt smell, at once clean and rotten. The tide was running out fast, pausing at the submerged rocks and spreading into yellowish foam, as though deliberating what to throw up next or leave behind, how many wrecks of ships and men, how many plastic bottles. It annoyed her that she could not remember exactly, although she had been told often enough, how much of the coast was eroded every year. Wally would supply the information immediately. Churches with peals of bells were under those waves, as well as the outskirts of a speculative building estate. Historians dismissed the legend, pointing out that there would have been plenty of time to save the bells, but perhaps they didn't know Hardborough. How many years had they left the Old House, when everyone knew it was falling to pieces?

Milo and Kattie – someone young, in any case, with bright red tights, so it could hardly be anyone else – were walking down the cliff path. When they got nearer, Florence could see that Kattie looked as though she had been crying, so the outing could hardly have been a success.

'Why are you sitting on a doorstep, Florence?' Milo asked.

'I don't know why I go out for walks at all. Walks are for the retired, and I'm going to go on working.'

'Is there room on your step for me to sit down?' Kattie asked. She was behaving nicely, trying to please and conciliate. Either she wanted Milo to see how readily she could charm other people, or she wanted to show him how kind she could be to a dull middle-aged woman, simply because Milo seemed to know her. Whichever it was, Florence felt deeply sympathetic. She made room on the step at once and

Kattie sat down neatly, pulling her short skirt down over her long red legs.

'Kattie wouldn't believe that there were ruins in Hardborough, so I brought her to see,' said Milo, looking down at both of them, and then at the pitiful houses. 'They were all ready to move into, weren't they? I wonder if the water's still connected.' He stepped over a pile of masonry into the remains of a kitchenette, and tried the taps. Rusty water, the colour of blood, gushed out. 'Kattie could live here perfectly well. She keeps saying she doesn't like our place.'

Florence, wishing to change the subject, asked Kattie about her work at the BBC. It was rather disappointing to find that she had nothing to do with television but checked the expenses sheets for the Recorded Programmes Department, which she referred to as RPD. Surely that couldn't be rewarding work for this intelligent-looking girl.

'We've been to lunch with Violet Gamart,' said Milo, balancing easily on the short grass at the very edge of the cliff. 'It was a chance for her not to disapprove of us.'

'Why can't you ever say anything agreeable about anybody?' Florence asked. 'Does she still want you to run, or look as though you're running, an Arts Centre in Hardborough?'

'That's a seasonal matter with her. It reaches a serious crisis every summer, when Glyndebourne and the Aldeburgh Festival get into the news. Now it's January. The pulse is low.'

'Mrs Gamart was very kind,' said Kattie, hugging herself rather as Christine sometimes did.

'I don't like kind people, except for Florence.'

'That doesn't impress me,' said Florence. 'You appear to me to work less and less. You must remember that the BBC is a Corporation, and that your salary is ultimately met out of public funds.'

94

'That's Kattie's business,' Milo replied. 'She does my expense sheets. We'll walk back with you.'

'Thank you, I'll stay here for a little longer.'

'Please come with us,' said Kattie. She appeared to be racking her brains. 'Won't you tell me about how you manage to wrap up the books? I'm always so hopeless with paper and string.'

Florence always used paper bags, and never remembered to have seen Kattie in the shop at all, but she agreed to accompany them back to Hardborough. Kattie kept picking little bits of plants and asking her deferentially what they were. Florence had to tell her that she wasn't sure of any of them, except thyme and plantains, until the flowers began to show, and that wouldn't be for a couple of months.

One day, when the top class of the Primary School were having their free activity, which in cold weather largely meant sitting at their desks and amiably exchanging whatever dirty words they had learned lately, a stranger appeared at the door.

'You needn't rise from your seats, children. I'm the Inspector.'

'No, you're not,' said the head boy.

Mrs Traill, who had been checking the attendance register, came back to the classroom. 'I don't think I know you,' she said.

'Mrs Traill? My name is Sheppard. Perhaps you'd care to glance at my certificate of appointment from the Education Authority, which entitles me, under the Shops Act of 1950, to enter any school in which I have reasonable cause to believe that children employed in any capacity in a shop are at present being educated.'

'Employed!' cried Mrs Traill. 'I daresay they'd like to be employed, but outside of family business and newspaper rounds, I'd like you to tell me what there is for them. You might like to try again at potato-lifting time. I don't remember your ever coming here before, by the way.'

'Due to staff shortages, our visits have not been as regular as we should like.'

'Who suggested that you should come here this time?' the headmistress asked. Receiving no answer, she added. 'There's only Christine Gipping who works regularly after school.'

'At what address?'

'The Old House Bookshop. Stand up, Christine.'

The Inspector checked his notebook. 'As I expect you're aware, I have the right to examine this girl as I think fit in respect to matters under the Shops Act.'

A storm of whistling broke out from the class.

'I've brought a lady colleague with me' said the Inspector grimly. 'She's just outside, checking the car's properly locked.'

'There won't be criminal interference, then,' the head boy said placidly.

Christine was unperturbed. She followed the female inspector, who hurried in, with explanatory gestures, from the yard, into the small room behind the piano where the dinner money was counted.

To: Mrs Florence Green, The Old House Bookshop

The Education Authority's Inspectors have examined Christine Gipping and have required her to sign a declaration of truth of the matters respecting which she was examined. Although there is no suggestion of irregularity in her school attendance, it appears that consequent to the arrival of a best-selling book she worked more than 44 hours in your establishment during one week of her holidays. Furthermore her health safety and welfare are at risk in your premises which are haunted in an objectionable manner. I quote from a deposition by Christine Gipping to the effect that 'the rapper doesn't come on so loud now, but we can't get rid of him altogether'. I am advised that under the provisions of the Act the supernatural would be classed with bacon-slicers and other machinery through which young persons must not be exposed to the risk of injury.

From: Mrs Florence Green

The Shop Acts which you quote only apply to young persons between the ages of fourteen and sixteen. Christine Gipping is just eleven, or what would she be doing in the Primary?

To: Mrs Florence Green, The Old House Bookshop

If Christine Gipping is, as you say, 11 years of age she is not permitted by law to serve in any retail business except a stall or moveable structure consisting of a board supported by trestles which is dismantled at the end of the day.

From: Mrs Florence Green

There is no room on the pavement of Hardborough High Street for boards supported by trestles to be dismantled at the end of the day. Christine, like a large proportion of the Primary School population of Suffolk, is, as you very well know, 'helping out'. She will be taking her 11+ in July and I expect her to proceed to Flintmarket Grammar School, when she will have no time for odd jobs after school.

No more was heard from the Authority's inspectors, and this complaint, wherever it had originated, died away like the earlier ones into silence. A brief note of congratulation came round from Mr Brundish. How could he have heard about it? He recalled that in his grandfather's day the Inspector had always come round the schools with a ferret in his pocket, ready to be of use in getting rid of the rats.

But the Old House Bookshop, like a patient whose crisis is over, but who cannot regain strength, showed less encouraging returns. This was to be expected in the months after Christmas. There would be more capital in hand after the warehouse was demolished and she could sell the site. Wilkins was being very slow, however. He had never been a speedy man, and of course the cold weather was against him. These old places looked as though they'd come down at a touch, but they could be stubborn. Florence was obliged to repeat this to the bank manager, who had asked her to step in for a chat, and had then asked her if she had noted how very little working capital she had at present.

'You are converting the oyster warehouse from a fixed into a current asset?'

'It isn't either at the moment,' Florence replied. 'Wilkins says the mortar's harder than the flint.'

Mr Keble observed that it was not a very favourable moment, perhaps, for selling a small building site which had always been known to be waterlogged. Florence didn't recall his having mentioned this when her loan had first been discussed.

'Rather less activity, I think, in your business at the moment? Perhaps it's just as well. At one point it seemed as though you were going to jolt us out of our old ways altogether. But all small businesses have their ups and downs. That's another thing you find easier to grasp in a position like mine, where you can take the broader view.'

Later that spring, Mrs Gamart's nephew, the member for

the Longwash Division, a brilliant, successful, and stupid young man, got his Private Bill through its first and second reading. It was an admirable bill from the point of view of his career. The provisions were acceptable to all parties – humanitarian, democratic, a contribution to the growing problem of leisure, and unlikely ever to be put into practice. Referred to as the Access to Places of Educational Value and Interest Bill, it empowered local councils to purchase compulsorily, and subject to agreed compensation, any buildings wholly or partly erected before 1549 and not used for residential purposes, provided there was no building of similar date on public show in the area. The buildings acquired were to be used for the cultural recreation of the public. Florence noticed a small paragraph about this in *The Times*, but knew that it could not affect her. Neither Hardborough nor Flintmarket councils had money for projects of any kind, and in any case, the Old House was in use for 'residential purposes' – she was still living there, although the words deflected her thoughts to the problems of upkeep. The winter had taken a large number of pegged tiles off the roof of the Old House, and a patch of damp was spreading across the bedroom ceiling, inch by inch, just as the sea was eating away the coast. There was more damp in the stock cupboard underneath the staircase. But it was the home of her books and herself, and they would remain there together.

The subject of the Bill had not been suggested to her nephew by Mrs Gamart, although she was gratified when he told her, over lunch at the House, that the idea had come to him at that party of hers last spring. As a source of energy in a place like Hardborough which needed so little, an energy, too, which was often expended in complaints, she was bound to create a widening circle of after-effects which went far beyond the original impulse. Whenever she realized this she was pleased, both for herself and for the sake of others, because she always acted in the way she felt to be right. She

99

did not know that morality is seldom a safe guide for human conduct.

She smiled at her nephew over the lunch table, and said that she would not have the fish. 'I'm afraid living in Hardborough spoils you for fish anywhere else,' she said. 'You get it so fresh down there.' She was a very charming woman, well-preserved too, and had come up to London that day to press for some charitable scheme, nothing at all do to with the Old House Bookshop. Her nephew could not quite call to mind what it was, but he would be reminded.

9

At Hardborough Primary School the eleven-plus exam was not marked in the usual way by the headmistress herself, after the children had gone home. The papers were exchanged with Saxford Tye Primary. This gave the necessary guarantee of impartiality to the closely observant little town, or, as Mrs Traill put it, saved her from being torn to pieces after it was over. She was, perhaps, not quite so sensitive in the matter of giving out the results. The acceptances from Flintmarket Grammar School came in square white envelopes. Those from the Technical came in long buff-coloured ones. Each child in the top form, when they arrived at school that summer's morning, looked at their own desk, saw their envelopes, and knew their destiny at once. So, too, did everyone else in the class.

Hardborough children, looking back in future years over a long life, would remember nothing more painful or more decisive than the envelopes waiting on the desks. Outside it was fine weather. Yellow gorse was in flower from end to end of the common. Summer had also invaded the classroom. The pupils had been asked to bring in some Nature for the elementary biology class. There were jam-jars of white campion, dog-roses and catchfly; loose straw was scattered on the teacher's desk, and on the window-sill an eel was swimming uncomfortably in a glass tank.

It was all over in a minute. Christine was one of the last into school. She looked at her envelope and knew at once that it was what she had always expected. She had a long buff one.

Mrs Gipping called round herself to the Old House Bookshop – a concession worth noting since, with her busy day, she emerged only when she thought it strictly necessary. She had come to tell Florence that Christine would not be working for her any more, but she saw at once that Florence realized this and there was no need to deliver the message. Instead, they sat down together in the backhouse. The shop was shut, and this year's holiday-makers could be heard faintly calling from the beach.

'The old rapper doesn't seem to manifest while I'm here,' Mrs Gipping remarked. 'That knows not to waste its time, I dare say.'

'I haven't heard it so much lately,' said Florence, and then remembering the vintage marrow, she suggested they might have a drink together. 'Let's have a glass of cherry brandy, Mrs Gipping. I never do, certainly not in the afternoon, but perhaps just today.'

She took down two small glasses and the bottle, which like many liqueur bottles was of a strange shape, defiantly waisted and curved, and demanding to be kept for special occasions only.

'You got that in the church raffle, I suppose,' said Mrs Gipping. 'It's been in three years without anyone drawing the ticket. The Vicar won't know what to do without it.'

Perhaps it would bring luck. Each of the two women took a sip of the bright red, terribly sickly liquid.

'They say Prince Charles is fond of this.'

'At his age!' Then, knowing that it was her duty, as hostess, to come to the point, Florence said, 'I was very sorry to hear about Christine.'

'She's the first of ours not to get to the Grammar. It's what we call a death sentence. I've nothing against the Technical, but it just means this: what chance will she ever have of meeting and marrying a white-collar chap? She won't ever be able to look above a labouring chap or even an unemployed chap and believe me, Mrs Green, she'll be pegging out her own washing until the day she dies.'

The image of Wally flitted through Florence's tired mind. Wally had been at the Grammar this past year, and it couldn't be denied that he had been seen about lately with a new girl friend, also at the Grammar. He was teaching her to swim. 'Christine is very quick and handy,' she said, trying for a brighter view. 'And very musical,' she added, remembering the dance at the Court of King Herod. 'She's sure to make something of her life, wherever she is.'

'I don't want you to think that anything's being held against you,' said Mrs Gipping. 'That's what I principally came to say. We none of us believe that Christine would have got her eleven plus, even if she hadn't worked here after school. More than that, it may turn out to be an advantage. Experience must count. The school-leavers all say, they won't take us without experience, but how do we set about getting it? But Christine, if she needs a reference, we tell her that she's only got to come to you for it.'

'Certainly. She only has to ask.'

'She doesn't want to give up earning altogether while she's at the Technical.'

'Of course not.'

'We've been looking around a bit. We reckon she might get taken on as a Saturday girl at that new bookshop at Saxford Tye.'

Mrs Gipping spoke with a kind of placid earnestness. She finished her cherry brandy in a way that showed that she knew very well how to make a small glass last a long time.

'That's disagreeably sweet,' she said. 'Still, you can't complain if it's for the church.'

After Mrs Gipping had gone, Florence took her car out of its garage in a disused boat-shed next to the Coastguards and drove over to Saxford Tye. She parked in the main street and walked quietly about in the dusk. It was quite true. In a

103

good position, next to the smartened-up Washford Arms, there was a new bookshop.

It had not been open long, so it could not account by itself for her diminished trade. She allowed the latest Trial Balance, hovering unpleasantly on the threshold of her mind, to come in and declare itself. In those days, the separate pounds, shillings and pence allowed three separate kinds of menace from their three unyielding columns. Purchases £95 10s. 6d. (far too high), cash sales £62 10s. 11¾d., wages 12s. 6d., general expenses £2 8s. 2d., no orders, returns inward £2 17s. 6d., cash in hand £102 0s. 4d., value of stock July 31 say £600, petty cash, as usual, inexplicable. The holiday-makers had not seemed to have so much to spend this year, or perhaps not so much to spend on books. In future, if they stopped at Saxford on the way through, there might be even less.

Although she had no way of knowing this, Saxford Tye Books was not an enterprise like her own, but an investment on behalf of the simple-minded Lord Gosfield, who had sallied out from his fen-bound castle to attend Mrs Gamart's party more than a year ago. Since that time, all his acquaintances seemed to be turning their spare cottages into holiday homes, and his first slow intention (since he owned a good deal of Saxford Tye) had been to do the same thing, but then that had proved impracticable, because no one had ever yet been known to spend a holiday there. Sunk between silos and piles of root vegetables, the village was unique in that part of Suffolk in not having even a picturesque church to offer the visitor. The church had, in fact, been carelessly burnt down during the celebrations of 1925, when the Sugar Beet Subsidy Act had been passed, saving the lethargic population from extinction. But the construction of a new main road had made the Gosfield Arms, which had two good coach yards, a reasonable stopping place for motorists on the way to Hardborough or Yarmouth. The adjoining properties could be developed as shops, and Lord Gosfield seemed to remember Violet Gamart, who, mind you, was a clever woman, saying something about a bookshop. He asked his agent whether this might not be a good scheme. In collusion with this agent, who had more wits about him than his master, the brewers had made it necessary for anyone who wanted to stretch their legs, in the sense of reaching the pub's shining new lavatories, to pass the side window of the new bookshop. This displayed horse-brasses and ash-trays in the shape of sugar-beets, as well as a type of novel which Florence never intended to stock. The place was still open at half-past six. Undoubtedly it would be much livelier for Christine.

'I shall miss you, Christine, and I wanted to ask you what you'd like for a present.'

'Not one of those books. Not the kind you have.'

'Well, then, what? I'm going into Flintmarket tomorrow. What about a cardigan?'

'I'd rather have the money.' Christine was implacable. She could only find relief in causing pain. Her resentment was directed against everyone who had to do with books, and reading, and made it a condition of success to write little compositions, and to know which picture was the odd one out. She hated them all. Mrs Green, who was supposed to understand these things, and had always told her she would pass, was no better than the rest of them. She wouldn't pay them the compliment of distinguishing between them.

'Well, I hope you'll come round to the shop and see me sometimes, in the evenings.'

'I shan't have that much time.'

'The school bus gets in about five, doesn't it? I could keep a look out for you?'

'Oh, I shouldn't strain yourself. They say it's not good for you after you've turned forty.'

105

Perhaps it wasn't. Florence had noticed one or two eccentricities in herself lately, which might be the result of hard work, or of age, or of living alone. When the letters came, for example, she often found herself wasting time in looking at the postmarks and wondering whoever they could be from, instead of opening them in a sensible manner and finding out at once.

The letters, however, were fewer, and her whole business life might be said to be contracting. The lending library, which after all had been a steady if modest source of income, was now closed for good. This was because for the first time in its history a Public Library has been established in Hardborough. The borough had been requesting this service for very many years, and it would be difficult to say who was to be congratulated on forcing the measure through the County Council at last. The new Library was an important amenity. Fortunately, suitable premises were available. The property acquired was that of Deben's wet fish shop.

The rapper made itself heard less frequently, although once Florence found the account books, on which she spent so much time nowadays, thrown violently face downwards on to the ground. The pages were scrawled and tangled. She felt somewhat awkward in showing them to Jessie Welford's niece, who, however, told her that she was afraid other arrangements would have to be made, as she'd been given promotion at the office and wouldn't have time in the future to give a hand at the Old House. A certain coldness reflected the feeling at Rhoda's. Only just at the end, when she was making sure that she hadn't left anything behind, did she relent a little.

'Of course, my business was only to check the transactions, and I should professionally be quite wrong to offer you any other advice – '

'If it would be quite wrong, my dear, I certainly mustn't

let you do it,' said Florence, watching the assured young woman settle and pat herself into her raincoat.

'Well, then, so that seems to be all. I hope I haven't left you with any of my goods and chattels. What was it my father used to say – if you're down in the mouth think of Jonah – he came out all right.'

She was having supper next door at Rhoda's, and hurried away, leaving Florence with these images of disaster and shipwreck. Fortunately there was the spring cleaning to do, and the mailing list, which the scouts had undertaken to do for her on their hand printing-press. It would mean getting up an hour or two earlier in the mornings. She looked with shame at the rows of patiently waiting unsold books.

'You're working too hard, Florence,' Milo said.

'I try to concentrate – Put those down, they've only just come in and I haven't checked them. Surely you have to succeed, if you give everything you have.'

'I can't see why. Everyone has to give everything they have eventually. They have to die. Dying can't be called a success.'

'You're too young to bother about dying,' said Florence, feeling that this was expected of her.

'Perhaps. I believe Kattie might die, though. She wastes so much energy.'

Three times a week, Florence thought. She sighed. 'How is Kattie?' she asked.

'I don't know. As a matter of fact, Kattie has left me. She's gone to live with someone else, in Wantage. He's in Outside Broadcasting. I'm confiding in you.'

'I expect you've told everybody else in Hardborough who'll listen to you.'

'It concerns you particularly, because I shall have so much more free time. I shall be able to work here part-time as your assistant. I expect you miss that little girl.'

Florence refused to be taken aback. 'Christine learned a

great deal while she was here,' she said, 'and she had quite a nice manner with the customers.'

'Not as nice as mine,' said Milo. 'She hit Violet Gamart, didn't she? I shouldn't do that. How much can you pay me?'

'I gave Christine twelve and six a week, and I don't feel able to offer any more than that at the moment.' Surely that would get rid of Milo, although Florence was quite fond of him. If everyone was like this at the television place at Shepherd's Bush, they must find it difficult to get anything done at all. They must all be persuading each other.

'If you're interested in the work' – we used to call it 'nosey' at Müller's, she thought – 'you're welcome to come in the afternoons and try the job for a few weeks. If you don't need the twelve and sixpence you can give it to the Lifeboat or the Coastguards' box. Only please remember that I didn't ask you to come. You asked yourself.'

When Parliament reassembled, the Private Bill brought in by the member for the Longwash Division passed its third reading and went straight to the Lords. It attracted even less attention this time. Very few of the great public in whose name it was promoted read any of its amended provisions. The ancient buildings, for example, were to be subject to compulsory purchase even if they were occupied at the moment, provided they had stood vacant at any time in the past for more than five years. Mrs Gamart's nephew had had the assistance of Parliamentary draftsmen. It was impossible to say who was responsible for this detail or that.

Everybody thought it was very obliging of young Mr North to help out at the Old House, particularly when the business was not doing nearly as well as it used to. It was regrettable, perhaps, that whenever Florence had to drive over to Flint-market to see if the new orders had arrived, he immediately shut up shop and could be seen sitting in the comfortable

108

chair, moved forward into the patch of afternoon sunlight which came through the front window. But if business was slack, how could you blame him? And he always had a book of poetry, or something of the kind, open in front of him.

As Milo never remembered on these occasions to lock the backhouse door, Christine was able to come straight in, approaching on soundless feet, wearing her new school blazer.

> 'Shower down thy love, O burning bright! for one
>> night or the other night
> Will come the Gardener in white, and gathered
>> flowers are dead, Christine.'

'You watch it, Mr North,' said Christine.

'What unpleasant expressions they teach you in that new school of yours!'

Christine turned very red.

'I didn't come here to mix it with your sort,' she said.

A kind of unease had brought her back and she was disappointed not to find Florence there, partly so that she could cheer her up a little, partly so that she could show that she wouldn't take the job on again at any price. Also, she might as well show her the cardigan which she had bought with the money she had been given. It buttoned up high, not like the old-fashioned sort.

'Why don't you help Mrs Green any more?' Milo asked. 'She misses you.'

'Well, she's got you, hasn't she, Mr North? You're always in and out.'

Hesitating, not wanting to seem to ask for information, she burst out: 'They say they won't let her go on keeping this bookshop.'

'Who are "they"?'

'They want the Old House for something else they've thought of.'

'Why should you mind about that, my dear?'

'They say she can't hold on to it, do they'll have her up. That'll mean County Court. She'll have to swear to tell the whole truth and nothing but the truth.'

'We must hope that it won't come to that.'

Christine hardly felt that she had reasserted her position as yet. She minced round, dusting here and there – the duster needed a wash, as usual, she said – and looking with a stranger's recognition at her old acquaintances on the shelves.

'These don't ought to be with the Stickers,' she said, heaving up the two volumes of the *Shorter Oxford Dictionary*.

'No one has offered to buy them.'

'Still, they're not Stickers. They're a stock line.'

There was nothing much more to do. Even now, at the end of the day, there was scarcely anything that needed putting to rights.

'I don't see so much wrong with this shop, give it's terribly damp, and you can't tell when the rapper'll start up.'

'Certainly there can't be much wrong with it, or I shouldn't be here.'

'How long are you going to stay, then?'

'I don't know. I might not have the energy to stay much longer.'

'You might not have the energy to get up and go,' said Christine, watching him, with scornful fascination, where he sat. It would do him good to get a bit of garden and work it, she thought, even if it was only a couple of rows of radishes.

'I never had time to sit about when I was assistant.'

'I'm sure you didn't. You're either a child or a woman, and neither of them have any idea how to relax.'

'You watch it,' said Christine.

10

The cold weather came on early after the fine summer of 1960. By the beginning of October Raven had begun to speak pessimistically about the cattle, who were coughing piteously. In the early morning the thick white vapour came up to the level of their knees, so that their bodies seemed to float detached above the mist. Their heads, with large ears at half-mast, turned slowly in a cloud of steamy breath towards the chance comer.

The mist did not lift until nearly mid-day and closed down again by four o'clock. It was madness for Mr Brundish to go out in such conditions; and yet at Holt House, entirely by himself, he was slowly getting ready to pay a visit. By a quarter to eleven he had assumed the appearance almost of a boulevardier, with a coat collared in fur, and a grey Homburg hat, rather higher in the crown than was usual in those years. The natives of Hardborough only breathed the autumn air through woollen scarves, and Mr Brundish also wore one of these, and took a stick from the many waiting in the hall.

Because of the mist, only the hat and upper three-quarters of Mr Brundish could be seen, bending down with an occasional terrifying gasp and wheeze, as he navigated the Ropewalk, the Sheepwalk and Anson Street. It was at first thought, by those at their windows, that he was heading for the doctor's, or, still more alarming, for the church. Mr Brundish had not atended a service for some years. He was pale, and seemed afflicted. It was thought that he looked very moderate.

If not the doctor's or the church, then it could only be The Stead. Improbable or impossible as it seemed, he was toiling up the front steps, and, clear of the mist at last, stood pressing the bell.

Mrs Gamart was making a morning entry in her diary, and had written *Wednesday: wretched weather for Oct. Hydrangea petiolara quite damped off.* She heard the bell and was ready to rise, making light of the interruption, when she realized who the visitor really was. Then she felt the same disbelief as the rest of Hardborough, who had watched the progress from Holt House. The young local girl who helped with the washing up and had answered the front door, looked half-stunned, as though she had witnessed trees walking.

To be accepted by this tiresome old man would be an entry into a new dimension of time and space – the past centuries of inhabited Suffolk, and its present silent and watchful existence. From the very first months of her arrival her invitations had been refused, on the steady excuse of ill-health. Yet, beyond question, there were little gatherings at Holt House, distinguished by visitors who stayed the night, as well as ancient cronies drawn from the deepest recesses of East Anglia. Men only perhaps, although it was said – but Mrs Gamart didn't believe it – that Mrs Green had been to tea, and her own husband had certainly never been included. The General, however, with the transparent complicity of the male sex, insisted that old Mr Brundish was a decent fellow. The inadequacy of this remark vexed Mrs Gamart into silence.

And now Mr Brundish had come. He made no apologies as he was shown in, for in his day none had been thought necessary for an eleven o'clock call. Without attempting to disguise his weakness, without pretending to stop for a few minutes to admire the proportions of the hall, he clung to the banisters, struggling for breath. His stick fell with a clatter to the shining floor.

112

'I shall recover my stick later. Fortunately I have retained all my faculties.'

Mrs Gamart, who had come out to meet him, thought it best to lead the way into the drawing-room. The sweeping French windows overlooked the sea, as misty as the land. They both sat down. Without any further reference to his health, Brundish went on:

'I have come to ask you something. That is not very good manners, but I do not know that I can put it any better. If you mind being asked, you must say so at once. I could speak to your husband, of course.'

From long habit, Mrs Gamart rejected the idea that her husband might be necessary for anything. The concentration of her visitor appeared to waver and cease. For what seemed a considerable time he sat with his eyes closed, while his face took on a curious slatey pallor, as though he had been bleached by the sea. Then he resumed:

'A curious experience, fainting. One can't tell if one is doing it properly. There is nothing to go on. One can't remember the last time. You had better offer me something,' he added loudly, and then, in precisely the same tone: 'The bitch cannot deny me a glass of brandy.'

Mrs Gamart looked doubtfully at the stricken man. If he was having some kind of attack, all that was necessary was to ring the doctor's. Then he would be taken away. He would be under an obligation, of course, as anyone must be who is taken ill in someone else's house, although Mr Brundish, she realized, might not recognize obligations. But he couldn't have made the painful transit from Holt House, on a day like this, simply to tell her that he wasn't well, unless he suddenly wanted to make amends for the short-sightedness of fifteen years. It would be better not to offer him stimulants, she thought.

'Shall I see about some coffee?' she asked.

'The woman is trying to poison me. The moment will

113

pass.' Mr Brundish opened and closed his hands, as though to grasp the air, yet even in that movement there was nobility. 'I want you to leave Florence Green alone,' he brought out.

Mrs Gamart was utterly taken aback. 'Did she ask you to come here?'

'Not at all. She is simply a woman, no longer young, who wants to keep a bookshop.'

'If Mrs Green has any cause to complain,' said Mrs Gamart, 'I suppose she could employ a solicitor. I believe that she is rather given to changing her legal advisers.'

'Why do you want her out of that house? I live in an oldish house myself, and I know how inconvenient they are. The bookshop is draughty, ineligible for a second mortgage, and, of course, haunted.'

Tact and good training had by this time come to Mrs Gamart's assistance.

'Hasn't it occurred to you, as someone who must care so much for the welfare and the heritage of this place, that a building of such historical interest could be put to a better use?'

This was a false move. Mr Brundish didn't care at all about the welfare or the heritage of Hardborough. He *was*, in a sense, Hardborough; it never occurred to him whether he cared or not.

'Old age is not the same thing as historical interest,' he said. 'Otherwise we should both of us be more interesting than we are.'

Mrs Gamart had realized by now that though her visitor might be conducting the conversation according to some kind of rules, they were not the ones she knew. Some different kind of defence would accordingly be needed.

'I say again, I want you to leave my friend Florence Green alone,' shouted Mr Brundish. 'Alone!'

'Your friend, you know, seems to have fallen foul of the

law, I rather think more than once. If that is the case, I, of course, can have nothing to say. If she goes on as she has begun, the law will have to take its course.'

'I don't know whether you are referring to a law that wasn't in existence a year ago, and crawled through Parliament while our backs were turned? I'm talking about an order for compulsory purchase. You may call it an eviction. That is a fairer term. Did you put your precious nephew up to that Private Bill of his?'

She would not lower herself so far as to pretend not to understand. 'It's true that my nephew's Bill may affect the bookshop, as there's a provision that the premises must have stood empty for five years. That would certainly apply to the Old House.' How had he come by this information? It seemed as though he had drawn it in through unseen roots, without moving from Holt House, without seeing or listening. 'There are so many authorities to consider, you know, Mr Brundish. Ordinary mortals like myself – ' she hesitated – 'and you, would scarcely know where to begin. I'm on the bench, and fairly well used to public service, but I should be quite out of my depth. We shouldn't even be able to find the right person to write to.'

'I know perfectly well, madam, who to write to. Over the past years, if I hadn't made it my business to know, I should have lost several hundred acres of my marshes, some farming land, and two pumping mills. Let me inform you that the purchaser of the Old House will have to be the Flintmarket Borough Council, and that they will proceed under the Acquisition of Land Authorisation Procedure Act of 1946, the Housing Act of 1957, and this grotesque effort of your nephew's. If nothing has been done so far, we can make common front against them. If notice has been served that they are willing to treat, we must call for a private hearing in front of a government inspector.'

The significance and weight of that 'we' could not be

mistaken. Violet Gamart perfectly understood the bargain that was being offered. An alliance was proposed, a working alliance at any rate, between Holt House and The Stead, and in return something was demanded which in fact she had no power to bring about. But did that matter? She would temporize. Mr Brundish would have to call again to undertake further persuasion, she must call on him to discuss details. His mind was not under complete control, he would forget what had been said last time, he would become a regular visitor. She would have yielded nothing and gained considerably. Meanwhile it would be wiser not to promise too much.

'We could certainly think of ways of making the move easier, if it has to come. There are still plenty of other shops to let, you know, in larger towns than Hardborough.'

'That's not what I am talking about! You must talk about what I am talking about! It was difficult for me to get here in this weather! – Either this woman is stupid, or else she is malevolent.'

'I wish I could do more.'

'I am to understand, then, that you will do nothing.'

This was exactly what she had meant, and what she intended. She had to restore the situation, and neither evasion nor frankness would answer; he saw through both of them. That frightful old men have hearts ready to be touched was, however, something that she had never questioned. She turned on him a delightful smile, which warmed her dark bright eyes and had moved many more important people than him.

'But you mustn't speak to me like that, Mr Brundish. You can't realize what you are saying. You must think me outrageous. Is that it?'

Mr Brundish gave the impression of carefully turning the words over in his mind, as though they were pebbles of which he must ascertain the value.

'I find that I cannot answer either "yes" or "no". By "outrageous" I take it that you mean "unexpectedly offensive". Certainly you have been offensive, Mrs Gamart, but you have been exactly as I expected.'

With some difficulty he rose, and propping himself on the various bits of furniture, not all of them adapted to bear his weight, he regained his hat and left The Stead. But half-way across the street – the mist having cleared by this time, so that he could be clearly seen by the inhabitants of Hardborough – Mr Brundish fell over and died.

The local tradespeople, in consultation with the Flintmarket Chamber of Commerce, decided not to close on the day of old Mr Brundish's funeral. It was market day, and there would be a fair chance of extra sales.

'I'm not going to close either,' Florence told Raven, who on occasion acted as sexton. Raven was surprised, because in his view she had a right to go to the ceremony, being able to claim better acquaintance with the deceased than many who'd be there. This was true, but she could not explain to him how much she wanted to be by herself, to think about her strange correspondent and champion. On what uncanny errand had he crossed the square, with his hat and stick, that day?

He was buried in the flinty soil of the churchyard among the Suffolk sea dead, midshipmen drowned at eleven years old, fishermen lost with all hands. The northeast corner of the acre was the family plot of the earth-loving Brundishes. Hardborough, huddled below the level of its marshes, was for one day at least a centre of interest. Who would have thought that old Mr Brundish would have known so many people, and that so many relatives would have turned up, and such a lot from London? He was a Fellow of the Royal Society, it seemed; how had that come about? The public houses had all applied for an extension, and there was a large cold lunch at The Stead, where the guests talked and laughed, and then subdued their laughs, and scarcely knew where to put them. It was known that the old man had died intestate, and Mr Drury had set out on the prolonged research which would dispose of Holt House and the marshes and pumping mills and the £2,705 13s. 7d. remaining in the current account.

While the church ceremony was still in progress, and Florence, without any expectation of customers, was slowly winding down the cash register, General Gamart came into the shop. He stood for a moment blocking the light. Then, evidently giving himself a command, he took three paces forward. At first, that seemed to exhaust the whole enterprise. He was speechless, and fidgeted with a pile of Noddy annuals. Florence Green did not much feel like helping him. He had not been in the shop for some months, and she presumed that he had been acting under orders. Then she relented, knowing that he had come on a kind impulse. In the end, she valued kindness above everything.

'You don't want a book, do you?'

'Not exactly. I just came in to say "A good man gone".'

The General cleared his throat. It was the best he could do. 'I believe you knew Edmund Brundish quite well,' he added hoarsely.

'I feel as though I did, but when I come to think of it, I've only spoken to him during one afternoon in my whole life.'

'Well, I've never spoken to the fellow at all. He was in the first show, of course, but not in the Suffolks, he was in the RFC, I believe – he wanted to fly. Odd, that.'

The General talked much more freely now that the sticky part, the condolences, were over.

'Another odd thing, he was calling on us that very morning.'

'He wanted to speak to your wife, I suppose.'

'Yes, you're quite right. Violet told me all about it. He

118

made a great effort to call on her, it seems, to congratulate her on her idea – her idea, I mean, about this Arts Centre. I'm sorry I didn't manage to get a word with him myself. I must say I shouldn't have thought Art was quite his line of country, but, well, a good man gone. Twelve years older than I am. I suppose any of us could collapse like that, when you come to think of it.'

There was nothing to stop him going on like this indefinitely. 'You mustn't be late for lunch, General Gamart.' She knew about the preparations at The Stead. He would be needed to open the wine.

Conscious of some want of tact, half relieved and half dissatisfied, he dismissed himself and withdrew.

A month or so later, the Old House was requisitioned under the new Act of Parliament. Since one of the provisions was that there should be no other uninhabited buildings of the same date in the area, the oyster warehouse could have been offered in its place, so it was unfortunate that Florence had given orders to have it pulled down. Wilkins had taken nearly a year over the demolition, but he was going ahead quite fast now.

Large numbers of pieces of paper were put through the brass letter-box of the bookshop. The postman apologized for bringing so many. On one of them the City of Flintmarket notified Florence Mary Green that they required to purchase and take under the provisions of the Act of 1959 or Acts or parts of Acts incorporated in the above Acts the lands or hereditaments mentioned and described in the schedule as delineated in the plan attached hereto (but they had forgotten to attach it) and thereon coloured pink, together with all mines and minerals in and under the said lands, other than coal, and that they were willing to treat with you and each and every of you for the purchase of the said lands and as to the compensation to be made to you and each and every of

119

you by reason of the taking of the said lands authorized as aforesaid. Florence felt, as she read this, that it was the moment for the rapper to manifest itself, and when it did not, she almost missed it.

The notice also appeared in the *Flintmarket, Kingsgrave and Hardborough Times,* making poor Florence feel like a wanted criminal. It was certainly not her imagination that old acquaintances avoided her in the street, and customers wore a surprised expression, saying, Oh, I thought I saw somewhere that you had closed down. Mr Thornton, Mr Drury and Mr Keble and their wives no longer came to the shop at all, for it was tainted.

She didn't mind so much as she had expected. It was defeat, but defeat is less unwelcome when you are tired. The compensation would be enough to pay off the bank loan and to put down a deposit on a rented property, perhaps somewhere quite else. Change should be welcome. And after all, as she now realized, Mr Brundish himself had come round to the idea of the new Centre. For some reason, this idea gave her more pain than the notice of Willingness to Treat.

Raven, in the bar of the Anchor, wanted to know how that lot at Flintmarket Town hall, who according to themselves never had a penny to spare, and couldn't even afford to drain their own marshes, had managed to raise the money to buy out Mrs Green at the Old House. But Flintmarket Urban District Council were no more ready to discuss their finances than any other public body. The Recreation Committee said in their report how heartening it was, that if anything was truly wanted and needed, a benefactor could always be found to step forward and make it possible.

Florence's solicitors in Flintmarket were at first greatly excited at the idea of handling, as they called it, one of the first cases under a new Act. They spoke of bringing an action for declaration, or applying for an order of *certiorari.*

'Would that do any good?'

120

'Well, there can't really be any legal grounds for challenging an administrative decision, but it's been held that in fact the public can do so, on the grounds of natural justice.'

'What is natural justice?' asked Florence.

After the solicitors found that their client had very little money, they gave up the order of *certiorari* and discussed the matter of compensation. Like all her other advisers, they took a gloomy and hostile view. There would be no claim for depreciation, as books were legally counted as ironmongery, as not losing value by being moved about. Nothing could be claimed for services, as it was a one-man business. Mr Thornton would have made a joke about its being a 'one-woman' business, but the Flintmarket solicitors did not do so. There remained the issue of compensation for the Old House itself.

When, after a few more weeks, she rang them up, they spoke of snags and delays. By this they meant, although they did not admit it for some time, that she was unlikely to get anything at all. Various Town and Country Planning Acts provided that if a house was so damp that it was unfit for human habitation and subsidence was threatened, no claim for compensation could be made.

'But the Old House has been there for centuries without subsiding. I'm inhabiting it, and I'm still human, and it's not as damp as all that – it dries out in the summer, and in midwinter. And anyway, what about the land?'

The solicitor referred to the land as 'the cleared site value', as though the Old House had already ceased to exist.

'That can only be estimated if it is in fact land, but an inspection of the cellars has established that the property is standing in half an inch of water.'

'What inspection? I wasn't notified about it.'

'Apparently on various dates when you were absent from the business, an experienced builder and plasterer, Mr John

121

Gipping, was sent in by the council to make an estimate of the condition of the walls and cellar.'

'John Gipping!'

'Of course, we assume that he made a peaceable entry.'

'I'm sure he did. He's not at all a violent man. What I should like to know is, who let him in?'

'Oh, your assistant, Mr Milo North. It will be assumed that he acted as your servant, and following your instructions. Have you any comments?'

'Only that I'm glad they gave the job to Gipping. He hasn't found it easy to get work lately.'

'What makes it very awkward for us is that Mr North has also signed a deposition to the effect that the damp state of the property has affected his health, and made him unfit for ordinary employment.'

'Why did you do it?' she asked Milo. 'Did somebody ask you to?'

'They did ask me rather often, and it seemed the easiest thing to do.'

Milo no longer came round to help in the bookshop; she happened to meet him crossing the common. He made no attempt to avoid her on this occasion. Indeed, he tried to make himself useful by suggesting that if she still wanted an assistant, Christine might well be free again, since, after only half a term at the Technical, she had been suspended by the headmaster. Milo said that he did not know the details, and Florence did not press for them.

There was not very much more that she could do. The bank manager, with some embarrassment, asked her if it would be convenient for her to make an appointment to see him as soon as possible. He wanted to know whether what he had heard was correct, that she had no legal right to compensation, and, in that case, what she intended to do about repayment of the loan.

'I was hoping to start again,' said Florence. 'I thought I could.'

'I should not advise you to try another small business. It's curious how many people look upon the bank as no more than a charitable institution. There comes a time when each of us must be content to call it a day. There is, of course, always the stock. If that could be liquidated, we should be well on the way out of our difficulty.'

'You mean that you want me to sell the books?'

'To clear off the loan, yes – the books and your car. I fear that will be absolutely necessary.'

Florence was left, therefore, without a shop and without books. She had kept, it is true, two of the Everymans, which had never been very good sellers. One was Ruskin's *Unto this Last*, the other was Bunyan's *Grace Abounding*. Each had its old bookmarker in it, *Everyman I will be thy guide, in thy most need to go by thy side,* and the Ruskin also had a pressed gentian, quite colourless. The book must have gone, perhaps fifty years before, to Switzerland in springtime.

In the winter of 1960, therefore, having sent her heavy luggage on ahead, Florence Green took the bus into Flintmarket via Saxford Tye and Kingsgrave. Wally carried her suitcases to the bus stop. Once again the floods were out, and the fields stood all the way, on both sides of the road, under shining water. At Flintmarket she took the 10.46 to Liverpool Street. As the train drew out of the station she sat with her head bowed in shame, because the town in which she had lived for nearly ten years had not wanted a bookshop.

Praise for Penelope Fitzgerald

"The finest British writer alive."

— RICHARD EDER, *Los Angeles Times/Newsday*

"Wonderfully accomplished and original."

— RICHARD HOLMES, *New York Review of Books*

"She writes the kind of fiction in which perfection is almost to be hoped for, as unostentatious as true virtuosity can make it, its texture a pure pleasure."

— FRANK KERMODE, *London Review of Books*

"No writer is more engaging than Penelope Fitzgerald."

— ANITA BROOKNER, *Spectator*

"Fitzgerald's special talent is stylistic, a mannered comic dryness that relishes absurdities without dwelling on them. She moves at speed, is full of sharp observations and inventions, and is very funny."

— ANTHONY THWAITE, *Observer*

"Where some writers like to build effects slowly, Fitzgerald prefers a quicksilver economy. Vivid . . . elegant . . . astonishing."

— MICHAEL DIRDA, *Washington Post Book World*

"One of the pleasures of reading her is the unpredictability of her intelligence, which never loses its quality but springs constant surprises."

— MICHAEL RATCLIFFE, *The Times*

"[Her] dry, shrewd, sympathetic, and sharply economical books are almost disreputably enjoyable . . . Fugitive scraps of insight and information — like single brushstrokes of vivid and true colors — convey much more reality than any amount of impasto description and research. In Mrs. Fitzgerald's novels, you can breathe the air and taste the water."

— MICHAEL HOFMANN, *New York Times Book Review*

Books by Penelope Fitzgerald

Fiction

THE GOLDEN CHILD

THE BOOKSHOP

OFFSHORE

HUMAN VOICES

AT FREDDIE'S

INNOCENCE

THE BEGINNING OF SPRING

THE GATE OF ANGELS

THE BLUE FLOWER

Nonfiction

EDWARD BURNE-JONES

THE KNOX BROTHERS

CHARLOTTE MEW
AND HER FRIENDS

Penelope Fitzgerald

Offshore

A MARINER BOOK
HOUGHTON MIFFLIN COMPANY
BOSTON • NEW YORK

First Mariner edition April 1998

First published in Great Britain in 1979
by William Collins Sons and Co., Ltd.

Reprinted by arrangement with Flamingo,
an imprint of HarperCollins Publishers

For information about permission to reproduce
selections from this book, write to Permissions,
Houghton Mifflin Company, 215 Park
Avenue South, New York, New York 10003.

Library of Congress Cataloging-in-Publication Data
Fitzgerald, Penelope.
Offshore / Penelope Fitzgerald.
— 1st Mariner ed.
p. cm.
"A Mariner book."
ISBN 0-395-47804-9
1. Mothers and daughters — England — London
— Fiction. 2. Battersea (London, England) —
Fiction. 3. Barges — England — Thames
River — Fiction. I. Title.
PR6056.I86O34 1998
823'.914 — dc21 97-50403 CIP

Printed in the United States of America

QUM 10 9 8 7 6 5 4 3 2 1

For *Grace*
and all who sailed in her

'che mena il vento, e che batte la pioggia,
e che s'incontran con sì aspre lingue.'

[1]

'Are we to gather that *Dreadnought* is asking us all to do something dishonest?' Richard asked.

Dreadnought nodded, glad to have been understood so easily.

'Just as a means of making a sale. It seems the only way round my problem. If all present wouldn't mind agreeing not to mention my main leak, or rather not to raise the question of my main leak, unless direct enquiries are made.'

'Do you in point of fact want us to say that *Dreadnought* doesn't leak?' asked Richard patiently.

'That would be putting it too strongly.'

All the meetings of the boat-owners, by a movement as natural as the tides themselves, took place on Richard's converted *Ton* class minesweeper. *Lord Jim*, a felt reproof to amateurs, in speckless, always-renewed gray paint, overshadowed the other craft and was nearly twice their tonnage, just as Richard, in his decent dark blue blazer, dominated the meeting itself. And yet he by no means wanted this responsibility. Living on Battersea Reach, overlooked by some very good houses, and under the surveillance of the Port of London Authority, entailed, surely, a certain standard of conduct. Richard would be one of the last men on earth or water to want to impose it. Yet someone must. Duty is what no-one else will do at the moment. Fortunately he did not have to define duty. War service in the RNVR, and his whole temperament before and since, had done that for him.

Richard did not even want to preside. He would have been

9

happier with a committee, but the owners, of whom several rented rather than owned their boats, were not of the substance from which committees are formed. Between *Lord Jim*, moored almost in the shadow of Battersea Bridge, and the old wooden Thames barges, two hundred yards upriver and close to the rubbish disposal wharfs and the brewery, there was a great gulf fixed. The barge-dwellers, creatures neither of firm land nor water, would have liked to be more respectable than they were. They aspired towards the Chelsea shore, where, in the early 1960's, many thousands lived with sensible occupations and adequate amounts of money. But a certain failure, distressing to themselves, to be like other people, caused them to sink back, with so much else that drifted or was washed up, into the mud moorings of the great tideway.

Biologically they could be said, as most tideline creatures are, to be 'successful.' They were not easily dislodged. But to sell your craft, to leave the Reach, was felt to be a desperate step, like those of the amphibians when, in earlier stages of the world's history, they took ground. Many of these species perished in the attempt.

Richard, looking round his solid, brassbound table, got the impression that everyone was on their best behaviour. There seemed to be no way of avoiding this, and since, after all, Willis had requested some kind of discussion of his own case, he scrupulously collected opinions.

'*Rochester? Grace? Bluebird? Maurice? Hours of Ease? Dunkirk? Relentless?*'

Richard was quite correct, as technically speaking they were all in harbour, in addressing them by the names of their craft. Maurice, an amiable young man, had realised as soon as he came to the Reach that Richard was always going to do this and that he himself would accordingly be known as *Dondeschiepolschuygen IV*, which was inscribed in gilt lettering on his bows. He therefore renamed his boat *Maurice*.

No-one liked to speak first, and Willis, a marine artist some sixty-five years old, the owner of *Dreadnought*, sat with his hands before him on the table and his head slightly sunken, so that only the top, with its spiky crown of black and gray hair, could be seen. The silence was eased by a long wail from a ship's hooter from downstream. It was a signal peculiar to Thames river – I am about to get under way. The tide was making, although the boats still rested on the mud.

Hearing a slight, but significant noise from the galley, Richard courteously excused himself. Perhaps they'd have a little more to contribute on this very awkward point when he came back.

'How are you getting on, Lollie?'

Laura was cutting something up into small pieces, with a cookery book open in front of her. She gave him a weary, large-eyed, shires-bred glance, a glance whose horizons should have been bounded by acres of plough and grazing. Loyalty to him, Richard knew, meant that she had never complained so far to anyone but himself about this business of living, instead of in a nice house, in a boat in the middle of London. She went home once a month to combat any such suggestion, and told her family that there were very amusing people living on the Thames. Between the two of them there was no pretence. Yet Richard, who always put each section of his life, when it was finished with, quietly behind him, and liked to be able to give a rational explanation for everything, could not account for this, his attachment to *Lord Jim*. He could very well afford a house, and indeed *Jim* had been an expensive conversion. And if the river spoke to his dreaming, rather than to his daytime self, he supposed that he had no business to attend to it.

'We're nearly through,' he said.

Laura shook back her dampish longish hair. In theory, her looks depended on the services of many employees, my hairdresser, my last hairdresser, my doctor, my other doctor who I went to when I found the first one wasn't doing me any

11

good, but with or without their attentions, Laura would always be beautiful.

'This galley's really not so bad, is it, with the new extractor?' Richard went on, 'A certain amount of steam still, of course...'

'I hate you. Can't you get rid of these people?'

In the saloon Maurice, who had come rather late, was saying something intended to be in favour of Willis. He was incurably sympathetic. His occupation, which was that of picking up men in a neighbouring public house, with which he had a working arrangement, during the evening hours, and bringing them back to the boat, was not particularly profitable. Maurice was not born to make a profit, but then, was not born to resent this, or anything else. Those who felt affection for him had no easy way of telling him so, since he seemed to regard friend and enemy alike. For example, an unpleasant acquaintance of his used part of Maurice's hold as a repository for stolen goods. Richard and Laura were among the few boat owners who did not know this. And yet Maurice appeared to be almost proud, because Harry was not a customer, but somebody who had demanded a favour and given nothing in return.

'I shall have to warn Harry not to talk about the leak either,' he said.

'What does he know about it?' asked Willis.

'He used to be in the Merchant Navy. If people are coming to look at *Dreadnought*, he might be asked his opinion.'

'I've never seen him speak to anyone. He doesn't come often, does he?'

At that moment *Lord Jim* was disturbed, from stem to stern, by an unmistakable lurch. Nothing fell, because on *Lord Jim* everything was properly secured, but she heaved, seemed to shake herself gently, and rose. The tide had lifted her.

At the same time an uneasy shudder passed through all those sitting round the table. For the next six hours – or a little less, because at Battersea the flood lasts five and a half hours, and the ebb six and a half – they would be living not on land, but on water. And each one of them felt the patches, strains and gaps in their craft as if they were weak places in their own bodies. They dreaded, and were yet painfully anxious, to get back and to see whether the last caulking had given way. A Thames barge has no keel and is afloat in the first few inches of shoal water. The only exception was Woodrow, from *Rochester*, the retired director of a small company, who was fanatical in the maintenance of his craft. The flood tide, though it had no real terrors for Woodie, caused him to fret impatiently, because *Rochester*, in his opinion, had beautiful lines below water, and these would not now be visible again for twelve hours.

On every barge on the Reach a very faint ominous tap, no louder than the door of a cupboard shutting, would be followed by louder ones from every strake, timber and weatherboard, a fusillade of thunderous creaking, and even groans that seemed human. The crazy old vessels, riding high in the water without cargo, awaited their owners' return.

Richard, like a good commander, sensed the uneasiness of the meeting, even through the solid teak partition. He would, if he had taken to the high seas in past centuries, never have been caught napping by a mutiny.

'I'd better see them on their way.'

'You can ask one or two of them to stay behind for a drink, if you like,' Laura said, 'if there's anyone possible.'

She often unconsciously imitated her father's voice, and, like him, was beginning to drink a little too much occasionally, out of boredom. Richard felt overwhelmed with affection for her. 'I got *Country Life* to-day,' she said.

He had noticed that already. Anything new was noticeable on shipshape *Lord Jim*. The magazine was lying open at the property advertisements, among which was the photograph of a lawn, and a cedar tree on it with a shadow, and a squarish house in the background to show the purpose of the lawn. A similar photograph, with variations as to size and county, appeared month after month, giving the impression that those who read *Country Life* were above change, or that none was recognised there.

'I didn't mean that one, Richard, I meant a few pages farther on. There's some smaller places there.'

'I might ask Nenna James to stay behind,' Richard said. 'From *Grace*, I mean.'

'Why, do you think she's pretty?'

'I've never thought about it.'

'Hasn't her husband left her?'

'I'm not too sure what the situation is.'

'The postman used to say that there weren't many letters for *Grace*.'

Laura said 'used' because letters were no longer brought by the postman; after he had fallen twice from *Maurice*'s ill-secured gangplank, the whole morning's mail soaked away in the great river's load of rubbish, the GPO, with every reason on its side, had notified the Reach that they could no longer undertake deliveries. They acknowledged that Mr Blake, from *Lord Jim*, had rescued their employee on both occasions and they wished to record their thanks for this. The letters, since this, had had to be collected from the boatyard office, and Laura felt that this made it not much better than living abroad.

'I think Nenna's all right,' Richard continued. 'She seems quite all right to me, really. I don't know that I'd want to be left alone with her for any length of time.'

'Why not?'

'Well, I'm not quite sure that she mightn't burst into tears, or perhaps suddenly take all her clothes off.' This had actually once happened to Richard at Nestor and Sage, the investment counsellors where he worked. They were thinking of re-designing the whole office on the more modern open plan.

14

The whole meeting looked up in relief as he came back to the saloon. Firmly planted on the rocking boat, he suggested, even by his stance in the doorway, that things, however difficult, would turn out reasonably well. It was not that he was too sure of himself, simply that he was a good judge of the possible.

Willis was thanking young Maurice for his support.

'Well, you spoke up . . . a friend in need . . .'

'You're welcome.'

Willis half got up from the table. 'All the same, I don't believe that fellow was ever in the Merchant Navy.'

Business suspended, thought Richard. Firmly, but always politely, he escorted the ramshackle assembly up the companion ladder. It was a relief, as always, to be out on deck. The first autumn mists made it difficult to see the whole length of the Reach. Seagulls, afloat like the boats, idled round *Lord Jim*, their white feathers soiled at the waterline.

'You'll probably have plenty of time to do something about your trouble anyway,' he said to Willis, 'it's quite a long business, arranging the sale of these boats. Your leak's somewhere aft, isn't it? . . . you've got all four pumps working, I take it . . . one in each well?'

This picture of *Dreadnought* was so wide of the mark that Willis found it better to say nothing, simply making a gesture which had something in common with a petty officer's salute. Then he followed the others, who had to cross to land and tramp along the Embankment. The middle reach was occupied by small craft, mostly laying up for the winter, some of them already double lashed down under weather-cloths. These were for fairweather people only. The barge-owners had to go as far as the brewery wharf, across *Maurice*'s foredeck and over a series of gangplanks which connected them with their own boats. Woodie had to cross *Maurice*, *Grace* and *Dreadnought* to rejoin *Rochester*. Only *Maurice* was made fast to the wharf.

One of the last pleasure steamers of the season was passing, with cabin lights ablaze, on its way to Kew. 'Battersea Reach, ladies and gentlemen. On your right, the artistic colony. Folk live on those boats like they do on the Seine, it's the artist's life they're leading there. Yes, there's people living on those boats.'

Richard had detained Nenna James. 'I wish you'd have a drink with us, Laura hoped you would.'

Nenna's character was faulty, but she had the instinct to see what made other people unhappy, and this instinct had only failed her once, in the case of her own husband. She knew, at this particular moment, that Richard was distressed by the unsatisfactory nature of the meeting. Nothing had been evaluated, or even satisfactorily discussed.

'I wish I knew the exact time,' she said.

Richard was immediately content, as he only was when something could be ascertained to the nearest degree of accuracy. The exact time! Perhaps Nenna would like to have a look at his chronometers. They often didn't work well in small boats – they were affected by changes of temperature – he didn't know whether Nenna had found that – and, of course, by vibration. He was able to give her not only the time, but the state of the tide at every bridge on the river. It wasn't very often that anyone wanted to know this.

Laura put the bottles and glasses and a large plateful of bits and pieces through the galley hatch.

'It smells of something in there.'

There was the perceptible odour of tar which the barge-owners, since so much of their day was spent in running repairs, left behind them everywhere.

'Well, dear, if you don't like the smell, let's go aft,' said Richard, picking up the tray. He never let a woman carry anything. The three of them went into a kind of snug, fitted with built-in lockers and red cushions. A little yacht stove gave out a temperate glow, its draught adjusted to produce exactly the right warmth.

Laura sat down somewhat heavily.

'How does it feel like to live without your husband?' she asked, handing Nenna a large glass of gin. 'I've often wondered.'

'Perhaps you'd like me to fetch some more ice,' Richard said. There was plenty.

'He hasn't left me, you know. We just don't happen to be together at the moment.'

'That's for you to say, but what I want to know is, how do you get on without him? Cold nights, of course, don't mind Richard, it's a compliment to him if you think about it.'

Nenna looked from one to the other. It was a relief, really, to talk about it.

'I can't do the things that women can't do,' she said. 'I can't turn over *The Times* so that the pages lie flat, I can't fold up a map in the right creases, I can't draw corks, I can't drive in nails straight, I can't go into a bar and order a drink without wondering what everyone's thinking about it, and I can't strike matches towards myself. I'm well educated and I've got two children and I can manage pretty well, there's a number of much more essential things that I know how to do, but I can't do those ones, and when they come up I feel like weeping myself sick.'

'I'm sure I could show you how to fold up a map,' said Richard, 'it's not at all difficult once you get the hang of it.'

Laura's eyes seemed to have moved closer together. She was concentrating intensely.

'Did he leave you on the boat?'

'I bought *Grace* myself, while he was away, with just about all the money we'd got left, to have somewhere for me and the girls.'

'Do you like boats?'

'I'm quite used to them. I was raised in Halifax. My father had a summer cabin on the Bras d'Or Lake. We had boats there.'

'I hope you're not having any repair problems,' Richard put in.

'We get rain coming in.'

'Ah, the weatherboarding. You might try stretching tarpaulin over the deck.'

Although he tried hard to do so, Richard could never see how anyone could live without things in working order.

'Personally, though, I'm doubtful about the wisdom of making endless repairs to these very old boats. My feeling, for what it's worth, is that they should be regarded as wasting assets. Let them run down just so much every year, remember your low outgoings, and in a few years' time have them towed away for their break-up value.'

'I don't know where we should live then,' said Nenna.

'Oh, I understood you to say that you were going to find a place on shore.'

'Oh, we are, we are.'

'I didn't mean to distress you.'

Laura had had time, while listening without much attention to these remarks, to swallow a further quantity of spirits. This had made her inquisitive, rather than hostile.

'Where'd you get your Guernsey?'

Both women wore the regulation thick Navy blue sailing sweaters, with a split half inch at the bottom of each side seam. Nenna had rolled up her sleeves in the warmth of the snug, showing round forearms covered with very fine golden hair.

'I got mine at the cut price place at the end of the Queenstown Road.'

'It's not as thick as mine.'

Laura leant forward, and, taking a good handful, felt the close knitting between finger and thumb.

'I'm a judge of quality, I can tell it's not as thick. Richard, like to feel it?'

'I'm afraid I can't claim to know much about knitting.'

'Well, make the stove up then. Make it up, you idiot! Nenna's freezing!'

'I'm warm, thank you, just right.'

'You've got to be warmer than that! Richard, she's your guest!'

'I can adjust the stove, if you like,' said Richard, in relief, 'I can do something to the regulator.'

'I don't want it regulated!'

Nenna knew that, if it hadn't been disloyal, Richard would have appealed to her to do or say something.

'We use pretty well anything for fuel up our end,' she began, 'driftwood and washed-up coke and anything that'll burn. Maurice told me that last winter he had to borrow a candle from *Dreadnought* to unfreeze the lock of his woodstore. Then when he was entertaining one of his friends he couldn't get his stove to burn right and he had to keep it alight with matchboxes and cheese straws.'

'It's bad practice to keep your woodstore above deck,' said Richard.

Laura had been following, for some reason, with painful interest. 'Do cheese straws burn?'

'Maurice thinks they do.'

Laura disappeared. Nenna had just time to say, I must be going, before she came back, tottering at a kind of dignified slant, and holding a large tin of cheese straws.

'Fortnums.'

Avoiding Richard, who got to his feet as soon as he saw something to be carried, she kicked open the top of the Arctic and flung them in golden handfuls onto the glowing bed of fuel.

'Hot!'

The flames leaped up, with an overpowering stink of burning cheese.

'Lovely! Hot! I've got plenty more! The kitchen's full of them! We'll make Richard throw them. We'll all throw them!'

19

'There's someone coming,' said Nenna.

Footsteps overhead, like the relief for siege victims. She knew the determined stamp of her younger daughter, but there was also a heavier tread. Her heart turned over.

'Ma, I can smell burning.'

After a short fierce struggle, Richard had replaced the Arctic's brass lid. Nenna went to the companion.

'Who's up there with you, Tilda?'

Tilda's six-year-old legs, in wellingtons caked with mud, appeared at the open hatch.

'It's Father Watson.'

Nenna did not answer for a second, and Tilda bellowed:

'Ma, it's the kindly old priest. He came round to *Grace*, so I brought him along here.'

'Father Watson isn't old at all, Tilda. Bring him down here, please. That's to say . . .'

'Of course,' said Richard. 'You'll have a whisky, father, won't you?' He didn't know who he was talking to, but believed, from films he had seen, that R.C. priests drank whisky and told long stories; that could be useful at the present juncture. Richard spoke with calm authority. Nenna admired him and would have liked to throw her arms round him.

'No, I won't come in now, thank you all the same,' called Father Watson, whose flapping trousers could now be seen beside Tilda's wellingtons against a square patch of sky. 'Just a word or two, Mrs James, I can easily wait if you're engaged with your friends or if it's not otherwise convenient.'

But Nenna, somewhat to the curate's surprise, for he seldom felt himself to be a truly welcome guest, was already half way up the companion. It had begun to drizzle, and his long macintosh was spangled with drops of rain, which caught the reflections of the shore lights and the riding lights of the craft at anchor.

'I'm afraid the little one will get wet.'

'She's waterproof,' said Nenna.

As soon as they reached the Embankment Father Watson began to speak in measured tones. 'It's the children, as you must be aware, that I've come about. A message from the nuns, a message from the Sisters of Misericord.' He sometimes wondered if he would be more successful in the embarrassing errands he was called upon to undertake if he had an Irish accent, or some quaint turn of speech.

'Your girls, Mrs James, Tilda here, and the eleven-year-old.'

'Martha.'

'A very delightful name. Martha busied herself about the household work during our Lord's visits. But not a saint's name, I think.'

Presumably Father Watson said these things automatically. He couldn't have walked all the way down to the reach from his comfortless presbytery simply to talk about Martha's name.

'She'll be taking another name at confirmation, I assume. That should not long be delayed. I suggest Stella Maris, Star of the Sea, since you've decided to make your dwelling place upon the face of the waters.'

'Father, have you come to complain about the girls' absence from school?'

They had arrived at the wharf, which was exceedingly ill-lit. The brewers to whom it belonged, having ideas, like all brewers in the 1960's, of reviving the supposed jollity of the eighteenth century, had applied for permission to turn it into a fashionable beer garden. The very notion, however, ran counter to the sodden, melancholy, and yet enduring spirit of the Reach. After the plans had been shelved, the whole place had been leased out to various small-time manufacturers and warehousemen; the broken-down sheds and godowns must still be the property of somebody, so too must be the piles of crates whose stencilled lettering had long since faded to pallor.

But, rat-ridden and neglected, it was a wharf still. The river's edge, where Virgil's ghosts held out their arms in

21

longing for the farther shore, and Dante, as a living man, was refused passage by the ferryman, the few planks that mark the meeting point of land and water, there, surely, is a place to stop and reflect, even if, as Father Watson did, you stumble over a ten-gallon tin of creosote.

'I'm afraid I'm not accustomed to the poor light, Mrs James.'

'Look at the sky, father. Keep your eyes on the lightest part of the sky, and they'll adapt little by little.'

Tilda had sprung ahead, at home in the dark, and anywhere within sight and sound of water. Feeling that she had given her due of politeness to the curate, the due exacted by her mother and elder sister, she pattered onto *Maurice*, and, after having a bit of a poke round, shot across the connecting gangplank onto *Grace*.

'You'll excuse me if I don't go any further, Mrs James. It's exactly what you said, it's the question of school attendance. The situation, you see, they tell me there's a legal aspect to it as well.'

How dispiriting for Father Watson to tell her this, Nenna thought, and how far it must be from his expectations when he received his first two minor orders, and made his last acts of resignation. To stand on this dusky wharf, bruised by a drum of creosote, and acting not even as the convent chaplain, but as some kind of school attendance officer!

'I know they haven't been coming to class regularly. But then, father, they haven't been well.'

Even Father Watson could scarcely be expected to swallow this. 'I was struck by the good health and spirits of your little one. In fact I had it in mind that she might be trained up to one of the women's auxiliary services which justified themselves so splendidly in the last war – the WRENS, I mean, of course. It's a service that's not incompatible with the Christian life.'

'You know how it is with children; she's well one day, not

so well the next.' Nenna's attitude to truth was flexible, and more like Willis's than Richard's. 'And Martha's the same, it's only to be expected at her age.'

Nenna had hoped to alarm the curate with these references to approaching puberty, but he seemed, on the contrary, to be reassured. 'If that's the trouble, you couldn't do better than to entrust her to the skilled understanding of the Sisters.' How dogged he was. 'They'll expect, then, to see both your daughters in class on Monday next.'

'I'll do what I can.'

'Very well, Mrs James.'

'Won't you come as far as the boat?'

'No, no, I won't risk the crossing a second time.' What had happened the first time? 'And now, I'm afraid I've somewhat lost my sense of direction. I'll have to ask you my way to dry land.'

Nenna pointed out the way through the gate, which, swinging on its hinges, no longer provided any kind of barrier, out onto the Embankment, and first left, first right up Partisan Street for the King's Road. The priest couldn't have looked more relieved if he had completed a mission to those that dwell in the waters that are below the earth.

'I've got the supper, Ma,' said Martha, when Nenna returned to *Grace*. Nenna would have felt better pleased with herself if she had resembled her elder daughter. But Martha, small and thin, with dark eyes which already showed an acceptance of the world's shortcomings, was not like her mother and even less like her father. The crucial moment when children realise that their parents are younger than they are had long since been passed by Martha.

'We're having baked beans. If Father Watson's coming, we shall have to open another tin.'

'No, dear, he's gone home.'

Nenna felt tired, and sat down on the keelson, which ran

from end to end of the flat-bottomed barge. It was quite wrong to come to depend too much upon one's children.

Martha set confidently to work in *Grace*'s galley, which consisted of two gas rings in the bows connected to a Calor cylinder, and a brass sink. Water came to the sink from a container on the deck, which was refilled by a man from the boat-yard once every twenty-four hours. A good deal of improvisation was necessary and Martha had put three tin plates to heat up over the hissing saucepan of beans.

'Was it fun on *Lord Jim*?'

'Oh, not at all.'

'Should I have enjoyed it?'

'Oh no, I don't think so. Mrs Blake threw cheese straws into the stove.'

'What did Mr Blake say?'

'He wants to keep her happy, to make her happy, I don't know.'

'What did Father Watson want?'

'Didn't he talk to you at all?'

'I daresay he would have done, but I sent him out to fetch you, with Tilda, she needed exercise.'

'So he didn't mention anything.'

'He just came down here, and I made him a cup of tea and we said an act of contrition together.'

'He wanted to know why you hadn't been to class lately.'

Martha sighed.

'I've been reading your letters,' she said. 'They're lying about your cabin, and you haven't even looked at most of them.'

The letters were Nenna's connection, not only with the land, but with her previous existence. They would be from Canada, from her sister Louise who would suggest that she might put up various old acquaintances passing through London, or find a suitable family for a darling Austrian boy, not so very much older than Martha, whose father was a kind

24

of Count, but was also in the import-export business, or try to recall a splendid person, the friend of a friend of hers who had had a very, very sad story. Then there were one or two bills, not many because Nenna had no credit accounts, a letter-card from an old schoolfriend which started Bet you don't remember me, and two charitable appeals, forwarded by Father Watson even to such an unpromising address as *Grace*.

'Anything from Daddy?'

'No, Ma, I looked for that first.'

There was no more to be said on that subject.

'Oh, Martha, my head aches. Baked beans would be just the thing for it.'

Tilda came in, wet, and black as coal from head to foot.

'Willis gave me a drawing.'

'What of?'

'*Lord Jim*, and some seagulls.'

'You shouldn't have accepted it.'

'Oh, I gave him one back.'

She had been waiting on *Dreadnought* to watch the water coming in through the main leak. It had come half way up the bunk, and nearly as far as Willis's blankets. Nenna was distressed.

'Well, it goes out with every tide. He'll have to show people round at low tide, and get them off before it turns.'

'Surely he can do some repairs,' said Martha.

'No, Fate's against him,' said Tilda, and after one or two forkfuls of beans she fell fast asleep with her head across the table. It was impossible, in any case, to bathe her, because they were only allowed to let out the bathwater on a falling tide.

By now the flood was making fast. The mist had cleared, and to the north-east the Lots Road Power Station discharged from its four majestic chimneys long plumes of white pearly smoke which slowly drooped and turned to dun. The lights dazzled, but on the broad face of the water there were innumerable V-shaped eddies, showing the exact position of whatever the river had not been able to hide. If the old Thames trades had still persisted, if boatmen had still made a living from taking the coins from the pockets of the drowned, then this was the hour for them to watch. Far above, masses of autumn cloud passed through the transparent violet sky.

After supper they sat by the light of the stove. Nenna was struck by the fact that she ought to write to Louise, who was married to a successful business man. She began, Dear Sis, Tell Joel that it's quite an education in itself for the girls to be brought up in the heart of the capital, and on the very shores of London's historic river.

[2]

Tilda was up aloft. *Grace*'s mast was fifteen foot of blackened pine, fitted into a tabernacle, so that it could be lowered to the deck in the days when *Grace* negotiated the twenty-eight tideway bridges between Richmond and the sea. Her mizzen mast was gone, her sprit was gone, the mainmast was never intended for climbing and Tilda sat where there was, apparently, nowhere to sit.

Martha, whose head was as strong as her sister's, sometimes climbed up as well, and, clinging on about a foot lower down, read aloud from a horror comic. But today Tilda was alone, looking down at the slanting angle of the decks as the cables gave or tightened, the passive shoreline, the secret water.

Tilda cared nothing for the future, and had, as a result, a great capacity for happiness. At the moment she was perfectly happy.

She was waiting for the tide to turn. Exactly opposite *Grace* a heap of crates which had driven up through the bends and reaches, twenty miles from Gravesend, was at rest in the slack water, enchanted apparently, not moving an inch one way or the other. The lighters swung at their moorings, pointing all ways, helpless without the instructions of the tide. It was odd to see the clouds move when the water was so still.

She blinked twice, taking the risk of missing the right few seconds while her eyes were shut. Then one end of a crate detached itself from the crates and began to steal away, edging slowly round in a half circle. Tilda, who had been holding her breath, let it go. A tremor ran through the boats' cables, the iron lighters, just on the move, chocked gently together. The great swing round began. By the shore the driftwood was still travelling upriver, but in midstream it was gathering way headlong in the other direction. The Thames had turned towards the sea.

Willis had frequently told her that these old barges, in spite of their great sails, didn't need a crew of more than two men, in fact a man and a boy could handle them easily. The sails had been tan-coloured, like the earth and dressed with oil, which never quite dried out. There were none left now. But *Grace* wouldn't need them to go out to sea on the ebb tide. She wouldn't make sail until she reached Port of London. With her flat bottom, she would swim on the tide, all gear dropped, cunningly making use of the hidden drifts. The six-year-old boy knew every current and eddy of the river. Long had he studied the secrets of the Thames. None but he would have noticed the gleam of gold and diamonds – the ring on the dead man's finger as his hand broke the surface. Farewell! He recognised it as the hand of his father, missing now for countless years. The *Grace*, 180 tons fully loaded, nosed her way through the low arches by the Middlesex bank, where there was no room for other craft, passing, or surpassing, all the shipping there. At Tower Bridge if four foot diameter discs bearing black and white signal stripes are displayed fourteen foot to landward of the signals, this is an indication that the bridge cannot be raised from mechanical or other cause. Only *Grace* could pass, not *Maurice*, not even *Dreadnought*, a sight never to be forgotten. Men and women came out on the dock to watch as the great brown sails went up, with only a six-year-old boy at the winch, and the *Grace*, bound for Ushant, smelt the open sea.

There was a scratching at the heel of the mast. A cat, with her mouth full of seagull feathers, was feebly trying to climb up, but after a few feet her claws lost purchase and she slithered back by gradual stages to the deck.

'Stripey!'

The ship's cat was in every way appropriate to the Reach. She habitually moved in a kind of nautical crawl, with her stomach close to the deck, as though close-furled and ready for dirty weather. The ears were vestigial, and lay flat to the head.

Through years of attempting to lick herself clean, for she had never quite lost her self-respect, Stripey had become as thickly coated with mud inside as out. She was in a perpetual process of readjustment, not only to tides and seasons, but to the rats she encountered on the wharf. Up to a certain size, that is to say the size attained by the rats at a few weeks old, she caught and ate them, and, with a sure instinct for authority, brought in their tails to lay them at the feet of Martha. Any rats in excess of this size chased Stripey. The resulting uncertainty as to whether she was coming or going had made her, to some extent, mentally unstable.

Stripey did not care to be fed by human beings, and understood how to keep herself warm in cold weather. She slept outside, on one or other of the stove pipes which projected out of the stacks on deck. Curled up on the pipe, she acted as an obstruction which drove the smoke down again into the barge, making it almost uninhabitable. In turn, Woodie, Willis, Nenna, Maurice and even his visitors could be heard coughing uncontrollably. But Stripey rarely chose to sleep in the same place two nights running.

From the masthead Tilda, having sailed out to sea with *Grace*, took a closer survey of the Reach. Her whole idea of the world's work was derived from what she observed there and had little in common with the circulation of the great city which toiled on only a hundred yards away.

No movement on *Lord Jim*. Willis was walking towards *Dreadnought* with the man from the boatyard, whose manner suggested that he was refusing to supply more tar, gas and water until the previous bill had been paid.

On *Rochester*, Woodie was getting ready to lay up for the

29

winter. It seemed that he was not, after all, a true barge dweller. His small recording company, as he explained only too often, had gone into voluntary liquidation, leaving him with just enough to manage nicely, and he was going to spend the cold weather in his house in Purley. Managing nicely seemed an odd thing to do at the north end of the Reach. Woodie also spoke of getting someone to anti-foul his hull, so that it would be as clean as *Lord Jim*'s. The other barges were so deeply encrusted with marine life that it was difficult to strike wood. Green weeds and barnacles were thick on them, and whales might have saluted them in passing.

Maurice was deserted, Maurice having been invited, as he quite often was, to go down for the day to Brighton. But his deckhouse did not appear to be locked. A light van drew up on the wharf, and a man got out and dropped a large quantity of cardboard boxes over the side of the wharf onto the deck. One of them broke open. It was full of hair dryers. The man then had to drop down on deck and arrange the boxes more carefully. It would have been better to cover them with a tarpaulin, but he had forgotten to bring one, perhaps. He wasted no time in looking round and it was only when he was backing the van to drive away that his face could be seen. It was very pale and had no expression, as though expressions were surplus to requirements.

Willis, walking in his deliberate way, looked at the boxes on *Maurice*, paused, even shook his head a little, but did nothing. Nenna might have added to her list of things that men do better than women their ability to do nothing at all in an unhurried manner. And in fact there was nothing that Willis could do about the boxes. Quite certainly, Maurice did not want the police on his boat.

'Ahoy there Tilda! Watch yourself!' Willis called.

Tilda knew very well that the river could be dangerous. Although she had become a native of the boats, and pitied the tideless and ratless life of the Chelsea inhabitants, she respected the water and knew that one could die within sight of the Embankment.

One spring evening a Dutch barge, the *Waalhaven*, from Rotterdam, glittering with brass, impressive, even under power, had anchored in midstream opposite the boats. She must have got clearance at Gravesend and sailed up on the ebb. Of this fine vessel the *Maurice*, also from Rotterdam, had once been a poor relation. The grounded barges seemed to watch the *Waalhaven*, as prisoners watch the free.

Her crew lined up on deck as gravely as if at a business meeting. A spotless meeting of well-regarded business men in rubber seaboots, conducted in the harmonious spirit which had always characterised the firm.

Just after teatime the owner came to the rails and called out to *Maurice* to send a dinghy so that he could put a party ashore. When nothing happened, and he realised that he had come to a place without facilities, he retired for another consultation. Then, as the light began to fail, with the tide running very fast, three of them launched their own dinghy and prepared to sail to the wharf. They had been waiting for high water so that they could sail alongside in a civilised manner. It was like a demonstration in small boat sailing, a lesson in holiday sport. They still wore their seaboots, but brought their shoregoing shoes with them in an oilskin bag. The gods of the river had, perhaps, taken away their wits.

The offshore wind was coming hard as usual through the wide gap between the warehouses on the Surrey side. Woodie, observing their gallant start, longed to lend them his Chart 3 and to impress upon them that there was one competent owner at least at this end of the Reach. Richard, back from work after a tiresome day, stopped on the Embankment to look, and remembered that he had once gone on board the *Waalhaven* for a drink when she put in at Orfordness.

Past the gap, the wind failed and dropped to nothing, the

dinghy lost way and drifted towards three lighters moored abreast. Her mast caught with a crack which could be heard on both sides of the river on the high overhang of the foremost lighter. The whole dinghy was jammed and sucked in under the stem, then rolled over, held fast by her steel mast which would not snap. The men were pitched overboard and they too were swallowed up beneath the heavy iron bottoms of the lighters. After a while the bag of shoes came up, then two of the men, then a pair of seaboots, floating soles upwards.

Tilda thought of this incident with distress, but not often. She wondered what had happened to the other pairs of boots. But her heart did not rule her memory, as was the case with Martha and Nenna. She was spared that inconvenience.

Willis called again, 'Ahoy there, Tilda! Don't shout down back to me!' Imagining her to be delicate, he was anxious for her not to strain her voice. Tilda and Martha both sang absolutely true, and Willis, who was fond of music, and always optimistic about the future of others, liked to think of them as concert performers. They could still manage *Abends, wenn wir schlafen gehen*, taught them by the nuns as a party piece, and then, indeed, they sounded like angels, though angels without much grasp of the words after the second line. More successful, perhaps, was *Jailhouse Rock*. But Tilda had taught herself to produce, by widening her mouth into the shape of an oblong, a most unpleasant imitation of a bosun's whistle, which could be heard almost as far as *Lord Jim*. The sound indicated that she was coming down the mast. Father Watson had been more than a little frightened by it, and had confided in the nuns that it was more like something produced by some mechanical contrivance, than by a human being. His words confirmed the opinion of the Sisters of Misericord that the two children, so clever and musical, were at risk on the boat, spiritually and perhaps physically, and that someone ought to speak much more seriously to Mrs James.

[3]

Below decks, *Grace* was shipshape, but after calling on *Lord Jim* Nenna always felt impelled to start cleaning the brightwork. They hadn't much – just the handholds of the companion, the locker hinges, and the pump-handle of the heads, which was part of the original equipment and was engraved with the date, 1905.

Nenna was thirty-two, an age by which if a blonde woman's hair hasn't turned dark, it never will. She had come to London after the war as a music student, and felt by this time that she was neither Canadian nor English. Edward and she had got married in 1949. She was still at the RSM then, violin first study, and she fell in love as only a violinist can. She didn't know if they had given themselves sufficient time to think things over before they married – that was the kind of question her sister Louise asked. Edward stayed in the Engineers for a bit, then came out and was not very successful in finding a job to suit him. That wasn't his fault, and if anyone said that it was, Nenna would still feel like poking a hole in them. They got a flat. People who asked her why she didn't make use of her talent and give singing lessons had perhaps not tried to do this while living in two rooms over a greengrocer's, and looking after young children. But Edward was said by his friends to have business sense, and to be able to make things work. That was why the launderette was so evidently a good investment. It was quite a new idea over here, you didn't do your washing at home but brought it out to these machines, and the courteous manager greeted you and put in the soap powder for you, and had the clothes all ready for you when you came back, but wasn't, alas, as it turned out, much of a hand at doing the accounts. The closing of the launderette had given rise to a case in the County Court, in which Edward and she had been held not to blame, but had been conscious of the contempt of their solicitor, who always seemed to be in a great hurry.

This, no doubt, was the reason that Nenna's thoughts, whenever she was alone, took the form of a kind of perpetual magistrate's hearing, in which her own version of her marriage was shown as ridiculously simple and demonstrably right, and then, almost exactly at the same time, as incontrovertibly wrong. Her conscience, too, held, quite uninvited, a separate watching brief, and intervened in the proceedings to read statements of an unwelcome nature.

'. . . Your life story so far, Mrs James, has had a certain lack of distinction. I dare say it seemed distinguished enough while you were living it – distinguished, at least, from other people's lives.'

'You put that very well, my lord.' She realised that the magistrate had become a judge.

'Now then . . . in 1959 your husband came to the conclusion, and I am given to understand that you fully agreed, that it would be a sensible step for him to take employment for 15 months with a construction firm in Central America, in order to save the larger part of his salary . . .'

Nenna protested that she had never exactly thought it sensible, it was the parting of lovers, which must always be senseless, but they'd both of them thought that David, Panama, would be a wretched place to take small children to. The words sounded convincing, the judge leaned forward in approbation. Encouraged, she admitted that she had been entrusted with their last £2000, and had bought a houseboat, in point of fact, the barge *Grace*.

'The children missed their father?'

'The older one did. Tilda didn't seem to, but no-one understands what she thinks except Martha.'

'Thank you, Mrs James, we should like you to confine yourself to first-hand evidence . . . you wrote to your husband, of course, to explain the arrangements you had made in his absence?'

'I gave him our new address at once. Of course I did.'

'The address you gave him was 626 Cheyne Walk, Chelsea S.W.10?'

'Yes, that's right. That's the address of the boatyard office, where they take in the letters.'

'. . . giving him the impression, as indeed it would to any-one who did not know the district, that you had secured a well-appointed house or flat in Chelsea, at a very reasonable figure?'

'Well-appointed' was quite unfair, but Nenna's defence, always slow to move, failed to contest it.

'I didn't want to worry him. And then, plenty of people would give a lot to live on the Reach.'

'You are shifting your ground, Mrs James . . .'

'When I sent photographs to my sister in Canada, she thought it looked beautiful.'

'The river is thought of as romantic?'

'Yes, that's so!'

'More so by those who do not know it well?'

'I can't answer that.'

'They may be familiar with the paintings of Whistler, or perhaps with Whistler's statement that when evening mist clothes the riverside with poetry, as with a veil, and the poor buildings lose themselves in the dim sky, and the tall chimneys become campanili, and the warehouses are palaces in the night, and the whole city hangs in the heavens, and fairyland is before us – then the wayfarer hastens home, and Nature, who, for once, has sung in tune, sings her exquisite song to the artist alone, her son and her master – her son, in that he loves

35

her, her master in that he knows her? . . . shall I read you that deposition again, Mrs James?'

Nenna was silent.

'Whistler, however, lived in a reasonably comfortable house?'

Nenna refused to give way. 'You soon get used to the little difficulties. Most people like it very much.'

'Mrs James. Did your husband, on his return to this country, where he expected to be reunited with his wife and family, like the houseboat *Grace* very much?'

'A number of these houseboats, or disused barges, including *Grace*, are exceedingly damp?'

'Mrs James. Do you like your husband?'

'Mrs James. Did your husband, or did he not, complain that the houseboat *Grace*, apart from being damp, needed extensive repairs, and that it was difficult if not impossible for you to resume any meaningful sexual relationship when your cabin acted as a kind of passageway with your daughters constantly going to and fro to gain access to the hatch, and a succession of persons, including the milkman, trampling overhead? You will tell me that the milkman has refused to continue deliveries, but this only adds weight to my earlier submission that the boat is not only unfit to live in but actually unsafe.'

'I love him, I want him. While he was away was the longest fifteen months and eight days I ever spent. I can't believe even now that it's over. Why don't I go to him? Well, why doesn't he come to us? He hasn't found anywhere at all that we could all of us live together. He's in some kind of rooms in the north-east of London somewhere.'

'42b Milvain Street, Stoke Newington.'

'In Christ's name, who's ever heard of such a place?'

'Have you made any effort to go and see the plaintiff there, Mrs James? I must remind you that we cannot admit any second hand evidence.'

So now it was out. She was the defendant, or rather the accused, and should have known it all along.

'I repeat. Have you ever been to Milvain Street, which, for all any of us know, may be a perfectly suitable home for yourself and the issue of the marriage?'

'I know it isn't. How can it be?'

'Is he living there by himself?'

'I'm pretty sure so.'

'Not with another woman?'

'He's never mentioned one.'

'In his letters?'

'He's never liked writing letters very much.'

'But you write to him every day. That is perhaps too often?'

'It seems I can't do right. Everyone knows that women write a lot of letters.'

To the disapproval and distaste of the court she was shouting.

'I only want him to give way a little. I only want him to say that I've done well in finding somewhere for us to be!'

'You are very dependent on praise, Mrs James.'

'That depends, my lord, on who it's from.'

'You could be described as an obstinate bitch?' That was an intervention from her conscience but she had never been known for obstinacy in the past, and it was puzzling to account, really, for her awkward persistence about *Grace*. In calmer moments, too, she understood how it was that Edward, though generous at heart, found it difficult to give way. He was not much used to giving at all. His family, it seemed, had not been in the habit of exchanging presents, almost inconceivably to Nenna, whose childhood had been gift-ridden, with much atonement, love and reconciliation conveyed in the bright wrappings. Edward had no idea of how to express himself in that way. Nor was he fortunate as a shopper. He had realised, for instance, when Martha was born, that he would do well to take flowers to the hospital, but not that if you buy an azalea in winter and carry it on a bus and through a number of cold streets, all the buds will drop off before you arrive.

Nenna had never criticised the bloomless azalea. It was the other young mothers in the beds each side of her who had laughed at it. That had been 1951. Two of the new babies in the ward had been christened Festival.

'Your attention, Mrs James.'

The first exhibit in her case was a painful quarrel, laid out before the court in its naked entirety. Edward had not come back from the construction firm at David with anything saved up, but then, she had hardly expected him to. If he had saved anything he would have changed character and would hardly have been the man she loved. And, after all, they had *Grace*. Nenna, who was of hopeful temperament, intended to ask Edward's mother to look after Martha and Tilda for a while. She and Edward would be alone on *Grace*, and they could batten down and stay in bed for twenty-four hours if they felt like it.

'Mrs James, are you asking the court to believe that you were sincere in this? You know perfectly well that your husband's mother lives at a considerable distance, in point of fact in a suburb of Sheffield, and that she has never at any time offered to look after your children.'

Edward had made the same objection. And yet this particular quarrel, now that it was under rigorous scrutiny, hadn't arisen over that matter at all, but over something else entirely, the question of where Nenna could possibly have put his squash racquets while he was away. They had both of them thought that the climate of Panama would be bad for the racquets, although it turned out in the end that he could perfectly well have taken them with him. If Nenna had brought them with her to *Grace*, they must certainly have been

38

ruined by the damp. But, worse still, they were not on *Grace*. Nenna was full of contrition. O my God, I am heartily sorry for having offended Thee. Thirty minutes of squash gives a man as much exercise as two hours of any other game. She had been entrusted with the racquets. They were, in a sense, a sacred trust. But she could not remember anything at all about them.

'You mislaid them deliberately?'

'I don't do anything deliberately.'

That seemed to be true. Some of her actions were defensive, others optimistic, more than half of them mistaken.

'On this occasion you lost your temper, and threw a solid object at Mr James?'

It had only been her bank book, and Edward had been quite right to say that it was not worth reading.

But then the exhibit, the quarrel, hateful and confusing in being exposed to other eyes, changed character and became, after all, evidence for the defence. In mid-fury Edward had asked what day of the week she imagined it was, for at the time, in the highly coloured world of the argument, this detail had become of supreme importance.

'Look here, is it Wednesday or Thursday?'

'I don't know, Ed, whichever you like.'

Given so much free choice, he had melted immediately, and by good fortune they had several hours alone on the boat. The girls were at school, and no misery that Nenna had ever felt could weigh against their happiness which flowed like the current, with its separate eddies, of the strong river beneath them.

Perhaps the whole case was breaking down, to the disappointment of the advocates, who, after all, could hardly be distinguished from the prosecution on both sides. So little was needed for a settlement, and yet the word 'settlement' suggested two intractable people, and they were both quite humble. Nor was it true, as their accusers impartially suggested, that she or Edward preferred to live in an atmosphere of crisis. They both needed peace and turned in memory towards their peaceful moments together, finding their true home there.

When Nenna was not in the witness box, she sometimes saw herself getting ready for an inspection at which Edward, or Edward's mother, or some power superior to either, gave warning that they might appear – she could only hope that it would be on a falling tide – to see where she could be found wanting. Determined not to fail this test, she let the image fade into the business of polishing the brasses and cleaning ship. The decks must be clear, hatches fastened, Stripey out of sight, and above all the girls ought to be back in regular education.

'You're both going in to school on Monday, aren't you, Martha?'

Martha, like her father, and like Richard, saw no need for fictions. She gave her mother a dark brown, level glance.

'I shall go in, and take Tilda with me, when the situation warrants it.'

'We shall have Father Watson round again.'

'I don't think so, Ma. He missed his footing on the gangplank last time.'

'I'm so tired of making excuses.'

'You should tell the truth.'

In what way could the truth be made acceptable? Tilda had initiated the train of events, as, with her careless mastery of life, she often did. Pressed by the nuns to complete a kettleholder in cross-stitch as a present for her father, she had replied that she had never seen her father holding a kettle and that Daddy had gone away.

The fact was that she had lost the six square inches of canvas allocated for the kettleholder when it was first given out to the class. Martha knew this, but did not wish to betray her sister.

Tilda had at first elaborated her story, saying that her

mother was looking for a new Daddy, but her observation, quick as a bird's flight, showed her that this was going too far, and she added that she and her sister prayed nightly to Our Lady of Fatima for her father's return. Up till that moment Tilda, in spite of her lucid gray eyes, showing clarity beneath clarity, which challenged the nuns not to risk scandalising the innocent, had often been in disfavour. She was known to be one of the little ones who had filled in their colouring books irreverently, making our Lord's beard purple, or even green, largely, to be sure, because she never bothered to get hold of the best crayons first. Now, however, she was the object of compassion. After a private conference with Mother Superior, the Sisters announced that there would be a special rosary every morning, during the time set aside for special intentions, and that the whole Junior School would pray together that Martha and Tilda's Daddy should come back to them. After this, if the weather was fine, there would be a procession to the life size model of the grotto of Lourdes, which had been built in the recreation ground out of a kind of artificial rock closely resembling anthracite. Sister Paul, who was the author of several devotional volumes, wrote the special prayer: Heart of Jesus, grant that the eyes of the non-Catholic father of Thy little servants, Martha and Matilda, may be opened, that his tepid soul may become fervent, and that he may return to establish himself on his rightful hearth, Amen.

'They are good women,' Martha said, 'but I'm not going to set foot in the place while that's going on.'

'I could speak to the nuns.'

'I'd rather you didn't, Ma. They might begin to pray for you as well.'

She glanced up, apparently casually, to see if Nenna had taken this too hard.

Tilda appeared with a ball of oozing clay in her arms which she flung down on the table. Apparently carrion, it moved and stretched a lean back leg, which turned out to be Stripey's.

'She's in voluntary liquidation,' said Martha, but she fetched a piece of old towelling and began to rub the cat, which squinted through the folds of white material like Lazarus through the grave-clothes.

'How did she get into this state?' Nenna asked. 'That isn't shore mud.'

'She was hunting rats on the wharf and she fell into a clay lighter, Mercantile Lighterage Limited, flag black diamond on broad white band.'

'Who brought her in, then?'

'One of the lightermen got off at Cadogan Stairs and walked back with her and gave her to Maurice.'

'Well, try to squeeze the water out of her tail. Gently.'

The clay rapidly set in a hard surface on the table and the floorboards underneath it. Martha mopped and scraped away for about half an hour, long after Tilda had lost interest. During this time it grew dark, the darkness seeming to rise from the river to make it one with the sky. Nenna made the tea and lit the wood stove. The old barges, who had once beaten their way up and down the East coast and the Channel ports, grumbled and heaved at their cables while their new owners sat back in peace.

Without warning, a shaft of brilliant light, in colour a sickly mauve, shone down the hatchway.

'It must be from *Maurice*,' said Martha, 'it can't be a shore light.'

They could hear his footsteps across the gangplank, then a heavier one as he dropped the eighteen inch gap on to *Grace's* deck.

'Maurice can't weigh much. He just springs about.'

'Cat-like?' Nenna asked.

'Heaven forbid,' said Martha.

'*Grace*!' Maurice called, in imitation of Richard, 'perhaps you'd like to come and have a look.'

Nenna and the two girls shook off a certain teatime drowsiness and went back on deck, where they stood astounded. On the afterdeck of *Maurice*, which lay slightly at an angle to *Grace*, a strange transformation had taken place. The bright light – this was what had struck them first – issued from an old street lamp, leaning at a crazy angle, rather suggesting an amateur production of *Tales of Hoffmann*, fitted, in place of glass, with sheets of mauve plastic, and trailing a long cable which disappeared down the companion. On the deck itself were scattered what looked like paving stones, and the lee-board winch had been somewhat garishly painted in red, white, and gold.

The wash of a passing collier rocked both boats and the enormous reverberation of her wailing hooter filled the air and made it impossible for them to speak. Maurice stood half in the shadow, half brightly purple, and at last was able to say:

'It'll make you think of Venice, won't it?'

Nenna hesitated.

'I've never been to Venice.'

'Nor have I,' said Maurice, quick to disclaim any pretence to superiority, 'I got the idea from a postcard someone sent me. Well, he sent me quite a series of postcards, and from them I was able to reconstruct a typical street corner. Not the Grand Canal, you understand, just one of the little ones. When it's as warm as it is tonight, you'll be able to leave the hatch open and imagine yourselves in the heart of Venice.'

'It's beautiful!' Tilda shouted.

'You don't seem quite certain about it, Nenna.'

'I am, I am. I've always wanted to see Venice, almost more than any other place. I was only wondering what would happen when the wind gets up.'

What she must not ask, but at the same time mustn't be thought not to be asking, was what would happen when Harry came next. As a depot for stolen goods *Maurice*, surely, had to look as inconspicuous as possible.

43

'I may be going abroad myself quite soon,' said Maurice casually.

'Oh, you didn't tell us.'

'Yes, I met someone the other night who made a sort of suggestion about a possible job of some kind.'

It wasn't worth asking of what kind; there had been so many beginnings. Sometimes Maurice went over to Bayswater to keep up his skating, in the hopes of getting a job in the ice show. Perhaps it was that he was talking about now.

'Would you be selling *Maurice*, then?'

'Oh yes, of course, when I go abroad.'

'Well, your leak isn't nearly as bad as *Dreadnought*.'

This practical advice seemed to depress Maurice, who was trying the paving stones in various positions.

'I must ask Willis how he's getting on . . . there's so much to think about . . . if someone wanted a description of this boat, I suppose the Venetian corner would be a feature . . .'

He switched off the mauve light. None of the barge-owners could afford to waste electricity, and the display was really intended for much later at night, but he had turned it on early to surprise and please them.

'Yes! I'll soon be living on land. I shall tell my friend to take all his bits and pieces out of my hold, of course.'

'Maurice is going mad,' said Martha, quietly, as they went back onto *Grace*.

[4]

Maurice's strange period of hopefulness did not last long. Tenderly responsive to the self-deceptions of others, he was unfortunately too well able to understand his own. No more was said of the job, and it rapidly became impossible to tell who was trying to please whom over the matter of the Venetian lantern.

'What am I to do, Maurice?' Nenna asked. She confided in him above all others. Apart from anything else, his working day did not begin till seven or eight, so that he was often there during the day, and always ready to listen; but there were times when his customers left early, at two or three in the morning, and then Maurice, somewhat exhilarated with whisky, would come over to *Grace*, magically retaining his balance on the gangplank, and sit on the gunwale, waiting. He never went below, for fear of disturbing the little girls. Nenna used to wrap up in her coat and bring out two rugs for him.

During the small hours, tipsy Maurice became an oracle, ambiguous, wayward, but impressive. Even his voice changed a little. He told the sombre truths of the lighthearted, betraying in a casual hour what was never intended to be shown. If the tide was low the two of them watched the gleams on the foreshore, at half tide they heard the water chuckling, waiting to lift the boats, at flood tide they saw the river as a powerful god, bearded with the white foam of detergents, calling home the twenty-seven lost rivers of London, sighing as the night declined.

45

'Maurice, ought I to go away?'

'You can't.'

'You said you were going to go away yourself.'

'No-one believed it. You didn't. What do the others think?'

'They think your boat belongs to Harry.'

'Nothing belongs to Harry, certainly all that stuff in the hold doesn't. He finds it easier to live without property. As to *Maurice*, my godmother gave me the money to buy a bit of property when I left Southport.'

'I've never been to Southport.'

'It's very nice. You take the train from the middle of Liverpool, and it's the last station, right out by the seaside.'

'Have you been back since?'

'No.'

'If *Maurice* belongs to you, why do you have to put up with Harry?'

'I can't answer that.'

'What will you do if the police come?'

'What will you do if your husband doesn't?'

Nenna thought, I must take the opportunity to get things settled for me, even if it's only by chance, like throwing straws into the current. She repeated –

'Maurice, what shall I do?'

'Well, have you been to see him yet?'

'Not yet. But of course I ought to. As soon as I can find someone to stay with the girls, for a night or two if it's necessary, I'm going to go. Thank you for making my mind up.'

'No, don't do that.'

'Don't do what?'

'Don't thank me.'

'Why not?'

'Not for that.'

'But, you know, by myself I can't make my mind up.'

'You shouldn't do it at all.'

'Why not, Maurice?'

'Why should you think it's a good thing to do? Why should it make you any happier? There isn't one kind of happiness, there's all kinds. Decision is torment for anyone with imagination. When you decide, you multiply the things you might have done and now never can. If there's even one person who might be hurt by a decision, you should never make it. They tell you, make up your mind or it will be too late, but if it's really too late, we should be grateful. You know very well that we're two of the same kind, Nenna. It's right for us to live where we do, between land and water. You, my dear, you're half in love with your husband, then there's Martha who's half a child and half a girl, Richard who can't give up being half in the Navy, Willis who's half an artist and half a longshoreman, a cat who's half alive and half dead . . .'

He stopped before describing himself, if, indeed, he had been going to do so.

Partisan Street, opposite the Reach, was a rough place, well used to answering police enquiries. The boys looked on the Venetian corner as a godsend and came every day as soon as they were out of school to throw stones at it. After a week Harry returned to *Maurice*, once again when there was no-one on the boat, took away his consignment of hair-dryers, and threw the lantern and the paving-stones overboard. Tilda, an expert mudlark, retrieved most of the purple plastic, but the pieces were broken and it was hard to see what could be done with them. Maurice appreciated the thought, but seemed not to care greatly one way or the other.

[5]

Willis deeply respected Richard, whom he privately thought
of as, and sometimes called aloud, the Skipper. Furthermore,
although he had been pretty well openly accused of dishonesty
at the meeting, his moral standards were much the same as
Richard's; only he did not feel he was well enough off to
apply them as often, and in such a wide range of conditions, as
the Skipper. It didn't, thank heavens, seem likely that a
situation would ever arise in which there was no hope for
Richard, whereas, on the other hand, Willis considered that
for himself there was scarcely any hope at all if he could not
sell *Dreadnought*. £2000 would, according to his calculations,
be more or less enough for him to go and spend the rest of his
days with his widowed sister. He could hardly go empty-
handed, and the benefits of the move had been pointed out to
him often.

'My sister's place is on gravel soil. You don't feel the damp
there. Couldn't feel it if you wanted to.'

Nor, however, did you see the river, and Willis would have
to find something else to fill the great gap which would be left
in his life when it was no longer possible to see the river traffic,
passing and repassing. Like many marine painters he had
never been to sea. During the War he had been an auxiliary
coastguard. He knew nothing about blue water sailing. But to
sit still and watch while the ships proceeded on their lawful
business, to know every class, every rig and every cargo, is to
make inactivity a virtue, and Willis from *Dreadnought* and
from points along the shore as far as the Cat and Lobster at

Gravesend had honourably conducted the profession of looking on. Born in Silvertown, within sound of the old boat-builders' yards, he disliked silence. Like Tilda, he found it easier to sleep when he could hear the lighters, like iron coffins on Resurrection Day, clashing each other at their moorings all night, and behind that the whisper of shoal water.

Tilda, in spite of her lack of success with the convent's colouring books, wished to be a marine painter also. Her object was to paint exactly like Willis, and to put in all the rigging with a ruler, and to get everything right. She also wanted to have a Sunday dinner, whenever possible, in the style of Willis, who followed the bargemen's custom of serving first sultana pudding with gravy, and then the roast.

As an artist, he had always made an adequate living, and Willises, carefully packed in stiff board and oiled paper, were despatched – since a number of his patrons were in the Merchant Navy – to ports all over the world for collection. But these commissions, mostly for the originals of jokes and cartoons which Willis had managed in former times to sell to magazines, had grown fewer and fewer in the last ten years, as, indeed, had the drawings themselves. After the war the number of readers who would laugh at pictures of seasick passengers, or bosuns getting the better of the second mate, diminished rapidly.

A few distant correspondents, untouched by time, still asked confidently for a painting of a particular ship. *Dear Willis – As I am informed by those who ought to know that you have 'taken the ground' somewhere near London River, I expect you can tell me the whereabouts of the dear old* Fortuna, *built 1892, rigged when I last saw her in 1920 as a square foresail brigantine. Old ships never die and doubtless she is still knocking around the East Coast, though I suppose old Payne may have made his last port by now. . . . I should be interested in an oil painting on canvas, or board (which I suppose would come a bit cheaper ! !) showing her beating round the Foreland under sail in fairly heavy weather, say Force 6* . . . Willis could only pray that the writers of such letters, stranded in ports which the war had passed by almost without notice, would never return, to be betrayed by so much change.

Willis sometimes took Tilda, in her character as an apprentice painter, to the Tate Gallery, about two and a half miles along the Embankment. There was no Tube then to Pimlico, and they proceeded by a series of tacks to Victoria. At Sloane Square Underground Station Willis pointed out the mighty iron pipe crossing high in the air above the passenger line.

'Look, that carries the River Westbourne, flowing down from Paddington. If that was to take and start leaking, we'd all have to swim for it.'

Tilda eyed the great pipe.

'Where does it come out?'

'The outfall? Well, it's one of the big sewers, my dear, I'll get the name right for you.' He made a note.

The other passengers drew back from the dishevelled river dwellers, so far out of their element.

Laura was doubtful whether the little girl ought to be allowed to go out like that alone with an old man, and not a very scrupulous one at that, for a whole afternoon. She told Richard a number of stories on the subject, some of them taken from the daily papers, and suggested that he might turn the matter over in his mind. But Richard said it wasn't necessary.

'You told me yourself that he was dishonest.'

'It isn't necessary.'

Willis and Tilda usually stopped on the way at a little shop in the Vauxhall Bridge Road, which seemed glad of any kind of custom, to buy a quarter of aniseed marbles. These were sold loose, but were put into a special paper bag overprinted with the words

COME ON, CHILDREN, HERE'S A NEW HIT!
FIRST YOU ROLL IT, THEN YOU CHEW IT.

Willis had never known many children, and until Nenna had come to the boats he had rather tended to forget there were such things. The very distinctive taste of the aniseed marbles, which were, perhaps, some of the nastiest sweets ever made, recovered time past for him.

Once at the Tate, they usually had time only to look at the sea and river pieces, the Turners and the Whistlers. Willis praised these with the mingled pride and humility of an inheritor, however distant. To Tilda, however, the fine pictures were only extensions of her life on board. It struck her as odd, for example, that Turner, if he spent so much time on Chelsea Reach, shouldn't have known that a seagull always alights on the highest point. Well aware that she was in a public place, she tried to modify her voice; only then Willis didn't always hear, and she had to try again, a good deal louder.

'Did Whistler do that one?'

The attendant watched her, hoping that she would get a little closer to the picture, so that he could relieve the boredom of his long day by telling her to stand back.

'What did he put those two red lights up there for? They're for obstruction not completely covered by water, aren't they? What are they doing there among the riding lights?'

'They don't miss much, do they?' the attendant said to Willis. 'I mean, your little granddaughter there.'

The misunderstanding delighted Tilda. 'Dear grandfather, are you sure you are not weary? Let us return to our ship. Take my arm, for though I am young, I am strong.'

Willis dealt with her admirably by taking almost no notice of what she said.

'Whistler was a very good painter. You don't want to make any mistake about that. It's only amateurs who think he isn't. There's Old Battersea Bridge. That was the old wooden bridge. Painted on a grey ground, you see, to save himself trouble. Tide on the turn, lighter taking advantage of the ebb.'

51

It was understood that on their return they would have tea on *Grace*.

'How old do you think I am, Mrs James?' Willis asked, leaning quietly forward. 'Don't tell me you've never thought about it. It's my experience that everybody thinks how old everybody else is.'

There was no help for it. 'Well, perhaps nearer seventy than sixty.'

Willis's expression never changed quickly. It seemed to be a considerable undertaking for him to rearrange the leathery brown cheeks and the stiff grey eyebrows which were apparently supported by his thick-lensed spectacles.

'I don't seem to feel my age while I'm on these little expeditions, or when I'm drawing.'

Now he wouldn't have time for either. Cleaning ship, and worrying about the visits of intending purchasers, occupied his entire horizon.

His ideas proceeded from simplicity to simplicity. If the main leak could be concealed by showing only at low tide, Willis thought that the equally serious problem of rain – for the weatherboards were particularly weak in one place – could be solved if he stood directly under the drip, wearing a sort of broad waterproof hat. He was sure he had one stowed away somewhere.

'He's no idea of how to sell anything except his drawings,' Woodie told Charles, 'and then I doubt whether he charges enough for them. I should describe him as an innocent.'

'He knows a fair amount about boats.'

'He lives in the past. He was asking me about some man called Payne who seems to have died years ago.'

Richard saw, with reservations, where his duty lay, and put *Dreadnought* on the market through the agency of an old RNVR friend of his, who had gone into partnership, on coming out of the forces, as an estate agent in Halkin Street. Perhaps 'acquaintance' would be a fairer description than 'friend', but the difference was clearer in peacetime than it had been during the war.

The agent was up-to-date and wished, as was fashionable in those years, to give an amusing turn to the advertisement, which he thought ought to appear, not where Willis had thought of putting it, in the *Exchange and Mart*, but in the A circulation newspapers.

'... Whistler's Battersea ... main water ... no? well, main electricity ... two cabins, one suitable for a tiny Flying Dutchman ... huge Cutty Sark type hold awaits conversion ... complete with resident Ancient Mariner ... might be persuaded to stop awhile if you splice the mainbrace ...'

The senior partner usually drafted these announcements himself, but all the partners felt that, given the chance, they could do it better.

'The *Cutty Sark* was a tea clipper,' Richard said. 'And I don't think there's any question of Willis staying on board. In fact, that's really the whole point of the transaction.'

'Did this barge go to Dunkirk?'

'A number of them were drafted,' Richard said, '*Grace* was, and *Maurice*, but not *Dreadnought*, I think.'

'Pity. It would have been a selling point. How would it be, Richard, if we were to continue this discussion over a very large pink gin?'

This remark, often repeated, had earned Richard's friend, or acquaintance, the nickname of Pinkie.

Since this meeting, Richard had had a further debate with his conscience. It was, of course, the purchaser's business to employ a surveyor, whether a house or a boat was in question, and Pinkie would not be offering *Dreadnought* with any kind of guarantee as to soundness, only, after all, as to quaintness. On the other hand, Pinkie seemed to have lost his head to a certain extent, perhaps at the prospect of making his mark by bringing in something novel in the way of business. Surely he hadn't been quite so irritating as a watchkeeping officer in the

Lanark? But the weakest element in the situation – the one most in need of protection, towards which Richard would always return – the weakest element was certainly Willis. He had begun to neglect himself, Laura said. She had gone along once to pay a casual visit and found one of Nenna's youngsters, the little one, cooking some kind of mess for him in *Dreadnought's* galley. Richard rather liked Willis's pictures, and had got him to do a pen and wash drawing of *Lord Jim*. He saw the old man as in need of what, by current standards, was a very small sum to enable him to wind up his affairs.

Richard was not aware that he was no longer reasoning, but allowing a series of overlapping images – the drawing of *Lord Jim*, Tilda cooking – to act as a substitute for argument, so that his mind was working in a way not far different from Maurice's, or Nenna's. But the end product would be very different – not indecisive and multiple, but single and decisive. Without this faculty of Richard's, the world could not be maintained in its present state.

Having explained carefully to Willis what he was about to do, Richard invited Pinkie out to lunch. This had to be at a restaurant, because the only club that Richard belonged to was Pratt's. He had got himself put up for Pratt's because it was impossible to have lunch there. There was, too, something unaccountable about Richard – perhaps the same wilfulness that induced him to live offshore although his marriage was in a perilous state – which attracted him to Pratt's because celebrations were only held there for the death of a king or a queen.

The restaurant to which Richard invited Pinkie was one at which he had an account, and there was, at least, no difficulty in knowing what drinks to order. Pinkie sucked in his drink in a curious manner, very curious considering how many gins he must have in the course of the week, as though his glass was a blowhole in Arctic ice and to drink was his only hope of survival.

54

'By the way, Richard, when are you and Laura going to give up this nonsense about living in the middle of the Thames? This is the moment to acquire property, I'm sure you realise that.'

'Where?' Richard asked. He wondered why Pinkie mentioned Laura, then realised with sinking heart that she was no longer keeping her discontent to herself, and the echo of it must have travelled for some distance.

'Where? Oh, a gentleman's county,' Pinkie replied, wallowing through his barrier of ice, 'say Northamptonshire. You can drive up every morning easily, be in the office by ten, down in the evening by half-past six. I calculate you could spend about 60 per cent of your life at work and 40 per cent at home. Not too bad, that. Mind you, these Jacobean properties don't come on the market every day. We just happen to be more lucky at laying hands on them than most. Or Norfolk, of course, if you're interested in small boats.'

Richard wondered why living on a largish boat should automatically make him interested in small ones.

'Not Norfolk, I think.' A number of Laura's relations lived there, but he had not come to the Relais to discuss them. 'You wouldn't make a profit on *Lord Jim* anyway,' he added, 'I don't regard her as an investment.'

'Then what in the name of Christ did you buy her for?'

This was the question Richard did not want to answer. Meanwhile, the waiter put a warm plate printed with a name and device in front of each of them and, after a short interval, took it away again, this, presumably, representing the cover for which the restaurant made a charge. Subsequently he brought various inedible articles, such as bread dried to a crisp, and questionable pieces of shellfish, and placed these in front of them. Pinkie chewed away at a raw fragment.

'We might call him an old shellback, if you think that'd go down better, instead of an Ancient Mariner.'

'Who?'

55

'This Willis of yours. It doesn't do to be too literary.'

The waiter invited them to choose between coq au vin and navarin of lamb, either of which, in other circumstances, would have been called stew.

'Knows his job, that fellow,' said Pinkie. Richard felt inclined to agree with him.

The wine, though Richard was not the kind of person whom the sommelier kept waiting, was not particularly good. Pinkie said nothing about this because he was dazed by gin, and was not paying, and Richard said nothing because, after a little thought, he concluded that the wine was good enough for Pinkie.

After they had been given the coq au vin the waiter shovelled on to their plates, from a mysteriously divided dish, some wilted vegetables, and Richard recognised that the moment had come to make his only point.

'I really haven't any particular interest in the sale, except that I want to do the best that I can for this retired artist, Sam Willis,' he said. 'I regard him as a friend, and you remember that apart from all this local colour, I gave you the specifications of his boat.'

'Oh, I dare say. They'll have those in the office. The invaluable Miss Barker. Well, proceed.'

'There wasn't any mention, I think I'm right in saying, of a survey – that rested with the purchaser.'

Another waiter brought round a trolley on which were a number of half-eaten gâteaux decorated with a white substance, and some slices of hard apple resting in water, in a glass bowl. The idea of eating these things seemed absurd, and yet Pinkie asked for some.

'Well, these specifications. I'll have to go back to the shop, and check up on them, as I said, but I imagine you won't grudge me a glass of brandy first.'

Richard gave the order. 'There's something which I didn't mention, but I want to make it absolutely clear, and that is that I've reason to believe that this craft, the *Dreadnought*, leaks quite badly.'

Pinkie laughed, spraying a little of the brandy which had been brought to him onto the laden air. 'Of course she does. All these old boats leak like sieves. Just as all these period houses are as rotten as old cheese. Everyone knows that. But age has its value.'

Richard sighed. 'Has it ever struck you, Pinkie, what it would be like to belong to a class of objects which gets more valuable as it gets older? Houses, oak-trees, furniture, wine, I don't care what! I'm thirty-nine, I'm not sure about you . . .'

The idea was not taken up, and half an hour later Richard signed the bill and they left the Relais together. Pinkie could still think quite clearly enough to know that he had very little prospect of a new commission. 'As you're fixed, Richard,' he said, half embracing his friend, but impeded by his umbrella, 'as you're fixed, and you're an obstinate bugger, I can't shake you, you're living nowhere, you don't belong to land or water?' As Richard did not respond, he added, 'Keep in touch. We mustn't let it be so long next time.'

The second or third lots of clients sent along by Pinkie, an insurance broker and his wife, who wanted somewhere to give occasional parties in summer, at high tide only, were very much taken with *Dreadnought*. It was raining slightly on the day of inspection, but Willis, who had not been able to lay hands on his waterproof 'tile', but made do with a deep-crowned felt hat, stood on duty under the gap in the weather-boards, while an unsuspecting clerk from the agency showed the rest of the boat. The galley was very cramped, but the ship's chests, still marked FOR 2 SEAMEN, and the deck-house, from which Willis had watched the life of the river go by, both made a good impression.

'You'll have noticed the quality of the bottom planking,' said the clerk. 'All these ends are $2\frac{1}{2}$ English elm for three strakes out from the centre, and after that you've got oak. That's what Nelson meant, you know, when he talked about wooden walls. Mind, I don't say that she hasn't been knocked about a bit . . . There may be some weathering here and there . . .'

After a few weeks which to Willis, however, seemed like a few years, the broker's solicitors made a conditional offer for the poor old barge, and finally agreed to pay £1500, provided that *Dreadnought* was still in shipshape condition six months hence, in the spring of 1962.

Six months, Willis repeated. It was a long time to wait, but not impossible.

Richard suggested that the intervening time could well be spent in replacing the pumps and pump-wells, and certain sections of the hull. It was difficult for him to realise that he was dealing with, or rather trying to help, a man who had never, either physically or emotionally, felt the need to replace anything. Even Willis's appearance, the spiky short black hair and the prize-fighter's countenance, had not changed much since he had played truant from Elementary school and gone down to hang about the docks. If truth were known, he had had a wife, as well as a perdurable old mother, a great bicyclist and supporter of local Labour causes, but both of them had died of cancer, no replacements possible there. The body must either repair itself or stop functioning, but that is not true of the emotions, and particularly of Willis's emotions. He had come to doubt the value of all new beginnings and to put his trust in not much more than the art of hanging together. *Dreadnought* had stayed afloat for more than sixty years, and Richard, Skipper though he was, didn't understand timber. Tinkering about with the old boat would almost certainly be the end of her. He remembered the last time he had been to see the dentist. Dental care was free in the 60's, in return for signing certain unintelligible documents during the joy of escape from the surgery. But when the dentist had announced that it was urgently necessary to extract two teeth Willis had got up and walked away, glad that he hadn't taken off his coat and so would not have to enter into any further discussion while he recovered it from the waiting-room. If one goes, he thought, still worse two, they all go.

'*Dreadnought* is good for a few years yet,' he insisted. 'And what kind of repairs can you do on oak?'

'Have you asked him about the insurance valuation?' Laura asked Richard.

'There isn't one. These old barges – well, they could get a quotation for fire, I suppose, but not against flood or storm damage.'

'I'm going home for a fortnight. It may be more than a fortnight – I don't really know how long.'

'When?'

'Oh, quite soon. I'll need some money.'

Richard avoided looking at her, for fear she should think he meant anything particular by it.

'What about *Grace*?' Laura went on.

'What about her?'

'Is *Grace* in bad condition?'

Richard sighed. 'Not as good as one would like. There the trouble is largely above the waterline, though. I've told Nenna time and again that she ought to get hold of some sort of reliable chap, an ex-Naval chippie would be the right sort, just to spend the odd day on board and put everything to rights. There aren't any partitions between the cabins, to start with.'

'Did Nenna tell you that?'

'You can see for yourself, if you drop in there.'

'What a very odd thing to tell you.'

'I suppose people have got used to bringing me their queries, to some extent,' said Richard, going into their cabin to take off his black shoes and put on a pair of red leather slippers, which, like all his other clothes, never seemed to wear out. The slippers made him feel less tired.

'There are more queries from *Grace* than from *Dreadnought*, aren't there?'

'I'm not sure. I've never worked it out exactly.'

'They're not worth talking about anyway. I expect they talk about us.'

'Oh, do you think so?'

'They say "There goes that Mrs Blake again. She turns me up, she looks so bleeding bored all day".'

Richard did not like to have to think about two things at once, particularly at the end of the day. He kissed Laura, sat down, and tried to bring the two subjects put to him into order, and under one heading. A frown ran in a slanting direction between his eyebrows and half way up his forehead. Laura's problem was that she had not enough to do – no children, though she hadn't said anything about this recently – and his heart smote him because he had undertaken to make her happy, and hadn't. Nenna, on the other hand, had rather too much. If her husband had let her down, as was apparently the case, she ought to have a male relation of some kind, to see to things. In Richard's experience, all women had plenty of male relations. Laura, for instance, had two younger brothers, who were not settling very well into the stockbrokers' firm in which they had been placed, and numerous uncles, one of them an old horror who obtained Scandinavian au pairs through advertisements in *The Lady*, and then, of course, her Norfolk cousins. Nenna appeared to have no-one. She had come over here from Canada, of course. This last reflection – it was Nova Scotia, he was pretty sure – seemed to tidy up the whole matter, which his mind now presented as a uniform interlocking structure, with working parts.

Laura was very lucky to be married to Richard, who would not have hurt her feelings deliberately for the whole world. A fortnight with her parents, he was thinking now, on their many acres of damp earth, must surely bring home to her the advantages of living on *Lord Jim*. Of course, it hadn't so far done anything of the kind, and he had to arrive at the best thing to do in the circumstances. He was not quite satisfied with the way his mind was working. Something was out of phase. He did not recognise it as hope.

'I want to take you out to dinner, Lollie,' he said.

'Why?'

'You look so pretty, I want other people to see you. I daresay they'll wonder why on earth you agreed to go out with a chap like me.'

'Where do you go when you take people out to lunch from the office?'

'Oh, the Relais, but that's no good in the evening. We could try that Provençal place. Give them a treat.'

'You don't really want to go,' said Laura, but she disappeared into the spare cabin, where, unfortunately, her dresses had to be kept. Richard took off his slippers and put on his black shoes again, and they went out.

[6]

Martha and Tilda were in the position of having no spending money, but this was less important when they were not attending school and were spared the pains of comparison, and they felt no bitterness against their mother, because she hadn't any either. Nenna believed, however, that she would have some in the spring, when three things would happen, each, like melting ice-floes, slowly moving the next one on. Edward would come and live on *Grace*, which would save the rent he was paying on his rooms at present; the girls, once they were not being prayed for at the grotto, would agree to go back to the nuns; and with Tilda at school she could go out herself and look for a job.

Martha could not imagine her mother going out to work and felt that the experiment was likely to prove disastrous.

'You girls don't know my life,' said Nenna, 'I worked in my vacations, wiping dishes, camp counselling, all manner of things.'

Martha smiled at the idea of these dear dead days. 'What did you counsel?' she asked.

The girls needed money principally to buy singles by Elvis Presley and Cliff Richard, whose brightly smiling photograph presided over their cabin. They had got the photograph as a fold-in from *Disc Weekly*. If you couldn't afford the original records, there were smaller ones you could buy at the Woolworths in the King's Road, which sounded quite like.

Like the rest of London's river children, they knew that the mud was a source of wealth, but were too shrewd to go into competition with the locals from Partisan Street for coins, medals and lugworms. The lugworms, in any case, Willis had told them, were better on Limehouse Reach. Round about *Grace* herself, the great river deposited little but mounds of plastic containers.

Every expedition meant crossing the Bridge, because the current on Battersea Reach, between the two bridges, sets towards the Surrey side. The responsibility for these outings, which might or might not be successful, had worn between Martha's eyebrows a faint frown, not quite vertical, which exactly resembled Richard's.

'We'll go bricking to-day,' she said. 'How's the tide?'

'High water Gravesend 3 a.m., London Bridge 4, Battersea Bridge 4.30,' Tilda chanted rapidly. 'Spring tide, seven and a half hour's ebb, low tide at 12.'

Martha surveyed her sister doubtfully. With so much specialised knowledge, which would qualify her for nothing much except a pilot's certificate, with her wellingtons over which the mud of many tides had dried, she had the air of something aquatic, a demon from the depths, perhaps. Whatever happens, I must never leave her behind, Martha prayed.

Both the girls were small and looked exceptionally so as they crossed the Bridge with their handcart. They wore stout Canadian anoraks, sent them by their Aunt Louise.

Below the old Church at Battersea the retreating flood had left exposed a wide shelf of mud and gravel. At intervals the dark driftwood lay piled. Near the draw dock some longshoremen had heaped it up and set light to it, to clear the area. Now the thick blue smoke gave out a villainous smell, the gross spirit of salt and fire. Tilda loved that smell, and stretched her nostrils wide.

Beyond the dock, an old wrecked barge lay upside down. It was shocking, even terrifying, to see her dark flat shining bottom, chine uppermost. A derelict ship turns over on her

63

keel and lies gracefully at rest, but there is only one way up for a Thames barge if she is to maintain her dignity.

This wreck was the *Small Gains*, which had gone down more than twenty-five years before, when hundreds of barges were still working under sail. Held fast in the mud with her cargo of bricks, she had failed to come up with the rising tide and the water had turned her over. The old bricks were still scattered over the foreshore. After a storm they were washed back in dozens, but most of them were broken or half ground to powder. Along with the main cargo, however, *Small Gains* had shipped a quantity of tiles. At a certain moment in the afternoon the sun, striking across the water from behind the gas works, sent almost level rays over the glistening reach. Then it was possible for the expert to pick out a glazed tile, though only if it had sunk at the correct angle to the river bed.

'Do you think Ma's mind is weakening?' Tilda asked.

'I thought we weren't going to discuss our affairs today.' Martha relented and added – 'Well, Ma is much too dependent on Maurice, or on anyone sympathetic. She ought to avoid these people.'

The two girls sat on the wall of Old Battersea churchyard to eat their sandwiches. These contained a substance called Spread, and, indeed, that was all you could do with it.

'Mattie, who would you choose, if you were compelled at gunpoint to marry tomorrow?'

'You mean, someone off the boats?'

'We don't know anybody else.'

Seagulls, able to detect the appearance of a piece of bread at a hundred yards away, advanced slowly towards them over the shelving ground.

'I thought perhaps you meant Cliff.'

'Not Cliff, not Elvis. And not Richard, he's too obvious.' Martha licked her fingers.

'He looks tired all the time now. I saw him taking Laura

64

out to dinner yesterday evening. Straight away after he'd come back from work! Where's the relaxation in that? What sort of life is that for a man to lead?'

'What was she wearing?'

'I couldn't make out. She had her new coat on.'

'But you saw the strain on his features?'

'Oh, yes.'

'Do you think Ma notices?'

'Oh, everybody does.'

When the light seemed about right, striking fire out of the broken bits of china and glass, they went to work. Tilda lay down full length on a baulk of timber. It was her job to do this, because Martha bruised so easily. A princess, unknown to all about her, she awaited the moment when these bruises would reveal her true heritage.

Tilda stared fixedly. It was necessary to get your eye in.

'There's one!'

She bounded off, as though over stepping stones, from one object to another that would scarcely hold, old tires, old boots, the ribs of crates from which the seagulls were dislodged in resentment. Far beyond the point at which the mud became treacherous and from which *Small Gains* had never risen again, she stood poised on the handlebars of a sunken bicycle. How had the bicycle ever got there?

'Mattie, it's a Raleigh!'

'If you've seen a tile, pick it up straight away and come back.'

'I've seen two!'

With a tile in each hand, balancing like a circus performer, Tilda returned. Under the garish lights of the Big Top, every man, woman and child rose to applaud. Who, they asked each other, was this newcomer, who had succeeded where so many others had failed?

The nearest clean water was from the standpipe in the churchyard; they did not like to wash their finds there, because the water was for the flowers on the graves, but Martha fetched some in a bucket.

As the mud cleared away from the face of the first tile, patches of ruby-red lustre, with the rich glow of a jewel's heart, appeared inch by inch, then the outlines of a delicate grotesque silver bird, standing on one leg in a circle of blue-black leaves and berries, its beak of burnished copper.

'Is it beautiful?'

'Yes.'

'And the dragon?'

The sinuous tail of a dragon, also in gold and jewel colours, wreathed itself like a border round the edge of the other tile.

The reverse of both tiles was damaged, and on only one of them the letters NDS END could just be made out, but Martha could not be mistaken.

'They're de Morgans, Tilda. Two of them at one go, two of them in one morning.'

'How much can we sell them for?'

'Do you remember the old lady, Tilda?'

'Did I see her?'

'Tilda, I only took you three months ago. Mrs Stirling, I mean, in Battersea Old House. Her sister was married to William de Morgan, that had the pottery, and made these kind of tiles, that was in Victorian days, you must remember. She was in a wheelchair. We paid for tea, but the money went to the Red Cross. We were only supposed to have two scones each, otherwise the Red Cross couldn't expect to make a profit. She explained, and she showed us all those tiles and bowls, and the brush and comb he used to do his beard with.'

'How old was she?'

'In 1965 she'll be a hundred.'

'What was her name?'

'Mrs Wilhemina Stirling.'

Tilda stared at the brilliant golden-beaked bird, about which there was something frightening.

'We'd better wrap it up. Someone might want to steal it.'

Sobered, like many seekers and finders, by the presence of the treasure itself, they wrapped the tiles in Tilda's anorak, which immediately dimmed their lustre once again with a film of mud.

'There's Woodie!'

Tilda began to jump up and down, like a cork on the tide. 'What's he doing?'

'He's getting his car out.'

There were no garages near the boats and Woodie was obliged to keep his immaculate Austin Cambridge in the yard of a public house on the Surrey side.

'I'm attracting his attention,' Tilda shouted. 'He can drive us home, and we can put the pushcart on the back seat.'

'Tilda, you don't understand. He'd have to say yes, because he's sorry for us, I heard him tell Richard we were no better than waifs of the storm, and we should ruin the upholstery, and be taking advantage of his kindness.'

'It's his own fault if he's kind. It's not the kind who inherit the earth, it's the poor, the humble, and the meek.'

'What do you think happens to the kind, then?'

'They get kicked in the teeth.'

Woodie drove them back across the bridge.

'You'll have to look after yourselves this winter, you know,' he said. 'No more lifts, I'm afraid, I shall be packed up and gone till spring. I'm thinking of laying up *Rochester* in dry dock. She needs a bit of attention.'

'Do you have to manage all that packing by yourself?' Tilda asked.

'No, dear, my wife's coming to give me a hand.'

'You haven't got a wife!'

'You've never seen her, dear.'

'What's her name?'

'Janet.' Woodie began to feel on the defensive, as though he had made the name up.

'What does she look like?'

'She doesn't much care for the river. She spends the summer elsewhere.'

'Has she left you, then?'

'Certainly not. She's got a caravan in Wales, a very nice part, near Tenby.' Although Woodie had given this explanation pretty often, he was surprised to have to make it to a child of six. 'Then in the winter we go back to our house in Purley. It's an amicable arrangement.'

Was there not, on the whole of Battersea Reach, a couple, married or unmarried, living together in the ordinary way? Certainly, among the fairweather people on the middle Reach. They lived together and even multiplied, though the opportunity for a doctor to hurry over the gangplank with a black bag and, in his turn, fall into the river, had been missed. *Bluebird*, which was rented by a group of nurses from the Waterloo Hospital, had been at the ready, and when the birth was imminent they'd seen to it that the ambulance arrived promptly. But, apart from *Bluebird*, the middle Reach would be empty by next week, or perhaps the one after.

Martha, who had decided to stop thinking about the inconvenience they were causing, asked Woodie not to stop at the boats; they would like to go on to the New King's Road.

'We want to stop at the Bourgeois Gentilhomme,' she said, with the remnants of the French accent the nuns had carefully taught her.

'Isn't that an antique shop, dear?'

'Yes, we're going to sell an antique.'

'Have you got one?'

'We've got two.'

'Are you sure you've been to this place before?'

'Yes.'

'I shall have to pull up as near as I can and let you out,' said Woodie. He wondered if he ought to wait, but he wanted to get back to *Rochester* before she came afloat. He watched the two girls, who, to do them justice, thanked him very nicely, they weren't so badly brought up when you came to think about it, approach the shop by the side door.

On occasions, Martha's courage failed her. The advantages her sister had in being so much younger presented themselves forcibly. She sharply told Tilda, who had planted herself in a rocking-chair put out on the pavement, that she must come into the shop and help her speak to the man. Tilda, who had never sat in a rocker before, replied that her boots were too dirty.

'And anyway, I'm old Abraham Lincoln, jest sittin and thinkin.'

'You've got to come.'

The Bourgeois Gentilhomme was one of many enterprises in Chelsea which survived entirely by selling antiques to each other. The atmosphere, once through the little shop-door, cut down from a Victorian billiard-table, was oppressive. Clocks struck widely different hours. At a corner table, with her back turned towards them, sat a woman in black, apparently doing some accounts, and surrounded by dusty furniture; perhaps she had been cruelly deserted on her wedding day, and had sat there ever since, refusing to have anything touched. She did not look up when the girls came in, although the billiard table was connected by a cord to a cow-bell, which jangled harshly.

'Where's Mr Stephen, please?'

Without waiting for or expecting a reply, Martha and the reluctant Tilda walked through into the back office. Here no conversion had been done to the wretched little room, once a scullery, with two steps down to a small yard stacked high with rubbish. Mr Stephen, sitting by a paraffin heater, was also writing on pieces of paper, and appeared to be adding things up. Martha took out the two tiles and laid them in front of him.

Well used to the treasures of the foreshore, the dealer wiped the gleaming surfaces free, not with water this time, but with something out of a bottle. Then, after carefully taking off his heavy rings, he picked each of the tiles up in turn, holding them up by the extreme edge.

'So you brought these all this long way to show me. What did you think they were?'

'I know what they are. I only want to know how much you can pay me for them.'

'Have you any more of these at home?'

'They weren't at home.'

'Where did you find them, then?'

'About the place.'

'And you're sure there aren't any more?'

'Just the two.'

Mr Stephen examined the gold and silver bird through a glass.

'They're quite pretty tiles, dear, not anything more than that.'

'Then why did you take off your rings so carefully?'

'I'm always careful, dear.'

'These are ruby lustre tiles by William de Morgan,' said Martha, 'with decoration in gold and silver – the "starlight and moonlight" lustre.'

'Who sent you in here?' Mr Stephen asked.

'Nobody, you know us, we've been in before.'

'Yes, but I mean, who told you what to say?'

'Nobody.'

'Mrs Wilhemina Stirling,' Tilda put in, 'ninety-seven if she's a day.'

'Well, whoever you're selling for, I'm sorry to disappoint you, but these tiles can't be by de Morgan. I'm afraid you just don't know enough about it. I don't suppose you looked at what's left of the lettering on the reverse. NDS END. William de Morgan had his potteries in Cheyne Walk, and later he moved his kilns to Merton Abbey. This is not the mark for either one of those.'

'Of course it isn't. These are part of a very late set. His very last pottery was at Sands End, in Fulham. Didn't you know that?'

Dignity demanded that the dealer should hand the tiles back with a pitying smile. But he could not resist holding the bird up to his desk lamp, so that the light ran across the surface and seemed to flow over the edges in crimson flame. And now Martha and he were united in a strange fellow feeling, which neither of them had expected, and which they had to shake off with difficulty.

'Well, I think perhaps we can take these. The bird is much the finer of the two, of course – I'm only taking the dragon to make a pair with the bird. Perhaps you'd like to exchange them for something else in my shop. There are some charming things out there in front – some very old toys. Your little sister here . . .'

'I hate very old toys,' Tilda said. 'They may have been all right for very old children.'

'A Victorian musical box . . .'

'It's broken.'

'I think not,' said the dealer, leaving the girls and hastening out front. He began to search irritably for the key. The woman sitting at the table made no attempt to help him.

'Tilda, have you been tinkering about with the musical box?'

'Yes.'

Martha saw that discovery, which could not be long delayed, would reduce her advantage considerably.

'We're asking three pounds for the two de Morgan lustre tiles. Otherwise I must trouble you to hand them back at once.'

Tilda's respect for her sister, whom she had never seen before in the possession of so much money, reduced her

71

almost to silence; in a hoarse whisper she asked whether they were going to get the records straight away.

'Yes, we will, but we ought to get a present for Ma first. You know Daddy always used to forget to give her anything.'

'Did she say so?'

'Have you ever actually seen anything that he's given her?'

They walked together down the King's Road, went into Woolworths, and were dazzled.

[7]

The same flood tide that had brought such a good harvest of tiles heaped a mass of driftwood onto the Reach. Woodie looked at it apprehensively. He wouldn't, of course, as he usually did, have to spend the months in Purley worrying about *Rochester*, and wondering whether she was getting knocked about by flotsam in his absence. There were only a few weeks now before she went into dry dock. Perhaps he half realised that the absence of worry would make his winter unendurable. As though clinging to the last moments of a vanishing pleasure, he counted the baulks of timber edging darkly towards the boats.

His wife had already arrived from Wales. He had in prospect a time of truce, while Janet, an expert manager, in a trouser suit well adapted to the task, gave him very real help with the laying-up, but at the same time made a series of unacceptable comparisons between the caravan and *Rochester*. These comparisons were never made or implied once they were both back in Purley. They arose only in the short uneasy period passed between land and water.

As he crossed *Grace*'s deck Woodie looked up with astonishment at *Dreadnought*, which was a bigger boat, and, having much less furniture on board, rode higher in the water. In the lighted deckhouse he could not only see old Willis, fiddling about with what looked like tins and glasses, but Janet, wearing her other trouser suit.

'It's a celebration,' said Nenna, coming up to the hatch, 'they're only waiting for you to come. It's because Willis has sold *Dreadnought*.'

73

'A provisional offer, I should call it. Still, it's not my object to spoil things. Aren't you going to come?'

'No, it's our turn tomorrow. The deckhouse only holds four.' And Woodie could see now that Maurice was in there as well. He never quite knew what to make of Maurice. Mrs James seemed to talk to him by the hour, in the middle of the night, sometimes, he believed, and so did the children. 'I left your two at an antique shop in the King's Road,' he said. 'They seemed to know exactly what they wanted.'

Nenna put on her jacket. She knew the Bourgeois Gentil-homme, and always feared that one day Martha might get into difficulties. If they weren't there, they were pretty sure to be in Woolworths. She started out to meet them.

Willis had noticed Woodie's return, and could be seen gesturing behind the window of the deckhouse, expressing joy, pointing him out to Janet, and waving to him to come on in.

Woodie was not feeling very sociable, as he had had, of course, to return his car to the Surrey side and walk home across the Bridge. But the deckhouse was certainly cosy, and the door, as he pulled it to behind him, cut out, to a considerable extent, the voices of the river. It was the only door on *Dreadnought* which could be considered in good repair. Even the daylong scream of the gulls was silent in here, and the hooters and sound signals arrived only as a distant complaint. For Willis, indeed, it was rather too quiet, but useful this evening when he had guests. 'We want to be able to make ourselves heard,' he said. Evidently he had toasts in mind.

In preparation, he had opened several bottles of Guinness, and one of the cans, which contained Long Life – the lady's drink – in compliment to Mrs Woodie. But he was distressed that he had no glasses.

'I shouldn't let Janet have a glass anyway,' cried Maurice, never at a loss. He explained that the lager was manufactured by the Danes, an ancient seafaring people, to be drunk straight out of the can, so that the bubbles would move straight up and down in the stomach to counteract the sideways rocking movement of the boat. To Woodie's surprise his wife laughed as though she couldn't stop. 'You never told me it was so social on the boats,' she said. He tried hard to get into the spirit of the thing. Why should a boat be less social than a caravan, for heaven's sake? He'd never seen Janet drinking out of a can before, either. But he mustn't forget that it was a great occasion for old Willis, who must be getting on for sixty-five, ready to take the knock any day now.

'It's good of you to come at such short notice, very good,' said Willis. 'I'd like to call you all shipmates. Is that passed unanimously? And now I'd like to ask how many of you go regularly to the fish-shop on Lyons Dock?'

At this moment the electricity failed, no surprise on *Dreadnought* where the wiring was decidedly a makeshift. They were all in the dark, only the river lights, fixed or passing, wavered over cans, bottles and faces.

'A bit unfortunate,' said Woodie.

'Forty years ago we wouldn't have said that!' Willis exclaimed, 'Not with the right sort of woman in the room! We'd have known what to do!'

Once again Janet and Maurice laughed uproariously. The place was becoming Liberty Hall. Woodie put his hand at once, as he invariably could, on his set of pocket screwdrivers, but before he felt that it was quite tactful to offer help, Willis had lit an Aladdin, which presumably he always kept ready, no wonder. Fixed in gimbals, the lamp gradually extended its radiant circle into every corner of the deckhouse.

Maurice sprang to his feet, slightly bending his head, so as to avoid stunning himself on the roof. Although the four of them were practically knee to knee, he made as if speaking in a vast auditorium. 'Can everybody see me clearly? . . . you at the back, madam? . . . can I take it, then, that I'm heard in all parts of the house?'

Willis opened more bottles. His spectacles shone, even his leathery cheeks shone.

'Now, I was saying something about the fish-shop on Lyons Dock. If you don't ever go there, you won't have had the chance of sampling their hot mussels. They boil them in an iron saucepan. Must be iron.'

'The river's oldest delicacy!' Maurice cried.

'Oh no, they're quite fresh. I've got some boiling down below. They should be just about done now.'

'Surely mussels aren't in season?' Woodie asked.

'You're thinking of whitebait, there's no season for mussels.'

'I'm under doctor's orders, to some extent.'

'First time I've heard of it,' Janet cried.

'Mussels are at their best in autumn,' said Maurice, 'that's what they continually say in Southport.'

Encouraged, Willis offered to fetch the mussels at once, and some plates and forks and vinegar, and switch on the radio while he was gone, to give them a bit of music. Woodie was surprised to learn that there were any plates on *Dreadnought*. 'May I have the first dance, Janet?' Maurice asked, up on his feet again. Couldn't he see that there was hardly room to sit?

As Willis went to the afterhatch it struck him that *Dreadnought* was rather low in the water, almost on a level with *Grace*. He looked across to see if he could catch a glimpse of Nenna and the girls, and ask them what they thought about it, but everybody seemed to have gone ashore.

The hold was very dark, but not quite as dark as Willis had expected. In fact, it was not as dark as it should be. There were gleams and reflections where none could possibly be. Half way down the companion he stopped, and it was as though the whole length of the hold moved towards him in a body. He heard the faintest splash, and was not sure whether it was inside or out.

76

'What's wrong?' he thought.

Then he caught the unmistakable dead man's stench of river water, heaving slowly, but always finding, no matter what the obstacle, the shortest way home.

How bad was it?

Another step down, and the water was slopping round his ankles. His shoes filled. He bent down and put a hand in the water, and swore when an electric shock ran through his elbow and shoulder. Now he knew why the lights were out. A pale blue light puzzled him for a moment, until he realised that it was the Calor gas stove in the galley. He could just make out the bottom of the iron saucepan in which the mussels were still boiling for his guests.

The main leak had given way at last. And Willis had it in his heart to be sorry for old *Dreadnought*, as she struggled to rise against the increasing load of water. It was like one of those terrible sights of the racecourse or the battle field where wallowing living beings persevere dumbly in their duty although mutilated beyond repair.

There was a box of matches in his top pocket, but when he got them out his hands were so wet that he could not make them strike. The only hope now was to reach the hand-pump in the galley and see if he could keep the level within bounds. About a foot below the outwale there was a pretty bad hole which he'd never felt concerned him, it was so far above the waterline. He could see the shore lights through it now. If *Dreadnought* went on sinking at the present rate, in ten minutes the hole wouldn't be above the waterline, but below.

Willis set out to wade through the rolling wash. Something made for him in the darkness and struck him a violent blow just under the knee. Half believing that his leg was broken, he stooped and tried to fend the object off with his hands. It came at him again, and he could just make out that it was part of his bunk, one of the side panels. That, for some reason, almost made him give up, not the pain, but the familiar bit of furniture, the bed he had slept in for fifteen years, now hopelessly astray and as it seemed attacking him. Everything that should have stood by him had become hostile. The case of ice that weighed him down was his best suit.

He lost his footing and went right under. Totally blinded, his spectacles streaming with water as he bobbed up, he tried to float himself into the galley. Then he realised that there was no chance of finding the hand-pump. The flood was up to the top of the stove already, and as the gas went out the saucepan went afloat and he was scalded by a stream of boiling water that mixed with the cold. There was no hope for *Dreadnought*. He would be lucky to get back up the companion.

Above in the deck-cabin the guests, for a while, noticed nothing, the music was so loud, and Maurice was so entertaining. It was said by his acquaintances in the pub that he gave value for money, but there was a touch of genius in the way he talked that night. With a keener sense of danger than the others, and finding it exhilarating, as they certainly would not, he had noticed at once that something was wrong, even before he had rubbed a clear patch on the steamy windows and, looking out into the night, had seen the horizon slowly rising, inch by inch. He made a rapid calculation. Give it a bit longer, we're all enjoying ourselves, he thought. Maurice had never learned to swim, but this did not disturb him. If only there was a piano, I could give them 'Rock of Ages' when the time comes, he said to himself.

Woodie's complaints had died down somewhat. 'Don't know about these shellfish. Taking his time about it, isn't he?'

'Never mind!' Maurice cried, 'it'll give me time to tell both your fortunes. I just glanced at both your hands earlier on, just glanced, you know, and I seemed to see something quite unexpected written there. Now, you won't mind extending your palm, will you, Janet? You don't mind being first?'

'Do you really know how to do it?'

Maurice smiled radiantly.

'I do it almost every night. You'd be surprised how many new friends I make in that way.'

'I've got a copper bracelet on, that I wear for rheumatism,' she said, 'will that affect your reading?'

'Believe me, it won't make the slightest difference,' said Maurice.

The door opened, and Willis stood there, like a drowned man risen from the dead, his spectacles gone, water streaming from him and instantly making a pool at his feet. *Dreadnought*'s deck was still a foot or so above the tide. He was able to escort his guests, in good order, across *Grace* for Maurice, while the Woodies retreated over the gangplank to *Rochester*.

It is said on the river that a Thames barge, once she has risen with the tide, never sinks completely. But *Dreadnought*, let alone all her other weak places, had been holed amidships by a baulk of timber, and before long the water poured into her with a sound like a sigh, and she went down in a few seconds.

The loss of *Dreadnought* meant yet another meeting of the boatowners on *Lord Jim*, more relaxed in atmosphere than the former one, because it seemed that Mrs Blake was away, but hushed by the nature of Willis's misfortune. And yet this too had its agreeable counterpart; their boats, however much in need of repair, had not gone down.

One glass of brown sherry each – the best, there was no second best on *Lord Jim* – restored the impression of a funeral. Richard consulted a list. He wrote lists on special blank pages at the end of his diary, and tore them out only when they were needed, so that they were never lost. With care, there was no need to lose anything, particularly, perhaps, a boat. The disaster having taken place, however, the meeting must concern itself only with practical remedies.

Grace had already taken in all that could be salvaged of

Willis's clothing, for drying and mending. The nuns, Nenna's nuns, what a very long time ago it seemed, in a class known as plain sewing, had taught her bygone arts, darning, patching, reinforcing collars with tape, which at last found their proper object in Willis's outmoded garments. Richard congratulated *Grace*. Nenna thought: I'm pleased for him to see that I can make a proper job of something. Why am I pleased?

Far greater sacrifices were required from *Rochester*, who volunteered to take Willis in as a lodger. At a reasonable rent, Richard suggested – but the Woodies wanted no payment. It would, after all, only be for a week or so, after that they were due back at Purley.

'That seems satisfactory, then – he can go straight to you after he comes out of hospital,' – Willis had been admitted to the Waterloo, where it was exceedingly difficult to get a bed, once more with the help of the nurses on *Bluebird*.

'And now, if you'll excuse me, I'm going on to the worst problem of the lot – Willis's financial position . . . Not the sort of thing any of us would usually discuss in public, but essential, I'm afraid, in the present case. I've been on to the P.L.A. and they confirm that *Dreadnought* has been officially classed as a wreck, and what's worse, I'm afraid, is that she's lying near enough to the shipping channels for them, to quote their letter, to exercise their statutory powers and remove her by means of salvage craft.'

'Will that matter?' Woodie asked. 'She'll never be raised again,' and Maurice suggested that Willis would be much better off if he didn't have to look at the wreck of *Dreadnought* at every low tide.

'I quite accept that, but, to continue, all expenses of salvage and towage will be recoverable from the owners of the craft. I'm not too sure, to be quite honest with you, that Willis will be able to pay any, let alone all, of these expenses. I can't see any way out but a subscription list, to be organised as soon as possible. If there are any other suggestions . . .'

There were none, and it being obvious who would have to head the subscribers, Richard wound up the meeting by reading aloud a letter from Willis, delivered by way of *Bluebird*, in which, addressing them all as shipmates, he sent them all a squeeze of the hand and God bless. The words sounded strange in Richard's level unassuming voice, which, however quiet, always commanded attention. The catastrophe had evidently relaxed Willis's habitual control, and he had spoken from the heart, but who could tell how much else survived?

Three days later, Richard came along to *Grace* early in the morning, and told her that there was a call for her. The only telephone on the Reach was on *Lord Jim*. If this was inconvenient, Richard did not say so, although to be called to the telephone, or wanted on the telephone, as Richard put it, always seemed a kind of reproach in itself. More awkward still, since Laura was not on board, he was obliged to lock up before going to the office, and had to wait on board, with his brief-case and umbrella, determinedly not listening, while Nenna went down to the saloon.

Nenna felt sure that there was no-one that it could be but Edward. Although it was very unlikely, he must have got the number from the boat company.

'Hullo, Nenna! This is Louise! Yes, it's Louise!'

'Louise!'

'Didn't you get my last letter?'

'I don't think so. They get lost sometimes.'

'How come?'

'People fetch them from the office and mean to take them round, and then they get lost or dropped in the water.'

'That's absolutely absurd, Nenna dear.'

'What does it matter anyway? Where are you, Louise, can I come right over and see you?'

'Not right now, Nenna.'

'Where are you calling from?'

'From Frankfurt on the Rhine. We're over here on a business trip. Too bad you didn't read my letters. Has Heinrich arrived?'

'God, Louise, who is Heinrich?'

'Nenna, I know all your intonations as well as I know my own, and I can tell that you're in a very bad state. Joel and I have a suggestion about that which we're going to put to you as soon as we get to London.'

'I'm quite all right, Louise. You're coming here, then?'

'And Edward. Exactly what is the position in regard to your marriage. Is Edward still with you?'

Nenna was a child again. She felt her responsibilities slipping away one by one, even her marriage was going.

'Oh, Louise, do you still have lobster sandwiches at Harris's?'

'Now, this boat of yours. What number is this I'm calling you on, by the way? Is that the yacht club?'

'Not exactly . . . it's a friend.'

'Well, this boat you and the children are living on. I understand very well how people live year round in houseboats on the Seine, but not on the Thames, isn't it tidal?'

'Why, yes, it is.'

'And this boat of yours – is she crewed, or is it a bareboat rental?'

'Neither really. I've bought her.'

'Where do you sail her then?

'She never sails, she's at moorings.'

'We were reading in the London *Times* that some kind of boat was sunk on the Thames the other day. In one of the small paragraphs. Joel reads it all through. He says it's so long since he saw you and the girls that he won't know you. In any case, as I said, we have certain plans which we'd like to put before you, and in the meantime I want you to say hello from us to young Heinrich.'

'Louise, don't ring off. Whatever it's costing. I've never met young Heinrich.'

'Well, neither have we, of course. Didn't you get my letter?'

'It seems not, Louise.'

'He's the son of a very good business friend of ours, who's sent him to school at Sales Abbey, that's with the Benedictines, and he's currently returning home, he has permission to leave school early this term for some reason and return home.'

'Does he live in Frankfurt on the Main?'

'On the Rhine. No, not at all, he's Austrian, he lives in Vienna. He just requires to spend one night in London, he's due to catch a flight to Vienna the next day.'

'Do you mean that he expects to come and stay on *Grace*?'

'Who is Grace, Nenna?'

'What's the name of this boy?' Nenna asked.

'His parents are a Count and Countess, in business as I told you, of course all that doesn't mean anything now, but they're in very good standing. He should have been with you last Friday.'

'Well, he wasn't. There must have been a misunderstanding about that . . . Oh, Lou, you don't know how it is to hear your voice . . .'

'Nenna, you're becoming emotional. Wouldn't you agree it's just about time that somebody helped you to restore some kind of order into your life?'

'Oh, please don't do that!'

'I hate to cut you short,' said Richard from the hatch, 'it's only that I can hardly expect my staff to be in time if I'm late myself.'

His voice was courteous to the point of diffidence, and Nenna, giving way a little, let herself imagine what it would be like to be on Richard's staff, and to be directed in everything else by Louise, and to ebb and flow without volition, in the warmth of love and politeness.

'Goodbye, Louise. As soon as you get to England. – Forgive

me, Richard, it was my sister, I don't know how she got your number, I haven't seen her in five years.'

'I sensed that she wasn't used to being contradicted.'

'No.'

'She was very firm.'

'That's so.'

'Are you sure she's your sister?'

'As far as he's concerned, I'm just a drifter,' Nenna thought, smiling and thanking him. Richard patted himself to see that he had some matches on him, a gesture which appealed to Nenna, and walked off up the Embankment to call a taxi.

I won't go down without a struggle, Nenna thought. I married Edward because I wanted to live with him, and I still do. While she ironed Willis's stiff underclothes which, aired day after day, never seemed to get quite dry, the accusations against her, not inside her mind but at some point detached from it, continued without pause. They were all the more tedious because they were reduced, for all practical purposes, to one question: why, after everything that has been put forward in this court, have you still made no attempt to visit 42b Milvain Street? Nenna wished to reply that it was not for the expected reasons – not pride, not resentment, not even the curious acquired characteristics of the river dwellers, which made them scarcely at home in London's streets. No, it's because it's my last chance. While I've still got it I can take it out and look at it and know I still have it. If that goes, I've nothing left to try.

She told Martha that she would be going out that evening and would quite likely not be back until the following day.

'Well, where do we stay?'

'On *Rochester*. I'll ask them.'

In less than a week the impeccable *Rochester* had been transformed into a kind of boarding-house. Nenna would

84

never have dreamed before this of asking them to look after the girls. Willis, on his return from hospital, had taken up his quarters there, though he was no trouble, remaining quietly in the spare cabin without even attempting to watch the river's daily traffic. He had not come up on deck when the P.L.A. tug arrived, and the poor wreck had been towed away, still under water, but surfacing from time to time as though she had still not quite admitted defeat.

'That's just a launch tug,' said Tilda, 'under forty tons. It didn't take much to move *Dreadnought*.'

The salvage men returned what they could, including the iron saucepan, but Willis's painting materials were past pair. Nothing was said about his next move, except that he could hardly expect his sister to take him in now, and that he was unwilling, under any circumstances, to move to Purley. Therefore the daily life of the Woodies, which had depended almost entirely on knowing what they would be doing on any given day six months hence, fell into disrepair. They had to resort to unpacking many of the things which they had so carefully stowed away. They repeated, however, that Willis was no trouble.

When Nenna told them that she had urgent business on the other side of London and that she would have to ask whether Martha and Tilda could stay the night, *Rochester* accepted without protest, and they went over, taking with them their nightdresses, Cliff records, the Cliff photograph and two packets of breakfast cereals, for they did not like the same kind. Tilda, who had been vexed at missing the actual shipwreck, went straight down to Willis's cabin to ask him if he would draw her a picture of it. Martha confronted her mother.

'You're going to see Daddy, aren't you?'

'I might be bringing him back with me. Would you like that?'

'I don't know.'

85

[8]

Better take a cheap all-day ticket, the bus conductor advised, if Nenna really wanted to get from Chelsea to Stoke Newington.

'Or move house,' he advised.

Although as she changed from bus to bus she was free at last of the accusing voices, she had time for a number of second thoughts, wishing in particular that she had put on other clothes, and had had her hair cut. She didn't know if she wanted to look different or the same. Her best coat would perhaps have been better because it would make her look as though she hadn't let herself go, but on the other hand her frightful old lumber jacket would have suggested, what was true enough, that she was worried enough not to care. But among all these doubts it had not occurred to her that if she got as far as 42b Milvain Street, and rang the bell, Edward would not open the door.

It was the b, perhaps, that was the trouble. b suggested an upstairs flat, and there was only one bell at 42. The yellowish-gray brick houses gave straight on to the street, which she had found only after turning out of another one, and then another. On some doorsteps the milk was still waiting to be taken in. She still missed the rocking of the boat.

He might be in or he might be out. There was a light on in the hall, and apparently on the second floor, though that might be a landing. Nenna struggled against an impulse to rush into the fish and chip shop at the corner, the only shop in the street, and ask them if they had ever seen somebody coming out of number 42b who looked lonely, or indeed if they had ever seen anyone coming out of it at all.

The figure turning the corner and walking heavily down the road could not under any circumstances have been Edward, but at least it relieved her from the suspicion that the street was uninhabited. When the heavily-treading man slowed down at number 42, she couldn't believe her luck. He had been out and was coming in, although the way he walked suggested that going out had not been a great success, and that not much awaited him at home.

As he stopped and took out two keys tied together, neither of them a car key, Nenna faced him boldly.

'Excuse me, I should like you to let me in.'

'May I ask who you are?'

The 'may I ask' disconcerted her.

'I'm *Grace*. I mean, I'm Nenna.'

'You don't seem very sure.'

'I am Nenna James.'

'Mrs Edward James?'

'Yes. Does Edward James live here?'

'Well, in a way.' He dangled the keys from hand to hand. 'You don't look at all how I expected.'

Nenna felt rebuked.

'How old are you?' he asked.

'I'm thirty-two.'

'I should have thought you were twenty-seven or twenty-eight at most.'

He stood ruminating. She tried not to feel impatient.

'Did Edward say what I looked like, then?'

'No.'

'What *has* he been saying?'

'As a matter of fact, I very rarely speak to him.'

Nenna looked at him more closely, trying to assess him as an ally. The cuffs of his raincoat had been neatly turned. Somebody must be doing his mending for him, as she was doing Willis's, and the idea gave her a stab of pain which she couldn't relate to her other feelings. She stared up at his broad face.

'We can't stand here all night on the pavement like this,' he said, still with the two keys in his hand.

'Then hadn't you better let me in?'

'I don't know that that would be quite the right thing to do.'

'Why not?'

'Well, you might turn out to be a nuisance to Edward.'

She mustn't irritate him.

'In what way?'

'Well, I didn't care for the way you were standing there ringing the bell. Anyway, he's out.'

'How can you tell? You're only just coming in yourself. Do you live here?'

'Well, in a way.'

He examined her more closely. 'Your hair is quite pretty.'

It had begun to rain slightly. There seemed no reason why they should not stand here for ever.

'As a matter of fact,' he said, 'I do remember you. My name is Hodge. Gordon Hodge.'

Nenna shook her head. 'I can't help that.'

'I have met you several times with Edward.'

'And was I a nuisance then?'

'This isn't my house, you see. It belongs to my mother. My mother is taking your husband in, at considerable inconvenience, as a kind of paying guest.'

'He's the lodger?'

'She only agreed to it because I used to know him at school.'

Abyss after abyss of respectability was opening beneath her. How could Edward be living in a house belonging to somebody's mother, and, above all, Gordon Hodge's mother?

'Why do you very rarely speak to him?'

'We're just living here quietly, with my mother, two quiet chaps working things out for ourselves.'

A wave of cold discouragement closed over her. The disagreement about where they were to live had come to seem the only obstacle. But perhaps Edward was altogether better without her. Perhaps he knew that. He must have heard her at the door.

'Well,' said Gordon, 'you'd better come inside, I suppose.' Once the key was in the lock, he pushed forward with both hands, one on the front door, one on Nenna's back, so that in the end she was propelled into no. 42. Gordon's mother had an umbrella stand and a set of Chinese temple bells in her hall.

'Carry on up.' They passed two landings, Gordon following her with majestic tread, but faster than one might expect, since although he had lost time in hanging up his raincoat in the hall, he reached the door first, and opened it without any kind of announcement, and Edward was standing, with his back to them at first, thinner and smaller than she remembered, but then she always made that mistake when she hadn't seen him for a bit – he turned round, protesting, and it was Edward.

Who else, after all, could it have been? But in her relief Nenna forgot the quiet reasonable remarks which she had rehearsed at the bus stops, and in the buses, all the way to Stoke Newington.

'Darling, darling.'

Edward looked at her with grey eyes like Tilda's, but without much expectation from life.

'Darling, aren't you surprised?'

'Not very. I've been listening to you ringing the bell.'

'How did you know it was me?'

'Nenna. Have you come all this way, after all this time, to try to get me to live on that boat?'

Nenna had forgotten about Gordon, or rather she assumed

that he must have gone away, but he had not. To her amazement, he was still planted just behind her.

'Edward, Nenna. You two seem to be having a bit of a difference of opinion. Yes, let's face it, you're in dispute. And in these matters it's often helpful to have a third party present. That's how these marriage counsellors make their money, you know.'

This must have been a joke, as he laughed, or perhaps any mention of marriage was a joke to Gordon, who walked past Nenna and settled himself between them in a small chair, actually a nursing chair, surviving from some earlier larger family home and much too low for him, so that he had to try crossing his legs in several positions. He creaked, as he settled, as a boat creaks. Had he really been at the same school as Edward? His feet were now stuck out in front of him and Nenna could read the word EXCELLA on the soles of each of his new shoes.

'Get out!'

Gordon sat quite still for a few seconds, then uncrossed his legs and went out of the room, a room in his own house, or rather his mother's. Because it was theirs, he knew how to shut the door, although it did not fit very well, without any irritating noise.

'You've always known how to get rid of my friends,' Edward muttered.

Nenna was no more able to deny this than any other woman.

'He's hateful!'

'Gordon's all right.'

'We can't talk while he's around.'

'His mother has been very good to me.'

'That's ridiculous! To be in a position where you have to say that someone's mother has been very good to you – that's ridiculous! Isn't it?'

'Yes.'

'Where did you meet these Hodges anyway? I never remember you ever talking about them.'

'I had to go somewhere,' Edward said.

They had plenty of time, and yet she felt that there was almost none.

'Eddie, I'll tell you what I came to say. Why won't you come over to us for a week, or even for a night?'

'That boat! It's not for me to come to you, it's for you to get rid of it. I'm not quarrelling with you about money. If you don't want to sell it, why can't you rent it out?'

'I don't know that I can, right away.'

'Why, what's wrong with it?'

'She's a thought damp. It would be easier in the spring.'

'Didn't I see something in the paper about one of them sinking? I don't even know if they're safe for the children!'

'Some of them are beautiful. *Lord Jim*, for instance, inside she's really better than a house.'

'Who lives on *Lord Jim*?' Edward asked with the discernment of pure jealousy, the true lover's art which Nenna was too distraught to recognise.

'I don't know, I don't care. Well, the Blakes do. Richard and Laura Blake.'

'Have they got money?'

'I suppose so.'

'They live on a boat because they think it's smart.'

'Laura doesn't.'

'What's this Richard Blake like?'

'I don't know. He was in the Navy, I think, in the war, or the RNVR.'

'Don't you know the difference?'

'Not exactly, Eddie.'

'I bet he does.'

Things were going as badly as they could. From the room immediately beneath them, somebody began to play the piano, a Chopin nocturne, with heavy emphasis, but the piano was by no means suitable for Chopin and the sound travelled upwards as a hellish tingling of protesting strings.

'Eddie, is this the only room you've got?'

'I don't see anything wrong with it.'

She noticed now that there was a kind of cupboard in the corner which was likely to contain a washbasin, and a single bed, tucked in with a plaid rug. Surely they'd do better making love on board *Grace* than on a few yards of Mackenzie tartan?

'You can't expect us to come here!'

It must be Gordon playing downstairs. There were pauses, then he banged the keys plaintively, going over the passages he hadn't been able to get right, then suddenly he put on a record of the Chopin and played along with it, always two or three notes behind.

'Eddie, what do you want? Why are you here? Why?'

He replied reluctantly, 'My job's up here.'

'I don't even know what you do. Strang Graphics! What are they?'

They were both still standing up, facing each other, at about the same height.

'Strang is an advertising firm. It's small, that's why it's up here, where the rents are low. They hope to expand later, then they'll move. I'm not going to pretend anything about my job. It's clerical.'

Edward's references from the construction firm when he left Panama had not been very good. Nenna knew that, but she was sure it couldn't have been Edward's fault, and at the moment she couldn't be bothered with it.

'You don't have to stay there! There's plenty of jobs! Anyone can get a job anywhere!'

'I can't.'

He turned his head away, and as the light caught his face at a certain angle Nenna realised in terror that he was right and that he would never get anywhere. The terror, however, was not for herself or for the children but for Edward, who might realise that what he was saying was true. She forgot whatever she had meant to tell him, went up close and took him tenderly by both ears.

'Shut up, Eddie.'

'Nenna, I'm glad you came.'

'You are?'

'Curious, I didn't mean to say that.'

She clung to him hard, she loved him and could never leave him. They were down on the floor, and one side of her face was scorched by Gordon's mother's horrible gas-fire, in front of which there was a bowl of tepid water. He stroked her face, with its one bright red cheek, one pale.

'You look as ugly as sin.'

'Wonderful.'

There was a tapping, just audible above the piano. 'Excuse me, Mrs James, I'm Gordon's mother, I thought I'd just look in, as I haven't had the pleasure of meeting you.'

Nenna got to her feet, trying to pull down her jersey.

'I hope you don't find the gas-fire too high,' said Mrs Hodge, 'it's easily lowered. You just turn the key down there on the right hand side.'

Not receiving any response, she added, 'And I hope the music doesn't disturb you. Gordon is something of a pianist.'

'No, he isn't,' said Nenna.

The mother's face crumpled up and withered, then corrected itself to the expression of one who is in the right. She withdrew. Nenna was ashamed, but she couldn't make amends, not now. In the morning she would beg sincerely for forgiveness, less sincerely praise Gordon as a pianist, offer to help pay to have the piano seen to.

Then she looked at Edward and saw that he was furious. 'You've only come here to hurt these people.'

'I didn't. I never knew they existed. Forgive!'

'It's not a matter of forgiveness, it's a matter of common politeness.'

93

They were quarrelling, but at first they were not much better at it than Gordon was at Chopin.

'I want you, Eddie, that's the one and only thing I came about. I want you every moment of the day and night and every time I try to fold up a map.'

'You're raving, Nenna.'

'Please give.'

'Give you what? You're always saying that. I don't know what meaning you attach to it.'

'Give anything.'

She didn't know why she wanted this so much, either. Not presents, not for themselves, it was the sensation of being given to, she was homesick for that.

And now the quarrel was under its own impetus, and once again a trial seemed to be in progress, with both of them as accusers, but both figuring also as investigators of the lowest description, wretched hirelings, turning over the stones to find where the filth lay buried. The squash racquets, the Pope's pronouncements, whose fault it had been their first night together, an afternoon really, but not much good in either case, the squash racquets again, the money spent on *Grace*. And the marriage that was being described was different from the one they had known, indeed bore almost no resemblance to it, and there was no-one to tell them this.

'You don't want me,' Edward repeated, 'if you did, you'd have been with me all this time. All you've ever cared about is being approved of, like a little girl at a party.'

He must have forgotten what Tilda's like, she thought, and she felt frightened. But Edward went on to tell her that she didn't really care for the children, she only liked to think she did, to make herself feel good.

So far neither of them had raised their voices, or only enough to be heard above Gordon's din. But when she made a last appeal, and told him, though feeling it was not quite true, that Martha had asked her to bring her father back,

94

and then, very unwisely, referred again to Mrs Hodge, and the house, and the single bed, and even the temple bells, and asked him why he didn't come to his senses and whether he didn't think he'd be happier living with a woman, whether she was on a boat or not, he turned on her, upsetting the bowl of water in front of the gas fire, and shouted:

'You're not a woman!'

Nenna was outside in the street. In leaving the room, swelling for the first time with tears, she had collided awkwardly with Gordon's mother, who supposed she could stand where she liked in her own house, and even if Edward had called after her, she would not have been able to hear him. She walked away down Milvain Street as fast as it was possible for her feet to hit the ground. The fish and chip shop was still lighted and open. She had expected to spend that night with Edward and wake up beside him, the left-hand side, that had become a habit and it was a mistake, no doubt, to allow marriage to become a matter of habit, but that didn't prove that she was not a woman.

She walked down street after street, always turning to the right, and pulled herself up among buses, and near a railway bridge. Seven Sisters Road. It was late, the station was shut. Her hands were empty. She realised now for the first time that she had left her purse behind in Edward's room. That meant that she had no money, and the all-day bus ticket was of course also in the purse.

Nenna set out to walk. A mile and a half down Green Lanes, half a mile down Nassington Green Road, one and a half miles the wrong way down Balls Pond Road, two miles down Kingsland Road, and then she was lost. As is usual in such cases, her body trudged on obstinately, knowing that one foot hurt rather more than the other, but deciding not to admit this until some sort of objective was reached, while her mind, rejecting the situation in time and space, became disjointed and childish. It came to her that it was wrong to pray for anything simply because you felt you needed it personally. Prayer should be beyond self, and so Nenna repeated a Hail Mary for everyone in the world who was lost in Kingsland Road without their bus fares. She had also been taught, when in difficulty, to think of a good life to imitate. Nenna thought of Tilda, who would certainly have got on to a late night bus and ridden without paying the fare, or even have borrowed money from the conductor. Richard would never have left anything behind anywhere, or, if he had, he would have gone back for it. Louise would not have made an unsuccessful marriage in the first place, and she supposed her marriage must be unsuccessful, because Edward had told her that she was not a woman.

Nenna had no more than an animal's sense of direction and distance, but it seemed to her that the right thing to do would be to try to reach the City, then, once she got to Blackfriars, she knew where the river was, and though that would be Lambeth Reach or King's Reach, a long way downstream of the boats, still, once she had got to the river she would be on the way home. She had worked in an office in Blackfriars once, before Tilda came.

That meant turning south, and she would have to ask which way she was headed. She began to look, with a some-what dull kind of hopefulness, for somebody friendly, not too much in a hurry, walking the opposite way, although it would be more reasonable, really, to ask somebody walking the same way. Handfuls of sleet were beginning to wander through the air. Radio shop, bicycle shop, family planning shop, funeral parlour, bicycles, radio spare parts, television hire, herbalist, family planning, a florist. The window of the florist was still lit and entirely occupied by a funeral tribute, a football goal, carried out in white chrysanthemums. The red ball had just been introduced into Soccer and there was a ball in the goal, this time in red chrysanthemums. Nenna

stood looking into the window, feeling the melted hail make
its way down the gap between the collar of her coat and her
body. One shoe seemed to be wetter than the other and the
strap was working loose, so, leaning against the ledge of the
shop window, she took it off to have a look at it. This made
her left foot very cold, so she twisted it round her right ankle.
Someone was coming, and she felt that she couldn't bear it if
he, because it was a man, said, 'Having trouble with your
shoe?' For an unbalanced moment she thought it might be
Gordon Hodge, pursuing her to see that she would not come
back, and make a nuisance of herself to Edward.

The man stood very close to her, pretended to look in the
window, advanced with a curious sideways movement and
said –

'Like flowers?'

'Not at the moment.'

'Fixed up for the night?'

Nenna did not answer. She was saddened by the number
of times the man must have asked this question. He smelled
of loneliness. Well, they always moved off in the end, though
they often stayed a while, as this one did, whistling through
their teeth, like standup comics about to risk another joke.

He snatched the shoe out of her hand and hurled it
violently away from her into the Kingsland Road.

'What you going to do now?'

Nenna shook off her other shoe and began half walking and
half running as fast as she could, not looking behind her,
Laburnum Street, Whiston Street, Hows Street, Pearson
Street, a group at the end of Cremers Street who stood laughing, probably at her. One foot seemed to be bleeding. I expect
they think I've been drinking.

Where the Hackney Road joins Kingsland Road a taxi
drew up beside her.

'You're out late.'

'I don't know what the time is.'

97

'A bit late for paddling. Where are you going?'

'To the river.'

'Why?'

'Why not?'

'People jump in sometimes.'

Nenna told him, without much expecting to be believed, that she lived on Battersea Reach. The driver twisted his arm backwards to open the door.

'You'd like a lift, wouldn't you?'

'I haven't any money.'

'Who said anything about money?'

She got into the warm interior of the taxi, reeking of tobacco and ancient loves, and fell asleep at once. The taxi-man drove first to Old Street, where there was a garage open all night for the trade, and bought a tankful of petrol. Then he turned through the locked and silent City and towards the Strand, where the air first begins to feel damp, blowing up the side streets with the dawn wind off the river.

'We can go round by Arthur's in Covent Garden and get a sandwich, if you want,' he said, 'that won't break the bank.'

Then he saw that his fare was asleep. He stopped and had a cup of tea himself, and explained to the Covent Garden porters, who wanted to know what he'd got in the back, that it was the Sleeping Beauty.

The taxi drew up opposite the Battersea Bridge end of the boats. Only the driver's expression showed what he thought of the idea of living in a place like that. But it might suit some people. Carefully, as one who was used to such endings, he woke Nenna up.

'You're home, dear.'

Then he made a U turn and drove away so rapidly that she could not make out his number, only the red tail light diminishing, at more than legal speed, down the deserted Embankment. She was, therefore, never able to thank him.

. . .

Although it must be three or four in the morning, there were still lights showing on *Lord Jim*. Richard was standing on the afterdeck, wearing a Naval duffle coat, Arctic issue.

'What are you doing, Nenna, where are your shoes?'

'What are you doing, Richard, standing there in your greatcoat?'

Neither of them was speaking sensibly.

'My wife's left me.'

She must have done, Nenna thought, or he wouldn't call Laura 'my wife'.

'Surely she's only gone to stay with her family. You told me so.'

Although it was very unlikely that they could be disturbing anyone they both spoke almost in whispers, and Nenna's last remark, which scarcely deserved an answer, was lost in the air, drowned by the wash of high tide.

'I haven't liked to say anything about it, but you must have noticed, that evening you stayed to have a drink with us, that my wife wasn't quite herself.'

'I thought she was,' said Nenna.

Richard was startled. 'Don't you like her?'

'I can't tell. I should have to meet her somewhere else.'

'You probably think I'm an obstinate swine to make her live here on *Lord Jim*. I couldn't really believe she wouldn't like it. I'm afraid my mind doesn't move very fast, not as fast as some people's. I wanted to get her right away from her family, they're a disrupting factor, I don't mind telling you.'

'Do they play the piano?' Nenna asked. She could no longer feel her feet, but, glancing down at them, not too obviously for fear Richard should feel that he ought to do something about them, she saw that both of them were now bleeding. A hint of some religious association disturbed her. In the convent passage the Sacred Heart looked down in reproach. And suppose she had left marks on the floor of the taxi?

'Of course I wouldn't have suggested taking her to live anywhere that was below standard. I had a very good man in to see to the heating and lighting, and the whole conversion was done professionally. But I suppose that wasn't really the point. The question really was, did being alone with me on a boat seem like a good idea or not?'

'She'll come back, Richard.'

'That won't alter the fact that she went away.'

Richard evidently felt that memory must keep to its place, otherwise how could it be measured accurately?

'Nenna, you've hurt your foot!'

Overwhelmed by not having noticed this earlier, by his failure of politeness, observation and helpfulness, all that had been taught him from boyhood up, Richard proceeded at the double onto the Embankment, to escort her on to *Lord Jim*.

'They're all right, honestly, Richard. It's only a scrape.' That was the children's word. 'Just lend me a handkerchief.'

Richard was the kind of man who has two clean handkerchiefs on him at half past three in the morning. From the hold, where everything had its proper place, he fetched a bottle of TCP and a pair of half-wellingtons. The boots looked very much too big, but she appreciated that he wouldn't have liked to lend a pair of Laura's. Or perhaps Laura had taken all her things with her.

'Your feet are rather small, Nenna.'

Richard liked things to be the right size.

'Smaller than standard, I think.' He seated her firmly on one of the lights, and, without mistake or apology, put each of her feet into one of the clean boots. Each foot in turn felt the warmth of his hands and relaxed like an animal who trusts the vet.

'I don't know why you're wandering about here in the dark anyway. Nenna, have you been to a party?'

'Do you really think I go to parties where everyone leaves their shoes behind?'

'Well, I don't know. You lead a bit of a Bohemian existence, I mean, a lot more Bohemian than I do. I mean, I know various people in Chelsea, but they don't seem very different from anyone else.'

'I've come from a bit farther than Chelsea tonight,' Nenna said.

'Please don't think I'm being inquisitive. You mustn't think I'm trying to find out about your private affairs.'

'Richard, how old are you?'

'I was born on June 2nd 1922. That made me just seventeen when the War broke out.' Richard only estimated his age in relationship to his duties.

Nenna sat moving her feet about inside the spacious wellingtons. It was the river's most elusive hour, when darkness lifts off darkness, and from one minute to another the shadows declare themselves as houses or as craft at anchor. There was a light wind from the north-west.

'Nenna, would you like to come out in the dinghy?'

Too tired to be surprised at anything, Nenna looked at the davits and saw that the dinghy must have been lowered away already. If everything hadn't been quite in order he wouldn't, of course, have asked her.

'We can go up under Wandsworth Bridge as far as the Fina Oil Depot and then switch off and drift down with the tide.'

'Were you going to go anyway?' asked Nenna. The question seemed of great importance to her.

'No, I was hoping someone might come along and keep me company.'

'You mean you'd left it to chance?' Nenna couldn't believe this.

'I was hoping that you might come.'

Well, thought Nenna.

They had to go down the rope side-ladder, Richard first. Her feet hurt a good deal, and she thought, though not wishing to be ungrateful, that she might have done better without the boots. However, she managed to step in amidships without rocking *Lord Jim*'s dinghy by an inch.

'Cast off, Nenna.'

She was back for a moment on Bras d'Or, casting off, coiling the painter up neatly, approved of by her father, and by Louise.

It had been a test, then, she remembered, of a day's success if the outboard started up first time. Richard's Johnson, obedient to the pressed button, came to life at once, and she saw that it had never occurred to him that it mightn't. Small boats develop emotions to a fine pitch, and she felt that she would go with him to the end of the world, if his outboard was always going to start like that. And indeed, reality seemed to have lost its accustomed hold, just as the day wavered uncertainly between night and morning.

'I've been wanting to tell you, Nenna, that I very much doubt whether you're strong enough to undertake all the work you do on *Grace*. And some of the things you do seem to me to be inefficient, and consequently rather a waste of energy. For example, I saw you on deck the other morning struggling to open the lights from the outside, but of course all your storm fastenings must be on the inside.'

'We haven't any storm fastenings. The lights are kept down with a couple of bricks. They work perfectly well.' Now she felt furious. 'Surely you don't watch me from *Lord Jim*.'

Richard considered this carefully.

'I suppose I do.'

She had been unjust. She knew that he was good, and kept an eye on everybody, and on the whole Reach.

'I shouldn't be any happier, you know, if everything on *Grace* worked perfectly.'

He looked at her in amazement.

'What has happiness got to do with it?'

The dinghy followed the left bank, passing close to the

entrance to Chelsea creek. They scanned the misty water, keeping a watch-out for driftwood which might foul up the engine.

'Do you talk a great deal to Maurice?' Richard asked.

'All day and half the night, sometimes.'

'What on earth do you talk about?'

'Sex, jealousy, friendship and music, and about the boats sometimes, the right way to prime the pump, and things like that.'

'What kind of pump have you got?'

'I don't know, but it's the same as Maurice's.'

'I could show you how to prime it any time you like.' But he was not satisfied. 'When you've finished saying all that you want to say about these things, though, do you feel that you've come to any definite conclusion?'

'No.'

'So that, in the end, you've nothing definite to show for it?'

'About jealousy and music? How could we?'

'I suppose Maurice is very musical?'

'He's got a nice voice and he can play anything by ear. I've heard him play Liszt's Campanello with teaspoons, without leaving out a single note. That wasn't music, but we had a good time . . . and then, I don't know, we do talk about other things, particularly I suppose the kind of fixes we're both in.'

She stopped, aware that it wouldn't be advisable for Richard to know about Harry's visits. The crisis of conscience and duty would be too painful. Yet she would have very much liked to keep nothing back from him.

'That leads up to what I've really often wanted to ask you,' Richard went on. 'It seems to me you find it quite easy to put your feelings in words.'

'Yes.'

'And Maurice?'

'Yes.'

'I don't. I'm amazed at the amount people talk, actually.

I can't for the life of me see why, if you really feel something, it's got to be talked about. In fact, I should have thought it lost something, if you follow me, if you put it into words.'

Richard looked anxious, and Nenna saw that he really thought that he was becoming difficult to understand.

'Well,' she said, 'Maurice and I are talkative by nature. We talk about whatever interests us perhaps for the same reason that Willis draws it and paints it.'

'That's not the same thing at all. I like Willis's drawings. I've bought one or two of them, and I think they'll keep up their value pretty well.'

Beyond Battersea Bridge the light, between gray and silver, cast shadows which began to follow the lighters, slowly moving round at moorings.

At a certain point, evidently prearranged, for he didn't consult Nenna and hardly glanced at the banks, Richard put about, switched off the engine and hauled it on board. Once he had fitted in the rudder to keep the dinghy straight against the set of the tide he returned to the subject. A lifetime would not be too long, if only he could grasp it exactly.

'Let's say that matters hadn't gone quite right with you, I mean personal matters, would you be able to find words to say exactly what was wrong?'

'I'm afraid so, yes I would.'

'That might be useful, of course.'

'Like manufacturers' instructions. In case of failure, try words.'

Richard ignored this because it didn't seem to him quite to the point. On the whole, he disliked comparisons, because they made you think about more than one thing at a time. He calculated the drift. Satisfied that it would bring them exactly down to the point he wanted on the starboard side of *Lord Jim*, he asked—

'How do you feel about your husband?'

The shock Nenna felt was as great as if he had made a

mistake with the steering. If Richard was not at home with words, still less was he at home with questions of a personal nature. He might as well capsize the dinghy and be done with it. But he waited, watching her gravely.

'Aren't you able to explain?'

'Yes, I am. I can explain very easily. I don't love him any more.'

'Is that true?'

'No.'

'You're not making yourself clear, Nenna.'

'I mean that I don't hate him any more. That must be the same thing.'

'How long have you felt like this?'

'For about three hours.'

'But surely you haven't seen him lately?'

'I have.'

'You mean tonight? What happened?'

'I insulted his friend, and also his friend's mother. He gave me his opinion about that.'

'What did your husband say?'

'He said that I wasn't a woman. That was absurd, wasn't it?'

'I should imagine so, yes. Demonstrably, yes.' He tried again. 'In any ordinary sense of the word, yes.'

'I only want the ordinary sense of the word.'

'And how would you describe the way you feel about him now?' Richard asked.

'Well, I feel unemployed. There's nothing so lonely as unemployment, even if you're on a queue with a thousand others. I don't know what I'm going to think about if I'm not going to worry about him all the time. I don't know what I'm going to do with my mind.' A formless melancholy overcame her. 'I'm not too sure what to do with my body either.'

It was a reckless indulgence in self-pity. Richard looked steadily at her.

'You know, I once told Laura that I wouldn't like to be left alone with you for any length of time.'

'Why did you?'

'I don't know. I can't remember what reason I gave. It must have been an exceptionally stupid one.'

'Richard, why do you have such a low opinion of yourself?'

'I don't think that I have. I try to make a just estimate of myself, as I do of everyone else, really. It's difficult. I've a long way to go when it comes to these explanations. But I understood perfectly well what you said about feeling unemployed.'

They were up to *Lord Jim*. With only the faintest possible graze of the fender, the dinghy drifted against her.

'Where shall I tie up?'

'You can make fast to the ladder, but give her plenty of rope, or she'll be standing on end when the tide goes down.'

Nenna knew this perfectly well, but she felt deeply at peace.

As Richard stood up in the boat, he could be seen to hesitate, not about what he wanted to do, but about procedures. He had to do the right thing. A captain goes last on to his ship, but a man goes first into a tricky situation. Nenna saw that the point had come, perhaps exactly as she tied up, when he was more at a loss than she was. Their sense of control wavered, ebbed, and changed places. She kicked off the Wellingtons, which was easy enough, and began to go up the ladder.

'Is the hatch open?' she asked, thinking he would be more at ease if she said something entirely practical. On the other hand, it was a waste of words. The hatch on *Lord Jim* was always locked, but Richard never forgot the key.

[9]

Nenna's children neither showed any interest in where she had been nor in why she did not come back until next morning. Back again on *Grace*, Tilda was messing about at the foot of the mast with a black and yellow flag, one of the very few they had.

'We haven't much line either,' she said, 'I shall have to fly it from the stays.'

'What's it mean, Tilda dear?'

'This is L, *I have something important to communicate*. It was for you, Ma, in case you were out when we got back.'

'Where were you going, then?'

'We're going to take him out and show him round.'

'Who?'

'Heinrich.'

Martha came up the companion, followed by a boy very much taller than she was. Nenna was struck by the difference in her elder daughter since she had seen her last. Her hair was out of its fair pony tail and curled gracefully, with a life of its own, over her one and only Elvis shirt.

'Ma, this is Heinrich. He was sixteen three weeks ago. You don't know who he is.'

'I do know. Aunt Louise told me, but there was some kind of confusion in that she told me that he was due last Friday.'

'The date was altered, Mrs James,' Heinrich explained. 'I was delayed to some extent because the address given to me was 626 Cheyne Walk, which I could not find, but eventually the river police directed me.'

107

'Well, in any case I'd like to welcome you on board, Heinrich, hullo.'

'Mrs James. Heinrich von Furstenfeld.'

Heinrich was exceptionally elegant. An upbringing designed to carry him through changes of regime and frontier, possible loss of every worldly possession, and, in the event of crisis, protracted stays with distant relatives ensconced wherever the aristocracy was tolerated, from the Polish border to Hyde Park Gate, in short, a good European background, had made him totally self-contained and able with sunny smile and the formal handshake of the gymnast to set almost anybody at their ease, even the flustered Nenna.

'I hope Martha has shown you where to put your things.'

Martha looked at her impatiently.

'There's no need for him to unpack much, he's got to go to the airport tomorrow. He arrived here very late, and they had to find a bunk for him on *Rochester*. Willis was much more cheerful and said it reminded him of a boarding house in the old days.'

'I must go and explain to Mrs Woodie.'

'Oh, it's quite unnecessary. And I've shown Heinrich all round *Grace*. He understands that he can only go to the heads on a falling tide.'

'I am not so very used to calculating the tides, Mrs James,' said Heinrich in a pleasant conversational tone. 'The Danube, close to where I live, is not tidal, so that I shall have to rely for this information upon your charming daughters.'

'What's your house like in Vienna?' Tilda asked.

'Oh, it's a flat in the Franciskanerplatz, quite in the centre of things.'

'What kind of things are you used to doing in Vienna?' said Nenna. 'If you've only got one day in London, we shall have to see what we can arrange.'

'Oh, Vienna is an old city – I mean, everybody remarks on how many old people live there. So that although my native place is so beautiful, I am very much looking forward to seeing Swinging London.'

'Heinrich has to stand here on the deck while you drone on,' said Tilda. 'He ought to be given a cup of coffee immediately.'

'Oh, hasn't he had breakfast?'

'Ma, where are your shoes?' asked Martha, drawing her mother aside and speaking in an urgent, almost tragic undertone. 'You look a mess. From Heinrich's point of view, you hardly look like a mother at all.'

'I don't know what his mother's like. I know his father's an old business acquaintance of Auntie Louise and Uncle Joel.'

'His mother is a Countess.'

Tilda had taken Heinrich below, and put a saucepan of milk on the gas for his coffee. To his dying day the young Count would not forget the fair hand which had tended him when none other had heeded his plight.

'Why is your mother barefoot?' Heinrich asked. 'But I won't press the query if it is embarrassing. Perhaps she is Swinging.'

'Oh, you'll get used to her.'

A diplomat by instinct, Heinrich considered which of his twenty or thirty smaller European cousins Tilda most resembled. The Swiss lot, probably. His tone became caressing and teasing.

'I shall have to take you back with me to Vienna, dear Tilda, yes, I'm sorry, I shan't be able to manage without you, fortunately you're so small they won't miss you here and I can take you for a Glücksbringer.'

Here he went astray, for Tilda did not at all like being so small. 'Get outside this,' she said, slamming the tin mug of coffee in front of him, and sawing away energetically at the loaf.

With a faint smile the young Count turned to thank his saviour, while some colour stealed, stole, back into his pale cheeks.

On deck, Martha and Nenna had been joined by Maurice, who had decided to consider himself on holiday, and had not been to the pub for several nights.

'Who's the boy-friend?' he asked Martha.

'He is the son of the friend of my aunt.'

'Have it your own way. Pretty face, at all events.'

'Maurice,' said Martha. 'Help me. I'm trying to get my mother to dress and behave properly.'

It was just ten minutes to nine, and Richard walked by on his way up to World's End to catch a bus to the office. Nenna thought, if he doesn't look my way I'll never speak to him again, and in fact I'll never speak to any man again, except Maurice. But as he drew level with *Grace* Richard gave her a smile which melted her heart, and waved to her in a way entirely peculiar to himself, half way between a naval salute and a discreet gesture with the rolled umbrella.

Maurice folded his arms. 'Congratulations, Nenna.'

'Oh, don't say that.'

'Why not?'

'God made you too quick-witted. I don't know what's happening to me exactly.'

'Weak-mindedness.'

'Self-reproach, really.'

'What's that, dear?'

Martha left them, and went down the companion. Armed at all points against the possible disappointments of her life, conscious of the responsibilities of protecting her mother and sister, worried at the gaps in her education, anxious about nuns and antique dealers, she had forgotten for some time the necessity for personal happiness. Heinrich at first seemed strange to her.

The three children sat round the table and discussed how they were to spend the day. Tilda, unwatched by the other two, shook out the packets of cereal, at the bottom of which small plastic tanks, machine-guns and images of Elvis had been concealed by the manufacturers. When she had found the tokens she shovelled back the mingled wheat and rye, regardless, into the containers.

'You have no father, then, it seems, Martha,' Heinrich said quietly.

'He's left us.'

This was no surprise to Heinrich. 'My father, also, is often absent at our various estates.'

'You're archaic,' said Martha. Heinrich, while continuing to eat heartily, took her hand.

'I really came to bring you a telegram,' Maurice said. 'I fetched it from the boatyard office.'

'Did you, well, thank you, Maurice. I seemed to have missed some mail lately, my sister kept asking me whether I hadn't received her letters.'

'They have to take their chance with wind and tide, my dear, like all of us.'

The telegram was from Louise. They'd arrived in London. They were at the Carteret Hotel and Nenna was to call her there as soon as possible.

'Hullo, can I speak with Mrs Swanson? Hullo, is that Mr Swanson's room? Louise, it's Nenna.'

'Nenna, I was just about to ring you on that number I called before, from Frankfurt.'

'I'd as soon you didn't ring there, Louise.'

'Why, is there anything wrong?'

'Not exactly.'

'Is Edward with you, Nenna?'

'No.'

'That's what I anticipated. We want you to come and have lunch with us, dear.'

'Look, Louise, why don't I come over and see you both right away?'

'Lunch will be more convenient, dear, but after that we've put the whole of the rest of the day aside to have a thorough discussion of your problems. There seems to be so much to be settled. Joel is of one mind with me about this. I mean of course about yourself and the little girls, the possibility of your returning to Halifax.'

'It's the first time you've ever even mentioned this, Louise.'

'But I've been thinking about it, Nenna, and praying. Joel isn't a Catholic, as you know, but he's told me that he believes there's a Providence not so far away from us, really just above our heads if we could see it, that wants things to be the way they're eventually going. Now that idea appeals to me.'

'Listen, Louise, I went to see Edward yesterday.'

'I'm glad to hear it. Did he see reason?'

Nenna hesitated. 'I'm just as much to blame as he is and more. I can't leave him with nothing.'

'Where is he living?'

'With friends.'

'Well, he has friends, then.'

'Louise, you mustn't interfere.'

'Look, Nenna, we're not proposing anything so very sensational. I think we have to admit that you've tried and failed. And if we're offering you your passage home, you and the children, and help in finding your feet once you get there, and a good convent school for the girls, so that they can go straight on with the nuns and won't really notice any difference, well, all that's to be regarded as a loan, which we're very glad to offer you for an extended period, in the hopes of getting you back among caring people.'

'But there are people who care for me here too, Lou. I do wish you'd come and see *Grace*.'

'We must try and make time, dear. But you were always the one for boats – I'm always thankful to remember how happy that made father, the way you shared his feeling for boats and water. Tell me about your neighbours. Do you ever go and visit any of them?'

'We haven't any money,' said Martha, 'so you'll have to share our limited notion of entertainment.'

'There is nothing to be ashamed of in being poor,' said Heinrich.

'Yes, there is,' Martha replied, with a firmness which she could hardly have inherited either from her father or her mother, 'but there's no reason why we shouldn't go and look at things. Looking is seeing, really. That's what we do most of the time. We can go this afternoon and look at the King's Road.'

'I should like to visit a boutique,' said Heinrich.

'Well, that will be best about five or six, when everybody leaves work. A lot of them don't open till then.'

Tilda had lost interest in what was being said and had gone to fetch Stripey, who was being pursued across *Maurice* by a rat. Maurice was constantly being advised by Woodie and Richard to grease his mooring-ropes, so that the rats could not get across them, but he always forgot to do so.

Later in the day they prepared for their expedition into Chelsea. 'And your mother?' enquired Heinrich.

'You're always asking about her!' Martha cried. 'What do you think of her?'

'She is a very attractive woman for her years. But on the Continent we appreciate the woman of thirty.'

'Well, she's gone to talk things over with Aunt Louise, who's also an attractive woman for her years, but a good bit older, and quite different. She lives in Nova Scotia, and she's wealthy and energetic.'

'What do they talk over?'

'I expect Ma's arranging to take us out to Canada. She hasn't said so, but I should think it's that.'

'Then I shall see you often. We have relations both in Canada and in the United States.'

Martha tried not to wish, as they set out, that they could leave Tilda behind. She hardly remembered ever feeling this before about her ragged younger sister.

Without the guidance of the nuns, Tilda seemed to have lost her last vestige of moral sense. Partisan Street, the first street on the way up from the boats, was, as has been said, considered a rough place – a row of decrepit two-up, two-down brick houses, the refuge of crippled and deformed humanity. Whether they were poor because they were lame, or lame because they were poor, was perhaps a matter for sociologists, and a few years later, when their dwellings were swept away and replaced by council flats with rents much higher than they could afford, it must be assumed that they disappeared from the face of the earth. Tilda, who knew them all, loved to imitate them, and hobbled up Partisan Street alternately limping and shuffling, with distorted features.

'Your sister makes me laugh, but I don't think it's right to do so,' Heinrich said.

Martha pointed out that everybody in the street was laughing as well. 'They've asked her to come and do it at their Christmas Club,' she said. 'I wish I could still laugh like that.'

They turned into World's End, and opened the door into the peaceful garden where the faithful of the Moravian sect lie buried.

'They're buried standing, so that on Judgment Day they can rise straight upward.'

'Men and women together?'

'No, they're buried separately.'

Shutting the door in the wall, they walked on, Martha conscious, through every nerve in her body, of Heinrich's hand under her elbow. She asked him what was the first sentence he had ever learned in English.

'I am the shoemaker's father.'

'And French?'

'I don't remember when I learned French. It must have been at some time, because I can speak it now. I can also get along in Polish and Italian. But I don't know that I shall ever make much use of these languages.'

'Everything that you learn is useful. Didn't you know that everything you learn, and everything you suffer, will come in useful at some time in your life?'

'You got that from Mother Ignatius,' Tilda interrupted. 'Once, in the closing years of the last century, a poor woman earned her daily bread by working long hours at her treadle sewing machine. Work, work, ah it was all work I'm telling you in them days. Up and down, up and down, went that unwearying right foot of hers. And so by incessant exercise, her right foot grew larger and broader, while the other remained the same size, and at length she feared to go out in the streets at all, for fear of tripping and falling flat. Yet that woman, for all her tribulations, had faith in the intercessions of our Lady.'

'Tilda,' said Martha, stopping suddenly and taking her sister by the shoulders, 'I'll give you anything you like, within reason, to go back to the boats and stay there.'

Between the sisters there was love of a singularly pure kind, proof against many trials. Martha's look of request, or appeal, between her shadowing lashes, was one that Tilda would not disregard. Her protests were formal only.

'There's a lot more of that sewing-machine story.'

'I know there is.'

'I shall be all by myself. Ma's gone into London.'

'You must go to *Rochester*.'

'I've just been there.'

'Mrs Woodie told me she never finds the little ones a worry.'

'Perhaps she wishes she hadn't said that.'

'Willis will be there.'

Tilda alternately nodded her head and shook it violently from side to side. This meant consent.

'You must promise and vow to go straight to *Rochester*,' Martha told her. 'You must swear by the Sacred Heart. You know you like it there. You don't like it in the King's Road, because they won't let you into the boutiques, and you're too young to try on the dresses.'

Tilda darted off, hopping and skipping.

In this, its heyday, the King's Road fluttered, like a gypsy encampment, with hastily-dyed finery, while stage folk emerged from their beds at a given hour, to patrol the long pavements between Sloane Square and the Town Hall. Heinrich and Martha went in and out of one boutique after another, Dressing Down, Wearwithal, Wearabouts, Virtuous Heroin, Legs, Rags, Bags. A paradise for children, a riot of misrule, the queer looking shops reversed every fixed idea in the venerable history of commerce. Sellers, dressed in brilliant colours, outshone the purchasers, and, instead of welcoming them, either ignored them or were so rude that they could only have hoped to drive them away. The customers in return sneered at the clothing offered to them, and flung it on the ground. There were no prices, no sizes, no way to tell which stock was which, so that racks and rails of dresses were transferred as though by a magic hand from one shop to another. The doors stood open, breathing out incense and heavy soul, and the spirit was that of the market scene in the pantomime when the cast, encouraged by the audience, has let the business get out of hand.

Heinrich and Martha walked through this world, which was fated to last only a few years before the spell was broken, like a prince and princess. At Wearwithal, Heinrich tried on a pair of pale blue sateen trousers, which fitted tightly. Martha, guarding his jeans while he changed, admired him more for deciding against them than if he had bought them.

'Won't they do?' she asked.

'Such trousers are not worn on the Continent.'

'I thought perhaps you hadn't enough money.'

Heinrich in fact had plenty of money, and his own cheque-book, but his delicacy, responding to Martha's pride, prevented him from saying so.

'We will go to a coffee bar.'

These, too, were something new in London, if not in Vienna. The shining Gaggia dispensed one-and-a-half inches of bitter froth into an earthenware cup, and for two shillings lovers could sit for many hours in the dark brown shadows, with a bowl of brown sugar between them.

'Perhaps they'll be annoyed if we don't have another cup.'

Heinrich again put his fine, long-fingered hand over hers. She was amazed at its cleanliness. Her own hands were almost as black as Tilda's.

'You must not worry. I am in charge. How does that suit you?'

'I'm not sure. I'll tell you later,' said Martha, who wished one of her school friends would come in and see her. They'd tell Father Watson and the nuns, but what did that matter, they must know why she was absent from school anyway.

'I expect, living here in Chelsea, you go out a great deal.'

'How can I? I've no-one to go out with.'

'I think you would like the cake-shops in Vienna, also the concerts. I should like to present you to my mother and great-aunts. They take subscription tickets every winter for all the concerts, the *Musikverein*, anything you can name. You're fond of music?'

'Of course,' said Martha impatiently. 'What music do your great-aunts like?'

'Mahler. Bruckner . . .'

'I hate that. I don't want to be made to feel all the time.'

Heinrich put his head on one side and half closed his eyes.

'You know, I think that you could be heading for a very

serious depression.' Martha felt flattered. It seemed to her that she had never been taken seriously before.

'You mean I could break down altogether?'

'Listen, Martha, the best thing would be for you to tell me about your worries. They are probably those with which your catechism class does not help. The nuns will not understand the physiological causes of your restlessness and priests do not know everything either. Perhaps you would rather I did not speak like this.'

'It's all right, Heinrich, go on.'

'I too, have many problems at school. About that you wouldn't understand very well, Martha. We are all of us youths between sixteen and eighteen years of age, and for month after month we are kept away from women. I, personally, have the number of days pasted up on the inside of my locker. All this can produce a kind of madness.'

'What do your teachers say?'

'The monks? Well, they comprehend, but they can't cover all our difficulties. A good friend of mine, in the same set for physics and chemistry, grew so disturbed that he took some scissors and cut all round the stiff white collars, which we have to wear on Sundays, and made them into little points.'

'Like a dog in a circus,' said Martha, appalled.

'He wanted to make himself grotesque. He has left school, but I received an air-letter from him recently. Now he is anxious to join the priesthood.'

'But are you happy there?'

Heinrich smiled at her consolingly. 'I shall not allow sex to dominate my life, I shall find a place for it, that is all. . . . But, my dear, we are here to talk about you.'

She could see that he meant it, and knew that there might never again be such an opportunity.

'There's a great deal of sin in me,' she began rapidly, 'I know that a great part of me is darkness, not light. I wish my father and mother lived together, but not because I care whether they're happy or not. I love Ma, but she must expect to be unhappy because she's reached that time of life. I want them to live together in some ordinary kind of house so that I can come and say, how can you expect me to live here! But I shall never lead a normal life because I'm so short – we're both short – that's why Tilda stands on the deck half the day, it's because somebody told her that you only grow taller while you're standing up. And then I don't develop. We had a class composition, My Best Friend, and the girl who was describing me put up her hand and asked to borrow a ruler because she said she'd have to draw me straight up and down.'

'That is not friendship,' said Heinrich.

'There might be something wrong with me. I might be permanently immature.'

'I am sure you aren't, my dear. Listen, you are like the blonde mistress of Heine, the poet Heine, *wenig Fleisch, sehr viel Gemüt*, little body, but so much spirit.' He leaned forward and kissed her cheek, which, from being cold when they entered the coffee-bar, was now glowing pink. This was quite the right thing to do in a coffee-bar in the King's Road. But afterwards they became, for the time being, rather more distant.

'It has been very pleasant to spend the day here, Martha, and to see your boat.'

'Yes, well, at least that's something you haven't got in Vienna.'

Heinrich's father was a member of the Wiener Yacht Club.

'Certainly, not such a large one.'

Outside the boutiques were still aglow with heaps of motley flung about the feet of the disdainful assistants. The music grew louder, the Chelsea Granada welcomed all who would like to come in and watch the transmission of *Bootsie and Snudge*. They wandered on together at random.

'Two people can become close in a very short time,' Heinrich said. 'It is up to them not to let circumstances get the better of them. It is my intention, as I think I told you, to shape my own life.'

Tilda had not gone straight onto *Rochester*. Aware of the not quite familiar atmosphere which had surrounded Martha and Heinrich and detached her sister, she felt, for the first time, somewhat adrift. Jumping defiantly onto *Grace*'s deck, she gathered up the surprised Stripey and hugged her close. Then she examined her more attentively.

'You've got kittens on you.'

Depositing the cat, who flattened out immediately into a gross slumber, she swarmed up the mast. Low tide. A tug passed, flying a white house flag with the red cross of St George, and with a funnel might have been either cream or white.

'Thames Conservancy. She oughtn't to be as far down river as this. What's she doing below Teddington?'

On *Maurice*, fifteen feet below her, Harry, in the owner's absence, was unusually busy. He was wiring up the main hatch above the hold, in a way that showed he was certainly not an electrician by trade, with the intention of giving a mild electric shock to anyone who might try to get into it.

Tilda did not understand what he was doing, but she stared at him from the height of the mast until he became conscious of her, and turned round. He put down his pliers and looked up at her. His eyes were curious, showing an unusual amount of the whites.

'Want some sweeties?'

'No.'

'Want me to show you a comic?'

'No.'

'Come on, you can't read, can you?'

'I can.'

'You could get over here, couldn't you? You can come and sit on my knee if you like, and I'll show you a comic.'

Tilda swung to and fro, supported by only one arm round the mast.

'Have you got Cliff Richard Weekly?'

'Oh, yes, I've got that.'

'And Dandy?'

'Yes, I've got that too.'

'This week's?'

'That's right.'

'I don't need showing.'

'You haven't seen the things I've got to show you.'

'What are they like?'

'Something you've never seen before, love.'

'You've no right on that boat,' Tilda remarked. 'She belongs to Maurice.'

'Know him, then?'

'Of course I do.'

'Know what he does for a living?'

'He goes out to work.'

'I'll show you what he does, if you like. You won't find that in a comic.'

Tilda persisted. 'Why are you putting up wires on *Maurice*?'

'Why? Well, I've got a lot of nice things in here.'

'Where did you get them from?'

'Don't you want to know what they are?'

'No, I want to know where you got them from.'

'Why?'

'Because you're a criminal.'

'Who told you that, you nasty little bitch?'

'You're a receiver of stolen goods,' Tilda replied.

She watched him sideways, her eyes alight and alive. After all, there were only two ways that Harry could come on to *Grace*, the gangplank across from *Maurice*, on which Stripey lay digesting uneasily, or back to the wharf and round by the afterdeck.

Harry bent down and with one hand lifted the gangplank so that it hung in mid-air. Stripey shot upwards, sprang, and missed her footing, falling spreadeagled on the foreshore.

'Your kitty's split open, my love.'

'No, she's not. She's been eating a seagull. If she was open you'd see all the feathers.'

Harry had a bottle in his hand.

'Are you going to get drunk?'

'The stuff in this bottle? Couldn't drink that. It would burn me if I did. It'd fucking well burn anybody.'

It was spirits of salt. He looked at her with the points of his eyes, the whites still rolling. The bottle was in his right hand and he swung it to and fro once or twice, apparently judging its weight. Then he moved towards the wharf, coming round to meet her on *Grace*.

Tilda clambered over the washboard, and clinging on by fingers and toes to the strakes, half slithered and half climbed down the side, gathered up the cat and skimmed across to *Rochester*. The side-ladder was out, as she very well knew.

'Oh, Mrs Woodie, will you look after me? Martha told me to come here. I came here straight away.'

'What's that you're carrying?' asked Mrs Woodie, resigned by now to almost anything.

'She's my pet, my pet, the only pet I've been allowed to have since I was a tiny kiddie.'

Mrs Woodie looked at the distended animal.

'Are you sure, dear, that she's not . . .'

'What do you mean, Mrs Woodie? I believe that there's an angel that guards her footsteps.'

The hold of *Rochester* had changed, in the last few weeks, from below decks to a cosy caravan interior. There was a good piece of reversible carpet put down, and Tilda seated herself, open-mouthed, in front of the television, where Dr Kildare flickered. Mrs Woodie began to cut sandwiches into neat squares. 'Where are you?' she called to her husband.

Woodie appeared, somewhat put out. 'I'll take a cup to Willis. He's still dwelling too much on the past, in my opinion.'

'Tell him Tilda's here.'

Willis came in quietly and sat beside the child on the locker, covered with brand new flower-patterned cushions.

'Where's your sister?'

'Out with Heinrich.'

'With the German lad? Well, he seems nice enough. He wouldn't remember the war, of course.'

Tilda began to tell him exactly what had been happening in Dr Kildare, so far. She said nothing about Harry, because, for the time being, she had forgotten all about him.

Richard came back from work that evening later than he had hoped. Disappointed that there were no lights showing on *Grace* – it had never occurred to him that Nenna would not be there tonight – he was turning to walk along the Embankment to *Lord Jim* when he caught sight of a stranger on *Maurice*. He therefore changed direction and went along the wharf.

'I'm a friend of the owner's,' he said. 'Good evening.'

There was no reply, and he noticed that the gangplank was down between *Maurice* and *Grace*. Something was not quite right, so without hesitation he dropped down on to the deck.

Harry did not look up, but continued paying out the flex until he rounded the corner of the deck-house and could see Richard without bothering to turn his head. He put down the pair of pliers he was holding and picked up a heavy adjustable spanner.

'What are you doing on this boat?' Richard asked.

'Who made you God here?' said Harry.

The light was fading to a point where the battlements of the Hovis tower could only be just distinguished from the pinkish-gray of the sky. When Richard came a couple of steps nearer – it would never have occurred to him to go back until the matter was satisfactorily settled – Harry, looking faintly surprised, as though he couldn't believe that anything could be quite so simple, raised the adjustable spanner and hit him on the left side of the head, just below the ear. Richard fell without much sound. He folded up sideways against the winch, and immediately tried to get up again. It would have been better if he had been less conscientious, because he had broken one of his ribs against the handle of the winch and as he struggled to his feet the sharp broken edge of the bone penetrated slightly into his lung. Harry watched him fall back and noted that a considerable quantity of blood was coming away at the mouth. He wiped the spanner and put it away with his other tools. He was reflecting, perhaps, that this had been an easier job than the electrical wiring. Carrying the bag of tools, he disappeared up the wharf towards Partisan Street and the King's Road.

Heinrich and Martha were walking back to the Reach hand in hand. 'That's Maurice's pub,' she told him, 'he'll be in there now,' and, as they got nearer, 'I wish the Venice lantern was still there, it looked nice at night,' but in reality there was no need to say very much.

The foreshore was dark as pitch, but the corner street lamps palely illuminated the deck of *Maurice*. The body of a man lay across the winch, with an arm drooped over the side.

'Martha, don't look.'

Often, as the night drew on, a number of people were seen to lie down in odd places, both in Partisan Street and on the Embankment. Maurice's customers, too, were unpredictable. But none of them lay still in quite this way.

'Perhaps it's Harry,' Martha said. 'If it is, and he's dead, it'll be a great relief for Maurice.'

They walked steadily nearer, and saw blood on the deck, looking blackish in the dim light.

124

'It's *Lord Jim*,' she whispered.

The sight of a lord, knocked out by criminals, exactly fitted in with Heinrich's idea of swinging London.

'It's Mr Blake,' said Martha.

'What should we do?'

Martha knew that with any luck the police launch would be at *Bluebird*. 'They go there to fetch the nurses on night shift and give them a lift down to hospital.'

'That would not be permitted in Vienna.'

'It's not permitted here.'

They were both running along the Embankment. Loud music, complained of by the neighbours on shore, thumped and echoed from cheerful *Bluebird* on the middle Reach. You could have told it a mile away. The river police duty-boat, smart as a whistle, was waiting alongside.

In this way Richard, still half-alive, was admitted to the men's casualty ward of the Waterloo hospital. One of the young probationers from *Bluebird* was on the ward, and came in with an injection for him, to help him to go to sleep.

'Isn't it Miss Jackson?' Richard said faintly. He had been trained to recognise anybody who had served under him, or who had helped him in any way. Miss Jackson had assisted with the removal of Willis. But Richard's polite attempt to straighten himself and to give something like a slight bow made the damage to his lung rather worse.

They patched him up, and he dozed through the night.

The long pallid hospital morning passed with interruptions from the nursing, cleaning, and auxiliary staff, all of whom gravitated to the bed, where they were received by the nice-looking Mr Blake, who was in terrible pain, with grave correctness. The probationers told him to remember that every minute he was getting a little better, and Ward Sister told him not to make any effort, and not to try to take anything by the mouth. 'I'm afraid I'm being a bit of a nuisance,'

Richard tried to say. 'You're not supposed to talk,' they said.

When he was left to himself his mind cleared, and he began to reflect. He remembered falling, and the deck coming up to hit him, which brought back the sensation – although it hadn't done so at the time – of the moment just before the torpedo hit *Lanark*. He also remembered the look of the adjustable spanner, and it seemed to him appropriate that having been knocked down with a spanner his whole body was now apparently being alternately wrenched and tightened. There must surely be some connection of ideas here, and he would get better quickly if he could be certain that everything made sense.

Next, having reviewed, as well as he could, his work at the office, and made a courageous but unsuccessful attempt to remember whether there was any urgent correspondence he hadn't dealt with, he let his thoughts return to Nenna. Yesterday, or was it the day before yesterday, or when was it, he had gone first up the ladder on to *Lord Jim*, but Nenna had gone first into the cabin. Thinking about this, he felt happier, and then quite at peace. It was rather a coincidence that she was wearing a dark blue guernsey exactly like Laura's, with a neck which necessitated the same blindfold struggle to get it off. About the whole incident Richard felt no dissatisfaction and certainly no regret. He could truly reflect that he had done not only the best, but the only thing possible.

At the end of the morning a very young doctor made his rounds and told Richard on no account to talk, he was only making a routine check-up. 'You can answer with simple signs,' he said reassuringly, 'we'll soon have you out of here and on four wheels again.' Less sensitive than the nurses, he evidently took Richard for a quarrelsome garage proprietor.

'No bleeding from the ears?'

The young doctor appeared to be consulting a list, and Richard, anxious to help a beginner, tried to indicate that he would bleed from the ears if it was the right thing to do. As to the exact locality of the pain, it was difficult to convey that it had grown, and that instead of having a pain he was now contained inside it. The doctor told him that they would be able to give him something for that.

'And absolute quiet, no police as yet. We had an officer here wanting you to make a statement, but he'll have to wait a couple of days. However,' he added unexpectedly, 'we're going to bend the regulations a little bit and let you see your children.'

From the no-man's land at the entrance to the ward, where the brown lino changed blue, Tilda's voice could be heard, asking whether she and her sister might be allowed to bring Mr Blake a bottle of Suncrush.

'Is he your Daddy, dear?'

'He is, but we haven't seen him for many, many years, for more than we can remember.'

'Well, if Dr Sawyer's given permission. . . .'

Tilda advanced, with Martha lingering doubtfully behind, and swept several plants from the loaded windowsill to make room for the Suncrush.

'Do you remember us, Daddy dear?'

Ward Sister was still complaining that children were not allowed to see the patients unattended. By good fortune, however, another visitor arrived; it was Willis, who took charge at once of the two girls. Richard's catastrophe had brought him to himself. Gratitude, felt by most people as a burden, was welcome to the unassuming Willis.

'Well, Skipper, it's sad to see you laid low. Not so long since I was in here myself, but I never dreamed . . .'

Willis had not quite known what to bring, so he'd decided on a packet of Whiffs. In his ward at the Waterloo they'd been allowed to smoke for an hour a day. 'But I can see it's different in here,' he said, as though this, too, was a mark of the superiority of Skipper. Richard did not smoke, but Willis had never noticed this.

'I think he wants to write something for you, dear,' the nurse said to Martha. Tilda, unabashed, was out in the pantry, helping the ward orderlies take the lids off the supper trays. Richard looked at Martha and saw Nenna's puzzled eyes, though they were so much darker. He painfully scrawled on the piece of paper which had been left for him: HOW IS YOUR MOTHER?

Martha wrote in turn – it didn't occur to her to say it aloud, although Richard could hear perfectly well – BUSY, SHE'S PACKING.

WHAT FOR?

WE'RE GOING TO CANADA.

WHEN?

But this Martha could not answer.

Laura was sent for, and arrived back in London the following afternoon. She dealt easily and efficiently with Richard's office, with the police, with the hospital. There she spoke only to Matron and the lung specialist. 'It's no use talking to the ward staff, they're so overworked, poor dears, they can't tell one case from another!' The ward sister had actually drawn her aside and asked her whether she did not think it would be a good idea to let her husband see his children more often in the future.

Richard was still not allowed to speak – he was not recovering quite so fast as had been expected – and he could make little reply when Laura told him that this was exactly the kind of thing she had expected all along, and that she would see about disposing of *Lord Jim* immediately. Her family, applied to, began to scour the countryside for a suitable house, within reasonable commuting distance from London, in good condition, and recently decorated, so that she could move Richard straight there as soon as he was discharged from the hospital.

Nenna felt that she could have made a better hand at answering Louise if only Edward had taken the trouble to return her purse. It wasn't only the money, but her library card, her family allowance book, the receipt from the repair shop without which she couldn't get her watch back, creased photographs, with Edward's own photograph among them, her address book, almost the whole sum of her identity.

After all, she thought, if she did go away, how much difference would it make? In a sense, Halifax was no further away than 42b Milvain Street, Stoke Newington. All distances are the same to those who don't meet.

Halifax was equally far from the Essex/Norfolk border, to which Laura had removed Richard. The FOR SALE notice nailed to *Lord Jim*'s funnel saddened her and if possible she approached *Grace* from the other direction. If she had told Richard about Harry, and about *Maurice*'s dubious cargo, he wouldn't have had to lie in a pool of blood waiting for her own daughter to rescue him. But curiously enough the regret she felt, not for anything she had done but for what she hadn't, quite put an end to the old wearisome illusion of prosecution and trial. She no longer felt that she needed to defend herself, or even to account for herself, there. She was no longer of any interest to Edward. The case was suspended indefinitely.

As Louise seemed unwilling to come to the boats, Nenna was obliged to take the girls to tea at the luxurious Carteret. It was an anxious business to make them sufficiently respectable. On the twelfth floor of the hotel, from which they could just get a view of the distant river, they were delighted with their prosperous-looking aunt. Taller, stronger, not so blonde but much more decisive than their mother, she still seemed perpetually astonished by life.

'Martha! Tilda! Well I'll be! I haven't seen you both for such a long time, and you're both of you just! Well, how are you going to like us in Canada?'

'Louise, that depends on such a number of things. We have to sell *Grace*, to begin with.'

'What would happen if I pressed that bell?' Tilda asked.

'Well, somebody would come along, one of the floor waiters, to ask if we wanted tea, or cakes, or any little thing like that. Go on, you can press it, honey.'

Tilda did so. The bell was answered, and their order arrived.

'Is that right, dear?'

'Yes, those are the things Martha and I like. Are there any boats in Canada?'

'No shortage of boats, no shortage of water.'

Tilda's mind was made up in favour of the New World.

'But I'm not sure that we ought to leave Maurice, though,' she said, licking each finger in turn. 'Now that he won't have Ma to talk to, and there's no Mr Blake to get up a subscription if he goes down, I'd say he might lose heart altogether. And then the police are always coming round to interrogate him.'

'Who's Maurice, dear?' asked her aunt rather sharply.

'Maurice is on *Maurice*, just like the Blakes were on *Lord Jim*.'

'Ah, yes, Richard Blake, he called me up.'

'How could he?' Nenna cried.

'You remember, he's the one I had to call his number to get you, that's when we were in Frankfurt. I told him then that when we came to England we'd be staying at this hotel. It suits us all right, although Joel keeps saying that the service was so much better before the war.'

'But what did he say?'

Nenna's question caused confusion, which Louise gradually sorted out. What had this Richard Blake said, well, she got the impression that he was counting on coming to a series of Transatlantic insurance conferences in the spring, and he was either coming to Montreal first, or to New York, she couldn't remember which order it was, search me, said Louise, she hadn't thought it mattered all that much.

'I don't know whether it does or not,' said Nenna. 'He was going to show me how to fold up a map properly.'

'Joel can do that for you, dear.'

'We shan't be able to take Stripey,' said Tilda, continuing the course of her own thoughts. 'She won't leave *Grace*. Mrs Woodie bought her a basket, a very nice one made by the blind, but she wouldn't get into it.'

'Mrs Woodie?'

'A kindly lady, somewhat advanced in years.'

'She'll enjoy being back at school with girls of her own age,' Louise quietly observed to Nenna.

Mr Swanson came in, greeted everybody, and ordered a rye.

'Well, von Furstenfeld called me today, their boy's arrived safely in Vienna, and they're more than pleased, Nenna, with the spirit of hospitality you and your family extended to him. I owe you a debt of gratitude there.'

Martha smiled, perfectly tranquil.

Joel Swanson did not understand, nor did he ever expect to understand, exactly what was going on, but the kind of activity he seemed to be hearing about, in snatches only, was more or less exactly what he'd expect from his wife's relatives. He smiled at them with inclusive good will.

With *Lord Jim* and *Grace* both on his books, Pinkie felt doubtful about his chance of selling either. Of course, they were at the opposite ends of the price range. But the market would be affected, particularly as the disappointed broker hadn't hesitated to tell everyone how lucky he'd been not to drop a packet on *Dreadnought*, which had gone straight to the bottom like a stone in a pond. It was awkward, too, from the sales point of view, that Richard had been aboard one of these barges when he got knocked over the head. Thank heavens he hadn't got to try and sell that one. Poor old Richard, torpedoed three times, and then finished off, near as a toucher, with an adjustable spanner. Pinkie consulted the senior partner.

'Not everyone's buy. But if someone's looking for an unusual night spot . . .'

On *Grace* there was, after all, not so very much to be done. The barges, designed to be sailed by one man and a boy, could be laid up in a few days. Only the mast gave trouble. Not all Woodie's efforts could succeed in lowering it. 'I've another idea about your mast,' he said every morning, coming brightly across, but the thick rust held it fast. As to the packing, Mrs Woodie, eager to give a hand, was disappointed to find so little to do. The James family seemed to have few possessions. Mrs Woodie felt half inclined to lend her some, so as to have more to sort out and put away.

Unperturbed, Stripey gave birth. The warm hold of *Rochester* was chosen by the sagacious brute, and Willis, always up very early, found her on the ruins of the new locker cushions, with five mud-coloured kittens. Martha presented all but one to Father Watson. The presbytery needed a cheerful touch, he had so often hinted at this. But the priest, who had a strong instinct of self-preservation, transferred the litter of river-animals to the convent, as prizes in the Christmas raffle. With relief, he discussed the emigration of the James family with the nuns; so much the best thing – if there was no chance of a reconciliation – all round.

The night before Nenna and her two daughters were due to leave England, storm weather began to blow up on the

Reach. There had been a good deal of rain, the Thames was high, and a north westerly had piled up water at the river's mouth, waiting for a strong flood tide to carry it up. Before dark the wind grew very strong.

A storm always seems a strange thing in a great city, where there are so many immoveables. In front of the tall rigid buildings the flying riff-raff of leaves and paper seemed ominous, as though they were escaping in good time. Presently, larger things were driven along, cardboard boxes, branches, and tiles. Bicycles, left propped up, fell flat. You could hear glass smashing, and now pieces of broken glass were added to the missiles which the wind flung along the scoured pavement. The Embankment, swept clean, was deserted. People came out of the Underground and, leaning at odd angles to meet the wind, hurried home from work by the inner streets.

Above the river, the seagulls kept on the wing as long as they could, hoping the turbulence would bring them a good find, then, defeated and battered, they heeled and screamed away to find refuge. The rats on the wharf behaved strangely, creeping to the edge of the planking, and trying to cross over from dry land to the boats.

On the Reach itself, there could be no pretence that this would be an ordinary night. Tug skippers, who had never before acknowledged the presence of the moored barges, called out, or gave the danger signal – five rapid blasts in succession. Before slack tide the police launch went down the river, stopping at every boat to give fair warning.

'Excuse me, sir, have you checked your anchor recently?'

The barge anchors were unrecognisable as such, more like crustaceans, specimens of some giant type long since discarded by Nature, but still clinging to their old habitat, sunk in the deep pits they had made in the foreshore. But under the ground they were half rusted away. *Dreadnought*'s anchor had come up easily enough when the salvage tug came to dispose of her. The mud which held so tenaciously could also give way in a moment, if conditions altered.

'And how much anchor chain have you got? The regulation fifteen fathoms? All in good condition?'

Like many questions which the police were obliged to put, these were a formality, it being clear that the barge-owners couldn't answer them. It could only be hoped that the mooring-ropes were in better case than the anchors. The visit was, in fact, a courteous excuse to leave a note of the nearest Thames Division telephone number.

'Waterloo Pier. WAT 5411. In all emergencies. Sure you've got that?'

'We'd have to go on shore to telephone,' said Woodie doubtfully, when his turn came. He was thinking of taking *Rochester*'s complement straight to Purley in the car, whether Willis agreed or not.

'What do you think of this weather, officer?'

The sergeant understood him, as one Englishman to another. The wind had ripped the tarpaulin off some of the laid-up boats, and huge fragments of oilcloth were flying at random, wrapping themselves round masts and rails.

'You want to look out for those,' he said. 'They could turn nasty.'

The Thames barges, built of living wood that gave and sprang back in the face of the wind, were as much at home as anything on the river. To their creaking and grumbling was added a new note, comparable to music. As the tide rose, the wind shredded the clouds above them and pushed a mighty swell across the water, so that they began to roll as they had once rolled at sea.

Nenna and Martha had absolutely forbidden Tilda to go above decks. Banished to the cabin, she lay there full of joy, feeling the crazy desire of the old boat to put out once again into mid-stream. Every time *Grace* rose on the swell, she was aware of the anchor chain tightening to its limit.

'We're all going ashore,' Nenna called, '*Rochester*'s gone already. We're just taking a bag, we'll come back for the rest when the wind's gone down.'

Tilda put on her anorak. She thought them all cowards.

No-one knew that Maurice was on board ship, because there were no lights showing. Certainly not a habitual drinker, he was nevertheless sitting that night in the darkness with a bottle of whisky, prepared for excess.

It wasn't the uncertain nature of his livelihood that worried him, nor the police visits, although he had twice been invited to accompany the officers to the station. So far they hadn't applied for a search warrant to go over the boat, but Maurice didn't care if they did. Still less did he fear the storm. The dangerous and the ridiculous were necessary to his life, otherwise tenderness would overwhelm him. It threatened him now, for what Maurice had not been able to endure was the sight of the emptying Reach. *Dreadnought*, *Lord Jim*, now *Grace*. Maurice, in the way of business, knew too many, rather than too few, people, but when he imagined living without friends, he sat down with the whisky in the dark.

When he heard steps overhead on deck, he switched on the light. Making two shots at it before he could manage the switch, he wondered if he'd better not drink any more. Of course, that rather depended on who was coming; he didn't know the footsteps. Someone was blundering about, didn't know the boat, probably didn't know about boats at all, couldn't find the hatch. Maurice, always hospitable, went to open it. His own steps seemed enormous, he floated up the steps, swimming couldn't be so difficult after all, particularly as he'd become weightless. Reaching the hatch at the same time as the stranger outside, he collided with it, and they fell into each other's arms. Not a tall man, quite young and thin, and just as drunk, to Maurice's relief, as he was.

'My name's James.'

'Come in.'

'This is a boat, isn't it?'

'Yes.'

'Is it *Grace*?'

'No.'

'Pity.'

'You said your name was James?'

'No, Edward.'

'Never mind.'

Edward took a bottle of whisky out of his pocket, and, unexpectedly, two glasses. The glasses made Maurice sad. They must have been brought in the hope of some celebration to which the way had been lost.

'Clever of you to come on the right night,' he said.

He was absorbed, as host, in the task of getting his guest safely below decks. Fortunately he had had a good deal of practice in this. As he filled the glasses his depression emptied away.

Edward, sitting down heavily on the locker, said that he wanted to explain.

'Doctors tell you not to drink too much. They're very insistent on this. They're supported by teams of physiologists and laboratory researchers.'

He steered his way round these words much as he had negotiated the deck.

'What these so-called scientists should be doing is to study effects. Take my case. If one whisky makes me feel cheerful, four whiskies ought to make me feel very cheerful. Agreed?'

'I'm with you.'

'They haven't. I've had four whiskies and I feel wretched. Bloody wretched. Take that from me. And now I'd like to leave you with this thought. . . .'

'Do you have to make many speeches in the course of your work?' Maurice asked.

For an instant Edward sobered up. 'No, I'm clerical.'

The barge took a great roll, and Maurice could hear the hanger with his good suit in it, waiting for the job which never came, sliding from one end of its rail to the other.

'I came to give Nenna a present,' Edward said. Out of the same pocket which had held the glasses he produced a small blue and gold box.

'There's a bottle of scent in this box.'

'What kind?'

'It's called L'Heure Bleue.'

'Do you mind if I write that down?' Maurice asked.

'Certainly. Have my biro.'

'It's the Russian for "pen", you know.'

'Hungarian.'

'Russian.'

'A Hungarian invented them.'

'He would have made a fortune if. What's so special about this scent? You brought it for Nenna. Does she wear it?'

'I don't know. I think perhaps not. I haven't much sense of smell.'

'I don't think Nenna uses scent at all.'

'Do you know her, then?'

They both emptied their glasses.

'The mother whose man I live of the house in suggested it,' said Edward.

'What?'

'Wasn't that clear? I'm afraid I'm losing my fine edge.'

'Not a bit of it.'

'Gordon said I ought to bring her some scent.'

From directly above them came a noise like an explosion in a slate quarry. Something heavy had been torn away and, bouncing twice, landed flat on the deck directly over their heads. The deck timbers screamed in protest. Edward seemed to notice nothing.

137

'I've brought her purse.'

This too he dragged and tugged out of his pocket, and they both stared at it as though by doing so they could turn it into something else.

'Do you think she'll take me back?'

'I don't know,' Maurice said doubtfully. 'Nenna loves everybody. So do I.'

'Oh, do you know Nenna, then?'

'Yes.'

'You must know her pretty well, living on the same boat.'

'The next boat.'

'I expect she sometimes comes to borrow sugar. Matches, she might borrow.'

'We're both borrowers.'

'She's not easy to understand. You could spend a very long time, trying to understand that woman.'

There was about a quarter of the bottle left, and Edward poured it out for both of them. This time the movement of the boat helped him, and *Maurice* rocked the whisky out in two curves, one for each glass.

'Do you understand women?'

'Yes,' said Maurice.

With a great effort, holding his concentration as though he had it in his two hands, he added,

'You've got to give these things to her. Give them, that's it, give them. You've got to go across to *Grace*.'

'How's that done?'

'It's not difficult. Difficult if you're heavy. Luckily we haven't any weight this evening.'

'How do I go?'

It was worse than ever getting up the companion, much worse than last time. The whole boat plunged, but not now in rhythm with the staggering of Maurice and Edward. They managed three steps. The hatch in front of them flew open and the frame, tilted from one side to the other, gave them a

sight of the wild sky outside. A rat was sitting at the top of the
companion. A gleam of light showed its crossed front teeth.
Edward struggled forward.

'Brute, I'll get it.'

'It's one of God's creatures!' cried Maurice.

Edward hurled all that he had in his hands, the purse, the
scent, which struck the rat in the paunch. Hissing loudly, it
swivelled on its hind legs and disappeared, the tail banging
like a rope on the top step as it fled.

'Did the scent break?'

'I can smell it, I'm afraid.'

'I came here to give her a present.'

'I know, James.'

'What do I give her now?'

Edward sat empty-handed on the companion. Maurice,
who still hadn't exactly made out who he was, suddenly cared
intensely about the loss.

'Another present.'

'What?'

'Hundreds. I've got hundreds.'

Clinging together they followed the line of the keelson to
the forward hatch.

'Hundreds!'

Record-players, electric guitars, transistors, electric hair-
curlers, electric toasters, Harry's hoard, the strange currency
of the 1960's, piled on the floor, on the bunks, all in their new
containers, all wrapped in plastic. Maurice snatched out a
pile and loaded them on to the reeling Edward.

'She'll find these useful on *Grace*.'

'How do I get there?'

How had they got back on deck? As the battering wind
seized them they had to stoop along in the darkness, fighting
for handholds, first the base of the old pulley, then the mast.
Three toasters sailed away like spindrift in the gale. It was

still blowing hard north-west. The gang-plank to *Grace* was missing. The crash above their heads had come when it was lifted bodily and flung across the deck.

'There's still the ladder.'

Maurice had a fixed iron ladder down the port side.

'Is that *Grace*?' Edward shouted above the wind.

'Yes.'

'Can't see any lights.'

'Of course you can't. It's dark.'

'I hadn't thought of that. Don't know much about boats.'

Edward was much more confused than Maurice and needed all the help he was getting as Maurice manhandled him to the top of the ladder. Maurice was still sober enough to know that he was drunk, and knew also that the water between the two boats was wilder than he had ever seen it. That something was dreadfully wrong was an idea which urgently called his attention, but it wavered beyond his grasp. It was to do with getting over to *Grace*.

'This isn't the usual way we go.'

Edward had dropped the whole cargo of gifts by the time he had got down the twenty iron rungs of the ladder. As he reached the bottom the whole boat suddenly heaved away from him, so that the washboard at the top rolled out of sight and a quite new reach of sky appeared.

'Look out!'

Maurice was half-collapsed over the gunwale. Even like that, hopelessly drunk and quite tired out, there was about him an appealing look of promise, of everything that can be meant by friendship.

'You must come again when the weather's better!'

He leaned out, perilously askew, just to catch a sight of Edward's white face at the bottom of the ladder. Edward shouted back something that the wind carried away, but he seemed to be saying, once again, that he was not very used to boats.

With that last heave, Maurice's anchor had wrenched clear of the mud, and the mooring-ropes, unable to take the whole weight of the barge, pulled free and parted from the shore. It was in this way that *Maurice*, with the two of them clinging on for dear life, put out on the tide.

Other books by Penelope Fitzgerald available in Mariner editions

The Blue Flower

"A masterpiece. How does she do it?"

A. S. BYATT

The Blue Flower is set in the age of Goethe, in the small towns and universities of late-eighteenth-century Germany. It tells the true story of the Romantic poet Novalis and his passion for his "heart's heart," his "spirit's guide" — a plain, simple child named Sophie von Kühn. A sublime meditation on the irrationality of love, *The Blue Flower* was named one of the eleven best books of 1997 by the *New York Times Book Review*. ISBN 0-395-85997-2

The Bookshop

"A brilliant little book — no, it is perfect."

Boston Sunday Globe

In 1959, Florence Green, a kindhearted widow with a small inheritance, opens a bookshop — the only bookshop — in the seaside town of Hardborough. Her modest venture is met with polite but ruthless local opposition, and soon her shop becomes a battleground. Shortlisted for the Booker Prize, *The Bookshop* is a classic study of stiff upper lip in the face of small-town nastiness. ISBN 0-395-86946-3

The Gate of Angels

"Vibrant with wonderful characters, ablaze with ideas."

Washington Post

It is 1912 at Cambridge University, where faith in one set of unobservables (God, the soul) is giving way to faith in another (the indivisible stuff of matter). Fred Fairly, a rational young physicist, lives the life of a secular monk — until he meets Daisy, a working-class girl who turns his philosophy upside down. As the *Daily Mail* said of this sparkling comedy, "Gilbert could have written it and Sullivan set it to music." ISBN 0-395-84838-5

Praise from England for
Penelope Fitzgerald's *The Blue Flower*

Published in London to unanimous critical acclaim, *The Blue Flower* was the most admired novel of 1995, chosen nineteen times as Book of the Year in the year-end newspaper roundups.

"*The Blue Flower* is a masterpiece. Fitzgerald writes with a mysterious clarity nobody else approaches." — A. S. BYATT

"A minor miracle of sympathy and crispness." — *Guardian*

"The writing is elliptical and witty . . . What could be a sad little love story is constantly funny and always absorbing, with a cast of characters both endearing and amusing. This novel is a jewel." — *Daily Telegraph*

"An extraordinary imagining. An original masterpiece."
— *Financial Times*

"Very beautifully done. Fitzgerald never seems to try too hard; she never bullies the reader; but her dry, small-scale prose manages to produce large-scale emotional effects." — *Mail on Sunday*

"She has total confidence in her characters . . . her sense of time and place is marvellously deft, done in a few words. A beautiful book."
— *Spectator*

"The story of a poet which, it is subtly suggested, is also the story of a remarkable moment in the history of civilisation. He is naive and provincial, but innocently intelligent, which enables him to entertain with uncorrupted enthusiasm ideas of all sorts — about nature, its purity and its symbolism, about God [and] the epiphanies vouchsafed to the elect, about the new and the old ideas combining at the great moment when it was possible to proclaim that the world must be romanticised. It is hard to see how the hopes and defeats of Romanticism, or the relation between inspiration and common life, between genius and mere worthiness, could be more deftly rendered than they are in this admirable novel." — *London Review of Books*

"The high romantic foreshadows our more recent tragicomic times. But what seems to fascinate Fitzgerald is the parochialism that preceded it: high-minded aspirations struggling with a daily life of petty formalities and rigid observance ... Fitzgerald writes about all this with affection and amused detachment ... The novel has an almost daunting authenticity. Lightly, delicately, she brings to life these lost manners and attitudes." — *Sunday Telegraph*

"How many historical novelists seem to view the past like someone scanning a brochure of Tuscan villas in a grey November! ... And when real historical figures are involved, how hard not to fall into the fallacy of assuming that they were either aware of or wholly unconcerned about the figures they would cut for us ... Penelope Fitzgerald does not just step safely through this minefield, she makes of it a dance arena ... Her past is as present, this being as unbearably 'light,' its search for meaning as urgent and provisional, as our own." — *Independent on Sunday*

Praise for Penelope Fitzgerald

Penelope Fitzgerald is "the best English writer who is at present at the prime of her power" (Richard Eder, *Los Angeles Times*). Her first novel, *The Golden Child*, was published in 1977, and of the eight that have followed, three have been shortlisted for the Booker Prize — *The Bookshop* (1978), *The Beginning of Spring* (1988), and *The Gate of Angels* (1990). She won the prize in 1979 for *Offshore*.

"No writer is more engaging than Penelope Fitzgerald."
— ANITA BROOKNER

"There are twenty perfectly competent novelists at work in Britain today, but only a handful producing what one could plausibly call literature. Of this handful, Penelope Fitzgerald possesses . . . the purest imagination." — A. N. WILSON

"The compression of her characterization is extraordinary; she can sum people up in a single sentence that begs as many questions as it answers but is worth pages of analysis." — VICTORIA GLENDINNING

"She writes the kind of fiction in which perfection is almost to be hoped for, as unostentatious as true virtuosity can make it, its texture a pure pleasure." — FRANK KERMODE

Books by Penelope Fitzgerald

Fiction

The Golden Child
The Bookshop
Offshore
Human Voices
At Freddie's
Innocence
The Beginning of Spring
The Gate of Angels
The Blue Flower

Nonfiction

Edward Burne-Jones
The Knox Brothers
Charlotte Mew and
Her Friends

THE
BLUE FLOWER

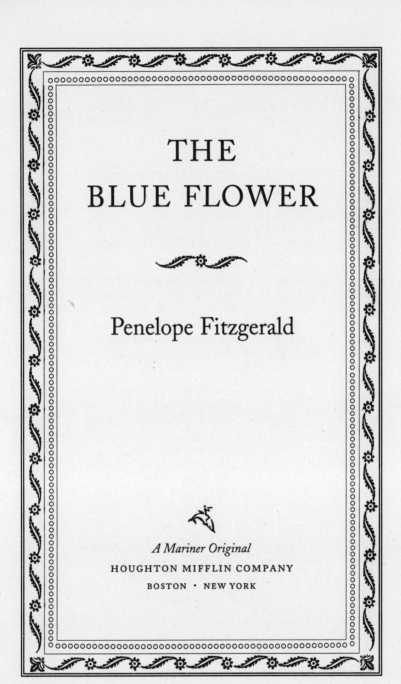

Penelope Fitzgerald

A Mariner Original

HOUGHTON MIFFLIN COMPANY

BOSTON · NEW YORK

FIRST U.S. EDITION
First published in Great Britain in 1995
by Flamingo, an imprint of HarperCollins Publishers

For information about permission to reproduce selections
from this book, write to Permissions, Houghton Mifflin Company,
215 Park Avenue South, New York, New York 10003.

For information about this and other Houghton Mifflin trade
and reference books and multimedia products, visit
The Bookstore at Houghton Mifflin on the World Wide Web
at http://www.hmco.com/trade/.

Library of Congress Cataloging-in-Publication Data
Fitzgerald, Penelope.
The blue flower / Penelope Fitzgerald. — 1st U.S. ed.
p. cm.
"A Mariner original."
ISBN 0-395-85997-2
1. Novalis, 1772–1801 — Fiction. 2. Poets, German —
18th century — Fiction. I. Title.
PR6056.186B58 1997
823'.914 — DC21   96-52911   CIP

The photographs on page 227, of Friedrich von Hardenberg's
gold engagement ring, are reproduced by kind permission
of the Museum Weissenfels/Saale.

Printed in the United States of America

QUM 10 9

Contents

Author's Note

This novel is based on the life of Friedrich von Hardenberg (1772–1801) before he became famous under the name Novalis. All his surviving work, letters from and to him, the diaries and official and private documents, were published by W. Kohlhammer Verlag in five volumes between 1960 and 1988. The original editors were Richard Samuel and Paul Kluckhohn, and I should like to acknowledge the debt I owe to them.

The description of an operation without an anaesthetic is mostly taken from Fanny d'Arblay's letter to her sister Esther Burney (September 30, 1811) about her mastectomy.

'Novels arise out of the shortcomings of history.'

F. von Hardenberg, later Novalis,
Fragmente und Studien, 1799–1800

I

Washday

Jacob Dietmahler was not such a fool that he could not see that they had arrived at his friend's home on the washday. They should not have arrived anywhere, certainly not at this great house, the largest but two in Weissenfels, at such a time. Dietmahler's own mother supervised the washing three times a year, therefore the household had linen and white underwear for four months only. He himself possessed eighty-nine shirts, no more. But here, at the Hardenberg house in Kloster Gasse, he could tell from the great dingy snowfalls of sheets, pillow-cases, bolster-cases, vests, bodices, drawers, from the upper windows into the courtyard, where grave-looking servants, both men and women, were receiving them into giant baskets, that they washed only once a year. This might not mean wealth, in fact he knew that in this case it didn't, but it was certainly an indication of long standing. A numerous family, also. The underwear of children and young persons, as well as the larger sizes, fluttered through the blue air, as though the children themselves had taken to flight.

'Fritz, I'm afraid you have brought me here at an inconvenient moment. You should have let me know. Here I am, a stranger to your honoured family, knee deep in your smallclothes.'

'How can I tell when they're going to wash?' said Fritz. 'Anyway, you're a thousand times welcome at all times.'

'The Freiherr is trampling on the unsorted garments,' said the housekeeper, leaning out of one of the first-floor windows.

'Fritz, how many are there in your family?' asked Dietmahler. 'So many things?' Then he shouted suddenly: 'There is no such concept as a thing in itself!'

Fritz, leading the way across the courtyard, stopped, looked round and then in a voice of authority shouted back: 'Gentlemen! Look at the washbasket! Let your thought be the washbasket! Have you thought the washbasket? Now then, gentlemen, let your thought be on *that* that thought the washbasket!'

Inside the house the dogs began to bark. Fritz called out to one of the basket-holding servants: 'Are my father and mother at home?' But it was not worth it, the mother was always at home. There came out into the courtyard a short, unfinished looking young man, even younger than Fritz, and a fair-haired girl. 'Here, at any rate, are my brother Erasmus and my sister Sidonie. Nothing else is wanted while they are here.'

Both threw themselves on Fritz. 'How many are there of you altogether?' asked Dietmahler again. Sidonie gave him her hand, and smiled.

'Here among the table-linen, I am disturbed by Fritz Hardenberg's young sister,' thought Dietmahler. 'This is the sort of thing I meant to avoid.'

She said, 'Karl will be somewhere, and Anton, and the Bernhard, but of course there are more of us.' In the house, seeming of less substance even than the shadows, was Freifrau von Hardenberg. 'Mother,' said Fritz, 'this is Jacob Dietmahler, who studied in Jena at the same time as myself and Erasmus, and now he is a Deputy Assistant to the Professor of Medicine.'

'Not quite yet,' said Dietmahler. 'I hope, one day.'

'You know I have been in Jena to look up my friends,' went on Fritz. 'Well, I have asked him to stay a few days with us.'

2

The Freifrau looked at him with what seemed to be a gleam
of terror, a hare's wild look. 'Dietmahler needs a little brandy,
just to keep him alive for a few hours.'

'He is not well?' asked the Freifrau in dismay. 'I will send
for the housekeeper.' 'But we don't need her,' said Erasmus.
'You have your own keys to the dining room surely.' 'Surely I
have,' she said, looking at him imploringly. 'No, I have them,'
said Sidonie. 'I have had them ever since my sister was married.
I will take you all to the pantry, think no more about it.' The
Freifrau, recollecting herself, welcomed her son's friend to the
house. 'My husband cannot receive you just at this moment,
he is at prayer.' Relieved that the ordeal was over, she did not
accompany them through the shabby rooms and even shabbier
corridors, full of plain old workmanlike furniture. On the
plum-coloured walls were discoloured rectangles where pictures must once have hung. In the pantry Sidonie poured the
cognac and Erasmus proposed the toast to Jena. *'Stosst an! Jena
lebe hoch! Hurra!'*

'What the Hurra is for I don't know,' said Sidonie. 'Jena is
a place where Fritz and Asmus wasted money, caught lice, and
listened to nonsense from philosophers.' She gave the pantry
keys to her brothers and went back to her mother, who was
standing at the precise spot where she had been left, staring out
at the preparations for the great wash. 'Mother, I want you to
entrust me with a little money, let us say five or six thaler, so
that I can make some further arrangements for our guest.' 'My
dear, what arrangements? There is already a bed in the room
he is to have.' 'Yes, but the servants store the candles there,
and they read the Bible there during their free hour.' 'But my
dear, why should this man want to go to his room during the
day?' Sidonie thought that he might want to do some writing.
'Some writing!' repeated her mother, in utter bewilderment.
'Yes, and for that he should have a table.' Sidonie pressed home
her advantage. 'And, in case he should like to wash, a jug of

3

water and a basin, yes, and a slop-pail.' 'But Sidonie, will he not know how to wash under the pump? Your brothers all wash so.' 'And there is no chair in the room, where he might put his clothes at night.' 'His clothes! It is still far too cold to undress at night. I have not undressed myself at night, even in summer, for I think twelve years.' 'And yet you've given birth to eight of us!' cried Sidonie. 'God in heaven spare me a marriage like yours!'

The Freifrau scarcely heeded her. 'And there is another thing, you have not thought – the Father may raise his voice.' This did not perturb Sidonie. 'This Dietmahler must get used to the Father, and to the way we do things, otherwise let him pack up and go straight home.'

'But in that case, cannot he get used to our guest-rooms? Fritz should have told him that we lead a plain, God-fearing life.'

'Why is it God-fearing not to have a slop-pail?' asked Sidonie.

'What are these words? Are you ashamed of your home, Sidonie?'

'Yes, I am.' She was fifteen, burning like a flame. Impatience, translated into spiritual energy, raced through all the young Hardenbergs. Fritz now wished to take his friend down to the river to walk up the towpath and talk of poetry and the vocation of man. 'This we could have done anywhere,' said Dietmahler. 'But I want you to see my home,' Fritz told him. 'It is old-fashioned, we are old-fashioned in Weissenfels, but we have peace, it is *heimisch*.' One of the servants who had been in the courtyard, dressed now in a dark cloth coat, appeared in the doorway and said that the Master would be glad to see his son's guest in the study, before dinner.

'The old enemy is in his lair,' shouted Erasmus.

Dietmahler felt a certain awkwardness. 'I shall be honoured to meet your father,' he told Fritz.

4

2

The Study

It was Erasmus who must take after his father, for the Freiherr, politely rising to his feet in the semi-darkness of his study, was unexpectedly a small stout man wearing a flannel nightcap against the draughts. Where then did Fritz – since his mother was no more than a shred – get his awkward leanness from, and his height? But the Freiherr had this in common with his eldest son, that he started talking immediately, his thoughts seizing the opportunity to become words.

'Gracious sir, I have come to your house,' Dietmahler began nervously, but the Freiherr interrupted, 'This is not my house. It is true I bought it from the widow of von Pilsach to accommodate my family when I was appointed Director of the Salt Mining Administration of Saxony, which necessitated my living in Weissenfels. But the Hardenberg property, our true home and lands, are in Oberwiederstadt, in the county of Mansfeld.' Dietmahler said politely that he wished he had been fortunate enough to go to Oberwiederstadt. 'You would have seen nothing but ruins,' said the Freiherr, 'and insufficiently fed cattle. But they are ancestral lands, and it is for this reason that it is important to know, and I am now taking the opportunity of asking you, whether it is true that my eldest son, Friedrich, has entangled himself with a young woman of the middle classes.'

'I've heard nothing about his entangling himself with any-one,' said Dietmahler indignantly, 'but in any case, I doubt if he can be judged by ordinary standards, he is a poet and a philosopher.'

'He will earn his living as an Assistant Inspector of Salt Mines,' said the Freiherr, 'but I see that it is not right to interrogate you. I welcome you as a guest, therefore as another son, and you will not mind my finding out a little more about you. What is your age, and what do you intend to do in life?'

'I am two and twenty and I am training to become a surgeon.'

'And are you dutiful to your father?'

'My father is dead, Freiherr. He was a plasterer.'

'I did not ask you that. Have you known what it was to have sad losses in your family life?'

'Yes, sir, I have lost two little brothers from scarlet fever and a sister from consumption, in the course of one year.'

The Freiherr took off his nightcap, apparently out of respect. 'A word of advice. If, as a young man, a student, you are tormented by a desire for women, it is best to get out into the fresh air as much as possible.' He took a turn round the room, which was lined with book-cases, some with empty shelves. 'Meanwhile, how much would you expect to spend in a week on spirits, hey? How much on books – not books of devotion, mind you? How much on a new black coat, without any expla-nation as to how the old one has ceased to be wearable? How much, hey?'

'Freiherr, you are asking me these questions as a criticism of your son. Yet you have just said that you were not going to interrogate me.'

Hardenberg was not really an old man – he was between fifty and sixty – but he stared at Jacob Dietmahler with an old man's drooping neck and lowered head. 'You are right, quite right. I took the opportunity. Opportunity, after all, is only another word for temptation.'

He put his hand on his guest's shoulder. Dietmahler, alarmed, did not know whether he was being pushed down or whether the Freiherr was leaning on him, perhaps both. Certainly he must be used to entrusting his weight to someone more competent, perhaps to his strong sons, perhaps even to his daughter. Dietmahler felt his clavicle giving way. I am cutting a mean figure, he thought, but at least he was on his knees, while Hardenberg, annoyed at his own weakness, steadied himself as he sank down by grasping first at the corner of the solid oak table, then at one of its legs. The door opened and the same servant returned, but this time in carpet slippers.

'Does the Freiherr wish the stove to be made up?'

'Kneel with us, Gottfried.'

Down creaked the old man by the master. They looked like an old married couple nodding over their household accounts together, even more so when the Freiherr exclaimed, 'Where are the little ones?'

'The servants' children, Excellency?'

'Certainly, and the Bernhard.'

3

The Bernhard

In the Hardenbergs' house there was an angel, August Wilhelm Bernhard, fair as wheat. After plain motherly Charlotte, the eldest, pale, wide-eyed Fritz, stumpy little Erasmus, easy-going Karl, open-hearted Sidonie, painstaking Anton, came the blonde Bernhard. To his mother, the day when he had to be put into breeches was terrible. She who hardly ever, if at all, asked anything for herself, implored Fritz. 'Go to him, go to your Father, beg him, pray him, to let my Bernhard continue a little longer in his frocks.' 'Mother, what can I say, I think Bernhard is six years old.'

He was now more than old enough, Sidonie thought, to understand politeness to a visitor. 'I do not know how long he will stay, Bernhard. He has brought quite a large valise.'

'His valise is full of books,' said the Bernhard, 'and he has also brought a bottle of schnaps. I dare say he thought there would not be such a thing in our house.'

'Bernhard, you have been in his room.'

'Yes, I went there.'

'You have opened his valise.'

'Yes, just to see his things.'

'Did you leave it open, or did you shut it again?'

The Bernhard hesitated. He could not remember.

'Well, it doesn't signify,' said Sidonie. 'You must, of course, confess to Herr Dietmahler what you have done, and ask his pardon.'

'When?'

'It should be before nightfall. In any case, there is no time like the present.'

'I've nothing to tell him!' cried the Bernhard. 'I haven't spoiled his things.'

'You know that Father punishes you very little,' said Sidonie coaxingly. 'Not as we were punished. Perhaps he will tell you to wear your jacket the wrong way out for a few days, only to remind you. We shall have some music before supper and after that I will go with you up to the visitor and you can take his hand and speak to him quietly.'

'I'm sick of this house!' shouted the Bernhard, snatching himself away.

Fritz was in the kitchen garden patrolling the vegetable beds, inhaling the fragrance of the broad bean flowers, reciting at the top of his voice.

'Fritz,' Sidonie called to him. 'I have lost the Bernhard.'

'Oh, that can't be.'

'I was reproving him in the morning room, and he escaped from me and jumped over the window-sill and into the yard.'

'Have you sent one of the servants?'

'Oh, Fritz, best not, they will tell Mother.'

Fritz looked at her, shut his book and said he would go out and find his brother. 'I will drag him back by the hair if necessary, but you and Asmus will have to entertain my friend.'

'Where is he now?'

'He is in his room, resting. Father has worn him out. By the way, his room has been turned upside down and his valise is open.'

'Is he angry?'

9

'Not at all. He thinks perhaps that it's one of our customs at Weissenfels.'

Fritz put on his frieze-coat and went without hesitation down to the river. Everyone in Weissenfels knew that young Bernhard would never drown, because he was a water-rat. He couldn't swim, but then neither could his father. During his seven years' service with the Hanoverian army the Freiherr had seen action repeatedly and crossed many rivers, but had never been put to the necessity of swimming. Bernhard, however, had always lived close to water and seemed not to be able to live without it. Down by the ferry he was forever hanging about, hoping to slip on board without paying his three pfennig for the crossing. The parents did not know this. There was a kind of humane conspiracy in the town to keep many matters from the Freiherr, in order to spare his piety on the one hand, and on the other, not to provoke his ferocious temper.

The sun was down, only the upper sky glowed. The mist was walking up the water. The little boy was not at the ferry. A few pigs and a flock of geese, forbidden to go by way of Weissenfels' handsome bridge, were waiting for the last crossing.

4

Bernhard's Red Cap

For the first time Fritz felt afraid. His imagination ran ahead of him, back to the Kloster Gasse, meeting the housekeeper at the front door – but, young master, what is that load you are carrying into the house? It is dripping everywhere, the floors, I am responsible for them.

His mother had always believed that the Bernhard was destined to become a page, if not at the court of the Elector of Saxony, then perhaps with the Count of Mansfeld or the Duke of Braunschweig-Wolfenbüttel. One of Fritz's duties, before long, would be to drag his little brother round these various courts in the hope of placing him satisfactorily.

The rafts lay below the bridge, close into the bank, alongside piles of gently heaving, chained pinewood logs, waiting for the next stage in their journey. A watchman was trying a bunch of keys in the door of a hut. 'Herr Watchman, have you seen a boy running?'

A boy was supposed to come with his dinner, said the watchman, but he was a rascal and had not come. 'Look, the towpath is empty.'

The empty barges laid up for repair were moored at their station on the opposite bank. Fritz pelted over the bridge. Everyone saw him, coat flying. Had the Freiherr no servants to send? The barges wallowed on their mooring ropes, grating against each other, strake against strake. From the quayside Fritz jumped down about four feet or so onto the nearest deck. There was a scurrying, as though of an animal larger than a dog.

'Bernhard!'

'I will never come back,' Bernhard called.

The child ran across the deck, and then, afraid to risk the drop onto the next boat, climbed over the gunwale and then stayed there hanging on with both hands, scrabbling with his boots for a foothold. Fritz caught hold of him by the wrists and at the same moment the whole line of barges made one of their unaccountable shifts, heaving grossly towards each other, so that the Bernhard, still hanging, was trapped and squeezed. A pitiful cough and a burst of tears and blood were forced out of him like air out of a balloon.

'How am I going to get you out of here?' demanded Fritz. 'What a pest you are, what a pest.'

'Let me go, let me die!' wheezed the Bernhard.

'We'll have to work our way along forward, then I can pull you up.' But the instinct to preserve life seemed for the moment to have deserted the child, Fritz must do it all, dragging and shuffling him along, wildly protesting, between the two gunwales. If they had been on the other bank there would have been passers-by to lend a hand, but then, Fritz thought, they'd think murder was being done. The boats grew narrower, he saw the glimmering water idling beneath them and hauled the child up like a wet sack. His face was not pale, but a brilliant crimson.

'Make an effort, do you want to drown?'

'What would it matter if I did?' squeaked the Bernhard. 'You said once that death was not significant, but only a change in condition.'

'Drat you, you've no business to understand that,' Fritz shouted in his ear.

12

'My *Mütze*!'

The child was much attached to his red cap, which was missing. So, too were one of his front teeth and his breeches. He had on only long cotton drawers tied with tape. Like most rescuers, Fritz felt suddenly furious with the loved and saved. 'Your *Mütze* has gone, it must be on its way to the Elbe by now.' Then, ashamed of his anger, he picked the little boy up and put him on his shoulders to carry him home. The Bernhard, aloft, revived a little. 'Can I wave at the people?'

Fritz had to make his way to the end of the line of barges, where perpendicular iron steps had been built into one bank and he could climb up without putting down the Bernhard.

How heavy a child is when it gives up responsibility.

He couldn't go straight back to the Kloster Gasse like this. But Sidonie and Asmus between them would be equal to explaining things away during the before-dinner music. Meanwhile, in Weissenfels, he had many places to get dry. After crossing the bridge again he walked only a short way along the Saale and then took two turns to the left and one to the right, where the lights were now shining in Severin's bookshop.

There were no customers in the shop. The pale Severin, in his long overall, was examining one of the tattered lists, which booksellers prefer to all other reading, by the light of a candle fitted with a reflector.

'Dear Hardenberg! I did not expect you. Put the little brother, I pray you, on a sheet of newspaper. Here is yesterday's *Leipziger Zeitung*.' He was surprised at nothing.

'The little brother is in disgrace,' said Fritz, depositing the Bernhard. 'He ran down onto the barges. How he came to get quite so wet I don't know.'

'*Kinderleicht, kinderleicht*,' said Severin indulgently, but his indulgence was for Fritz. He could not warm to children, since all of them were scribblers in books. He went to the very back of the shop, opened a wooden chest, and took out a large knitted shawl, a peasant thing.

'Take off your shirt, I will wrap you in this,' he said. 'Your brother need not return it to me. Why did you cause all this trouble? Did you hope to sail away and leave your father and mother behind you?'

'Of course not,' said the Bernhard scornfully. 'All the boats on that mooring are under repair. They could not sail, they have no canvas. I did not want to sail, I wanted to drown.'

'That I don't believe,' replied Severin, 'and I should have preferred you not to say it.'

'He loves water,' said Fritz, impelled to defend his own.

'Evidently.'

'And, indeed, so do I,' Fritz cried. 'Water is the most wonderful element of all. Even to touch it is a pleasure.'

Perhaps Severin did not find it a pleasure to have quite so much water on the floor of his bookshop. He was a man of forty-five, 'old' Severin to Fritz, a person of great good sense, unperturbed by life's contingencies. He had been poor and unsuccessful, had kept himself going by working very hard, at low wages, for the proprietor of the bookshop, and then, when the proprietor had died, had married his widow and come into the whole property. Of course the whole of Weissenfels knew this and approved of it. It was their idea of wisdom exactly.

Poetry, however, meant a great deal to Severin – almost as much as his lists. He would have liked to see his young friend Hardenberg continue as a poet without the necessity of working as a salt mine inspector.

For the rest of his journey home the Bernhard continued to complain about the loss of his red *Mütze*. It was the only thing he had possessed which indicated his revolutionary sympathies.

'I don't know how you got hold of it,' Fritz told him. 'And if Father had ever caught sight of it he would in any case have told the servants to throw it on the rubbish heap. Let all this be a lesson to you to keep yourself from poking about among the visitors' possessions.'

'In a republic there would be no possessions,' said the Bernhard.

5

The History of Freiherr Heinrich von Hardenberg

Freiherr von Hardenberg was born in 1738, and while he was still a boy came into the properties of Oberwiederstadt on the River Wipper in the county of Mansfeld, and the manor and farm of Schlöben-bei-Jena. During the Seven Years' War he served, as a loyal subject, in the Hanoverian Legion. After the Peace of Paris he gave up his commission. And he married, but in 1769 there was an epidemic of smallpox in the towns along the Wipper, and his young wife died. The Freiherr nursed the infected and the dying, and those whose families could not afford a grave were buried in the grounds of Oberwiederstadt which, having once been a convent, still had some consecrated earth. He had undergone a profound religious conversion – but I have not! said Erasmus, as soon as he was old enough to ask about the rows of green mounds so close to the house. 'I have not – does he ever think of that?'

On each grave was a plain headstone, carved with the words: *He, or she, was born on——, and on—— returned home*. This was the inscription preferred by the Moravians. The Freiherr now worshipped with the Moravian Brethren, for whom every soul is either dead, awakened, or converted. A human soul is converted as soon as it realises that it is in danger, and what that danger is, and hears itself cry aloud, *He is my Lord.*

A little over a year after his wife's death the Freiherr married his young cousin Bernadine von Böltzig. 'Bernadine, what an absurd name! Have you no other?' Yes, her second name was Auguste. 'Well, I shall call you Auguste henceforward.' In his gentler moments, she was Gustel. Auguste, though timorous, proved fertile. After twelve months the first daughter, Charlotte, was born, and a year later, Fritz. 'When the time comes for their education,' the Freiherr said, 'both shall be sent to the Brethren at Neudietendorf.'

Neudietendorf, between Erfurt and Gotha, was a colony of the Herrnhut. The Herrnhut was the centre where fifty years earlier the Moravians, refugees from persecution, had been allowed to settle down in peace. To the Moravians, a child is born into an ordered world into which he must fit. Education is concerned with the status of the child in the kingdom of God.

Neudietendorf, like the Herrnhut, was a place of tranquillity. Wind instruments, instead of bells, summoned the children to their classes. It was also a place of total obedience, for the meek are the inheritors. They must always go about in threes, so that the third might tell the Prediger what the other two had found to talk about. On the other hand, no teacher might give a punishment while he was still angry, since an unjust punishment is never forgotten.

The children swept the floors, tended the animals and made the hay, but they were never allowed to strive against each other, or take part in competitive games. They received thirty hours a week of education and religious instruction. All must be in bed by sunset, and remain silent until they got up at five the next morning. After any communal task had been completed – say, whitewashing the henhouses – the long trestle tables were brought out for a 'love-feast', when all sat down together, hymns were sung and a small glass of home-made liqueur was handed to everyone, even the youngest. The boarding fees were eight thaler for a girl, ten thaler for a boy (who ate more, and needed a Latin and a Hebrew grammar).

Charlotte von Hardenberg, the eldest, who took after her mother, did very well at the House of Maidens. She married early, and had gone to live in Lausitz. Fritz had been born a dreamy, seemingly backward little boy. After a serious illness when he was nine years old, he became intelligent and in the same year was despatched to Neudietendorf. 'But in what has he fallen short?' demanded the Freiherr, when only a few months later he was requested by the Prediger, on behalf of the Elders, to take his son away. The Prediger, who was very unwilling to condemn any child absolutely, explained that Fritz perpetually asked questions, but was unwilling to receive answers. Let us take – said the Prediger – the 'children's catechism'. In the course of this the instructor asks, 'What are you?'

A *I am a human being.*
Q Do you feel it when I take hold of you?
A *I feel it well.*
Q What is this, is it not flesh?
A *Yes, that is flesh.*
Q All this flesh which you have is called the body. What is it called?
A *The body.*
Q How do you know when people have died?
A *They cannot speak, they cannot move anymore.*
Q Do you know why not?
A *I do not know why not.*

'Could he not answer these questions?' cried the Freiherr.

'It may be that he could, but the answers he gave in fact were not correct. A child of not quite ten years old, he insists that the body is not flesh, but the same stuff as the soul.'

18

'But this is only one instance —'

'I could give many others.'

'He has not yet learned —'

'He is dreaming away his opportunities. He will never become an acceptable member of Neudietendorf.'

The Freiherr asked whether not even one sign of moral grace had been detected in his son. The Prediger avoided a reply.

The mother, poor Auguste, who soon become sickly (although she outlived all but one of her eleven children) and seemed always to be looking for someone to whom to apologise, begged to be allowed to teach Fritz herself. But what could she have taught him? A little music perhaps. A tutor was hired from Leipzig.

6

Uncle Wilhelm

While they were living at Oberwiederstadt, the Hardenbergs did not invite their neighbours, and did not accept their invitations, knowing that this might lead to worldliness. There was also the question of limited means. The Seven Years' War was expensive – Friedrich II was obliged to open a state lottery to pay for it – and for some of his loyal landholders, quite ruinous. In 1780 four of the smaller Hardenberg properties had to be sold, and at another one, Möckritz, there was an auction of the entire contents. Now it stood there without crockery, without curtains, without livestock. As far as the low horizon the fields lay uncultivated. At Oberwiederstadt itself, you saw through the narrow ancient windows row after row of empty dovecotes, and a *Gutshof* too vast to be filled, or even half-filled, which had once been the convent chapel. The main building was pitiable, with missing tiles, patched, weatherbeaten, stained with water which had run for years from the loosened guttering. The pasture was dry over the old plague tombstones. The fields were starved. The cattle stood feeding at the bottom of the ditches, where it was damp and a little grass grew.

Smaller and much more agreeable was Schlöben-bei-Jena, to which the family sometimes made an expedition. At Schlöben, with its mill-stream and mossy oaks, 'the heart,'

Auguste said tentatively, 'can find peace'. But Schlöben was in almost as much difficulty as the other properties. There is nothing peaceful, the Freiherr told her, about a refusal to extend credit.

As a member of the nobility, most ways of earning money were forbidden to the Freiherr, but he had the right to enter the service of his Prince. In 1784 (as soon as the existing Director had died) he was appointed Director of the Salt Mines of the Electorate of Saxony at Dürrenberg, Kösen and Artern, at a salary of 650 thaler and certain concessions of firewood. The Central Saline Offices were at Weissenfels, and in 1786 the Freiherr bought the house in the Kloster Gasse. It was not like Schlöben, but Auguste wept with relief, praying that her tears were not those of ingratitude, at leaving the chilly solitude and terribly out-of-date household arrangements of Oberwiederstadt. Weissenfels had two thousand inhabitants – two thousand living souls – brickyards, a prison, a poor-house, the old former palace, a pig-market, the river's traffic and the great clouds reflected in the shining reach, a bridge, a hospital, a Thursday market, drying-meadows and many, many shops, perhaps thirty. Although the Freifrau had no spending allowance of her own and had never been into a shop, indeed rarely left the house except on Sundays, she received a faltering glow, like an uncertain hour of winter sunshine, from the idea of there being so many things and so many people quite close at hand.

It was at Weissenfels that the Bernhard was born, in the bitter February of 1788. Fritz by then was nearly seventeen, and was not at Weissenfels on this occasion, but at his Uncle Wilhelm's, in Lucklum in the Duchy of Braunschweig-Wolfenbüttel. The boy had outgrown his tutor, who had to sit up late into the night reading mathematics and physiology in order to catch up with him. 'But this is not wonderful, after all,' the uncle wrote. 'Tutors are a poor-spirited class of men, and all this Herrnhuterei is nothing but hymn-singing and housework, quite unsuitable for a von Hardenberg. Send Fritz, for a time at least, to live in my household. He is fifteen or sixteen, I don't know which, and must learn to understand wine, which he can't do at Weissenfels, where the grapes are only fit to make brandy and vinegar, and to find out what grown men talk about when they are in decent company.' The Freiherr was, as always, infuriated by his brother's remarks and still more by their tone. Wilhelm was ten years older than himself, and appeared to have been sent into the world primarily to irritate him. He was a person of great distinction – 'in his own eyes' the Freiherr added – Governor of the Saxon division of the German Order of Knighthood (Lucklum branch). Round his neck, on very many occasions, he wore the flashy Maltese cross of the order, which was also embroidered, in plush and braid, on his greatcoat. The Hardenberg children knew him as the 'Big Cross', and His Mightiness. He had never married, and was graciously hospitable not only to his fellow landowners but to musicians, politicians, and philosophers – those who should be seen round the table of a great man, to offer their opinions and to agree with his own.

After a stay of only a few months, Fritz was returned to his father at Weissenfels, taking with him a letter from his uncle.

Lucklum, October 1787
I am glad that Fritz has recovered himself and got back on to the straight path, from which I certainly shall never try to remove him again. My way of life here is pitched too high for his young head. He was much too spoiled, and saw too many strange new people, and it could not be helped if a great many things were said at my table which were not helpful or salutary for him to know . . .

The Freiherr wrote to his brother to thank him for his hospitality, and to regret that he could not thank him more. The white waistcoat, breeches and broad-cloth coat which had been made for Fritz by his uncle's tailor, apparently because those he had brought with him were not considered smart enough for the dinner-table, would now be sent to the Moravian Brethren for distribution to charity. There would be no occasion for him to wear them in Weissenfels, where they lived simply.

'Best of Fritzes, you were lucky,' said fourteen-year-old Erasmus.

'I am not sure about that,' said Fritz. 'Luck has its rules, if you can understand them, and then it is scarcely luck.'

'Yes, but every evening at dinner, to sit there while these important people amused themselves by giving you too much to drink, to have your glass filled up again and again with fine wines, I don't know what . . . What did they talk about?'

'Nature-philosophy, galvanism, animal magnetism and free-masonry,' said Fritz.

'I don't believe it. You drink wine to forget things like that. And then at night, when the pretty women come creaking on tiptoe up the stairs to find the young innocent, and tap at your door, *TRIUMPH!*'

'There were no women,' Fritz told him. 'I think perhaps my uncle did not invite any.'

'No women!' cried Erasmus. 'Who then did the washing?'

7

The Freiherr and the French Revolution

Were things worse at Weissenfels when a letter from the Big Cross arrived, or when the Mother's elder brother, Captain August von Böltzig, happened to come to the house? Von Böltzig had fought in the same battalion as the Freiherr in the Seven Years' War, but had come to totally different conclusions. The King of Prussia, whom he admired without reservations, had supported total freedom in religious belief, and the Prussian army was notably fearless and morally upright. Must one then not conclude –

'I can see what you have in mind to say next,' said the Freiherr, his voice still just kept in check. 'You mean that you accept my reasoning,' said von Böltzig. 'You admit that there is no connection, or none that can be demonstrated, between religion and right conduct?'

'I accept that you, August von Böltzig, are a very great fool.' The Freifrau felt trapped between the two of them, like a powder of thinly-ground meal between the mill-stones. One of her night fears (she was a poor sleeper) was that her brother and the Uncle Wilhelm might arrive, unannounced, at the same time. What would she be able to do or say, to get decently rid of one of them? Large though the house was, she always found guests a difficulty. The bell rang, you heard the servants crossing the hall, everything was on top of you before you could pray for guidance.

In 1790, by which time the young Fritz had matriculated at the University of Jena, the forces of history itself seemed to take a hand against Auguste. But here her narrowness of mind was an advantage, in that she saw them as no more and no less important than the worn bed-linen, or her brother's godlessness. Like the damp river-breeze, which made the bones ache, the disturbances in France seemed to her no more than a device to infuriate her husband.

Breakfast at Weissenfels was taken in a frugal style. On the dining room stove, at six o'clock in the morning, there were ranks of earthenware coffee-pots, the coffee being partly made, for economy's sake, out of burnt carrot powder. On the table stood large thick cups and saucers and a mountain of white rolls. The family, still in their nightclothes, appeared in ones and twos and, like sleepwalkers, helped themselves from the capacious earthenware pots. Some of the coffee they drank, some they sucked in through pieces broken off from the white rolls. Anyone who had finished turned his or her cup upside-down on the saucer, calling out decisively, '*Satt!*'

As the boys grew older, Auguste did not like them to linger in the dining room. 'What are you speaking of, young men?' Erasmus and Karl stood warming themselves, close to the stove. 'You know that your father does not like . . .'

'He will be quite happy with the Girondins,' said Karl.

'But Karl, these people may perhaps have new ideas. He does not like new ideas.'

In the January of 1793, Fritz arrived from Jena in the middle of the breakfast, in a blue cloth coat with immense brass buttons, patched across the shoulder-blades, and a round hat. 'I will change my clothes, and come and sit with you.'

'Have you brought a newspaper?' Erasmus asked. Fritz looked at his mother, and hesitated. 'I think so.' The Freiherr, on this occasion, was sitting in his place at the head of the table. He said, 'I think you must know whether you have brought a newspaper or not.' Fritz handed him a copy, many times folded, of the *Jenaer Allgemeine Zeitung.* The paper was still cold from the freezing journey, in Fritz's outside pocket, from Jena.

The Freiherr unfolded it and uncreased it, took out his spectacles and in front of his silent family bent his attention on the closely printed front page. At first he said, 'I don't understand what I am reading.'

'The convention have served a writ of accusation on Louis,' said Fritz courageously.

'Yes, I read those words, but they were altogether beyond me. They are going to bring a civil action against the legitimate king of France?'

'Yes, they accuse him of treason.'

'They have gone mad.'

The Freiherr sat for a moment, in monumental stillness, among the coffee-cups. Then he said, 'I shall not touch another newspaper until the French nation returns to its senses again.'

He left the room. '*Satt! Satt! Satt!*' shouted Erasmus, drumming on his saucer. 'The revolution is the ultimate event, no interpretation is possible, what is certain is that a republic is the way forward for all humanity.'

'It is possible to make the world new,' said Fritz, 'or rather to restore it to what it once was, for the golden age was certainly once a reality.'

'And the Bernhard is here, sitting under the table!' cried the Freifrau, openly weeping. 'He will have heard every word, and every word he hears he will repeat.'

'It is not worth listening to, I know it already,' said the Bernhard, emerging from the tablecloth's stiff folds. 'They will cut his head off, you will see.'

'He does not know what he is saying! The king is the father, the nation is his family.'

'When the golden age returns there will be no fathers,' murmured the Bernhard. 'What is he saying?' asked poor Auguste.

She was right, however, in believing that with the French Revolution her troubles would be greatly increased. Her husband had not absolutely forbidden the appearance of newspapers in the house, so that she would be able to say to herself, 'It is only that he wants not to catch sight of them at table, or in his study.' For some other way had to be devised by which he could satisfy his immense curiosity about the escapades of the French which meant – if she was to tell the truth – nothing to her whatsoever. At the Saline offices, she supposed, and at the club – the Literary and Scientific Athenaeum of Weissenfels – he would hear the topics of the day discussed, but she knew, with the insight of long habit, so much more reliable than love, that whatever had happened would not be real to him – that he would not be able to feel he truly possessed it until he had seen it on the grey pages of a daily newspaper. 'Another time, dear Fritz, when you give your greatcoat to the servants to be brushed, you could leave your newspaper showing, just a few inches.'

'Mother, after all these years you don't know my Father. He has said he will not read the paper, and he will not.'

'But Fritz, how will he inform himself? The Brethren won't tell him anything, they don't speak to him of worldly matters.'

'*Weiss Gott!*' said Fritz. 'Osmosis, perhaps.'

8

In Jena

The Freiherr thought it best for his eldest son to be educated in the German manner, at as many universities as possible: Jena for a year, Leipzig for a year, by which time Erasmus would be old enough to join him, then a year at Wittenberg to study law, so that he would be able, if occasion arose, to protect whatever property the family had left through the courts. He was also to begin on theology, and on the constitution of the Electorate of Saxony. Instead of these subjects, Fritz registered for history and philosophy.

As a result he attended on his very first morning in Jena a lecture by Johann Gottlieb Fichte. Fichte was speaking of the philosophy of Kant, which, fortunately, he had been able to improve upon greatly. Kant believed in the external world. Even though it is only known to us through our senses and our own experience, still, it is there. This, Fichte was saying, was nothing but an old man's weakness. We are all free to imagine what the world is like, and since we probably all imagine it differently, there is no reason at all to believe in the fixed reality of things.

Before Fichte's gooseberry eyes the students, who had the worst reputation for unruliness in Germany, cowered, transformed into frightened schoolboys. 'Gentlemen! withdraw into yourselves! Withdraw into your own mind!' Arrogant and drunken in their free time, they waited, submissive. Each unhooked the little penny inkwell on a spike from behind a lapel of his jacket. Some straightened up, some bowed themselves over, closing their eyes. A few trembled with eagerness. 'Gentlemen, let your thought be the wall.' All were intent. 'Have you thought the wall?' asked Fichte. 'Now, then, gentlemen, let your thought be *that* that thought the wall.'

Fichte was the son of a linen-weaver, and in politics a Jacobin. His voice carried without effort. 'The gentleman in the fourth seat from the left at the back, who has the air of being in discomfort . . .'

A wretched youth rose to his feet.

'Herr Professor, that is because the chairs in the lecture-rooms of Jena are made for those with short legs.'

'My appointment as Professor will not be confirmed until next May. You are permitted to ask one question.'

'Why . . . ?'

'Speak up!'

'Why do we imagine that the wall is as we see it, and not as something other?'

Fichte replied, 'We create the world not out of our imagination, but out of our sense of duty. We need the world so that we may have the greatest possible number of opportunities to do our duty. That is what justifies philosophy, and German philosophy in particular.'

Late into the windy lamp-lit autumn night Jena's students met to *fichtisieren*, to talk about Fichte and his system. They appeared to be driving themselves mad. At two o'clock in the morning Fritz suddenly stood still in the middle of the Unterer Markt, letting the others stagger on in ragged groups without him, and said aloud to the stars, 'I see the fault in Fichte's system. There is no place in it for love.'

'You are outside his house,' said a passing student, sitting down on the cobblestones. 'His house is 12a. 12a is where Professor Fichte lives.'

'He is not a Professor until May,' said Fritz. 'We can serenade him until then. We can sing beneath his window, "We know what is wrong with your system . . . There is no place in it, no place in it for love."'

There were lodgings of all sorts in Jena. Some of the very poor students were entitled to eat free, as a kind of scholarship. They chose their eating-house, and could have their dinner only there and only up to a certain amount, a frightening sight, since the inn-keepers hurried them on, in order to clear the tables, and they were obliged to cram and splutter, snatching at the chance, like fiends in hell, of the last permitted morsel. But every one of them, no matter how wretched, belonged to a *Landsmannschaft*, a fellowship of their own region, even if that was only a hometown and numberless acres of potatoes. In the evenings, groups of friends moved from pothouse to smoky pothouse, looking for other friends and then summoning them, in the name of their *Landsmannschaft*, to avenge some insult or discuss a fine point of Nature-philosophy, or to get drunk, or, if already drunk, then drunker.

Fritz could have lived at Schlöben, but it was two hours away. He lodged at first – since she charged him nothing – with his Aunt Johanna Elizabeth. Elizabeth complained that she saw very little of him. 'I had so much looked forward to having a poet at my table. I myself, when I was a young woman, composed verses.' But Fritz, that first winter, had to spend an undue amount of time with his history teacher, the celebrated Professor Schiller. 'Dear Aunt, he is ill, it is his chest, a weakness has set in, all his pupils are taking it in turns to nurse him.'

'Nephew, you haven't the slightest idea how to nurse anyone.'
'He is a very great man.'
'Well, they are the most difficult to nurse.'

The Professor of Medicine and principal doctor to the University, Hofrat Johann Stark, was called in. He was a follower, like most of his colleagues, of the Brownian system. Dr Brown, of Edinburgh, had cured a number of patients by refusing to let blood, and by recommending exercise, sufficient sex, and fresh air. But he held that to be alive was not a natural state, and to prevent immediate collapse the constitution must be held in perpetual balance by a series of stimuli, either jacking it up with alcohol, or damping it down with opium. Schiller, although himself a believer in Brownismus, would take neither, but propped himself up against the bedstead, calling on his students to get paper and ink and take down notes at his dictation: 'To what end does man study universal history?'

It was at this time, when Fritz was emptying the sick room chamberpots, and later, watching the Professor at length put a lean foot to the floor, that he was first described in a letter by the critic Friedrich Schlegel. Schlegel was writing to his much more successful, elder brother, August Wilhelm, a professor of literature and aesthetics. He was in triumph at having discovered someone of interest whom his brother did not know. 'Fate has put into my hands a young man, from whom everything may be expected, and he explained himself to me at once with fire – with indescribably much fire. He is thin and well-made, with a beautiful expression when he gets carried away. He talks three times as much, and as fast, as the rest of us. On the very first evening he told me that the golden age would return, and that there was nothing evil in the world. I don't know if he is still of the same opinion. His name is von Hardenberg.'

9

An Incident in Student Life

'I shall not forget it,' said Fritz, thinking of an early morning in May, towards the end of his year in Jena. His Aunt Johanna had died of pneumonia in the bitter spring winds which Professor Schiller had just survived, and Fritz had lodgings in Schustergasse 4 (second staircase up), which he shared with a distant cousin – but where was this cousin when Fritz woke up, having been dragged out of bed half naked?

'He and some others are in the students' prison,' said the visitor, not a friend, hardly an acquaintance. 'You all went out together yesterday evening –'

'Very good, but in that case why am I not in the Black Hole along with them?'

'You have a better sense of direction than they have, and you were not arrested. But now you must come with me, you're needed.'

Fritz opened his eyes wide. 'You are Diethelm. You are a medical student.'

'No, my name is Dietmahler. Get up, put on your shirt and jacket.'

'I have seen you in Professor Fichte's lectures,' said Fritz, grasping the water-jug. 'And you wrote a song: it begins "In Distant Lands the Maiden . . ."'

'I am fond of music. Come, we have not much time.'

Jena being in a bare hollow, at the foot of a cliff, you can only get out of it by walking steadily uphill. It was still only four o'clock in the morning, but as they tramped up in the direction of Galgenberg they could feel the whole stagnant little town beginning to steam in its early summer heat. The sky was not quite light, but seemed to be thinning and lifting into a cloudless pallor. Fritz had begun to understand. There must have been a quarrel last night, or at least a dispute, about which he remembered nothing. If a duel was to be fought, which in itself was a prison offence, you needed a doctor, or since no respectable doctor could be asked to attend, then a medical student.

'Am I the referee?' Fritz asked.

'Yes.'

The referee in a Jena duel had to decide the impossible. The students' sword, the *Schläger*, was triangular, but rounded towards the point, so that only a deep three-cornered wound was allowed to score.

'Who has challenged who?' he asked.

'Joseph Beck. He sent me a note to say he must fight, who or why he did not say. Only the time and place.'

'I don't know him.'

'Your rooms were the nearest.'

'I am glad he has so true a friend.'

They were now above the mist level, where the dew was beginning to dry, and turned through a gate into a field which had been cleared of young turnips. Two students were hard at it, with flapping shirt-tails, attacking each other without grace or skill on the hardened, broken, yellowish ground.

'They started without us,' said Dietmahler. 'Run!'

As they crossed the field one of the duellists cut and ran for it to a gate in the other direction. His opponent left standing, dropped his *Schläger*, then fell himself, with his right hand masked in blood, perhaps cut off.

'No, only two fingers,' said Dietmahler, urgently bending down to the earth, where weeds and coarse grass were already beginning to sprout. He picked up the fingers, red and wet as if skinned, one of them the top joint only, one with a gold ring.

'Put them in your mouth,' said Dietmahler. 'If they are kept warm I can perhaps sew them back on our return.'

Fritz was not likely to forget the sensation of the one and a half fingers and the heavy ring, smooth and hard while they were yielding, in his mouth.

'All Nature is one,' he told himself.

At the same time (his own common sense told him to do this, without instructions from Dietmahler) he gripped the blubbering and spouting Joseph Beck under the right elbow, to hold up his forearm and keep the veins at the back of the hand empty. Meanwhile the whole sky, from one hilltop horizon to the other, was filled with light, and the larks began to go up. In the next meadow hares had stolen out to feed.

'As long as his thumb is saved, his hand may still be of use to him,' Dietmahler remarked. Fritz, with no way of swallowing his own saliva, mixed with earth and blood, thought, 'This is all of interest to him as a doctor. But, as a philosopher, it doesn't help me.'

They returned to Jena in a woodcutter's cart which was providentially going downhill. Even the woodcutter, who normally paid no attention to anything that did not concern him directly, was impressed by the cries and groans of poor Beck. 'The gentleman is perhaps a singer?'

'Drive straight to the Anatomy Theatre,' Dietmahler told him. 'If it is open, I may be able to find needles and gut.'

An Incident in Student Life

It was too early to buy either schnaps or opium, though Dietmahler, who was also a disciple of Brownismus, was impatient to pour quantities of both down his patient.

IO

A Question of Money

In the Michaelmas of 1791 Fritz began the second stage of his
university education, at Leipzig. He was nineteen, and Leipzig, with fifty thousand inhabitants, was the largest town he
had ever lived in. He found it impossible to manage on the
allowance that could be spared for him.

'I must speak to Father,' he told Erasmus.

'He will be displeased.'

'How many people are pleased when they are asked for
money?'

'What have you done with it, Fritz?'

'Well, I have spent what I had on the necessities of life.
There is the soul, and there is the flesh. But the old one too,
when he was a student, must have had these necessities.'

'That would be before he was awakened,' said Erasmus
gloomily. 'You cannot expect sympathy from him now. Nineteen years should have taught you that much.'

On his next return to Weissenfels, Fritz said: 'Father, I am
young, and, speaking with due respect, I cannot live like an
old man. I have kept myself under extreme restraint in Leipzig,
I have ordered one pair of shoes only since I have been there.
I have grown my hair long to avoid expense at the barber. In
the evening I eat only bread . . .'

36

'In what respects do you find that you cannot live like an old man?' asked the Freiherr.

Fritz shifted his ground.

'Father, there is not a student in Leipzig who does not owe money. I cannot manage on what you allow me at the moment. There are six of us still at home, I know, but we still have estates at Oberwiederstadt, and at Schlöben.'

'Did you think I had forgotten them?' asked the Freiherr.

He passed his hand over his face.

'Go to Oberwiederstadt, and see Steinbrecher. I will give you a letter to him.'

Steinbrecher was the revenue steward.

'But isn't he at Schlöben?'

'He deals now with all our properties. This month he is at Oberwiederstadt.'

Fritz took a place in the diligence, which left the Stag in Weissenfels at four in the morning, and went by way of Halle and Eisleben. The German diligence was the slowest in Europe, since all the luggage, which was loaded onto a kind of creaking extension of the floor extending over the back axle, had to be unloaded and re-loaded every time a passenger got in or out. While the conductor supervised this work the driver fed himself and his horses, on loaves of coarse brown bread.

At the Black Boy at Eisleben a farm servant was sitting on the bench outside, waiting for him.

'*Grüss dich*, Joseph,' said Fritz, remembering him from seven years back. 'Let us go into the grocer's and take a glass of schnaps.' In Saxony the inns were not allowed to sell spirits.

'I should be sorry to see your father's son diverting himself in such a way,' Joseph replied.

'But, Joseph, I was hoping to divert *you*.' This, it was clear, was not possible. The inn provided horses, and in silence they rode to Oberwiederstadt.

The revenue steward was waiting for them, although by now

37

it was dark. Fritz presented his father's letter, and waited for him to read it through twice. Then, feeling the awkwardness of silence, he said, 'Herr Revenue Steward, I think my Father has commissioned you to give me some money.'

Steinbrecher took off his spectacles.

'Young Freiherr, there is no money.'

'He sent me a long way to be told that.'

'I imagine that he wanted you to remember it.'

II

A Disagreement

Fritz walked the thirty-two miles back to Weissenfels. When he reached the Kloster Gasse his father had returned from the offices of the Salt Mines Administration, but he was not alone.

'His Highmindedness, the Uncle Wilhelm, is here,' Sidonie told him. 'The Big Cross himself. They are discussing your affairs. How did you get on with Steinbrecher? I'll tell you what I think, it's this: if some people were not older than others, and young people were as rich as old ones –'

'But, Sidonie, I really believe now that we are much poorer even than we thought.'

'You don't ask me what I believe,' said Sidonie. 'I am here in the house, I have more opportunity to think about it than you do.'

'It depends on all of us now, but on myself in particular –' Fritz began, but the Bernhard, who had made his appearance, interrupted: 'I am the chief sufferer. When the Big Cross is here, my mother brings me forward, believing that I am his favourite. In fact he dislikes children, and myself in particular.'

'He will expect better wine and more company than we usually have,' said Sidonie. 'He mentioned that, you know, the last time he honoured us with a visit.'

'Last time I was called upon to recite,' the Bernhard

The Blue Flower

continued, 'my uncle shouted: "For what reason has he been taught such idiocies?"'

'My mother is not in the salon,' said Sidonie. 'What shall I tell her to do?'

'Nothing,' said Karl, who was lying at ease on the only sofa. His position was unassailable. In a week he was off to begin his military training as a cadet with a regiment of carabiniers in the service of the Elector of Saxony. He was therefore approved of by his Uncle Wilhelm, even though he had never been invited to Lucklum. Fritz appeared not to be listening. Some urgency, some private resolution seemed to possess him. Sidonie had not noticed it when he first walked in, she had perhaps been too pleased to see him, but now it was unmistakable, as though he had brought an embarrassing stranger in with him, who was waiting for the moment of introduction.

In the reception room the Big Cross did not take a chair, but walked rapidly up and down, displaying each time he turned back into the room the dazzling emblem on his dark blue cloak. The Freiherr, tired after a day of disputes at the Inspectorate, sat in his roomy elbow-chair, thinking that if his brother did not take off his outer garment, there was some hope that he would soon go. 'But where is your wife, where is Auguste?' enquired Wilhelm.

'I don't imagine she will appear this afternoon.'

'Why is that ? She need not fear me, I am not a spook.'

'She needs rest, she is delicate.'

'If a woman keeps working, she will find she is never tired.'

'You have never married, Wilhelm. But here, at least, is Friedrich.' Fritz, pale as clay, came into the salon, and after greeting his father and his uncle not quite attentively enough began at full pitch.

'I want to tell you that I have decided what I am to do with my

40

life. It came to me on the journey back from Oberwiederstadt.'

'How fortunate that I am here,' said the Big Cross, 'just when my advice is most needed.'

'During my studies at Jena and now at Leipzig you, Uncle, have taken it amiss because I preferred philosophy and history to law, and you Father, have been offended when I said that even law would be preferable to theology. But now I want both of you to put these anxieties away from you – to blow them away, as if they were dust from the earth. I see now that my duty is to be a soldier. Everything points to it. In that way I shall cost you nothing. And I know now that I need discipline. I have romantic tendencies. In a barracks these will be corrected by the practical, unromantic duties of my daily life – the shit house, the fever ward, the route march, foot inspection. Later, when I see action, I shall have nothing to fear, because life, after all, is a goal, not a means. I have it in mind to apply to the Cuirassiers of the Elector's Guard.'

'*Scheisskerl*, shut your muzzle!' bellowed the Big Cross.

'That is not the way to address my son, or any decent man's son,' said the Freiherr. 'But it's true that he's talking like an idiot.'

'But Karl –' Fritz broke in.

'– is a smart young fellow, anxious to start life on his own account,' the Uncle cried. 'Whereas you! – The Cuirassiers! – I have heard you say at my own table, when you were the age that Karl is now, that life would be better if it were a dream, and that perhaps it will become one. Where is your practical ability? You've never even seen a man wounded!'

Fritz left the room. 'Whatever you have been talking about, you have put things much too strongly,' said Sidonie, coming past with two of the servants carrying coffee and bread and butter, which the Uncle, in disgust, waved away from a distance.

'At least they are agreed,' said Fritz. 'They are at one in thinking me incapable, and possibly a coward.'

Sidonie pressed his elbow in sympathy. But through the open doors of the salon the Uncle and the Father could be seen to turn towards each other in furious confrontation.

'Leave your son's concerns to me. You know absolutely nothing of these matters.'

'You forget that I served seven years in the Hanoverian Legion,' cried the Freiherr.

'But without acquiring the slightest military competence.'

Karl and Sidonie took the dejected Fritz into the garden, and down to the orchard. 'We're going to have pears and plums innumerable this year,' said Sidonie. 'Wherever did you get such a stupid idea? Why should you think you would ever make a soldier?'

'Where is your sense?' added Karl.

'I don't know. Tell me, Karl, what makes a man a soldier?'

'I, myself, wanted to enter the service of my Prince. I also wanted to get away from home,' said Karl.

'Won't you miss us, Karl?' asked Sidonie.

'I cannot afford to think about that sort of thing. I am of more use to you all, in any case, out in the world. And you, Sido, will soon be married, and forget about your brothers.'

'Never!' cried Sidonie.

The Sense of Immortality

Once he had got rid of the Uncle and his travelling entourage of body-servants and cooks, who had been infesting the kitchen quarters, Freiherr von Hardenberg summoned his eldest son and told him that after his year at Leipzig and a further year at Wittenberg to study chemistry, geology and law he would be ready to take his first steps as a trainee clerk in the Directorate of Salt Mines. Erasmus would be sent from Leipzig to Hubertusberg, where he would enrol in the School of Forestry, a wholesome, open-air life for which so far he had shown no inclination whatsoever. Karl had already seen action, at the age of sixteen. He had been with his regiment when the French were driven out of Mainz. He expected to come home frequently. It was not at all difficult to get army leave. Officers on leave were not paid, so that until they reported back, the regiment was able to save money.

If Fritz sometimes took the diligence, or walked long distances, it was because he rarely had a decent horse to ride. If ever he managed to hire or borrow one, he noted it down in his diary. His own horse, known only as the Gaul (the Crock), he could remember at Oberwiederstadt, although he had been too young to ride him until they moved to Weissenfels. How old was the

Gaul? Age had brought him cunning, rather than wisdom, and he had arrived with his master at an elaborate creaturely bargain as to place and time – when he might slow down, when he might stop, when consent to go on. Fritz did not disturb himself about his own appearance, or about the shabbiness of his horse, as long as they could get from one point to another.

From the age of seventeen he had been in almost perpetual motion, or the Gaul's unhurried version of it, back and forth, though not over a wide area. His life was lived in the 'golden hollow' in the Holy Roman Empire, bounded by the Harz Mountains and the deep forest, crossed by rivers – the Saale, the Unstrut, the Helme, the Elster, the Wipper – proceeding in gracious though seemingly quite unnecessary bends and sweeps past mine-workings, salt-houses, timber-mills, waterside inns where the customers sat placidly hour after hour, waiting for the fish to be caught from the river and broiled. Scores of miles of rolling country, uncomplainingly bringing forth potatoes and turnips and the great whiteheart pickling cabbages which had to be sliced with a saw, lay between hometown and hometown, each with its own-ness, but also its welcome likeness to the last one. The hometowns were reassuring to the traveller, who fixed his sights from a distance on the wooden roof of the old church, the cupola of the new one, and came at length to the streets of small houses drawn up in order, each with its pig sty, its prune oven and bread oven and sometimes its wooden garden-house, where the master, in the cool of the evening, sat smoking in total blankness of mind, under a carved motto: ALL HAPPINESS IS HERE or CONTENTMENT IS WEALTH. Sometimes, though not often, a woman, also, found time to sit in the garden-house.

When Fritz rode back southwards from Wittenberg at the end of his year's studies, it was a day in a thousand, crystal-clear, heavenly blue. They were just beginning the potato-lifting, with which he had so often helped, willingly enough, as a child with the Brethren at Neudietendorf.

Between Rippach and Lützen he stopped where a stream crossed the road, to let the Gaul have a drink, although the horse usually had to wait for this until the end of the day. As Fritz loosened the girths, the Gaul breathed in enormously, as though he had scarcely known until that moment what air was. Fritz's valise, tied to the crupper, rose and fell with a sound like a drum on his broad quarters. Then, deflating little by little, he lowered his head to the water to find the warmest and muddiest part, sank his jaws to a line just below the nostrils, and began to drink with an alarming energy which he had never displayed on the journey from Wittenberg.

Fritz sat by the empty roadside, on the damp Saxon earth which he loved, and with nothing in view except a convoy of potato-wagons and the line of alders which marked the course of the Elster. His education was now almost at an end. What had he learned? Fichtean philosophy, geology, chemistry, combinatorial mathematics, Saxon commercial law. One of his greatest friends in Jena, the physicist Johann Wilhelm Ritter, had tried to show him that the ultimate explanation of life was galvanism, and that every exchange of energy between the mind and the body must be accompanied by an electric charge. Electricity was sometimes visible as light, but not all light was visible, indeed most of it was not. 'We must never judge by what we see.' Ritter was almost penniless. He had never attended a university, never in fact been to school. A glass of wine was immeasurable encouragement to him. After that, lying in his wretched lodgings, he could see the laws of electricity written in cloudy hieroglyphs on the whole surface of the universe, and on the face of the waters, where the Holy Spirit still moved.

— My teachers did not agree with each other, my friends did not agree with my teachers, Fritz thought, but that is only on a superficial level, they were men of intellect and passion, let me believe in them all.

The children of large families hardly ever learn to talk to themselves aloud, that is one of the arts of solitude, but they often keep diaries. Fritz took out his pocket journal. Certain words came readily to him — *weaknesses, faults, urges, striving for fame, striving against the crushing, wretched, bourgeois conditions of everyday life, youth, despair.* Then he wrote, 'But I have, I can't deny it, a certain inexpressible sense of immortality.'

13

The Just Family

'You have heard me speak of Kreisamtmann Coelestin Just of Tennstedt,' said the Freiherr. Fritz thought that he had. 'He is of course the local presiding magistrate, but also, which is not always the case, supervisor of the tax collection for his district. I have arranged for you to study with him at Tennstedt in order to learn administration and practical office management, of which you know nothing.' Fritz asked if he should take lodgings. 'No, you will lodge with the Justs themselves. The Kreisamtmann has a niece, Karoline, a very steady young woman who keeps house for him, and in addition he has married, at the age of forty-six, the widow of Christian Nürnberger, the late Professor of Anatomy and Botany at Wittenberg. Very likely you may have met her there, during the past year.'

In the University towns it might be different, but no woman in Weissenfels, Tennstedt, Grüningen or Langensalza tried to look younger than they were or knew of any way of doing so. They accepted what the years sent.

Karoline Just saw, when she looked in her glass, the face of a woman of twenty-seven, uniformly smooth and pale, with noticeably dark eyebrows. She had been housekeeping for her

Uncle Coelestin Just at his house in Tennstedt for four years. It had not been thought that her uncle would ever marry, but only six months ago he had done so. 'My dear, you will be glad for me and for yourself,' he had said. 'If at any time now the question arises of your making a home of your own, you will be able to be sure that you are not deserting me.'

'The question has not arisen,' said Karoline.

That Karoline had nowhere else to go, except back to Merseburg (where her father was Pronotary of the Cathedral Seminary) did not strike Just as a difficulty. In either place she was truly welcome. Meanwhile he congratulated himself that his Rahel was not only that most eligible of German women, a Professor's widow, but also, at thirty-nine, most likely past the age of child-bearing. The three of them could live peaceably together without unwelcome change or disturbance.

In Tennstedt they said — Now he has two women under one roof. Well, there's a proverb . . . Who, then, is going to give the orders and spend the Kreisamtmann's money? — About the expected lodger — expected because the servants were talking about him, and because an extra bedstead had been purchased — they knew that he was said to be twenty-two years of age.

At the Universities the professors often arranged for their daughters to marry their likeliest pupil. Everywhere master carpenters, printers and bakers were satisfied when a daughter, or a niece, married one of their apprentices. The Kreisamtmann was neither a professor nor a skilled craftsman, he was a magistrate and an area tax-inspector, and such an arrangement might never have occurred to him, but now that he was a married man, they said, he had someone else to do the thinking for him.

Fritz arrived on foot, a day after he was expected, and at a time when Coelestin Just was at his office. 'The Long-Expected is here,' said Rahel to Karoline. She herself remembered him very well from Wittenberg, but was distressed to see him so dishevelled. 'You find the exercise healthy, Hardenberg?' she asked anxiously as she brought him into the house. Fritz looked at her vaguely, but with a radiant smile. 'I don't know, Frau Rahel. I hadn't thought about it, but I will think about it.' Once in the parlour, he looked round him as though at a revelation. 'It is beautiful, beautiful.'

'It's not beautiful at all,' said Rahel. 'You are more than welcome here, I hope that you will learn a great deal and you are free, of course, to form whatever opinions you like, but this parlour is not beautiful.'

Fritz continued to gaze around him.

'This is my niece by marriage, Karoline Just.'

Karoline was wearing her shawl and housekeeping apron.

'You are beautiful, gracious Fräulein,' said Fritz.

'We expected you yesterday,' said Rahel, dryly, 'but you see, we are patient people.' When Karoline had gone out, as she very soon did, to the kitchen, she added, 'I am going to take the privilege of someone who met you so often when you were a student, and welcomed you, you remember, to our Shakespeare evenings, and tell you that you ought not to speak to Karoline quite like that. You did not mean it, and she is not used to it.'

'But I did mean it,' said Fritz. 'When I came into your home, everything, the wine-decanter, the tea, the sugar, the chairs, the dark green tablecloth with its abundant fringe, everything was illuminated.'

'They are as usual. I did not buy this furniture myself, but –'

Fritz tried to explain that he had seen not their everyday, but their spiritual selves. He could not tell when these transfigurations would come to him. When the moment came it was as the whole world would be when body at last became subservient to soul.

Rahel saw that, whatever else, young Hardenberg was serious. She allowed herself to wonder whether he was obliged, on medical advice, to take much opium? For toothache, of course, everyone had to take it, she did not mean that. But she soon found out that he took at most thirty drops at bedtime as a sedative, if his mind was too active – only half the dose, in fact, that she took herself for a woman's usual aches and pains.

14

Fritz at Tennstedt

Fritz's luggage arrived a day later on the diligence. It consisted largely of books. Here were the hundred and thirty-three necessary titles, the earlier ones mostly poetry, plays and folktales, later on the study of plants, minerals, medicine, anatomy, theories of heat, sound and electricity, Mathematics, the Analysis of Infinite Numbers. They are all one, said Fritz aloud, warming his hands over a candle in his cold attic bedroom at Tennstedt. All human knowledge is one. Mathematics is the linking principle, just as Ritter told me that electricity is the link between body and mind. Mathematics is human reason itself in a form everyone can recognise. Why should poetry, reason and religion not be higher forms of Mathematics? All that is needed is a grammar of their common language. And if all knowledge was to be expressed through symbols, then he must set to work to write down every possible way the operation could be performed.

'*Triumph!*' exclaimed Fritz in his icy room (but he had never in his life – nor had anyone he knew – worked or slept in a room that was not exceedingly cold).

His second load of books began with Franz Ludwig Cancrinus' *Foundations of Mining and Saltworks*, Volume 1. Part 1: In What Mineralogy Consists. Part 2: In What the Art

of Experiment Consists. Part 3: In What the Specification of
Aboveground Earth Consists. Part 4: In What the Specification
of Belowground Earth Consists. Part 5: In What the Art of
Mine Construction Consists. Part 6: In What Arithmetic,
Geometry and Ordinary Trigonometry Consists. Part 7,
Section 1: In What Mechanics, Hydrostatics, Aerometrics and
Hydraulics Consists, Section 2: In What the Construction of
Mountain Machinery Consists. Part 8, Section 1: In What the
Smelting and Precipitation of Metals from Ore Consists,
Section 2: In What the Smelting of Half-metals Consists, Sec-
tion 3: In What the Preparation of Sulphur Consists. Part 9,
Section 1: In What the Examination of Salt and the Geological
Description of Salt-Bearing Mountains Consists, Section 2: In
What the Art of Salt-Boiling and the Construction of New
Saltworks Consists. Volume 2, What is Understood by Mining
and Salt Law.

The servants reported to Rahel that the young Freiherr was
talking aloud to himself in his room. 'He goes up there immediately after breakfast,' Rahel told her husband, 'and you have
seen that he also studies after dinner.' Just asked Karoline
whether they could not have a little music one evening, as a
relaxation. 'You must take pity', he suggested, 'on the unfortunate young man.'

'I know nothing about his trouble,' said Karoline. She found
herself very busy with the work of the forewinter – sausage-
making, beating flax for the winter spinning, killing the
geese (who had already been plucked alive twice) for their
third and last crop of down. After this it was necessary to eat
baked goose for a week. But she took her place that evening
in the parlour when Fritz, appealed to by Rahel, came downstairs, carrying a book – he had been persuaded to read
aloud to them – or no, it was not a book, but a folder of
manuscripts.

'You must not think that this was written to anyone in particular. I was at Jena. I was younger than I am now.

Accept my book, accept my little rhymes,
Care for them if you can and let them go
Do you want more? My heart, perhaps, my life?
Those you had long ago.'

He looked up – 'That would be very suitable to copy out in a young lady's album,' said Rahel. 'I'm afraid however we don't have anything of the sort in the house.'

Fritz tore the sheet of paper in half. Karoline put down the pillow-case she was mending. 'Please read more, read on.' Her Uncle Coelestin looked quietly at the glow from the stove, whose doors were slightly ajar. He had been told that young Hardenberg was a poet, but had only just realised that he intended to read his verses aloud. He could not pretend to be a judge of them. Singing was a different matter. Like everyone else he knew, Just sang himself, belonged to two singing clubs, and listened to singing indoors in winter and in summer in the open air, the woods, the mountains and the streets. Yes, and a friend of Karoline's, a high soprano, had possessed such a beautiful voice that at her wedding dinner, when all the notables of Tennstedt were present, Coelestin himself had been cajoled into appearing as an old bird-seller, with an armful of empty cages painted to represent gold, and into singing a comical country song, imploring the bridegroom 'not to take away their nightingale'. Yes, that was Else Wangel, only three years ago, three years since her wedding, and she was broad enough nowadays to fill a doorway.

Karoline was speaking to him reproachfully. 'Why are you talking of Else Wangel?'

'My dear, I did not know I was speaking aloud. All of you must pardon an old man.'

Just was forty-six. The melancholy of approaching mortality had been one of his reasons, first, for sending for his niece, then, in good time, for his marriage.

'Uncle, you have not been listening, you understood nothing.'

15

Justen

Karoline was in charge (Rahel having divided up the responsibilities with watchful tact) of the household accounts, which included collecting Fritz's weekly payment for board and lodging, also for stabling the Gaul, who had arrived from Weissenfels. On the very first Saturday, however, there was confusion. 'Fräulein Karoline, my father's cashier is due at Tennstedt to bring me my allowance from now until the end of November, but he has perhaps made a mistake and gone straight to Oberwiederstadt. I shall have to ask you I am afraid to wait for what is owing.'

'I don't think we can wait,' Karoline told him, 'but I will make it up, for the time being, from the housekeeping.' She had changed colour – which she scarcely ever did – at the idea of his embarrassment. 'How will he manage?' she asked Rahel. Rahel said, 'I dare say that in spite of attending three universities he has not been taught how to manage. He is the eldest son, and has not been protected from himself.'

Although the cashier arrived the next day, Karoline felt as if she had made some kind of a stand, but in reality she had no defences against Hardenberg, because, from the evening of the poetry-reading onwards he asked so much from her. He gave her his entire confidence, he laid the weight of it upon her. She was his friend — Karoline did not contradict this — and although he could live without love, he told her, he could not live without friendship. All was confessed, he talked perpetually. Neither the sewing not the forewinter sausage-chopping deterred him. As she chopped, Karoline learned that the world is tending day by day not towards destruction, but towards infinity. She was told where Fichte's philosophy fell short, and that Hardenberg had a demon of a little brother of whom he was fond, and a monstrous uncle who disputed with his father, but then, so did they all.

'Your mother also?'

'No, no.'

'I am sorry you are not happy at home,' said Karoline.

Fritz was startled. 'I have given you the wrong idea, there is love in our home, we would give our lives for each other.'

His mother was young enough too, he added, to bear more children; it was his absolute duty to start earning as soon as possible. Then he returned to the subject of Fichte, fetching his lecture notes to show to Karoline — page after page of triadic patterns. 'Yes, these are some of Fichte's triads, but I will tell you what has suddenly struck me since I came to Tennstedt. You might look at them as representing the two of us. You are the thesis, tranquil, pale, finite, self-contained. I am the antithesis, uneasy, contradictory, passionate, reaching out beyond myself. Now we must question whether the synthesis will be harmony between us or whether it will lead to a new impossibility which we have never dreamed of.'

Karoline replied that she did not dream very much.

About Dr Brown, whom he spoke of next, she did know something, but she had not realised that Brownismus was an improvement on all previous medical systems, or that Dr Brown himself had lectured with a glass of whisky and a glass of laudanum in front of him, sipping from each in turn, to demonstrate the perfect balance. She did not even know what whisky was.

Fritz also told her that women are children of nature, so that nature, in a sense, is their art. 'Karoline, you must read *Wilhelm Meister*.'

'Of course I have read *Wilhelm Meister*,' she said.

Fritz was disconcerted for a few seconds, so that she had time to add, 'I found Mignon very irritating.'

'She is only a child,' cried Fritz, 'a spirit, or a spirit-seer, more than a child. She dies because the world is not holy enough to contain her.'

'She dies because Goethe couldn't think what to do with her next. If he had made her marry Wilhelm Meister, that would have served both of them right.'

'You are very severe in your judgments,' said Fritz. He sat down to write a few verses on the subject. Karoline, with the kitchen-maid, was putting lengths of string through dried rings of apple. 'But Hardenberg, you have written about my eyebrows!'

> *Karoline Just has dark eyebrows*
> *And from the movements of her eyebrows*
> *I can gather good advice.*

'I shall give you a pet-name,' he said. 'You haven't got one?' Most Carolines and Karolines (and it was the commonest name in North Germany) were called Line, Lili, Lollie or Karolinchen. She shook her head. 'No, I have never had one.'

'I shall call you Justen,' he said.

16

The Jena Circle

Tennstedt had the advantage, from Just's point of view, of being over fifty miles from Jena. Young Hardenberg still had many friendships there, but, in Just's opinion, would be better off without them. For example, the physicist Johann Wilhelm Ritter — if that was what he was — should probably be committed, for his own good, to an asylum. But Ritter was an innocent. What struck Just in particular was the behaviour of the Jena women. Friedrich Schlegel, one of Hardenberg's earliest friends, was a great admirer of his brother August's wife, Caroline. This same wife had been the lover of George Forster, the librarian. Forster's wife Thérèse had left him for a journalist, complaining that when their baby died of smallpox, Forster had not consoled her but had simply 'taken strenuous steps to replace it'. Again, Friedrich Schlegel lived with a woman ten years older than himself. She was Dorothea, daughter of the philosopher Moses Mendelssohn, a kind and motherly woman, apparently, but she had a husband already, a banker, whose name Just couldn't remember. Whoever he was, he was well out of it.

They were all intelligent, all revolutionaries, but since each of them had a different plan, none of it would come to anything. They talked continually of going to Prussia, to Berlin, but they stayed in Jena. As Just saw it, this was because Jena was so much cheaper.

To the Jena circle Fritz was a kind of phenomenon, a country boy, perhaps still growing, capable in his enthusiasm of breaking things, tall and awkward. Friedrich Schlegel stuck to it that he was a genius. 'You must see him,' they told their acquaintances. 'Whatever you read of Hardenberg's you won't understand him nearly as well as if you take tea with him once.'

'When you write to him,' said the wild Caroline Schlegel to her sister-in-law Dorothea, 'tell him to come at once, and we will all *fichtisieren* and symphilosophise and *sympoetisieren* until the dawn breaks.'

'Yes,' said Dorothea, 'we must have the whole congregation together again in my front sitting room. I shall not be content until I see this. But in any case, why is our Hardenberg dragging round like a clerk under the orders of some tedious Kreisamtmann?'

'Oh, but the Kreisamtmann has a niece,' said Caroline.

'How old is she?' asked Dorothea.

17

What is the Meaning?

Now that the Gaul was in the Justs' stable, Fritz would be able to accompany the Kreisamtmann on circuit. There he was to act as his legal clerk, and to pick up business methods, as his father had specified, as he went.

In spite of his sober clothes, bought at second hand, Fritz did not look quite right, not quite like a clerk of any kind, and the Gaul also struck a jarring note. But the Kreisamtmann, from the moment he first saw Fritz, had taken him to his heart. The only precaution he thought necessary before they set out together on official business was to ask him whether he still felt as Just understood he once had about the sequence of events in France?

'The Revolution in France has not produced the effects once hoped for,' was how he put it to Fritz. 'It has not resulted in a golden age.'

'No, they've made a butcher's shop of it, I grant you that,' said Fritz. 'But the spirit of the Revolution, as we first heard of it, as it first came to us, could be preserved here in Germany. It could be transferred to the world of the imagination, and administered by poets.'

'It seems to me,' said Just, 'that as soon as you are settled into your profession, you would be well advised to take up politics.'

'Politics are the last thing that we need. This at least I learned with the Brethren at Neudietendorf. The state should be one family, bound by love.'

'That does not sound much like Prussia,' said the Kreis-amtmann.

To the Freiherr von Hardenberg he wrote that the whole relationship between himself and the son who had been entrusted to him was extremely successful. Friedrich was show-ing much application. Who would have guessed that he, the poet, would spare no pains to turn himself into a businessman, to do the same piece of work two or three times over, to go over the resemblances and differences in the words of newspaper articles about business matters so as to be sure he had judged them correctly, and all this as diligently as he read his poetry, science and philosophy. 'Of course, your son learns very quickly, twice as fast as other earthly mortals.'

'It is a curious thing that although I am supposed to be instructing him,' Just's letter went on, 'and *am* instructing him, he is teaching *me* even more, matters to which I never paid attention before, and in the process I am losing the narrow-mindedness of an old man. He has advised me to read *Robinson Crusoe* and *Wilhelm Meister*. I told him that up till this time I had never felt the least temptation to read a work of fiction.'

'What are these matters,' the Freiherr wrote back to him, 'to which you never paid attention before? Be good enough to give me one example.' Just replied that Fritz Hardenberg had spoken to him of a fable, which he had found, so far as Just could remember, in the works of the Dutch philosopher Franz Hemsterhuis — it had been about the problem of universal language, a time when plants, stars and stones talked on equal terms with animals and with man. For example, the sun com-municates with the stone as it warms it. Once we knew the words of this language, and we shall do so again, since history always repeats itself. '– I told him, that is of course always a possibility, if God disposes.'

The Freiherr replied that his son would not need a different language from German to conduct his duties as a future salt mine inspector.

Since winter often left the roads impassable, Coelestin Just and his probationary clerk did as much of their travelling as possible before the end of the forewinter. 'But there is something else which I have written and which I want to read to you while I still have time,' Fritz told Karoline. 'It will not truly exist until you have heard it.'

'Is it then poetry?'

'It is poetry, but not verse.'

'Then it is a story?' asked Karoline, who dreaded the reappearance of Fichte's triads.

'It is the beginning of a story.'

'Well, we will wait until my Aunt Rahel comes back from the evening service.'

'No, it is for you only,' said Fritz.

'His father and mother were already in bed and asleep, the clock on the wall ticked with a monotonous beat, the wind whistled outside the rattling window-pane. From time to time the room grew brighter when the moonlight shone in. The young man lay restlessly on his bed and remembered the stranger and his stories. "It was not the thought of the treasure which stirred up such unspeakable longings in me," he said to himself. "I have no craving to be rich, but I long to see the blue flower. It lies incessantly at my heart, and I can imagine and think about nothing else. Never did I feel like this before. It is as if until now I had been dreaming, or as if sleep had carried me into another world. For in the world I used to live in, who would have troubled himself about flowers? Such a wild passion for a flower was never heard of there. But where could this stranger have come from? None of us had ever seen such a man before. And yet I don't know how it was that I alone was truly caught and held by what he told us. Everyone else heard what I did, and yet none of them paid him serious attention."'

'Have you read this to anyone else, Hardenberg?'

'Never to anyone else. How could I? It is only just written, but what does that matter?'

He added, 'What is the meaning of the blue flower?'

Karoline saw that he was not going to answer this himself. She said, 'The young man has to go away from his home to find it. He only wants to see it, he does not want to possess it. It cannot be poetry, he knows what that is already. It can't be happiness, he wouldn't need a stranger to tell him what that is, and as far as I can see he is already happy in his home.'

The unlooked-for privilege of the reading was fading and Karoline, still outwardly as calm as she was pale, felt chilled with anxiety. She would rather cut off one of her hands than disappoint him, as he sat looking at her, trusting and intent, with his large light-brown eyes, impatient for a sign of comprehension.

What distressed her most was that after waiting a little, he showed not a hint of resentment or even surprise, but gently shut the notebook. *'Liebe Justen*, it doesn't matter.'

18

The Rockenthiens

In November, the Kreisamtmann took Fritz on a series of expeditions to local tax offices, whose drowsing inhabitants were brought to reluctant life by their young visitor, on fire to learn everything as rapidly as possible. 'The management of an office is not so difficult,' Just told him. 'It is largely a matter of knowing firstly, what is coming in, secondly, what is not yet attended to, thirdly, what has been dealt with and is ready to go out, and fourthly, what has in fact gone out. Everything must be at one of these four stages, and there will then be no excuse of any document being mislaid. For every transaction there must be a record, and of that record you must be able to lay your hand immediately on a written copy. The civilized world could not exist without its multitude of copying clerks, and they in turn could not exist if civilization did not involve so many pieces of paper.'

'I do not think I could endure life as a copying clerk,' said Fritz. 'Such occupations should not exist.'

'A revolution would not remove them,' said Coelestin Just, 'you will find that there were copy clerks at the foot of the guillotine.'

As they plodded on together, drops of moisture gathered and slowly fell from their hat-brims, the ends of their noses and the hairy tips of the horses' ears which the animals turned backwards as a kind of protest against the weather. Earth and air were often indistinguishable in the autumn mist, and morning seemed to pass into afternoon without a discernible mid-day. By three o'clock the lamps were already lit in the windows.

It was one of the year's thirteen public holidays, when in Saxony and Thuringia even bread was not baked, but at Greussen Just had asked the local head tax-clerk to keep the office open for an hour or so in the morning. Fritz was explaining how, with the help of chemistry, the copying of documents might perhaps be done automatically. Just sighed.

'Don't suggest any improvements here.'

'The office managers, perhaps, don't welcome our visits,' said Fritz, to whom this idea occurred for the first time, for they were still a strange species to him.

After Greussen, Grüningen, where Just told his young probationary clerk they would take, 'if it is offered', a little refreshment. They turned out of the town up a long drive, bordered with shivering trees and sodden pastures where the autumn grass-burning was still smouldering, sending thin fragrant columns of smoke up to the sky.

'This is the Manor House of Grüningen. We are calling on Herr Kapitän Rockenthien.'

It was a very large house, quite recently built, plastered with yellow stucco.

'Who is the Kapitän Rockenthien?'

'Someone who keeps his doors open,' said the Kreisamtmann.

Fritz looked ahead and saw that the gate into the coach-yard under the high yellow stone arch, and the great entrance doors on the south side of the house, were in fact standing open. From every tall window the lights shone extravagantly. Perhaps they were expected at Schloss Rockenthien. Fritz never discovered whether that had been so or not.

Two men came out to take their horses, and they went up the three front steps.

'If Rockenthien is at home you will hear him laugh,' said Just, seeming to brace himself up a little, and at that moment, shouting to the servants not to bother, Rockenthien appeared, holding out his broad arms to them, and laughing.

'Coelestin Just, my oldest friend, my best friend.'

'I'm nothing of the sort,' said Just.

'But why did you not bring your niece, the estimable Karoline?'

'I have brought with me this young man, who I am training in business management. Herr Johann Rudolf von Rocken-thien, formerly Captain in the army of his Highness Prince Schwarzburg-Sondeshausen, may I present Freiherr Georg Philipp Friedrich von Hardenberg.'

'My youngest friend!' roared von Rockenthien. The good cloth of his jacket strained and creaked as he held out his arms once again. 'You will not be out of place here, I assure you.' His remarks were not quite drowned by the pack of large dogs which had stationed itself in the hall in case something edible was dropped by the goers-in or -out.

'*Platz!*' shouted their master.

Now they were in the *Saal*, which was heated by two great fireplaces, burning spruce and pine. The large number of chairs and tables gave the room the air of a knockdown furniture sale. Who were all these people, all these children? Rockenthien himself scarcely seemed to know, but, as a great joke – like everything else he had said so far – began counting on his fingers. 'My own little ones – Jette, Rudi, Mimi –'

'He will not remember their ages,' called out a peaceful looking blonde woman, not young, lying on a sofa.

'Well, their ages, that is your business, rather than mine. This is my dear wife, Wilhelmine. And here are some, but not all of my stepchildren – George von Kühn, Hans von Kühn, and our Sophie must also be somewhere.'

Fritz looked round about him from one to another, and

bowed to the Frau von Rockenthien, who smiled but did not get up, while her husband jovially continued, introducing a French governess, said to have forgotten how to speak the language herself, and a number of callers – our physician, Dr Johann Langermann 'who, unfortunately for himself, can never find anything wrong with us', Herr Regierungsrat Hermann Müller, his wife Frau Regierungsrat Müller, two local attorneys, an instructor from the Luther Gymnasium – all these last, as was clear enough, putting in an hour at the Schloss without any definite invitation. There was, probably, nowhere else much to go in Grüningen.

Young George, who had dashed out of the room as soon as the new visitors were announced, now came back and tugged at the sleeve of Fritz's jacket.

'Heigh-ho, Freiherr von Hardenberg, I've been out to the stable to have a look at your horse. He's no good. Why don't you buy another one?'

Fritz did not heed either George or the company, who like the incoming tide on a shallow beach parted and re-formed behind the interesting newcomer with the object of cutting him off and trying out what he was made of. But he remained fixed, gazing intently down the room.

'His so good manners, where have they gone?' thought Coelestin, who was talking to the Regierungsrat.

At the back of the room, a very young dark-haired girl stood by the window, tapping idly on the glass as though she was trying to attract the attention of someone outside.

'Sophie, why has no-one put up your hair?' called Frau von Rockenthien from her sofa, in an undemanding, indeed soothing tone. 'And why are you looking out of the window?'

'I'm willing it to snow, mother. Then we could all amuse ourselves.'

'Let time stand still until she turns round,' said Fritz, aloud.

67

'If the soldiers came past, we could throw snow at them,' said Sophie.

'Söphgen, you are twelve years old, and at your age – you don't seem to notice, either, that we have guests,' her mother said.

At this she did turn round, as though caught by a gust, as children do in the wind. 'I'm sorry, I'm sorry.'

19

A Quarter of an Hour

Herr Rockenthien never had quite the air of one to whom the big house at Grüningen – or indeed any house – belonged. At forty, he was large and loose, with impulses as benevolent and ill-directed as a badger-hound's as he trundled through Schloss Grüningen's long corridors.

In point of fact the place had been built fifty years earlier by the father of his wife's first husband, Johann von Kühn. Rockenthien, therefore, had only come into it in 1787, when he married. But he was not the kind of man whose behaviour would be affected by coming into property, or indeed by losing it, and he was not intimidated by finding himself responsible for a large number of other lives.

The district tax office had been established in a relatively small front room to the left of the main entrance. There Rockenthien, in principle, as inheritor of the *Rittergut*, presided, but, though far from a weak man, he was too restless to preside for long over anything. Coelestin Just, with a clerk, rapidly got through the business.

Fritz told Just: 'Something happened to me.'

Just replied that whatever it was, it must happen later, since his job, indeed his duty, was to come to the front office, where in former days the tenants of Schloss Grüningen had brought

69

in their corn, their firewood and their geese, and now wrestled over their payments in compensation for the field work they no longer did for the Elector of Saxony.

'We have arrived in good time, Hardenberg, but should start at once. It will take us certainly all this morning, then we may expect a good dinner, have no fear of that, then the *Nachtisch*, when we may all talk and express ourselves freely, and the after-dinner sleep, and we may expect to be at work again from four until six.'

'Something has happened to me,' Fritz repeated.

Fritz wrote immediately to Erasmus at the School of Forestry at Hubertusberg, sending the letter by mail coach. Erasmus replied: 'I was at first amazed when I received your letter, but since they have done away with Robespierre in Paris I have become so used to extraordinary happenings that I soon recovered.

'You tell me, that a quarter of an hour decided you. How can you understand a Maiden in a quarter of an hour? If you had said, a quarter of a year, I should have admired your insight into the heart of a woman, but a quarter of an hour, just think of it!

'You are young and fiery, the Maiden is only fourteen and also fiery. You are both sensual human beings and now a tender hour comes and you kiss one another for all you're worth, and when that's over you think, well, this was a Maiden, like other Maidens! But let's suppose you get over all the obstacles, you get married. Then you can indulge as you never could before. But satisfaction makes for weariness, and you end up with that you've always so much dreaded, boredom.'

Fritz was obliged to admit to his brother, from whom he had never had any concealments, that Sophie was not fourteen, but only twelve, and that he hadn't had a tender hour, only the quarter of an hour he had mentioned, surrounded by other people, standing at the great windows of the *Saal* at Schloss Grüningen.

'I am Fritz von Hardenberg,' he had said to her. 'You are Fräulein Sophie von Kühn. You are twelve years of age, I heard your gracious mother say so.'

Sophie put her hands to her hair. 'Up, it should be up.'

'In four years time you will have to consider what man would be fortunate enough to hope to be your husband. Don't tell me that he would have to ask your stepfather! What do you say yourself?'

'In four years time I don't know what I shall be.'

'You mean, you don't know what you will become.'

'I don't want to become.'

'Perhaps you are right.'

'I want to be, and not to have to think about it.'

'But you must not remain a child.'

'I am not a child now.'

'Sophie, I am a poet, but in four years I shall be an administrative official, receiving a salary. That is the time when we shall be married.'

'I don't know you!'

'You have seen me. I am what you see.'

Sophie laughed.

'Do you always laugh at your guests?'

'No, but at Grüningen we don't talk like this.'

'But would you be content to live with me?'

Sophie hesitated, and then said:

'Truly, I like you.'

Erasmus was not reassured. 'Who can guarantee', he wrote, 'that if she is unspoiled now, she will stay unspoiled when she comes out into the world? A commonplace, you will tell me, but commonplaces aren't always wrong. And how can you tell, since you say that she is so beautiful and is sure to be courted by many others, that she won't be untrue to you? Girls act on instinct at thirteen (he still could not quite believe she was any younger), although at twenty-three they are cleverer than we are. Remember what you have said to me so often on this subject – yes, even two months ago, in Weissenfels. Have you forgotten so soon?'

Erasmus went on to say that what had hurt him above all in Fritz's letter was his 'coldly determined manner'. But if he was determined to go ahead, then he could rely on Erasmus for help – his love for his brother was unchanging, its only limit was death. The Father was sure to prove difficult, 'but then we have discussed so often the place of a father in the scheme of things.'

'By the way,' he added, 'what has happened to your friendship with Karoline Just? Fare well! Your true friend and brother, Erasmus.'

20

The Nature of Desire

Fritz asked whether he might spend Christmas at Tennstedt. 'That I am quite sure you can, if your own family will not be disappointed,' said Karoline. 'My uncle and aunt will make you heartily welcome, and we shall of course be killing the pig.'

'Justen, something has happened to me.'

He was ill, she had always feared it. 'Tell me what is wrong.'

'Justen, people might say that we haven't known each other for long, but your friendship — I cannot tell you — even when I am away I have such a clear remembrance of you that I feel as though you are still near me — we are like two watches set to the same time, and when we see one another again there has been no interval — we still strike together.'

She thought: But I could think of nothing to say after he read me the beginning of his Blue Flower. Thank God, he doesn't remember that.

'I have fallen in love, Justen.'

'Not at Grüningen!'

She felt as though her body had been hollowed out. Fritz was perplexed. 'Surely you know the family quite well. Herr von Rockenthien welcomed your uncle as his oldest friend.'

'Surely I do know them. But none of the older girls are at home just now, only Söphgen.' She had made this calculation already, when she had heard that her uncle was taking him to Grüningen.

Fritz looked at her steadily.

'Sophie is my heart's heart.'

'But Hardenberg, she can't be much more than . . .' she struggled for moderation. 'And she *laughs*.'

He said, 'Justen, so far you have understood everything, you have listened to everything. But it would be wrong of me to ask too much of you. I see that there is one thing, the most important of all, unfortunately, that you don't grasp, the nature of desire between a man and a woman.'

Karoline could not tell, either then or afterwards, why it was impossible for her to let this pass. Perhaps it was vanity – which was sinful – perhaps the cold fear of losing his confidence for ever.

'Not everyone can speak about what they suffer,' she said. 'Some are separated from the only one they love, but are obliged to remain silent.'

That was not a lie. She had not mentioned herself. But Fritz's generous sympathy and instant rush of fellow-feeling was very painful to her. What strong force had spoken with her voice and told him something which, after all, *was* a lie and intended as a lie? As the dear Fritz talked on, gently but eagerly, about the obstacles to happiness (he would of course ask her nothing more, what she had told him was sacred) – the obstacles which drew them even more closely together – she saw that between them they had created out of nothing a new and most unwelcome entity. So that now there were four of them, the poet, the much-desired Sophie screaming with laughter, herself, the sober niece-housekeeper, and now her absent, secret, frustrated lover, doubtless a respectable minor official of more than thirty, probably – as Karoline increasingly clearly saw him – in sober clothes of hard-wearing material, almost certainly a married man, or he might, perhaps, be a pastor. He was so real at that

74

moment that she could have put out a hand and touched him. And he had been born entirely from the wound that Hardenberg had dealt her, when he told her that she did not understand the nature of desire.

'Words are given us to understand each other, even if not completely,' Fritz went on in great excitement.

'And to write poetry.'

'Yes that's so, Justen, but you mustn't ask too much of language. Language refers only to itself, it is not the key to anything higher. Language speaks, because speaking is its pleasure and it can do nothing else.'

'In that case it might as well be nonsense,' objected Karoline.

'Why not? Nonsense is only another language.'

21

Snow

But Fritz, after all, was obliged to spend Christmas at Weissenfels. Sidonie wrote to him that not only would the Bernhard
be much disappointed if he did not come, but that he must see
his new brother. In the warmth of the great curtained patriar-
chal goose-featherbed at Weissenfels Nature's provisions continued, so that last year Amelie had been conceived and born,
and this year, Christoph. The Bernhard had received the news
without enthusiasm. 'There are now two more younger than
myself, it will be hard for me to attract sufficient attention.'

'But you love little Christoph,' said Sidonie patiently. 'You
are only a child yourself, Bernhard, you are still in your days
of grace.'

'On the whole, I hate little Christoph. When does Fritz
come? Will he be here for Christmas Eve?'

At Tennstedt, Karoline and Rahel together saw to the cabbages buried in sand in the cellar, and the potatoes buried in
earth in the yard. The surplus provisions were arranged in a
deep cupboard just inside the kitchen for distribution to the
poor, together with double rations of schnaps which harboured
in every coarse, consoling mouthful the memory of the heat of
summer.

About Hardenberg they only remarked to each other that it

was a pity, after all, that he could not spend Christmas with
them.

On his way to Weissenfels, Fritz was somewhat delayed. He
had arranged to call in for a few hours at Schloss Grüningen.
But that evening, all over the administrative district of
Thuringia and Saxony, it began to snow. The north-east
wind outlined every twig, every cart-shaft, every cabbage-
stump, with a rim of crystalline white. Then that disappeared
and there was nothing but a white blindness that seemed at
the same time to be rising from the ground and falling from
the heavy sky.

While Karoline was helping to clear a path to the outside
pump, a letter arrived from Hardenberg, from Grüningen.
'So he has got no further!' In it he told her, perhaps not very
tactfully, that being marooned, he was sleeping and eating 'in
the most hospitable house in the world'. The snow was so deep,
he alleged, that he couldn't go out without danger, and to take
pointless risks was unworthy of a responsible man. 'I shall, I
will, I must, I ought, I can stay here, who can do anything
against Fate? I have decided that I am a Determinist. Fate
might not be so kind another time.'

'In that great house there must be someone who can clear
the carriageway,' Karoline told herself. 'But he has always talked
a great deal of nonsense. When he first came here, he said my
hands were beautiful, also the tablecloth and the tea-tray.'

He had enclosed some verses, which ended,

Allow me a glimpse of the future, when our hearts
Are no longer full of anxiety and resignation, and Love and
   Fortune
Reward us at last for our sacrifices, and far behind us
Roars youth's wild ocean.
Some day, in the noon-tide of life, we shall both sit at table,
Each of us will be married, with the one we love beside us,

Then we shall look back to how it was in the morning.
Who would have dreamed of this? Never does the heart sigh
in vain!

Karoline knew that 'Never does the heart sigh in vain!' was
the sort of thing that they printed on sweet papers. But the
last verse caused her anguish. There he was, her non-existent
admirer, the unloved *Verliebte*, conjured out of her own
unhappiness, sitting at table with her, indeed, all four of them
were there. But the poem, at least, was for her and her alone.
The title was 'Reply to Karoline'. She put it in the drawer
where she kept such things, and turned the key. Then she
clasped her arms round her body as if to ward off the cold.

22

Now Let Me Get to Know Her

During his two days with the Rockenthiens, Fritz marvelled at the difference between daily life in the Kloster Gasse at Weissenfels and at Schloss Grüningen. At Grüningen there were no interrogations, no prayer-meetings, no anxiety, no catechisms, no fear. Anger, if any, evaporated within a few moments, and there was a good deal of what, at Weissenfels, would be called time-wasting. At breakfast time, no-one at Grüningen slammed down their coffee-cups, and cried out '*Satt*!' The constant coming and going round the tranquil Frau Rockenthien (who, like the Freifrau von Hardenberg, had a new baby to nurse) seemed an image of perpetual return, so that time scarcely declared itself an enemy.

At Grüningen, mention of the goings-on of the French caused no distress. When George appeared in a tricolour waistcoat there was not even a murmur of surprise. With pain Fritz compared the Demon George, easy-going and noisy, with the strangeness of the Bernhard. Then again, Uncle Wilhelm's visits at Weissenfels were an occasion of dread, one prayed for him to leave, while at Grüningen relations and friends poured in indiscriminately, all of them greeted, even if they had been there only yesterday, as if they had not been seen for many months.

'When summer comes we have the *Nachtisch* outside, under
the lilacs,' Frau Rockenthien told him. 'Then you must read
aloud to us.' At Weissenfels, after meals, everyone dispersed
as soon as grace was said. Fritz was not sure whether there
were any lilacs in the garden or not. He was inclined to think
not.

Snowed-up for probably not more than a day or two, Fritz
knew he must use his time wisely. 'You have your wish now,
Fräulein Sophie,' he said, watching her stand by the same
window in the *Saal*. Her child's pink mouth was just open, as
without knowing it she put out her tongue a very little, longing
to taste the crystal flakes on the far side of the glass. Herr
Rockenthien, thundering past with George and Hans at his
heels, paused to ask Fritz about his studies. He asked everyone
he met, with genuine interest, about their occupations, a habit
he had picked up during his service with the Prince of
Schwarzburg-Sondeshausen as a commissioning officer. Fritz
talked eagerly about chemistry, geology and philosophy. He
mentioned Fichte. 'Fichte explained to us that there is only one
absolute self, one identity for all humanity.'

'Well, this Fichte is lucky,' cried Rockenthien. 'In this household I have thirty-two identities to consider.'

'Papa hasn't a care in the world,' said George. 'Today, when
he was desperately needed by the head gardener to give instructions about the blocked ditches, he was out shooting in the
snow.'

'My career has been in the army, not in the vegetable patch,'
said Rockenthien good-humouredly. 'As to shooting, it is not
a passion with me. I was out with my gun early this morning
in order to feed my family.' With the air of a conjuror, he
drew out of his pocket what he had evidently forgotten until now,
a string of small dead birds connected head to tail with a length
of thread. It seemed as though the procession – one or two of
them stuck, and he had to tug and heave – would go on forever.

'Linnets! They won't go far!' shouted George. 'Three at a time I could crunch them.'

'All feel that I have nothing to do,' said Herr Rockenthien, 'although in truth this is one of our busiest times, and it will be one of my responsibilities to see that order is kept during the Advent Fair.'

'Where is this fair?' asked Fritz – it's not in order to *fichtisieren* here, he told himself – better to say no more about it.

'Oh, at Greussen, two miles away,' cried Sophie. 'It is the only thing that ever happens here, except the summer and the autumn fairs, and they also are at Greussen.'

'But you haven't yet been to the Leipzig fair?' Fritz asked her.

No, Sophie had never even so much as been to Leipzig. At the very thought of it her eyes shone, her lips parted.

What or whom does she look like? he thought, with this rich hair, and her long, pretty nose, not at all like her mother's. Nor were her arched eyebrows. In the third volume of Lavater's *Physiognomische Fragmente* there was an illustration, after a copperplate by Johann Heinrich Lips, of Raphael's self-portrait at the age of twenty-five. This picture had exactly the air of Sophie. From the copperplate, of course, you couldn't tell the colour, or the tonality of the flesh, only that the expression was unworldly and humane and that the large eyes were dark as night.

In his first quarter of an hour, at the window of the great *Saal*, Fritz had already opened his heart to Sophie. Now let me get to know her, he thought. How difficult will that be?

'If we are going to spend our lives together,' he said, 'I should like to learn everything about you.'

'Yes, but you must not call me *du*.'

'Very well, I will not, until you give me permission.'

He thought, let's make the attempt, even though it's possible that she would rather play with the little brother and sister. They were on the long, broad terrace between the house and the garden, which had been swept almost clear of snow. Mimi and Rudi, young and obstreperous, ran beside them with their iron-bound hoops. '*Lass das*, Freiherr, you don't know how to hit it,' Rudi had cried sharply, but Fritz did know, having been brought up in a house of many hoops, and he whacked first one and then the other hard and true so that they spun away and had to be pursued almost out of sight.

'Now, tell me what you think about poetry.'

'I don't think about it at all,' said Sophie.

'But you would not want to hurt a poet's feelings.'

'I would not want to hurt anyone's feelings.'

'Let us speak of something else. What do you like best to eat?'

Cabbage soup, Sophie told him, and a nice smoked eel.

'What is your opinion of wine and tobacco?'

'Those, too, I like.'

'Do you smoke, then?'

'Yes, my stepfather gave me a pipe.'

'And music?'

'Ah, that I love. A few months ago there were some students in the town and they played a serenade.'

'What did they play?'

'They played "Wenn die Liebe in deinen blauen Augen". That of course could not be for me, my eyes are dark, but it was very beautiful.'

Singing, yes. Dancing, yes, most certainly, but she was not permitted to attend the public balls until she was fourteen.

'Do you remember the question I asked you when I first met you, by the window?'

'No, I don't remember it.'

'I asked you whether you had thought at all about marriage.'

'Oh, I am afraid of that.'

'You did not say that when we spoke of it by the window.'

She repeated, 'I am afraid of that.' After Rudi, with Mimi

82

whimpering after him, had returned and been dismissed again ('Poor souls! They are getting out of breath!' said Sophie.) he asked her about her faith. She answered readily. They kept the days of penitence, of course, and on Sundays they went to the church, but she did not believe everything that was said there. She did not believe in life after death.

'But Sophie, Jesus Christ returned to earth!'

'That was all very well for him,' said Sophie. 'I respect the Christus, but if I was to walk and talk again after I was dead, that would be ridiculous.'

'What does your stepfather say when you tell him you don't believe?'

'He laughs.'

'But when you were younger, what did your teacher tell you? Surely you must have had a teacher?'

'Yes, until I was eleven.'

'Who was he?'

'The Magister Kegel from the seminary here in Grüningen.'

'Did you pay him attention?'

'Once he was angry with me.'

'Why?'

'He could not believe that I could understand so little.'

'What could you not understand?'

'Figures, and numbers.'

'Numbers are not more difficult to understand than music.'

'Ach, well, Kegel beat me.'

'Surely not, Sophie.'

'Yes, he struck me.'

'But what did your stepfather say to that?'

'Ach, well, it was difficult for him. A teacher must be obeyed.'

'What did the Magister Kegel do?'

'He collected the money that was owing to him, and left the house.'

'But what did he say?'

'"*On reviendra, mam'zell.*"'

'But he did not come back?'

'No, now I am too old to learn anything.'

She looked at him a little anxiously and added, 'Perhaps if I saw a miracle, as they did in the old days, I should believe more.'

'Miracles don't make people believe!' Fritz cried. 'It's the belief that is the miracle.'

He saw that, having done her best, she looked disappointed, and went on: 'Sophie, listen to me. I am going to tell you what I felt, when I first saw you standing by the window. When we catch sight of certain human figures and faces . . . especially certain eyes, expressions, movements – when we hear certain words, when we read certain passages, thoughts take on the meaning of laws . . . a view of life true to itself, without any self-estrangement. And the self is set free, for the moment, from the constant pressure of change . . . Do you understand me?'

Sophie nodded. 'Yes, I do. I have heard of that before. Some people are born again and again into this world.'

Fritz persevered. 'I did not quite mean that. But Schlegel, too, is interested in transmigration. Should you like to be born again?'

Sophie considered a little. 'Yes, if I could have fair hair.'

Herr von Rockenthien pressed young Hardenberg to stay longer. If he noticed that this son of an ancient house was courting his stepdaughter, he was not at all against it, although it might be said that his temperament led him to encourage almost everything. Frau von Rockenthien, serene and apparently in radiant health, but supported by cushions numberless, also nodded kindly. She mentioned, however, that Sophie's elder sister, Friederike von Mandelsloh, would soon be coming back home to Grüningen on a long visit, and would be a companion for Söphgen.

'Let them all come back to us, I say,' Rockenthien declared. 'Partings are painful! Isn't that what they sing at Jena at the end of the year, when the students leave?'

'They do,' said Fritz, and Rockenthien, in a voice as deep as the third level of a copper-mine, but with inappropriate cheerfulness, broke into the plaintive song: '*Scheiden und meiden tut weh* . . .'

'Now that I am leaving your hospitable roof, I should like your permission to write a letter to your stepdaughter Sophie,' said Fritz. Rockenthien broke off his song, and gathering the tattered remnants of his responsibilities around him, said that there would be no objection, as long as her mother opened it and read through it first.

'Of course. And I should like her, if you see fit, to be permitted to write an answer.'

'Permission! If that is all that is needed, I permit!'

23

I Can't Comprehend Her

Fritz wrote in his journal, 'I can't comprehend her, I can't get the measure of her. I love something that I do not understand. She has got me, but she is not at all sure she wants me. Her stepfather is an influence upon her, and I see now that jollity is as relentless as piety. Indeed she has told me that she would always like to see me cheerful. He also, of course, gave her a tobacco pipe.

'August Schlegel wrote that "form is mechanical when, through external force, it is imparted merely as an accidental addition without reference to its quality: as, for example, when we give a particular shape to a soft mass so that it may retain the same when it hardens. Organic form is innate: it unfolds itself from within, and acquires its determination at the same time as the perfect development of the germ."

'That, surely, is what is happening with Sophie. I do not want to change her, but I admit that I should like to feel that I could do so if necessary. But, in twelve years, during which she did not know that I existed on this earth, she has "acquired her determination". I should be happier if I could see one opening, the shadow of an opening, where I could make myself felt a little.

'To decide that she does not believe in the life to come. What insolence, what enormity.

'She said, "Truly, I like you."'

'She wants to please everyone, but will not adapt herself. Her face, her body, her enjoyment of life, her health, that which she likes to speak of. Her little dogs. Has her temperament woken up yet? Her fear of ghosts, her wine-drinking. Her hand on her cheek.'

At the house in the Kloster Gasse his mother was still lying in after the birth of Christoph, who was thriving only moderately, in spite of a capacious wet-nurse brought in from one of the villages. Uncomplaining as always on her own account, she was distressed now only for her infant, and for the Bernhard. Someone might be disillusioning him — (she feared this every Christmas) — and, without intending to do so, destroy his belief in Knecht Rupert.

'I don't remember the Bernhard ever believing in Knecht Rupert,' said Fritz to Sidonie. 'He always knew it was old Dumpfin, from the bakery, in a false beard.'

He had confided his secret only to Karoline Just, to Erasmus, and to Sidonie, who agreed that it would not do at the moment, or indeed at any moment, to agitate their mother. Fritz dragged Sidonie to his own room, where he took down the third volume from his own set of Lavater's *Physiognomie*. 'That is my Söphgen to the life. It is Raphael's self-portrait, of course . . . But how can a girl of twelve look like a genius of twenty-five?'

'That is easy,' said Sidonie. 'She cannot.'

'But you have never so much as seen her.'

'That's true. But I *shall* see her, I suppose, and when I do I shall tell you exactly the same thing.'

He shut the book. 'My pockets are full of things I've bought.' He took out handfuls of gingerbread, needle-cases, eau de Cologne, a bird-charmer and a catapult. 'Where can I put them, Sidonie? You don't know how uncomfortable they are. Torment!'

'In the library, that's where I'm going to have the gift-giving.' Sidonie, while attentive to the timid and plaintive requests occasionally brought to her from her mother's room, was entirely in charge. She had already made the stable-boys bring fir-tree boughs into the house and heap them up in the library. She kept the key herself. Whenever she opened the door an overwhelmingly spicy green breath crowded out into the passage, as though the forest had marched into the house.

'I bought all these on the way, at Freyburg,' Fritz said. 'I suppose you've been getting up every morning before it's light, as you always did, making things.'

'I hate sewing,' said Sidonie, 'and I am not good at it, and never shall be, but yes, I have.'

Where was Erasmus? Karl had arrived, Anton was there, the Freiherr had been obliged to go over to the salt mines at Artern, but would be back on Christmas Eve. 'That is what is so strange, Fritz, Asmus set off to ride to Grüningen to meet you.'

'Ride! What is he riding?'

'Oh, Karl's orderly brought a second horse with him, from the remount section.'

'That's fortunate.'

'Not so fortunate for Asmus, because he can't manage this horse, he has already fallen off twice.'

'Someone will pick him up, the roads are crowded now that the snow is clearing. But why is he going to Grüningen? *Weiss Gott*, it's idiotic!'

Sidonie arranged and rearranged the pile of bright things which Fritz had brought with him.

'I think he wanted to see for himself what your Sophie looked like.'

24

The Brothers

'Fritz!'

Erasmus caught up with his brother on the front door steps, racing after him up the right-hand flight, dislodging Lukas, the houseman, and his broom.

'Fritz, I have seen her, yes, I've been to Grüningen! I talked to your Sophie and to a friend of hers, and to the family.'

Fritz stood as if turned to ice, and Erasmus called out, 'Best of brothers, she won't do!'

He threw his arms round his so much taller brother. 'She won't do at all, my Fritz. She is good-natured, yes, but she is not your intellectual equal. Great Fritz, you are a philosopher, you are a poet.'

Lukas disappeared with his broom, hastening to the kitchen door to repeat what he had heard.

'Who gave you permission to present yourself at Grüningen?' asked Fritz, so far almost calm.

'Fritz, Sophie is stupid!'

'Mad, Erasmus!'

'No, I'm not mad, best of all Fritzes!'

'I said, who gave you permission —'

'Her mind is empty —'

'Better silence —! '

'Empty as a new jug, Fritz —'

'Silence!'

Erasmus clung on. And there, on the front steps of the house in the Kloster Gasse, the two of them were on show, and once again the people of Weissenfels, as they went by at a foot's pace, were scandalised, as they had been by the Bernhard's escapade on the banks of the river. There were the eldest of the Hardenberg boys, the Freiherr's pride, almost at blows.

Erasmus was by far the more upset of the two. His breath steamed up like a kettle in the winter's air. Without effort Fritz, trying for calm, pinned him against the iron handrail. 'You mean well, *Junge*, I am sure you do. Your feelings are those of a brother. You think I have been taken in by a beautiful face.'

'No, I don't,' Erasmus protested. 'You are taken in, yes, but not by a pretty face. Fritz, she is not beautiful, she is not even pretty. I say again this Sophie is empty-headed, moreover at twelve years old she has a double chin —'

'Gracious Freiin, your brothers are knocking each other's teeth out on the front steps,' announced Lukas. 'Peace and fellowship have been forgotten, indeed they are now at full length in the Kloster Gasse.'

'I will go to them at once,' said Sidonie.

'Shall I inform the Freifrau?'

'Don't be a fool, Lukas.'

Erasmus had been warmly received on his entirely unannounced visit to Grüningen. He was welcome for his brother's sake, and Frau Rockenthien had a special tenderness for small and insignificant young people, believing that they could be transformed, by giving them plenty to eat, into tall and stout ones. But Sophie herself, to his horror, he found was no more than a very noisy, very young girl, not at all like his own sisters.

During the scant two hours of his visit she and a friend of hers, a Jette Goldacker, had invited him to walk with them down to the path by the River Helbe, since they must not go alone, and see the Hussars, who were quite drunk, and were toppling over on the ice, the Regimental Sergeant too, and everything was going flying pitsch! patsch! It was Jette, true, who had drawn attention to a corporal unbuttoning himself, but Sophie had not reproached her. For *morgen*, Sophie said *morchen*, for *spät* she said *späd*, for Hardenberg, 'Hardenburch'. Well, Erasmus did not care a snap how she spoke. He did not set himself up as a teacher of elocution. But never had he met a young maiden of good family with so little restraint.

Fritz must have lost his senses. 'You're intoxicated. It's a *Rausch*, think of yourself as *im Rausch*. It will wear off, in the course of nature it must.'

Because of the Christmas gathering and because the Freiherr might come back at any moment, no more could be said between them, and after all the quarrel arose not from enmity but from love, although that was not likely to make it easier to settle. A truce was called.

'I know that I am receiving moral grace. How can that be intoxication?' Fritz wrote.

> *Am I to be kept apart from her for ever?*
> *Is the hope of being united*
> *With what we recognised as our own*
> *But could not quite possess completely*
> *Is that too to be called intoxication?*
> *All humanity will be, in time, what Sophie*
> *Is now for me: human perfection — moral grace —*
> *Life's highest meaning will then no longer*
> *Be mistaken for drunken dreams.*

25

Christmas at Weissenfels

'What are the boys saying?' asked the Freifrau doubtfully. She had been permitted to move out of the large shabby marital bedroom and upstairs, with the baby, to somewhere much smaller, almost an attic, which was sometimes used for storing apples, so that, in spite of the cold, it never lost its lazy, bittersweet apple smell. Only the wet nurse and a lady's maid who had come with her from her old home when she married, creaked up the stairs as far as this – Sidonie, too, of course, on flying feet.

'Ah, Sidonie, my dear, I thought I heard their voices raised, though not so much to-day as yesterday . . . Tell me, what is Fritz talking about?'

'About moral grace, mother.'

At this watchword of the Herrnhut the Freifrau sank back in relief against the starched pillows.

'And you have got the library ready – you know your father likes to –'

'Of course, of course,' said Sidonie.

'Tell me whether you think little Christoph is any better.'

Sidonie, an expert, removed several layers of shawls and looked closely at her frail brother. He scowled at her manfully, she brightened. 'Yes, truly, he is much better.'

'Thank God, thank God, I should not say this, she is another Christian soul, but I do not at all like the wet nurse.'

'I will speak to her at once,' said Sidonie, 'and send her back to Elsterdorf.'

'And then —? ' Sidonie thought her mother was worrying about a replacement, but saw it was not so. 'You are thinking about moving back to your bedroom downstairs. No, you are not well enough yet for that. I will send for your coffee.'

The Freiherr followed the old custom, which most of Weissenfels' households had given up, of the Christmas reckoning. The mother spoke to her daughters, the father to his sons, and told them first what had displeased, then what had pleased most in their conduct during the past year. In addition, the young Hardenbergs were asked to make a clean breast of anything that they should have told their parents, but had not. The Freifrau would not be well enough to undertake this duty, and the Freiherr, it was thought, might arrive from Artern later than he had calculated. But he arrived precisely at the time he had said.

Christmas Eve was bright and windless. All day the knocker of the kitchen door echoed through the yards. No-one who asked for charity at the Hardenbergs' house was ever turned away empty-handed, but on this day they could expect something more substantial. At Oberwiederstadt the pressure had been much greater. The house had been very near the border, and many who had no permission to cross into Prussia, and indeed were not particularly welcome in any of the states – the vagrants, old soldiers, travelling theatrical companies, pedlars – all these silted up on the frontier like floating rubbish on a river's banks. In Weissenfels there were only the town poor and the town mad, and later the girls with unwanted pregnancies, who could not afford the services of the Angel-maker, the back-street abortionist. These girls did not come to the kitchen door until it was quite dark.

In the library candles had been attached, waiting to blaze, on every sprig of the heaped-up fir branches. The tables were laid with white cloths, a table for each soul in the household. On each table was placed a name, made out of almond paste and baked brown. The presents themselves were not labelled. One must guess, or perhaps never know, who were the givers.

'What are we expected to sing for Christmas Eve?' Karl asked.

'I don't know,' said Sidonie. 'Father likes Reichardt's "Welcome to this Vale of Sorrow."'

'Bernhard,' said Karl, 'you are not to eat the almond-paste letters.'

The Bernhard was wounded. It had been almost two years now since he cared anything about sweets.

'I dare say too that this is the last year I shall be called upon to sing a treble solo,' he said. 'Pubescence is at the door.'

'What I want to know is this,' cried Erasmus, 'I want to know from you, our Fritz, what you will say when Father asks us to confess what we have done during the year. You know what I have already written to you, that you can rely upon me in everything. But are you going to tell him, as you have told me, not that you are in love, that needs no more apology than a bird needs an apology to fly, no, but that you have committed yourself to a little girl of twelve who laughs through her fingers to see a drunk in the snow?'

'Of this you have told me nothing,' said Karl reproachfully. Bernhard, although attached to Fritz, was in ecstasies, foreseeing embarrassments of all kinds.

'I shall tell him nothing that is unworthy of Sophie,' Fritz declared. 'Her name means wisdom. She is my wisdom, she is my truth.'

'Freiin, the lights,' said Lukas, hurrying in. 'Your gracious father is coming down to the library.'

'Well, help me, then, Lukas.' He had left the door open

94

and they saw the household assembled outside, their aprons patches of white in the shadows of the hall. At Grüningen they would have been in uproar on a holiday like this, but not in the Kloster Gasse.

Inside the library the myriad fiery shining points of light threw vast shadows of the fir branches onto the high walls and even across the ceiling. In the warmth the room breathed even more deeply, more resinously, more greenly. On the tables the light sparkled across gold-painted walnuts, birds in cages, dormice in their nests, dolls made of white bread twisted into shape, hymnbooks, Fritz's needle-cases and little bottles of *Kölnischwasser*, Sidonie's embroidery, oddments made out of willow and birch, pocket-knives, scissors, pipes, wooden spoons with curious handles which made them almost unusable, religious prints mounted on brilliant sheets of tin. By contrast with this sparkle and display how worn, as he came in, how haggard in spite of its roundness, was the face of the Freiherr von Hardenberg. As he paused at the door to give some instructions to Lukas, Fritz said to Karl, 'He is old, but I cannot bring myself to make things easy for him.'

The Freiherr came in, and quite against precedent, sat down in the elbow chair. His family looked at him in dismay. It had been his habit on Christmas Eve to stand behind the large leather-covered desk, always kept clear of presents and candles, in the very centre of the library.

'Why does he do this?' muttered Erasmus.

'I don't know,' said Fritz. 'Schlegel tells me that Goethe has bought one of these chairs, but when he sits in it he can't think.'

As their father began to speak he beat his hand, as though marking time, on the embracing arm of the chair.

'You expect me to consider your conduct for the past year, both the progress you have made and your backsliding. You expect me to question you about anything that has been concealed from me. You expect – indeed it would be your duty – to answer me truthfully. You expect these things, but you are mistaken. On this Christmas Eve, the Christmas Eve of the year 1794, I shall want no confessions, I shall make no interrogations. What is the reason for this? Well, in reality, while at Artern I received a letter from a very old friend, the Former Prediger of the Brethren at Neudietendorf. It was a Christmas letter, reminding me that I was fifty-six years of age and could not, in the nature of things, expect more than another few years on this earth. The Prediger instructed me for once not to reprove, but to remember only that this is a day of unspeakable joy, on which all men and women should be no more, and no less, than children. And therefore,' he added, looking slowly round at the sparkling tables, the wooden spoons, the golden nuts, 'I myself have become, during this sacred time, wholly a child.'

Anything less childlike than the leathery, seamed, broad, bald face of the Freiherr and his eyes, perplexed to the point of anguish under his strong eyebrows, could hardly be imagined. Probably the Prediger had not tried to imagine it. The Brethren were experienced in joy, and perhaps sometimes forgot what a difficult emotion it is, and how unfamiliar to many. Heavily the Freiherr von Hardenberg looked up from the desk.

'Are we not to have music?'

The Bernhard, disappointed at his father's strange mildness, but pleased to see his elders disconcerted, shinned up the library steps used for the highest shelves, and began to sing, in what was still a child's voice of absolute purity, 'He is born, let us love him.' The angelic voice was taken as a signal for the patiently-waiting household to come in, bringing with them the two-year-old Amelie, who advanced with determination on anything that shone, and a bundle of wrappings, which was the infant Christoph. The candle-flames began to burn low and catch the evergreens, there was a snapping and hissing and trails of sweet smoke as they were calmly extinguished by

Sidonie. The room was still, in alternate patches, brilliant and shadowy as everyone went to search for their own tables.

Erasmus stood close to Fritz. 'What will you tell Father now?'

26

The Mandelsloh

Nothing. Fritz would accept what Fate and Chance sent and take the opportunity to say nothing. The distance between himself and Erasmus distressed him far more than any falling-out with his father.

At Neudietendorf he had learned, even when he thought he was refusing to learn, the Moravian respect for chance. Chance is one of the manifestations of God's will. If he had stayed on among the Brethren, even his wife would have been chosen for him by lot. Chance had brought the Prediger's letter to Artern quicker than could have been expected, and made it possible for him to delay discussing his marriage to Sophie until somewhat nearer the time when he might expect to earn his own living. But chance, as he knew, might at any moment restore his father to his usual state of furious impatience. He had only spoken of being joyous, after all, for one day.

On Silvesterabend, six days after Christmas, Fritz received a letter from Sophie.

> Dear Hardenberg,
> In the first place I thank you for your letter secondly
> for your hair and thirdly for the sweet Needle-case
> which has given me much pleasure. You ask me

98

whether you may be allowed to write to me? You can be assured that it is pleasant to me at All Times to read a letter from you. You know dear Hardenberg I must write no more.

Sophie von Kühn

'She is my wisdom,' said Fritz.

Back on a day's visit to Grüningen, in the New Year of 1795, Fritz asked the Hausherr Rockenthien, 'Why must she write no more? Am I then dangerous?'

'My dear Hardenberg, she must write no more because she scarcely knows how to. Send for her schoolmaster and enquire of him! Certainly she ought to have studied more, ha! ha! Then she could well have written correctly a sweetheart's letter.'

'I don't want correctness, but I should like them a good deal longer,' said Fritz.

His next letter from Sophie ran: 'You gave me some of your Hair and I wrapped it nicely in a little Bit of paper and put it in the drawer of a table. The other day when I wanted to take it out neither the Hair nor the Bit of paper was to be seen. Now please have your Hair cut again, and in particular the Hair of your head.'

The next time he was at Grüningen, a strong blonde young woman came into the room, carrying a bucket. 'God help me, but I've forgotten what I meant to do with this,' she said, slamming it down on the painted wooden floor.

'This is my elder sister Friederike,' said Sophie eagerly. 'She is the Frau Leutnant Mandelsloh.'

She is not like her mother, Fritz thought, and not at all like her sister.

'Frieke, he wants me to write him another letter.'

Fritz said, 'No, Frau Leutnant, I want her to write me many hundreds of letters.'

'Well, the attempt shall be made,' said the Mandelsloh. 'But she will need some ink.'

'Is there none in the house?' Fritz asked. 'It is the same with us, we are often short of soap, or some other commodity.'

'Here there is plenty of everything,' said the Mandelsloh. 'And there is ink in my stepfather's study, and in several other rooms. Everywhere we may take what we like. But Söphgen does not use ink every day.'

Sophie was gone. Left alone with this large-boned, fair-haired creature, Fritz followed his instinct, turning to her at once for advice. 'Frau Leutnant, would you recommend me to ask your stepfather whether he would consent to an engagement between myself and –'

'About that I can't advise you at all,' she said calmly. 'You must see how much courage you have. The difficulty is not what to ask people, but when. I suppose your father, too, must be taken into account.'

'That is so,' said Fritz.

'Well, perhaps the two of them will sit down comfortably together and enjoy a good pipe of tobacco.' Fritz tried, but failed, to imagine this. 'In that way everything may be settled without tears. My own husband was an orphan. There was no-one he had to consider when he came to discuss matters with my stepfather, except his unmarried sister, whom of course he must support.'

'I thank you for your advice,' said Fritz. 'I think, indeed, that women have a better grasp on the whole business of life than we men have. We are morally better than they are, but they can reach perfection, we can't. And that is in spite of the fact that they particularise, we generalise.'

'That I have heard before. What is wrong with particulars? Someone has to look after them.'

Fritz paced the room. Conversation had the same effect on him as music.

'Furthermore, I believe that all women have what Schlegel finds lacking in so many men, a beautiful soul. But so often it is concealed.'

'Very likely it is,' said the Mandelsloh. 'What do you think of mine?'

Having said this, she looked startled, as though someone else had spoken. Fritz, who had reached the point nearest to her and to her bucket, stopped and fixed on her his brilliant, half-wild gaze.

'Don't look so interested!' she cried. 'I am very dull. My husband is very dull. We are two dull people. I should not have mentioned us. Even to think of us might make you weep from boredom.'

'But I don't find –'

She put her hands over her ears.

'No, don't say it! We who are dull accept that intelligent persons should run the world and the rest of us should work six days a week to keep them going, if only it turns out that they know what they are doing.'

'We are not talking about myself,' cried Fritz. 'We are talking about your soul, Frau Leutnant.'

Sophie reappeared, without pen, paper or ink. It seemed that she had been playing with some new kittens in the house-maids' pantry. 'So that is where they are,' said the Mandelsloh. She was reminded now that she had brought the bucket of water to drown these kittens. The servants were faint-hearted about their duty in this respect.

Friederike von Mandelsloh had been living in the garrison town of Langensalza, with her husband, a leutnant in Prince Clemens' Regiment. She had come back home to Grüningen, about ten miles away, because he had been sent to France with the Rheinfeld expeditionary force. She lamented that she had never been able to live long enough anywhere to have a carpet laid properly (and she did possess a large Turkish carpet). But then, she was a soldier's wife. Although she was, of course, no real relation to Hausherr Rockenthien she was, of all the younger generation, his favourite. In spite of her brusque semi-military manner, developed since she married at the age of sixteen, her china-blue eyes suggested her mother's assurance, her mother's calm. 'You are the best of the lot,' he told Friederike. 'You should never have left the house. It amounted to cruelty to myself.'

Every man, Rockenthien thought, deserved such a presence in his house. The Mandelsloh would check over the wines in the cellar, do his accounts, drown the kittens, keep an eye, if necessary, on Söphgen. And Friederike did take charge, not (as Sidonie did at Weissenfels) out of pity and painful anxiety, but simply as the result of her mother's smiling ability to impose on her. Frau Rockenthien's only positive action since Günther was born and Hardenberg had attached himself to Sophie had been to get Friederike back into the house. Beyond that, however, nothing was really necessary.

27

Erasmus Calls on Karoline Just

Karoline Just had never met Erasmus, but even at the door, before the servant announced him she knew who he must be. He was short and slight, his face was round, his eyes were neither large nor bright, but he was Fritz's brother. She also knew from what she had been told about him that he must be due back, overdue perhaps, for his next term at Hubertusberg.

Coelestin and Rahel Just were out. They were very much occupied at the moment with the purchase of a garden plot within walking distance of their street. They would grow asparagus, yes, and melons, and build a garden house, an earthly Paradise. They had gone out to drink coffee with the neighbours and to discuss the project, about which everybody already knew everything. Karoline, of course, was invited. But she did not go out very much these days.

'I am afraid there is no-one but myself to welcome you,' she said. 'Your brother of course is still lodging with us, but he is on a visit to Grüningen.'

Erasmus had come on a wave of tenderness and an impulse of conscience towards Karoline, or rather towards Karoline as he imagined her, which should properly have been felt by Fritz. He needed, too, to share his dismay at the intrusion into his life of such a creature as Sophie with someone who would surely understand him. He hoped at the same time to find out rather more about her, since his dispute with his brother meant that they could no longer discuss the matter, even in a letter.

'Fräulein, I speak to you in all sincerity.'

She asked him to call her Karoline.

'You must know Schloss Grüningen quite well, isn't that so? Your Uncle Just goes there, and must sometimes have taken you with him.'

'Yes, he has,' said Karoline. 'What do you want to know about it?' But Erasmus broke out, 'What do you think of her? Who is she, truly?'

'I was naturally more the friend of her eldest sister, who has married now and left home.'

'Speak to me honestly, Karoline.'

She asked him, 'Have you never met Sophie von Kühn?'

'I have. I went to Schloss Grüningen and knocked at the door, as I have knocked at yours. I no longer have any decent manners, or any explanation for my conduct. Perhaps I am going mad.'

'So, you have seen her. She is mature for her age, in some ways. She walks gracefully. She has pretty hair, dark hair, that is a good point.' For the first time she looked frankly at Erasmus. 'How could he?'

'I hoped that you would answer that. I came here in the hope that you might tell me that, and also because –'

Karoline collected herself enough to pull the bell. 'I am going to ask them to bring some refreshments, which we don't want.'

'Of course we do not,' said Erasmus, who, however, when it arrived, ate large quantities of *Zwieback*, and drank some wine.

He is twenty years only, she thought. He pities me. Never

again will he have such sympathy for another human being whom he does not even know. But she did not want to be pitied. 'Wait here a minute.' She left him sitting there, uncertain what to do – he did not like to go on eating while she was out of the room – and came back with the verses which Hardenberg had sent her:

Some day, in the noon-tide of life, we shall both sit at table,
Each of us will be married, with the one we love beside us,
Then we shall look back to how it was in the morning –
Who would have dreamed of this? Never does the heart sigh
  in vain!

Erasmus sat there, almost beyond words humiliated and embarrassed. 'Four of you then, Karoline, I make it four of you, sitting round this table. Then there is someone else you know and care for.'

'That is what the poem says,' Karoline told him cautiously. 'You may read it for yourself if you like.'

She handed him the verses, dashingly written over two whole sheets. 'So much waste! The back of the paper not used!'

'He always writes like that.'

'Did you think I was in love with Hardenberg?'

'God forgive me, I did,' Erasmus said at last. 'He has spoken of you so often. I expect I admire my brother too much. I deceive myself into thinking that everyone must feel about him in the same way. I am truly glad I was wrong – but we both continue, don't we, to feel the same about – you mustn't think I would be unjust to a young girl, and you must understand that although I have always shared Fritz's life I have also known that the time must come when I will lose the greater half of him, and I have always hoped that when that time comes I shall have strength enough to content myself with what's left for me

– but Karoline, disappointment must have its limits – we continue, surely, to feel the same about –'

Karoline covered her face with her hands. 'How could he? How could he?'

28

From Sophie's Diary, 1795

January 8

Today once again we were alone and nothing much happened.

January 9

Today we were again alone and nothing much happened.

January 10

Hardenburch came at mid-day.

January 13

Today Hardenburch went away and I had nothing to amuse me.

March 8

Today we all decided to go to church but the weather held us up.

March 11

Today we were all alone and nothing much happened.

March 12

Today was like yesterday and nothing much happened.

March 13

It was a day of penance and Hartenb. was there.

March 14

Today Hartenber. was there he got a letter from his brother.

29

A Second Reading

The 17th of March, 1795 was Sophie's 13th birthday. Two days earlier she had promised Fritz that she would marry him.

On the 16th of June the always obliging Karl sent a pair of gold rings from Lützen (where he was stationed) to his brother in Tennstedt.

On the 21st of August he wrote again from Lützen, where, he said, he had been 'vegetating' since the Peace of Basle. 'I am sending the stirrup with its leather, and both the straw hats, on one of which I have left the ribbon, which is the latest fashion. The other one can be worn according to taste.' One was for Erasmus to give to Karoline, one was for Sophie; the distribution was left to Fritz. There was also a workbox for the Mother, and, for the second time, Fritz's gold ring, which had been sent back to Lützen and had now been engraved, as he had asked, with an S. This could not have been done by a jeweller in Tennstedt – a place so small that they evidently didn't know the fashion in straw hats, and indeed had no straw hats to sell – and certainly not in Weissenfels, where it would have caused notice and comment. The Freiherr von Hardenberg had not even been asked for his permission. The very name of Sophie von Kühn had not been mentioned to him.

The Rockenthiens, on the other hand, had scarcely needed

109

to be asked. They were overjoyed, in the first place, simply by the new happiness in the house. Fritz was asked to be little Günther's godfather. George told him that if he was thinking of marrying it would be absolutely necessary for him to buy a new horse. The Gaul could go for cats' meat.

The Hausherr, rather surprisingly, seemed to take no offence at the idea that the Rockenthiens might be thought not good enough for the Hardenbergs. 'She is too young to marry as yet. I do not know even if her periods are regularly established. By the time she is fifteen, we shall find a way out of our difficulties.' Fritz had thought that Coelestin Just, his father's good friend, might be let into their confidence and act as a kind of emissary between Weissenfels and Grüningen. 'Oh, I think that wouldn't serve,' Herr Rockenthien said amiably. 'The Kreis-amtmann, as you probably noticed, thinks of me as a fool.'

Almost as soon as he had offered Sophie her ring, and seen her – since she could not wear it openly – hang it round her neck, Fritz asked if he might read her the opening chapter of *The Blue Flower*. 'It is the introduction', he told her, 'to a story which I cannot write as yet. I do not know even what it will be. I have made a list of occupations and professions, and of psychological types. But perhaps after all it will not be a novel. There is more truth, perhaps, in folktales.'

'Well, I like those,' said Sophie, 'but not if people are to be turned into toads, for that's not amusing.'

'I shall read my introduction aloud, and you must tell me what it means.' Sophie evidently felt weighed down by this responsibility.

'Do you not know yourself?' she asked doubtfully.

'Sometimes I think I do.'

'But has no-one else read it?'

Fritz searched his memory.

'Yes, Karoline Just.'

'Ah, she is clever.'

The Mandelsloh came in, said that she too would listen and handed Sophie her day's sewing. Even in this prosperous household they were turning the sheets and pillow slips sides to middle, which meant that they would last another ten years. Sophie was diverted for a moment by her needle-case. – 'You gave me this, dear Hardenberg!' – but then fell silent.

'His father and mother were already in bed and asleep, the clock on the wall ticked with a monotonous beat, the wind whistled outside the rattling window-pane. From time to time the room grew brighter when the moonlight shone in. The young man lay restlessly on his bed and remembered the stranger and his stories. "It was not the thought of the treasure which stirred up such unspeakable longings in me," he said to himself. "I have no craving to be rich, but I long to see the Blue Flower. It lies incessantly at my heart, and I can imagine and think about nothing else. Never did I feel like this before. It is as if until now I had been dreaming, or as if sleep had carried me into another world. For in the world I used to live in, who would have troubled himself about flowers? Such a wild passion for a flower was never heard of there. But where could this stranger have come from? None of us had ever seen such a man before. And yet I don't know how it was that I alone was truly caught and held by what he told us. Everyone else heard what I did, and yet none of them paid him serious attention."'

Not sure how much more he was going to read, the two women sat without speaking, with their sewing on their laps. Sophie was pale, her mouth was pale rose. There was the gentlest possible gradation between the colour of the face and the slightly open, soft, fresh, full, pale mouth. It was if nothing had reached, as yet, its proper colour or its full strength – always excepting her dark hair.

The Mandelsloh, who had given the reading her serious

attention, said, 'This is only the beginning of the story. How will it end?'

'I should like you to tell me that,' Fritz answered.

'So far, it is a story for children.'

'That is not against it,' cried Sophie.

'Why do you think this young man can't sleep?' he asked her urgently. 'Is it the moon? Is it the ticking of the clock?'

'Oh, no, that doesn't keep him awake. He only notices it because he is not asleep.'

'That is true,' said the Mandelsloh.

'But would he have slept well, if the stranger had not talked about the Blue Flower?'

'Why should he care about a flower?' Sophie asked. 'He is not a woman, and he is not a gardener.'

'Oh, because it is blue, and he has never seen such a thing,' said the Mandelsloh. 'Flax, I suppose, yes, and linseed, yes, and forget-me-nots and cornflowers, but they are commonplace and have nothing to do with the matter, the Blue Flower is something quite other.'

'Please, Hardenberg, what is the name of the flower?' asked Sophie.

'He knew once,' said Fritz. 'He was told the name, but he has forgotten it. He would give his life to remember it.'

'He can't sleep, because he is alone,' continued the Mandelsloh.

'But there are many in the house,' said Sophie.

'But he is alone in his room. He looks for another dear head on the pillow.'

'Do you agree?' asked Fritz, turning towards Sophie.

'Certainly I should like to know what is going to happen,' she said doubtfully.

He said, 'If a story begins with finding, it must end with searching.'

*　　*　　*

Sophie did not possess many books. She had her hymnal, her
Evangelium, and a list, bound with ribbon, of all the dogs that
her family had ever had, although some of them had died so
long ago that she could not remember them. To this she now
added the introductory chapter of the story of the Blue Flower.
This was in the handwriting of Karoline Just, who did all
Fritz's copying for him.

'Söphgen likes listening to stories,' Fritz wrote in his notebook. 'She doesn't want to be embarrassed by my love. My
love weighs down on her so often. She cares more about other
people and their feelings than about her own. But she is cold
through and through.'

'What I have written down about her does not make sense,'
he said to the Mandelsloh. 'One thing contradicts another. I
am going to ask you to write a description of her, as you have
known her all her life – a portrait of her, as a sister sees her.'

'Not possible!' said the Mandelsloh.

'I am asking too much of you?'

'Very much too much.'

'Do you never keep a journal?' he asked her.

'What if I do? You keep a diary, but could you describe
your brother Erasmus?'

'He describes himself,' said Fritz. His distress remained.
There was not even a passable likeness of Sophie in the house,
except for a wretched miniature, in which her eyes appeared to
bulge like gooseberries, or like Fichte's. Only the hair, falling
defiantly over her white muslin dress, was worth looking at.
The miniature caused the whole family, Sophie above all, to
laugh immoderately.

Fritz asked the Hausherr whether he might find a portrait
painter to come to the house, at his expense, to make a likeness
of Sophie as she really was. It would be necessary for him to
stay a few days to make sketches, but the portrait could be
finished in the studio.

'I daresay it will turn out, after all, to be at *my* expense,' said Rockenthien that night to his wife. 'I am not sure that, at the moment, Hardenberg is earning anything.' He himself had never earned anything either, except for his irregularly paid wages as an infantry captain. But he was of course securely married to a wife with a very good property of her own.

30

Sophie's Likeness

Fritz wanted to find a young painter. He wanted one who painted from the heart, and he settled on Joseph Hoffmann from Köln, who had been recommended to him by Severin.

Hoffmann arrived at Grüningen in late summer, when the roads and the evening light were still good, carrying his knapsack, his necessary, his valise, brushes and portfolio. His fee was to be six thaler, which Fritz intended to meet by selling some of his books. Fritz himself was not at Grüningen, having set himself to work immoderately hard, though he intended to come as soon as possible. The painter was late, because the diligence was late. The Rockenthien family were already at table. All were introduced, but it had not occurred to them to wait for him.

The servants had already brought in the soups, one made of beer, sugar and eggs, one of rose-hips and onions, one of bread and cabbage-water, one of cows' udders flavoured with nutmeg. There was dough mixed with beech-nut oil, pickled herrings and goose with treacle sauce, hard-boiled eggs, numerous dumplings. It is dangerous – on this, at least, all Germany's physicians were agreed – not to keep the stomach full at all times.

Good appetite!

A towering Alp of boiled potatoes, trailing long drifts of steam, was placed in the exact centre of the table, so that all might spear away at it with outstretched silver forks. Rapidly, as though in an avalanche, it subsided into ruin.

'I don't want you to look at me now, Herr Maler,' Sophie called across the table. 'Don't study me now, I am about to fill my mouth.'

'Gracious Fräulein, never would I do such a thing in the first few minutes of acquaintance,' said Hoffmann quietly. 'All I am doing is glancing round the table and assessing the presence, or absence, of true soul in the countenance of everyone here.'

'Ach Gott, I should not think you are often asked out to dinner twice,' said the Mandelsloh.

'I will offer you some advice,' said Herr Rockenthien, leaning forward to help himself to potatoes. 'That is my elder stepdaughter. Don't answer her, if what she says offends you.'

'Why should it offend me? I think that the Frau Leutnant is very probably not used to artists.'

'We know Hardenberg,' said the Mandelsloh. 'He is a poet, which is much the same as an artist. It is true that we are not quite used to him yet.'

Both the Hausherr and his wife were 'from the land'. They were country people. The painter Joseph Hoffmann had been born and brought up in a back street of Köln. His father had been a ladies' shoemaker who had taken to drink and lost any skill he once possessed. Hoffmann had come to the Dresden Academy as a very poor student and was not much more than that now, making a living by selling sepia drawings of distant prospects and bends in the river with reliably grazing cattle. After his sorties into the country he would hurry back to the reassuring close greasy pressure of his home town. Here at Schloss Grüningen he felt a foreigner. He could not eat these

vast quantities, he had never formed the habit, and he could
not make out who most of the people at table were. But he did
not allow this to disconcert him. This is my time, he thought,
and I shall seize my chance. The world will see what I can
do.

He had determined to paint Fräulein Sophie standing in the
sunshine, just at the end of childhood and on the verge of a
woman's joy and fulfilment, and to include in his portrait the
Mandelsloh, her sister, the soldier's wife, likely to be widowed,
sitting in shadow, the victim of woman's lot. He intended to
ask them to pose for him near one of the many small wayside
monuments, put up to the memory of local landlords and bene-
factors, which he had noticed on the way to Grüningen. They
acted as landmarks and were used as scratching-posts by the
cattle. The lettering on the monument would be seen, but,
because of the way the light fell, not clearly. The pressure of
these ideas, which urged themselves upon him with the force
of poetry, caused him to lay down his knife and fork and to
say distinctly, without the least reference to the loud voices
around him.

'Yes, there, exactly there.'

'Where?' asked Frau Rockenthien, who saw him by now as
one more object for compassion.

'I should like to paint your two daughters near a fountain —
sitting on stone steps — broken, time-worn stone. In the distance, a glimpse of the sea.'

'We are some way from the sea,' said Rockenthien doubtfully. 'I would say about a hundred and eighty miles. Strategi-
cally, that will always be one of our problems.'

'Strategy does not interest me,' said the young painter. 'Blood-
shed does not interest me. Apart from that, what does the sea
suggest to you?'

But to no-one present did it suggest anything, except salt
water. Indeed none of them, except Rockenthien, who had once

been stationed with the Hanoverian Regiment at Ratzeburg, had ever seen it.

Frau Rockenthien said peaceably that when she was young, sea air had been thought very unhealthy, but she was not quite sure what doctors said about it nowadays.

31

I Could Not Paint Her

The whole household wondered how Sophie was to be kept sitting still for the necessary length of time. The miniaturist, an elderly relative, had not required her to keep still at all, but had made do with tracing her shadow on a piece of white pasteboard. Hoffmann, however, made only a few sketches on the wing – Fräulein von Kühn running, Fräulein von Kühn pouring milk from a jug. He appeared, after this, to go into a kind of trance, and spent much time in his room.

'Heartily I wish Hardenberg were here,' said Rockenthien. 'This painter is welcome among us, and I thought we had done pretty well in giving him one of the top-floor drying rooms for a studio, but I can't say that he seems at home. The women, however, must manage these things.' By 'the women' he meant, of course, the Mandelsloh, but she had little patience with Hoffmann. 'He has been trained, I suppose, as a cobbler is trained to mend shoes, or a soldier to shoot his enemies. Let him take out his pencils and brushes, and set to.'

'Yes, but perhaps he can't get a likeness,' said Rockenthien. 'It's a trick, you know. You can't learn it, you're born with it. That's how these fellows – Dürer, Raphael, all those fellows – that's how they made their money.'

'I don't think that so far Hoffmann has made much money,' said the Mandelsloh doubtfully.

'Again, that's the trick of it. They have much more money than they let on, that's to say, if they can get a likeness.'

Sophie was sorry for Hoffmann, and the instinct to console which she inherited from her mother led her to ask to see all the drawings which he had brought with him in his portfolio and to praise everything in turn, and indeed she did consider them as marvels. Finally Hoffmann sighed. 'You, too, have studied drawing, I am sure, gracious Fräulein. You must show me what you have done.'

'No, that I won't do,' said Sophie. 'As soon as the drawing-master was gone, I tore them all up.'

She is not such a fool, thought Hoffmann.

Sophie's Diary:

Tuesday September 11

Today the painter did not come down in the morning for breakfast. My stepmother sent up one of the menservants with his coffee, but he said through the door, namely that he wished to be allowed to think.

Wednesday September 12

We began pickling the raspberries.

Thursday September 13

Today was hot and there was thunder and nothing happened and Hardenburch did not come.

Friday September 14

Today no-one came and nothing happened.

I Could Not Paint Her

Saturday September 15

The painter did not come downstairs, to drink schnaps with us.

Sunday September 16

The painter did not come to the Lord's service with us.

Monday September 17

My stepfather said, is that painter fellow still upstairs, let us hope he has not got any of the maids to bed with him.

Anxious to see whether this was the case, George commandeered a ladder from the stables and propped it against the painter's window, open to catch what breeze there was. Such a thing would have been impossible to imagine at Weissenfels. On the other hand George, unlike the Bernhard, would never have gone through a visitor's luggage.

A stable lad was told to hold the ladder steady, and George shinned up. 'Do you see anything?' bawled the lad, with whom George shared most of his activities.

'I'm not sure, it's dark inside. Hang on, Hansel, I think I can hear the bedsprings creaking.'

But Hansel lost his nerve and did not hang on. The ladder toppled sideways, slowly at first, then sickeningly faster. George, bellowing for help, had the sense to jump clear, but fell with the back of his head on the flagstones. The brass buttons on the tails of his jacket rang against the stones, and a moment later his head struck them grossly, like an unwanted parcel. He was lucky only to break a collar-bone, but was not present when the painter, on the next day, left Schloss Grüningen.

Waiting forlornly in the vestibule, Hoffmann, again with his valise, portfolio, brushes, and necessary, was seen off with

121

genuine kindness by Rockenthien, who said, 'I am sorry you have not found it possible to do more, Herr Maler. You must allow me to recompense you for the time you have spent.'

'No, no, my commission was from Hardenberg, and I shall explain myself to him. In any case,' he added firmly, 'you must not think I am without resources.'

This confirmed Rockenthien in his conviction that painters knew a trick or two, and he felt less uneasy. 'I am sorry you had to stay so much upstairs. But they sent up whatever you wanted, eh? They fed you, eh?'

'I have received every hospitality,' said Hoffmann. 'I should like to wish Master George a rapid recovery.'

George was soon up and about, but furious that while he had been laid up, Hansel had been given a good beating by the head coachman, and was to be dismissed. Against the head coachman's decisions nobody, and certainly not the Hausherr, dared to make any representation. 'There is no justice in this house,' George cried. 'This artist has failed entirely to paint my sister, and yet he receives nothing but compliments. As for Hansel, he only did what he was told.'

'No-one told him to let go of the ladder,' said the Hausherr.

Weissenfels was on Hoffmann's road back to Dresden. Although he never took much to drink, he felt by that time in need of a stimulant, and when the diligence halted he got down and went into the Wilde Mann, where he found Fritz.

This is not what I wanted, he thought, and yet I must explain myself at some time. Fritz threw his arms round him. 'The portrait-painter!'

'I came here because I thought that if you were in Weissenfels at all, you would be at your house, and I could not face meeting you.'

'Don't look so wretched, Hoffmann. I have already had a note from Sophie herself, no less, and I know that you have not finished the portrait or even begun it. Shall I send out for schnaps?'

'No, no, a glass of plain beer, if you are so good.' Hoffmann never took anything strong, fearing to follow the same road as his father.

'Well, let us talk. You have surely made sketches?'

'I have, and they are yours if you want them, but I am not satisfied.'

'Evidently it can't be easy to draw my Sophie. But do you know the engraving from Raphael's self-portrait in the third volume of Lavater's *Physiognomie*?'

'Yes, I know it.'

'And do you not think that the Raphael is the image of my Sophie?'

'No,' said Hoffmann. 'Except for the eyes, which are dark in both cases, there is very little resemblance.' His mind became steadier as he sipped at the dreary *Einfaches*, which resembled the water in which beans have been cooked.

'Hardenberg, I hope you do not doubt my skill. I received eight years' training in Dresden before I was even admitted to the life class. But the truth is that I have been defeated by Fräulein von Kühn. At first I was concerned with the setting – the background – but very soon that no longer mattered to me. It was the gracious Fräulein who puzzled me.'

'The artist's feeling justifies him,' said Fritz. 'That must always be true, for art and nature follow the same laws.'

'That is so. Pure sensations can never be in contradiction to nature. Never!'

'I don't altogether understand Söphgen myself,' Fritz went on. 'That is why I required a good portrait of her. But perhaps we shouldn't have expected that you –'

'Oh, I can see at once what she is,' Hoffmann broke out recklessly. 'A decent, good-hearted Saxon girl, potato-fed, with the bloom of thirteen summers, and the coarser glow of thirteen winters.' He overrode whatever protest it was that Fritz had begun, or rather he ignored it in the intensity of his wish to be understood. 'Hardenberg, in every created thing, whether it is alive or whether it is what we usually call inanimate, there is an attempt to communicate, even among the totally silent. There is a question being asked, a different question for every entity, which for the most part will never be put into words, even by those who can speak. It is asked incessantly, most of the time however hardly noticeably, even faintly, like a church bell heard across meadows and enclosures. Best for the painter, once having looked, to shut his eyes, his physical eyes though not those of the spirit, so that he may hear it more distinctly. You must have listened for it, Hardenberg, for Fräulein Sophie's question, you must have strained to make it out, even though, as I think very probable, she does not know herself what it is.'

'I am trying to understand you,' said Fritz.

Hoffmann had put his hand to his ear, a very curious gesture for a young man.

'I could not hear her question, and so I could not paint.'

32

The Way Leads Inwards

Fritz did not risk taking the painter to the Kloster Gasse, where he would surely say something to his parents about Sophie. There was no alternative to seeing him off from the Wilde Mann when the diligence left for Köln.

He did not want to go straight home, but walked a little way out of the town and into a churchyard which he knew well. It was by now the very late afternoon, pale blue above clear yellow, with the burning clarity of the northern skies, growing more and more transparent, as though to end in revelation.

The entrance to the churchyard was a large iron gate, with gilt letters on it, intertwined. The municipality of Weissenfels had intended to run to an iron fence as well, but at the moment the gate was set in wooden palings which more or less served to keep the cows in the pastor's front yard away from the graves. Knee-deep in the presbytery dung-heap they watched the passers-by without curiosity. Fritz walked among the grass mounds which were now, with the green alleys between them, almost disappearing in the rising mist. As in most graveyards, there were a number of objects left lying about – an iron ladder, a dinner basket and even a spade, as though work here were always in progress, and always liable to be interrupted. The crosses, iron and stone, appeared to grow out of the earth, the smaller ones struggling to get as tall as the others. Some had fallen. You could not say that the churchyard, which was a place for family walks on public holidays, was neglected, but neither was it well kept. There were weeds and a few geese. Stinging insects from the dungheaps and from God's acre joined in triumphant clouds in the strong sickly air.

The creak and thump of the pastor's cows could still be heard far into the burial ground where the graves and the still empty spaces, cut off from each other now by the mist, had become dark green islands, dark green chambers of meditation. On one of them, just a little ahead of him, a young man, still almost a boy, was standing in the half darkness, with his head bent, himself as white, still, and speechless as a memorial. The sight was consoling to Fritz, who knew that the young man, although living, was not human, but also that at the moment there was no boundary between them.

He said aloud, 'The external world is the world of shadows. It throws its shadows into the kingdom of light. How different they will appear when this darkness is gone and the shadow-body has passed away. The universe, after all, is within us. The way leads inwards, always inwards.'

When he got back to the Kloster Gasse, with the impulse to tell somebody about what he had seen, Sidonie immediately asked him who was that man who had been talking to him with so much feeling at the Wilde Mann – Gottfried had seen them – Oh, so it was the poor painter! – Why poor? Fritz asked – Gottfried had given it as his opinion that there were tears in his eyes. Well, Erasmus asked, has he done the portrait? No, Fritz said, he has not been successful. He had done his best to forgive Erasmus. They never, in the ordinary way of things, discussed Sophie. He regarded his brother as an obstinate heathen.

'Are there no sketches?' Sidonie asked.

'Yes, a few,' Fritz told her. 'But they are a kind of notation only – a few lines, a cloud of hair. He declares she is undrawable. What distresses me is my ring, for it was to have a smaller version of the portrait inside it, when it was ready. Now I must content myself with that misbegotten miniature.'

'You can't leave that ring alone,' said the Bernhard, who had come in, silent-footed, from school. 'Always engraved and re-engraved. It would be much better plain.'

'You have never seen it,' said Sidonie. 'None of us has ever seen it.' She smiled at her eldest brother. 'I daresay after all that you are not sorry to think that your Sophie is undrawable.'

Sidonie was making anxious calculations about Gottfried. He might be asked about the stranger in the Wilde Mann, and it would be impossible for him, if asked, to do anything less than tell the truth to the Freiherr. But then, Gottfried did not know that the man he had seen was a painter, and Sidonie was reassured also by the thought that her father never gave his concentrated attention to more than one subject at a time. Lately, to her mother's relief, he had once again allowed the *Leipziger Zeitung* into the house. At the moment he was anxious to hear how much Fritz had gathered from his visit to the salt-works and pan-houses of Artern, then he wished to discuss, or rather to give his opinions, on Buonaparte, who, on the whole, he thought, showed signs of competence. That should last them at least until tomorrow.

Fritz went in through the shabby darkly-polished house, where the sound of the early evening hymn-singing could be heard from behind the shut doors of the kitchen quarters. First to his mother and little Christoph, thin as a shadow with summer fever. 'Are you well, Fritz? Is there anything you want? Are you happy?' He would have liked to ask her to give him something, or to tell him something, but could think of nothing. She asked unexpectedly, 'Are you concealing anything from

127

your father?' Fritz took her hand. 'You must trust me, mother! I shall tell him everything – that is, everything that –' With quite unaccustomed energy she cried, 'No, in heaven's name, whatever it is, don't do that!'

33

At Jena

Before starting work in earnest, but having realised at Artern what it would be like when he did, Fritz went to see his friends at Jena. The Gaul could do the necessary thirty miles, though without enthusiasm. He had not been to see them, Caroline Schlegel had been saying, for centuries.

'We shall hope to hear him talking, as he used to do, before he gets round the corner of Grammaische Strasse,' said Dorothea Schlegel, 'saying something about the Absolute.'

Johann Wilhelm Ritter, a guest in her house as so often, reminded her that Hardenberg could not be judged by any ordinary standards, not even the ordinary standards of Jena, where fifteen out of every twenty inhabitants were said to be Professors. 'For him there is no real barrier between the unseen and the seen. The whole of existence dissolves itself into a myth.'

'But that is the trouble,' interrupted Caroline. 'He used, of course, to say that every day the world was drawing nearer to infinity. Now, we are told, he interests himself in the extraction and refinement of salt and brown coal, which can't be dissolved into a myth, no matter how hard he tries.'

'Goethe himself undertook to administer a silver mine for the Duke of Saxe-Weimar,' said her husband.

'Very unsuccessfully. Goethe's mine went bankrupt. However, I believe that Hardenberg will manage his efficiently, and that is what I can't forgive him. *Enfin*, he will become totally *merkantilistisch*. He will marry the niece of the Kreisamtmann and in good time he will become a Kreisamtmann himself.'

'I am sorry that he allows himself to become an object of jest,' said Ritter.

'That is not on account of his philosophy, or even his mania for salt. It is because he has such large hands and feet,' said Caroline. 'We all love him.'

'Dearly we love him,' said Dorothea.

In Jena, in autumn, friends walked together in the pine woods above the little town, or in Paradise, Jena's name for its towpath along the Saale. Sometimes Goethe, who often spent the summers here, was to be seen in Paradise, also walking, his hands clasped behind his back, in reverie. He was now forty-six years old, and was referred to by the Schlegel women as His Ancient and Divine Majesty. Goethe did not like to meet too many people at once. As he advanced, groups dexterously broke up before he was obliged to meet them. Fritz hung back, not aspiring to the attention of so great a man.

'And yet you have plenty to say,' Caroline told him. 'You could speak to him, as a young man, a coming poet, to one who seems almost indestructible.'

'I have nothing good enough to show him.'

'Never mind,' she said. 'You may talk to me, Hardenberg. Talk to me about salt.'

The musical evenings and *conversazione* at Jena were crowded, but not everyone said brilliant things, or indeed, anything at all. Some of the guests stood uneasily, certain that they had been invited, but not, now that they had arrived, that their names had been remembered.

'Dietmahler!'

'Hardenberg! I knew you as soon as you came into the room.'

'How do I come into a room?'

Dietmahler scarcely liked to say, You still look ridiculous and everyone is still glad to see you. He felt, like a wound, the irrecoverable gap between student days and those that follow.

'Are you a surgeon now?' Fritz asked him.

'Not quite, but soon. You see I have not moved far from Jena. When I qualify, I shall not do so badly. My mother is alive, but I have no younger brothers now and no sisters.'

'*Gott sei Dank*, I have plenty of both,' cried Fritz, on an impulse. 'Come and stay with us in Weissenfels. Dear friend, pay us a visit.'

It was in this way that Dietmahler witnessed the Great Wash at Weissenfels, and told the Freiherr von Hardenberg, in all sincerity, that he knew nothing about his son's entanglement with a young woman of the middle class, or, indeed, with any other woman.

34

The Garden-House

At Tennstedt, Karoline Just heard that the Rockenthiens had asked Fritz to stand godfather to Günther, the new baby. She thought, 'They are trying to bind him to them with links of iron.'

Erasmus, who wrote to her from Hubertusberg, was her only ally. 'I am prepared to resign myself, as I explained to you, to taking a much smaller place in Fritz's life,' he told her, 'at least, I tell myself that I am resigned. But not to having him taken away from us by a greedy infant. If Sophie von Kühn is an infant, however, by the way, she will not stay constant, she will change her mind. And yet I don't quite like the idea of that either.'

Fritz came back to Tennstedt, and went into the kitchen, saying he was too dusty from the summer's roads for the front room. 'Where is the Kreisamtmann? Where is Frau Rahel?'

What does it matter where they are? Karoline felt like answering. You have been away for so long, now is your opportunity to speak to someone who truly understands you. Didn't you say that we were like two watches, set to the same time? She said aloud, 'They are in their garden-house. Yes! It is finished at last.'

'That I must see,' said Fritz. He was washing his face and

132

hands under the pump, but as she put on her shawl he added, in a voice of great tenderness, 'Dear Justen, you must not think I have forgotten the things we talked about not so long ago.' Karoline did think he had forgotten all or most of it. Then as he dried himself he repeated, 'Never does the heart sigh in vain, Justen,' and she scarcely knew whether to be unhappy or not. In her mouth was something bitter, that tasted like the waters of death.

She would have twenty minutes alone with him on the walk down to the garden, which was in an area on the outskirts called the Runde. He would give her his arm. But they would have to stop and talk on the way to many neighbours and acquaintances, all of whom would say: 'Ah, Freiherr, so you are back from Jena.' 'Yes, back from Jena.' 'We are glad that your health has been spared, we are glad to see you back from Jena.' Many of these people would get up in Tennstedt, and go to bed again there at the end of the day, perhaps in all eighteen thousand or so times.

'How good it is to be alive,' several of them said, 'in this warm weather.'

The Justs' plot was small, and had no trees, but they had bought it already cultivated and it was planted up with vegetables, honeysuckle and centifolia roses. The garden-house itself was one of an accepted pattern, which could be ordered from either of the two master carpenters in Tennstedt, and was handsomely framed in carved and gilded wood. Its name was conspicuous, *Der Garten Eden*.

The Justs sat in a cloud of smoke from the Kreisamtmann's pipe, side by side on a new bench at the new entrance. There was no room for anyone else. This, too, was part of the accepted design of a garden-house. They looked happily outwards towards the Runde, half-asphyxiated by the fragrance of hop-vines, honeysuckle and tobacco. 'Hail, ever-blessed pair!' cried Fritz, from a distance.

133

Just, as he himself very well knew, had lately become almost absurdly absorbed by the details of design and installation. He had taken Fritz to Artern, as part of his apprenticeship, to listen to both sides in a disagreement between the different brotherhoods of salt workers. But although he had told Fritz to take careful notes, he had returned with impatience to the matter of the exact placing of the *Vorbau*, or porch, on the garden-house. At what angle would it receive most morning sun? Afternoon sun, of course, was to be avoided.

Even now, while Rahel was asking after her former friends in Jena (but without, Fritz thought, her old hint of sharpness), the Kreisamtmann once again introduced the subject of the *Vorbau*. It had always seemed to Fritz that Coelestin Just knew what contentment was, but not passion, and could therefore be accounted a happy man. He saw now how mistaken he had been. It was discontent that, at last, was making Just truly happy. Although, short of dismantling and re-constructing the entire garden-house nothing could now be done about the *Vorbau*, he would never be quite satisfied with it, never cease to build and rebuild it in his mind. The universe, after all, is within us.

35

Sophie is Cold Through
and Through

Sophie to Fritz – '. . . I have coughs and sneezes,
but it seems to me that I feel quite well again when
you are in my mind. Your Sophie.'

In the autumn of 1795 Fritz plodded over to Grüningen to
find Sophie without cares. She was playing with Günther, whose
experience of life must so far have been favourable, since he
smiled at anything in human form. 'He is stronger by far than
our Christoph,' said Fritz with a pang of regret. Günther did
nothing by halves. He had caught the household's cough, but
reserved it for the night-time, when it echoed, like a large dog
barking, down the corridors.

'Yes, he smiles and coughs at us all alike,' said Fritz, 'and
yet I'm flattered when my turn comes. It is so much more
pleasant to deceive oneself.'

'Hardenberg, why have you not written to me?' Sophie
asked.

'Dear, dear Söphgen, I wrote to you every day this week.
On Monday I wrote to explain to you that although God created
the world it has no real existence until we apprehend it.'

'So all this unholy muddle is our own doing,' said the Mandelsloh. 'What a thing to tell a young girl!'

'Things of the body aren't our own doing,' said Sophie. 'I have a pain in my left side, and that is not my own doing.'

'Well, let us all complain to each other,' said Fritz, but the Mandelsloh declared that she was always well. 'Did you not know that? It is generally agreed that I was born to be always well. My husband is quite sure of it, and so is everyone in this house.'

'Why did you not come earlier, Hardenburch?' asked Sophie.

'I have to work very seriously now,' he told her. 'If we are ever to get married, I must apply myself. I sit up late at night, reading.'

'But why do you do all this reading? You are not a student any more.'

'He would not read if he was,' said the Mandelsloh. 'Students do not read, they drink.'

'Why do they drink?' Sophie asked.

'Because they desire to know the whole truth,' said Fritz, 'and that makes them desperate.'

Günther, who had been half asleep, came to, and protested.

'What would it cost them,' Sophie asked, 'to know the whole truth?'

'They can't reckon that,' said Fritz, 'but they know they can get drunk for three groschen.'

She is thirteen, she will be fourteen, fifteen, sixteen. It takes time. One would say that God has stopped his clock.

But she is cold, cold through and through.

36

Dr Hofrat Ebhard

At Grüningen, when Fritz was gone, the Mandelsloh asked why Sophie had mentioned the pain in her left side. 'You told me we were not to say anything about it.'

'He is not to know,' said Sophie earnestly.

'Then why did you speak of it?'

'Just for the pleasure of talking about it while he was there. He took no notice, you know, Frieke, I laughed and so he did not notice it.'

The pain was no better by the beginning of November. It was Sophie's first serious illness, the first illness in fact that she had ever had. At first they thought it better not to notify Fritz, but on the 14th of November, when he went back to the Justs' house at mid-day, the maid Christel, when she brought him his coffee, told him that there was a messenger waiting for him. The messenger was from Grüningen. Christel's feelings about this were mixed, for she wanted at all costs to keep the young Freiherr in the house. He had come to them, and she considered him theirs, and indeed hers.

'I was not too frightened at first,' Fritz wrote to Karl, 'but when I heard that she was ill – my Philosophy was ill – I notified Just (we had been starting on the year's accounts) and without any further enquiry left for Grüningen.'

'What am I to tell Fräulein Karoline?' Christel had asked. 'She has gone to the market.'

'Tell her what you told me, she will feel exactly the same as I do,' he had said.

Sophie's pain was the first symptom of a tumour on her hip related to tuberculosis. Such pains can disappear, it is said, of their own accord. The doctor, Hofrat Friedrich Ebhard, relied a good deal on this possibility, and a good deal on experience. Of Brownismus he had never had the opportunity to learn anything.

In his *Elementae Medicinae* Brown gives a Table of Excitability for the main disorders, the correct balance being indicated by the figure 40. Phthisis, the early stage of consumption, is shown in his table as coming well below 40. Brown, therefore, in cases of phthisis, would prescribe that the wish to go on living should be supported by electric shocks, alcohol, camphor and rich soups.

None of these things suggested themselves to Ebhard, but he made no mistake in his diagnosis. This was not surprising, since one in four of his patients died of consumption. Fräulein von Kühn was young, but youth in these cases was not always on the patient's side. He had never had the chance to hear the opening of *The Blue Flower*, but if he had done so he could have said immediately what he thought it meant.

37

What is Pain?

Sophie's cough soon put Günther's into the shade. It came with an immense draught of breath which reminded her of laughing, so that in fact she would have been hard put to it, except for the pain, not to laugh.

What if there were no such thing as pain? When they were all children at Grüningen, Friederike, not yet the Mandelsloh, but already on duty, used to collect them together after the evening service to tell them a Sunday story.

'There was a certain honest shopkeeper,' she said, 'who unlike the rest of us, felt no pain. He had never felt any since he was born, so that when he reached the age of forty-five he was quite unaware that he was ill and never thought to call the doctor, until one night he heard the sound of the door opening, and sitting up in his bed saw in the bright moonlight that someone he did not know had come into his room, and that this was Death.'

Sophie had been unable to grasp the point of the story.

'He was so lucky, Frieke.'

'Not at all. The pain would have been a warning to him that he was ill, and as it was he had no warning.'

'We don't want any warnings,' the children told her. 'We get into enough trouble as it is.'

'But he had no time to consider how he had spent his life, and to repent.'

'Repentance is for old women and arse-holes,' shouted George.

'George, no-one can tolerate you,' said Friederike. 'They ought to whip you at school.'

'They do whip me at school,' said George.

The Hofrat ordered the application of linseed poultices to Sophie's hip, which were so scalding hot that they marked the skin for good. The linseed smelled of the open forest, of solid furniture, of the night-watchman's heavy oiled boots, specially issued to him by the town councillors because he had to patrol the streets in all weathers, of pine trees and green spruce. Unmistakeably, Sophie began to get better.

'*Liebster, bester Freund,*' Rockenthien wrote to Fritz. 'How are you? Here it is the same old story. Söphgen dances, jumps, sings, demands to be taken to the fair at Greussen, eats like a woodcutter, sleeps like a rat, walks straight as a fir-tree, has given up whey and medicine, has to take two baths a day by way of treatment, and is as happy as a fish in water.'

'Sometimes, I wish that I were the Hausherr,' Fritz wrote to Karl from Tennstedt, 'the world is not a problem to him, and yet this time what he says is true. My dear, treasured Philosophy had had sleepless nights, burning fever, had been bled twice, was too feeble to move. The Hofrat – by the way, it is possible that he is a fool – spoke of inflammation of the liver. And now, since the 20th of November, we are told and indeed we can see with our own eyes that all danger is past.' He asked Karl to send, by a good messenger, two hundred oysters – these to go straight to Grüningen, as a delicacy for the invalid – and to Tennstedt, Fritz's winter trousers, his woollen stockings, his *santés* (the comforters that went under the waistcoat), material for a green jacket, white cashmere for a waistcoat and trousers, a hat, and the loan of Karl's gold epaulettes. He would explain later why he wanted these things, and he would come to Weissenfels and settle up while *der Alte* was meeting old friends, as he did once a year, at the fair in Dresden.

38

Karoline at Grüningen

Even Tennstedt had its fair, specialising in *Kesselfleisch* – the ears, snout and strips of fat from the pig's neck boiled with peppermint schnaps. Great iron kettles dispersed the odours of pig sties and peppermint. There was music of sorts, and the stall-keepers, who had come in from the country, danced with each other to keep warm. Karoline had been accustomed to go to the fair at first with her uncle, then with her uncle and step-aunt, and she did so again this year. – A fine young woman still, what a pity she has no affianced to treat her to a pig's nostril!

Her uncle said, 'You will want to call at Schloss Grüningen, to congratulate them on their daughter's renewed health. Why do you not come with me next week, when I have to see Rockenthien on business?'

Karoline had never asked him, and did not now ask, what he thought of Hardenberg's engagement, although he must surely know about it, and how he felt about the Freiherr being kept so long in the dark. She was sure that it must give him pain to conceal anything from his old friend, and in this case the Freiherr had trusted him, after all, to supervise his eldest son. But she knew also that her uncle, like most men, believed that what had not been put into words, and indeed into written words, was not of great importance.

For their visit to the Rockenthiens, Coelestin had hired a horse and trap. They broke their journey at Gebesee, where the manor house belonged, he told Karoline, to the von Oldershausen family – the family, that was, of the Freiherr's long dead first wife. 'The property is now in ruins. They have not been fortunate.'

At the Black Boy, he sent out for schnaps, and looked at his niece attentively for the first time for months, since though he was no less fond of her than ever, her health and well-being could now fairly be left to Rahel. He felt that he should, perhaps, be sorry about something.

'My dear, you must be very tired of hearing about my garden and my garden-house.'

She smiled. That was not the trouble, then, Just thought to himself. Try again. At different ages, women had different troubles, but always there was something. 'I had meant to tell you that in Treffurt, a few weeks ago, I saw your cousin Carl August.'

She gave the same smile.

'And my sister, your Aunt Luisa, and I . . .'

'You thought the two of us might make a respectable match. But, you know, I haven't seen Carl August for years, and he is younger than I am.'

'One would never think it, Karolinchen. You are always rather pale, but . . .'

Karoline put a lump of sugar and a small amount of hot water in her glass. 'Don't make any arrangements for me with Tante Luisa, Uncle. Wait until all hope is gone, until behind me roars youth's wild ocean.'

'Is that from some poem or other?' asked Just doubtfully.

'Yes, from some poem or other. To tell you the truth, I don't like my cousin.'

'My dear, you said yourself you hadn't seen him for some time. I think I can tell you exactly when.'

In one of the top inside pockets of his winter coat, Just kept his minutely written diary for the last five years, and he began now to pat the outside of his pocket, as though expecting it to call out to him in response.

'My cousin was very irritating then, and he will be very irritating now,' Karoline went on. 'I am sure he prides himself on his consistency.'

'You must not let yourself become too difficult, my Karoline,' said her uncle, in some distress, and she reflected that he was being a little more frank than he had no doubt intended, and that she must not let him worry, as he would probably soon begin to do, that he had hurt her feelings. But it was never difficult to distract him. 'I daresay Hardenberg has spoiled me,' she said. 'I daresay talking to a poet has turned my head.'

At Schloss Grüningen she was relieved to find that Rockenthien had already gone to his office. The Kreisamtmann followed him there. Karoline paid her respects to the tranquil mistress of the house, and admired Günther, to whom she had sent an ivory teething ring, with a porcelain sweet-box for Sophie, marzipan and *pfefferkuchen* for Mimi and Rudi, and a brace of hares for the household.

'You are a good, generous girl,' said Frau Rockenthien. 'Your lodger, Hardenberg, is here, you know, and his brother Erasmus, yes, Erasmus this time. He often brings one of his brothers with him.'

Karoline's heart seemed to open and shut.

'I expect Hardenberg will return with us to Tennstedt this evening,' she said.

'Ach, well, they are in the morning room now. All are welcome, it is no matter and it is no trouble, whoever comes,' said Frau Rockenthien, and indeed for her it was not. 'I don't know, however, why Hardenberg has sent quite so many oysters. Do you care for oysters, my dear? Of course, they do not keep for ever.'

*   *   *

The morning room. Hardenberg, Erasmus, Friederike Mandelsloh, George trying, apparently for the first time, to play the flute, a pack of little dogs, Sophie in a pale pink dress. When Karoline had last seen her she had thought of her as one of the children. She still thought of her as one of the children. Every night she prayed that she might be spared to have children of her own, though not, perhaps, children quite like Sophie.

Hardenberg stayed beside his Philosophy, with his large feet stowed away under his chair. Erasmus came over at once to Karoline, delighted, not having expected to see her. Sophie was in raptures, absolutely genuine, over her sweet-box; she was going to give up chewing tobacco altogether, only sweets from now on.

'They will give you colic,' said the Mandelsloh.

'Ach, I have colic already. I tell Hardenburch he must call me his little wind-bag.'

Karoline turned to Erasmus, as though to another survivor from drowning. 'This is really all I need,' she thought, 'one moment only with someone who feels as I do.' And Erasmus took her hand in his warm one, and seemed about to say something, but in another moment he had turned back towards Sophie with an indulgent smile, half-senseless, like a drunken man.

Karoline perceived that Erasmus also had fallen in love with Sophie von Kühn.

39

The Quarrel

In his poem for her thirteenth birthday Fritz wrote that he could hardly credit that there had been a time when he had not known Sophie and when he was 'the man of yesterday,' careless, irresponsible, and so forth. The man of yesterday was now set, once and forever, on the right path. 'But he has been hateful to me,' Sophie told the Mandelsloh, 'we have quarrelled, it is all over.'

This was all the more unjust because she had looked forward to her first quarrel, having been told by her friend, Jette Gold-acker, that she and Hardenberg certainly ought to have one. It was the right thing for lovers to do, the Goldacker had said, and afterwards the ties between them would be strengthened. But what can we quarrel about? Sophie asked. About any little thing, it seemed, the more unimportant the better. But after they had been sitting together talking for about half an hour, perhaps not quite so long, her Hardenberg broke out, as though something in him had been overstretched and worked ruinously loose: 'Sophie, you are thirteen years old. How have you spent your time so far? Your first year was passed, I suppose, in smiling and sucking, as little Günther does now. During your second year, as girls are more forward than boys, you learned to speak. Your first words – what were they? "I want!" At three

146

you became still greedier, and finished off the sweet wine from the grown-ups' glasses. At four you began to laugh, and finding that pleasant, you laughed at everything and everybody. At five years old they started to try to educate you. At eleven, having learned nothing, you discovered you had become a woman. You were frightened, I daresay, and went to your gracious mother, who told you not to disturb yourself. Then it came to you that those succulent looks of yours, not quite blonde, not quite brunette, made it unnecessary for you to know, still less to say, anything rational. And now, of course, you're crying, sensibility itself, I suppose, let us see how long you can cry for, my Philosophy –'

He had no manners, Sophie had wept. That was what they said to her when she was in disgrace, the strongest reproach she knew. Fritz replied that he had been to the Universities of Jena, Leipzig and Wittenberg, and knew somewhat more about manners than a thing of thirteen.

'A thing of thirteen, Frieke! Can you believe that, can you explain that?'

'How did he explain it himself?'

'He said I was a torment to him.'

In his next letters to Sophie, Fritz called himself inexcusable, uncultivated, ungracious, impolite, incorrect, intolerable, impertinent and inhuman.

The Mandelsloh advised him to stop it. 'Whatever the cause of the trouble was, she has forgotten it.'

'There was no cause,' Fritz told her.

'That makes it more difficult, still, she has forgotten it.'

He set about applying to Prince Friedrich August III, in Dresden, for consideration as a salaried salt mine inspector designate in the Electorate of Saxony.

40

How to Run a Salt Mine

It was still Fritz's business to take the minutes and pick up what he could, in silence, at the meetings of the Direction Committee, which were held at the Salt Offices in Weissenfels. Freiherr von Hardenberg presided, assisted by Salt Mine Director Bergrath Heun and Salt Mine Inspector Bergrath Senf. The Bernhard delighted in this name – Salt Mine Inspector Mustard! – and he alone – although everybody knew about it – referred openly to the unfortunate episode when, as a result of falsifying the receipts for official building work and spending unauthorised sums on his own private house, Senf had been sentenced to two years in the common convicts' jail, subsequently reduced to eight weeks' normal imprisonment. 'That was a pity,' said the Bernhard. 'We could have chatted to him about it, it would have been interesting to know what it was like to live on bread and water.' 'You may make the experiment here at home, at any time you like,' said Sidonie.

Heun was of a very different character from Senf. Only a few years older than his two colleagues, he seemed ancient, and referred to himself as 'old Heun, the living archive of the salt mines'. In his long coat of coarse stuff, in which dust seemed to be incorporated, he suggested one of those elementals of the caves and passages of the inner earth, who emerge only reluctantly, and not with good omen, into daylight. The idea partly arose from his blanched skin and frequent blinking and creaking. 'The living archive has, perhaps, a touch of the rheumatismus.' Heun, given time, could answer on every point. He consulted the ledgers only to see that they confirmed the details and figures he had given. 'They would not dare to do otherwise,' thought Fritz.

Senf, on the other hand, smouldered with the suppressed energy of a very intelligent man who, as the result of a foolish miscalculation, was never likely to be able to profit from his intelligence again. At certain fixed intervals everyone connected with the mines and the salt works was permitted to submit their suggestions for improvement in writing. In an elaborate scheme, to which he still hoped his name would be one day attached, Senf had proposed that the salt of Thuringia and Saxony should no longer be evaporated in iron pans over wood fires at eighty degrees centigrade, but by the sun's warmth only. Very many fewer salt workers would be needed and there would be no necessity for them to have houses on the premises. His projects for solar power passed over, Senf put forward a new proposal for doubling the number of wheels on the pulleys which drew the salt water to the surface. 'When the Director, Freiherr von Hardenberg, had considered this scheme,' Fritz wrote in his minutes, 'his comment was, *Quod potest fieri per pauca, non debet fieri per plura* (Manage with as little as you can).' Salt Mine Inspector Senf replied with much warmth that this was not the way forward, and that these mean economies led rather to inertia and stagnation. In any case, with the coming of the nineteenth century, a time when, as Kant had foreseen, men would at last have learned to govern themselves, pulleys and tread wheels would in all probability have no place. Salt Mine Director Heun remarked that in that event, they need not waste more time in discussing them. Inspector Senf said that he was obliged to accept the Director's decision, but could not pretend that he felt satisfied.

'I have applied myself to everything you asked for,' Fritz told his father, 'and I shall do so even more earnestly in the future. You cannot expect me, in a few months, to become like old Heun.'

'Unfortunately I cannot and do not,' said the Freiherr. 'Even if you are granted a long life, I do not think you will ever resemble Wilhelm Heun.'

Formerly when he rode across country Fritz had admired the ancient mountains. Now he looked at the foothills and the coal-bearing ranges with a prospector's eye for copper, silver, and lignite. He intended to be a practical engineer and went, as often as he could manage it, down the shafts of the *Bergwerke*, wearing a miner's grey jacket and trousers.

'Your son would like to live underground,' Just told the Freiherr. 'Only reluctantly he returns to the light of day . . . I warned him, of course, that he must not shake hands with the miners, as they would consider that it brought bad luck. This disappointed him.'

Fritz covered sheet after sheet of paper with schemes for discovering new lignite beds and improving the supervision of tile-kilns and lime-kilns, with meteorological records which might help to bring the refinement of brine to a higher standard, and with notes on the legal aspect of salt manufacture. But he also saw himself as a geognost, a natural scientist, who, as he put it, had come 'to an entirely new land, and dark stars'. The mining industry, it seemed to him, was not a science, but an art. Could anyone but an artist, a poet, understand the relationship between the rocks and the constellations? The mountain ranges, and the foothills with their burden of precious metals, coal and rock salt, were perhaps no more than traces of the former paths of stars and planets, who once trod this earth.

'What has been, must be again,' he wrote. 'At what point in

history will they return to walk among us as they once did?'

Patiently Karoline Just listened to everything he had learned and therefore needed to repeat to another intelligence. She continued to sew while Fritz ploughed through a *Continuation of the Report on the Purchase of Coal-bearing Plots of Land at Mertendorf.* 'When these data are correlated, one cannot be in any doubt as to the future scheme of acquisition, in the course of which we freely confess that the peasants, by all accounts, will make, in relation to the old prices, fairly high demands . . .'

'Of course they will,' said Karoline, 'but when did you make this report?'

'I did not make it, it was made some time ago. I have to train myself by making reports on reports. That, after all, is what your uncle taught me to do.'

'You have been his best pupil. Indeed, I don't think that he will ever want another one.'

'And yet I don't think that as yet my father takes me seriously.'

'You don't take him seriously,' said Karoline.

'It is my father who must make the application to the administration to consider me for a salaried post. I might hope in the first instance to receive 400 thaler.' She had paused to rethread her needle. 'Justen, how often you must have tried to calculate whether *you* and *he* could keep house on such a sum!'

She realised that his imagination had sped on far ahead of her own, and that the cruel separation between herself and the Unwanted had now become a question of money. The Unwanted, evidently, had no salaried post. This vexed her. Bitterly though she had regretted the whole pretence from its very first moment, it was nevertheless hers. She had created, even if she hadn't meant to, the Unwanted, and she resented his being made into a failure (for he must be more than thirty), and unable to support her as a wife. She felt he had been slighted. She had an impulse to disconcert Hardenberg.

Usually that was easy enough. She told him now – quite truthfully – that although she wished him well, from the bottom of her heart, in his search for a post, she must admit to some doubts about the profession itself. Erasmus was to be a forestry official, well and good, if he ever finished at St Hubertusberg. Karl and Anton were to be soldiers and about that she knew nothing and had nothing to say, but mining, the extraction of minerals and salts from the earth – well, she had been more than once to the salt-refineries at Halle and Artern, and she had seen, and smelled, the clouds of dark yellowish smoke from the amalgam works near Freiberg, and she could not help thinking of them as an offence against Nature, which could never create such ugliness. 'So often, Hardenberg, we have spoken of Nature. Only on Wednesday evening you were saying at table that although human culture and industry may grow, Nature remains the same, and our first duty is to consider what she asks of us.' Taking a risk which she had forbidden herself, she went on, 'You have spoken of Sophie as Nature herself.'

Karoline shut her eyes for a moment as she said this, not being anxious to see the effect. Fritz cried – 'No, Justen, you have not understood. The mining industry is not a violation of Nature's secrets, but a release. You must imagine that in the mines you reach the primal sons of Mother Earth, the age-old life, trapped in the ground beneath your feet. I have seen this process as a meeting with the King of Metals, who waits underground, listening in hope for the first sounds of the pick, while the miner struggles through hardships to bring him up to the light of day. Release, Justen! What must the King of Metals feel when he turns his face to the sunlight for the first time?'

She meant to say, 'I wonder if you have mentioned these ideas to the Direction Committee' – but she could not bring herself to it. She recognised the voice in which he had read to her the opening chapter of *The Blue Flower*. Meanwhile he had

152

opened his file again, and taken out another page of his delicate crocketed writing, another report on a report, this time a summary, in tabular form, of the boiling-points of cooking-salt and salt fertilisers.

41

Sophie at Fourteen

Two days before Sophie's fourteenth birthday, on the 15th of March 1796, the anniversary of his engagement – still not authorised, and indeed not discussed so far, with his father – Fritz went to the jewellers in Tennstedt to have yet another alteration to his ring. It was to contain a tiny likeness of Sophie, he explained, taken from the miniature which had disappointed everybody – that couldn't be helped. Her startled, eager expression was there at least, and her mixture of darkness and brightness. On the reverse, he told them to engrave the words – *Sophie sey mein schuz geist* – Sophie be my guardian spirit. In her birthday poem he wrote:

> *What I looked for, I have found:*
> *What I found, has looked for me.*

In the June of 1796 Fritz wrote to both his father and his mother.

> Dear Father,
> Not without great unease do I send this letter which
> I have dreaded for so long. Long ago I would have
> sent it, if unfavourable circumstances had not arisen.
> All my hopes depend on your friendliness and

154

sympathy. There is nothing wrong with what lies in my heart, but it is a subject on which parents and children often do not understand each other. I know that you always want to be a patron and friend to your children, but you are a Father, and often fatherly love contradicts the son's inclination.

I have chosen a maiden. She has little wealth, and although she is equal to the nobility, she is not of ancient lineage. She is Fräulein von Kühn. Her parents, of whom the mother is the property owner, lie in Grüningen. I got to know her on an official visit to her stepfather's house. I enjoy the friendship and confidence of the whole family. But Sophie's answering choice long remained doubtful.

Long since would I have sought your confidence and consent, but at the beginning of November Sophie became grievously ill, and even now she is only recovering slowly. You can give back my peace. I beg from you consent and authorisation of my choice.

More by word of mouth. It all depends on you, to make this the happiest period of my life. True, my sphere of activity would be reduced by this match, but I rely for my future on industry, faith and economy, and on Sophie's intelligence and good management. She has not been grandly brought up − she is content with little − I need only what she needs. God bless this important, so anxious, so difficult-to-pass-through hour. It is good to speak out and say what you mean, but you can make me happy only through your consenting Father's voice.

Fritz

Dear little Mother,
I will wait for you at nine in the evening on Wednesday two weeks from now, alone in our garden at
Weissenfels. I do not need to ask for anything more,
for I know your tender heart.

Fritz

It was true that Hofrat Ebhard had not much idea what to do
next, but he was quite used to this. It did strike him that at
Schloss Grüningen his patient had too much company, too much
excitement, too many little dogs and cage birds, too many visits
from the wildly-talking Hardenberg. He sent her for a few
days to a rest-home in which he had a part interest, at Weis-
sensee. It was unfortunately damper and much less airy than
Schloss Grüningen. 'The house is deserted,' complained Rockenthien, for George also, just as he was beginning to turn into a
decent shot, was to be sent away to school in Leipzig. There
would be only twenty-six people left at home. His worries he
shoved to the back of his mind, as one puts a rat-trap on
a shelf, when, for the time being at least, it is no longer
needed.

'Well, what does he say, the Freiherr?' asked the Mandelsloh.
'I have written to him,' said Fritz, 'and to my mother, and
I have explained to them –'
'– what they certainly know already. You have told me that
even when your friend from Jena, Assistant Practitioner Dietmahler, came to stay with you, your father questioned him on
the subject. It's only Söphgen's name perhaps, that he won't
know until he gets your letter.'
'There is something I have to ask you,' said Fritz urgently.
'Let us speak heart to heart. Suppose my father were to refuse
his permission. Suppose that he tries to separate me from my

Philosophy, my heart's blood. Living here in this paradise you scarcely know what unjust authority means.'

'I know what it is to be separated,' said the Mandelsloh.

'My father himself has been married twice. I am twenty-four years old and there is no law that can be invoked against me in the Electorate of Saxony if I marry without his permission, or indeed against my Sophie, as soon as she reaches her fourteenth birthday. Would she come with me, Friederike, do you think she would defy the world and want no more of it in order to be with me?'

'On what would you support yourself?'

'I would earn the little we need as a soldier, a copying-clerk, a journalist, a night-watchman.'

'These occupations are all forbidden to the nobility.'

'Under another name —'

'— and, I suppose, in another country, if you could get your papers — would you not want to go south?'

'Ah, Frieke, the south, do you know it?'

'Far from it,' said the Mandelsloh, 'who would ever take me there? I shall have to wait until the Regiment is posted to the land where the lemon-trees flower.'

'Well, but you have not answered me.'

'You want her to leave her home, where for as long as she can remember — for God's sake . . .'

'You don't think, then, that she has the courage?'

'Courage when you don't understand what it is that you have to face is no better than ignorance.'

'Treason, Frieke! Courage is more than endurance, it is the power to create your own life in the face of all that man or God can inflict, so that every day and every night is what you imagine it. Courage makes us dreamers, courage makes us poets.'

'But it would not make Söphgen into a competent house-keeper,' said the Mandelsloh. Fritz ignored this and repeated wildly, 'Would she come with me? Could she bear the parting? – my love would make that easy – would she come?'

'God forgive me, I'm afraid she might.'

'Why are you afraid?'

'I forbid you to ask her.'

'You forbid me –'

'– if I don't, another will.'

'But who could that be?'

'Is it possible that you don't know?'

The Freifrau in the Garden

The Freiherr von Hardenberg wrote to Kreisamtmann Just.

Who was this von Kühn, the actual father of this
Sophie? They tell me that he is the son of Wilhelm
Kühn, who acquired in 1743, let us say fifty years
ago, the proprietorship of Grüningen and Nieder-
Topfstedt, and, after that, somehow managed to get a
patent of nobility. In good time his son, this Sophie's
father, installs himself at Grüningen. His first wife
is called Schmidt; she dies. His second wife is called
Schaller, then *he* dies. The widow takes up with a
certain Captain Rockenthien, I think from the Prince
of Schwarzburg's Regiment, thus he in turn becomes
the master of Grüningen and Nieder-Topsftedt. I
do not think that as yet Rockenthien himself has had
the assurance to apply for a patent of nobility.

Kreisamtmann Just replied to Freiherr von Hardenberg.

I can only repeat what I have said before, that I have
taught your son all the routine that he needs to know

for an official career, and in talking to him I, too, have glimpsed new horizons.

The Freiherr von Hardenberg to Kreisamtmann Just.

Glimpse what horizons you like, but why, in God's name, did you take him to the Rockenthiens?

He took Fritz's letter to Leipzig, where he sat with old friends in the club reserved for nobility, stifling in summer, since the members forbade the waiters to open the steam-clouded windows facing the street. There he consulted old friends, as to how he should answer his eldest son. He button-holed the old Count Julius von Schweinitz and the only slightly younger Graf von Loeben, and asked them what they themselves should do if either of their eldest sons should insist on marrying a grocer's daughter. His mind was, perhaps, beginning to give way a little.

Fritz had asked his mother to meet him in the garden simply so that they would not be overseen by his father, without reflecting what an extraordinary thing it would be for her to do. Auguste nowadays scarcely ever went out at all, never alone, never at night, and certainly never without the Freiherr's considered permission. When she told her maid to get out her black shawl, because she was going out by herself into the garden, the old woman began to say her prayers. Still, by the time the Freifrau had made her way down the unfamiliar back stairs, the alert had been given to everyone in the kitchens and the yard. At the bottom of the steps which led into the upper part of the garden the head gardener was waiting in the dusk with a light to open the gate. That was as well, because she had no key and had given no thought to how she should get in.

In the ordinary way she would have excused or explained

herself, but not to-night. She was absorbed not so much in
anxiety for Fritz as in gratification at being wanted and needed
and told to meet him in the garden.

She stood just inside the gate, listening to the shifting and
creaking and strange repeated ticking which birds, in their
restless half-sleep, make all night. They lodged in the great
cherry tree, which produced two hundred pounds of fruit in a
good summer, so that at first light they could start gorging
themselves before the gardener's boy arrived. The cherries were
almost black, but could still be distinguished from the mass of
leaves, gently stirring although there seemed to be no wind.

Fritz was there already, coming towards her up the path
from the lower garden. 'Mother, you know I would not keep
you waiting.'

The numberless times he had done so no longer existed.
'Dear Fritz, have you been to see your father?'

'Not yet.'

They sat on two of the old wooden chairs left out all summer
under the cherry tree. When Fritz had been born, sickly and
stupid, she had been given the blame, and had accepted it.
When after months of low fever he had become tall and thin
and, as they all said, a genius, she had not been given any
credit, and had not expected any. He asked her why she was
wearing her winter shawl.

'It's June, mother. Otherwise I should never have asked you
to meet me outside.'

Auguste saw now that the shawl was ridiculous. 'But Fritz,
I feel safe in it.' He smiled, and did not need to say, 'You are
safe with me.'

An extraordinary notion came to the Freifrau Auguste, that
she might take advantage of this moment, which in its half-
darkness and fragrance seemed to her almost sacred, to talk to
her eldest son about herself. All that she had to say could be
put quite shortly: she was forty-five, and she did not see how

she was going to get through the rest of her life. Abruptly Fritz leaned towards her and said, 'You know that I have only one thing to ask. Has he read my letter?'

Immediately she came to herself. 'Fritz, he surely must have done, but I can't tell. He has never shown me his letters, but then, God forgive me, I did not show him yours. However, the whole household are to join in a prayer meeting tomorrow evening to consider an important family question.'

'But, mother, you are on my side, tell me that is so. You approve of what I have done, and what I am going to do. I am following my heart and my soul, you cannot be against me.'

She cried, 'No! No!' but when he went on, 'In that case, why don't you tell my father what you feel?' she answered, 'But I have to obey him, that is natural.'

'Nonsense, in the world of Nature the female is often stronger than the male, and dominates him.'

'You mean among the birds and insects,' said the Freifrau timidly. 'But, Fritz, they know no better.'

Paying attention only to her mindless tenderness for him, he said, 'You must tell my father that it is not enough for him only to agree to my engagement. We must have somewhere to live, for Sophie and myself to live, the two of us, alone and together. You understand me, you are not too old to have forgotten.'

Auguste allowed herself to remember what she had felt when she and the Freiherr were left, for the first time, alone and together. But what mattered now was her son, almost, for the moment, in the overwhelming summer night, a stranger. 'Indeed, yes, Fritz, of course.'

She could be seen to be struggling with a small package, which she had hidden in the pocket of her top under-petticoat.

'Fritz, my dearest, this is my gold bracelet. Well! I have others, but this is truly mine, it was not given to me by your father, I received it from my godmother when I was twelve,

on the occasion of my confirmation. It has been enlarged since
then, but only a little, I wish you to have it altered, and made
into your engagement rings.'

'The rings have already been made, mother. Look!'

Sophie sey mein schuz geist.

'Indeed, mother, I must not take your bracelet, I do not
need it, put it away, consider yourself, or keep it, if anything,
for Sidonie.'

Thoughtfulness can be much more painful than neglect. The
Freifrau, however, had had very few opportunities to learn
this.

Back in her room, which was still at the top of the house, she
let herself reflect that if only Fritz could always be at home,
even with a new wife, she would want no further earthly happiness. Then she prayed for forgiveness, because she must have
forgotten, if only for a moment, the welfare of the Bernhard.

The Bernhard himself, however, thought of it unremit-
tingly. 'What will become of us, Sidonie?' he asked plaintively.
'To whom will you yourself be married? You're difficult, you
felt nothing at all for that medical fellow who came on the
washday, although he couldn't stop looking at you. You may
well be left a spinster. Karl and Anton, I know, are provided
for, and Asmus is supposed to have passed his first exams as a
forester . . .'

'I *have* passed them,' said Erasmus. 'The principal congratulated me, so did my father, so did Fritz. He sent me a copy
of *Robinson Crusoe.*'

'So, please lend it to me.'

'It's in English,' said Erasmus. 'You can't read English.'

'That is true,' said Bernhard with a deep sigh. 'In those wild
forests of words I am lost.'

'In any case,' said Anton, 'you should never lend a book or
a woman. There's no obligation to return either.'

'Anton, you are trying to talk like Karl,' said Sidonie. 'But you have not got it quite right.'

'It's simply that I feel the time approaching when a decision will be made about me,' said the Bernhard, standing up among them with the air of the boy Jesus among the Elders in the print on his bedroom wall.

'You know you're to be a page,' said Anton. 'The Electoral Courts of Thuringia and Saxony little know what's coming to them.'

'I appeal to all of you,' the Bernhard cried. 'Who in their senses would think of me as a page? Whatever it is that a page is obliged to do, I know that I could not do it.'

Tears ran down his face, and yet the Hardenbergs were at a kind of ease. Fritz, after he had spoken to his mother, had not stayed even for a night. The Freiherr had departed for a few days, taking with him as a confidential servant the pious Gottfried. Throughout the house there could be sensed, as when music changes not its theme but its key, a little less concentration on the soul, a little more on the body. Today, at half past eight in the morning, they were all still at breakfast. The Freifrau had not come down. Erasmus and Anton sprawled on their chairs. The windows were open down to the ground, the air brought in the scent of the cherry-trees – even of the amarelles, grown for making kirsch, which would not fruit till the autumn – and, from beyond Weissenfels, of the first hay-cutting. All four of them, even the Bernhard, knew that they were not unhappy that morning, but had too much good sense to say anything, even to themselves, about it.

The Freiherr had gone to the Brethren at Neudietendorf to consult the Prediger. At the risk of worldliness, he had spoken of his family properties – bankrupt Oberwiederstadt, the four lost estates, sold to strangers, and Schlöben, the beloved Schlöben-bei-Jena with its poplars and mill-stream, where he hoped to live in his retirement, making it a centre for some of the older Brethren.

'Meanwhile, my eldest son ignores my wishes. If Ober-wiederstadt and Schlöben were to be settled upon him, I cannot tell what he would do. It would be only decent for him to marry into the nobility and to find a woman with adequate wealth. Don't tell me I am always thinking about money, it is precisely that I don't want to have to think about it at all. But since the recent events in France the world is turned upside down, and a father's necessities no longer weigh with his sons.'

The Prediger nodded, and said that he would give his advice if Hardenberg would undertake to follow it. The Freiherr gave his word. The next day he rode back to Weissenfels with Gottfried. They stopped at no inns, and exchanged very few words. Silence between them said more.

> *Leipziger Zeitung*, 13 July 1796
> Christiane Wilhelmine Sophie v. Kühn
> Georg Philipp Friedrich v. Hardenberg
> betrothed
> Grüningen   Weissenfels

43

The Engagement Party

Servants appeared out of the yard gate of the house in the Kloster Gasse. The carrier had brought a pianoforte, ordered by the Freiherr, from Leipzig.

Everyone knows how best to move a piano, or rather, how it should be moved. Not up the front steps, you triple fool! – A little to the right. – It would be easier if we could take off the legs.

When the piano had reached its resting place in the salon and stood unwrapped from its straw and sackcloth, it could be seen to be a thing of beauty, rare in that austere household. Already, however, it had caused trouble enough, since the Father, although he had made up his mind some time ago to replace the harpsichord, had not been able to decide whether to order from Gottlieb Silbermann or Andreas Stein. 'Silbermann's pianos are more sonorous,' wrote the Uncle Wilhelm, 'but the touch is heavier than Stein's. For Stein's, on the other hand, one must send to Vienna.'

'This from Wilhelm,' shouted the Freiherr, 'who scarcely knows one note from another. The horses in his stable recognise more tunes than Wilhelm.' He continued to take, and discard, advice. 'The French manufacturers are the best,' old Heun assured him. 'They escaped the unpleasant situation in Paris, they have all taken refuge in London, where they live in the British Museum. You may enquire of them there.'

If the Freifrau had been consulted she would have said that she did not care for the pianoforte, as an instrument, at all, and thought it dull in comparison with the sparkling chatter of the harpsichord, which reminded her of her girlhood. The harpsichord, which had now been moved out of the house, was in fact the one she had brought with her to Oberwiederstadt on the occasion of her marriage. It was French, and had a picture of a ruined temple by moonlight on the inside of the lid. But the relentless damp of Weissenfels, where the Saale secretively chose its own time, at any season of the year, to flood its banks, had mouldered it gradually away. The painting had become almost invisible, the jacks were like a row of ageing teeth, some missing. It had come to need re-tuning every evening, and by the morning the pitch was gone. Bits of it, too, appeared to have come unscrewed. 'I dare say I shall be blamed,' said the Bernhard. And in fact Karl complained that they had allowed the Angel to make a *Pfuscherei* of the harpsichord while he was with his regiment. 'But in any case you cannot play it as well as Anton,' said the Bernhard, 'and it is being sold for firewood.'

The Freiherr bought a piano by Johannes Zumpe, one of Silbermann's apprentices, which had been advertised in the *Zeitung*. In this way he succeeded in not following his brother Wilhelm's advice.

Anton was called upon. Anton, who had been thought to have not much interest in life beyond following Karl's example, was now the necessary person. All the family could play – Erasmus could play anything by ear, Sidonie was truly musical, but they could not play like Anton.

The Zumpe piano had a third pedal, which allowed the three lowest octaves to be sustained, while the treble was damped in the ordinary way. Anton sat alone, refusing any help, in the

167

salon. Although it hadn't been one of the Freiherr's requirements when he bought the house, the Hardenbergs' salon had
been built originally as a music room and for nothing else, and
the airy space faithfully carried every note, balanced it, and let
it fall reluctantly.

The Freiherr now told his wife to invite suitable guests from
Weissenfels and the surrounding neighbourhood to a *soirée*.
'He is so good-hearted, Sidonie. He cannot rest until he has
shared the beauty of the new music.' Hardenberg went out so
little, except to meetings of the Brethren and on tours of inspection, that he did not realise that a piano was anything but a
novelty at Weissenfels. Chief Magistrate von Lindenau even
had a Broadwood, ordered from England to his own specifications.

'Surely what we are sharing is my father's heartfelt pleasure
in Fritz's engagement,' said Sidonie.

'Of course, my dear.'

'The party from Grüningen — we can't tell how many will
come — cannot, of course, return home the same night. They
must all stay here, and you will have to consider about the
rooms.'

'How fortunate that we bought the slop-pails!'

No-one in Weissenfels looked forward very much to the
Hardenbergs' invitations, but they were so rare — this was not
thought of as meanness, everyone knew of their piety and
charity — and so formally expressed, that they seemed less of a
celebration than a register of slowly passing time, like mortality
itself. Most of the guests would be town officials, all would
know each other. But none of them would have met the Rockenthiens, except of course the Justs. The Justs had the farthest to
come, but would spend the night at the house of old Heun,
who was Rahel's uncle.

Lukas was at the door, Gottfried in charge of the *Vorzimmer*,

which led into the great downstairs reception room. His last
trip with the Freiherr to Neudietendorf seemed to have left
him in a position of mild, almost benign authority, which had
not been so noticeable before. Erasmus thought it possible that
he had been drinking.

'Inconceivable,' said Sidonie. 'You have been too long away
from home.'

Small groups of people, in threes and fours, lingered in
the Kloster Gasse to watch the Hardenbergs' guests arrive,
particularly the rarely-seen country nobility. Old Count Julius
von Schweinitz und Krain was driven up in a great barouche
like a coffin. 'Take me to some quiet place.' Gottfried gave him
an arm to the study.

In the reception room the servants slowly circulated, offering
small glasses of arrack. Fritz kept a watch for those whom he
thought of as his own friends, and for those who understood
poetry – for example, Friedrich Brachmann, the advocate, who
had studied with him in Leipzig. Brachmann was crippled
from birth, but he walked so carefully, you wouldn't know it
(everyone in Weissenfels knew it). Brachmann was hoping to
enter the tax department. His limp would not matter there, his
ideas about aesthetics would not matter much either. Fritz put
an arm through his, and the other one round Frederick Severin.

'Ah, best of friends, I congratulate you,' said Severin. 'And
how is the little brother who likes the water?'

'I think he is not supposed to be downstairs,' replied Fritz,
'but I daresay he is.'

Louise, Brachmann's sister, was the dear friend of Sidonie,
who moved towards her as her name was announced by Gottfried. Louise was twenty-nine, and a poet.

Both girls were in white, run up by the same dressmaker,
but Sidonie seemed to be moving in flight or in a drift of
whiteness, delicate, weightless, strange to the onlookers of Weissenfels, while Louise could only hope not to hear, at least for

this summer, the suggestion that it was perhaps time Fräulein Brachmann should give up wearing white altogether.

'Oh Louise, Louise, I have spoken to Fritz: he is going to send your poems to Friedrich Schiller, only you must keep copies, my dear, because these great men frequently lose what is sent to them.'

Sidonie's eyes shone with the pleasure of pleasing. Louise did not reply.

'But that was what you wanted, Lu?'

'Is your brother not going to read them himself?'

Sidonie faltered.

'I am sure he must have done.'

'What did he say to you about them?' Then, after a moment. 'It does not signify, they are only words, the broken words of a woman.'

Sidonie wished that the party from Grüningen would arrive, and fix the attention of the lot of them: then the piano would surely draw them all together. That the Rockenthiens had set out she knew, since the Mandelsloh had had the good sense to send off the stable-boy (the new stable-boy) as messenger the moment they started. The boy, covered with a thick coating of dust, had now arrived, and was being petted in the kitchen. Meantime here were the Justs, Coelestin magnificent in the dark green ceremonial uniform of his rank. Heun, who came with them, was also entitled to a uniform, though not, apparently, one that fitted him. Karoline, who rarely took anything, swallowed half a glass of arrack, and went to stand with Fritz, Erasmus, Severin and Brachmann.

'Where is Sidonie?' she asked.

'With Louise, with poor Louise,' said Erasmus. 'But all that matters is that you have arrived. You are the best friend any of us have, the very best. You are the conciliator. Not even Sidonie can do it so well.'

'That is so,' said Fritz. 'Where Justen is, one can be at peace.'

'Then I hope, *mademoiselle*, you will visit my bookshop,' said Severin.

'Of course she will,' Fritz cried. 'She knows as much about books as I do, and far more about music.'

'There is nothing to know about music,' said Karoline, smiling.

'You must play for us later on.'

'I would not dream of it.'

Fritz bowed and excused himself, having duties everywhere. Karoline looked slowly round her, not allowing herself to watch where he went. She saw the guests as drifts of grey, black, and brown, with the uniforms (since most of those who wore them preferred to talk to each other) as knots of glittering colour, becoming less harsh as the evening light began to fade. The twilight, God be thanked, merciful to us all. The white dresses, now the most conspicuous of all, still lingered on the outer edge of the groups, except for Sidonie's. She had hurried to the side of Senf, who was standing entirely by himself, wearing, to mark his consciousness of his former disgrace (although he had plenty of good clothes), a patched swallow-tail coat. Sidonie was shaking her head at him, and laughing. This seemed extraordinary, for Senf had never been known to say anything amusing. He looked surprised, almost bewitched.

Fritz himself was for the moment with Louise, bending over her awkwardly, but with an instinct of true kindness. The poetess gaped up at him like a fish.

Brachmann drew Erasmus aside a little, towards the windows, and said, 'You know, I have never met Fräulein Just before. She is no longer quite young, but she has worth and serenity.' He paused. 'Do you think she would consider a lame man for a husband?

Erasmus, staggered, was able to answer, 'Oh, but her affections are engaged – I don't know where and I don't know who to, but I do know that much.'

171

What an embarrassing pair they are, he thought, this brother and sister. It would be much easier if they could marry each other.

'You were asking about the Bernhard,' said Karoline, left alone with Severin. 'I believe Hardenberg is truly interested in his younger brother. Indeed, he is altogether very fond of children.'

'Quite possibly he is,' said Severin. 'As to Bernhard, you must remember that not all children are child-like.'

44

The Intended

Perhaps there would never be another evening quite like this in Weissenfels. The guests were waiting, although they were not accustomed to it: even in this great airy room, most of their faces had turned a comfortable fruit-red, but they were unable to settle down to their familiar inspection of each other's costume, followed by discussion, slight advance, slight retreat, circulation, repetition, deep and thick gossip, then indulgence in pickled goose legs, black ham, fruit liqueurs, sweet cakes, more spirits, an amiable progress home, an uncertain climb up to bed. Tonight they could not quite count on anything. Uncertainty and expectancy moved among the guests like the first warning of fever, touching even the most stolid.

Still no Rockenthiens, still no Affianced. In the kitchen, the cook induced the protesting stable-boy, who felt that he was held in some way to blame, to kneel down and pray for his employers' safe arrival.

'They will come,' he blubbered, 'but Fräulein Sophie cannot be hurried, she has been ill.'

The Freiherr was unperturbed, for it had never crossed his mind, since the day when he had agreed to the engagement, to alter any of the arrangements he had made. In fifteen minutes they would all go upstairs to hear the piano, then supper, at

173

which he would not take his place at the head of one of the tables, but would move about, pausing now at one chair, now at another, while Fritz and his Intended sat side by side, then music, and if Sophie's health permitted it, dancing. There were six-and-a-half minutes to go until they adjourned to the music room; he allowed himself a short visit to his old friend Schweinitz und Krain, who was still half-slumbering where Gottfried had left him.

'Hardenberg, what is this I am drinking? Is this what they call punch?'

'Yes, I am told Fritz mixed it up himself.'

'It has to be mixed up?'

'Yes, it seems so.'

'Time wasted, Hardenberg.'

'I will get them to bring you something else.'

'Hardenberg, who are these Rockenthiens?'

The Freiherr shook his head.

'Alas! my old friend!' said the Count.

They had all been swept up the great central staircase, all were seated on faded and tattered chairs brought from all over the house. Most of the candles had been extinguished. Anton, still only fourteen, with raw wrists protruding from his first cadet's uniform, sat down at the Zumpe, where the brightest light fell.

'I will begin with something by Johann Friedrich Reichardt,' he announced boldly. 'I will play one of his revolutionary songs.'

'What is that, boy?' called out the Freiherr.

'Anton, you will start with some religious music,' cried the mother, with the authority of anguish. 'You will play "Wie sie so sanft ruhn".'

Anton turned towards her and nodded. Then the piano lifted its voice, so peaceable, so clear.

The gentle air continued, cut off from any noise in the

Kloster Gasse. But then the doors of the music room were thrown open, and light poured in from the broad passage-way outside. Gottfried, although clearly in doubt as to the interruption, introduced Frau von Rockenthien, beautiful but sleepy-looking in a pale violet dress, the Hausherr, a chastened George. But where is She?

'They gave me orders to go ahead,' bellowed Rockenthien. 'My stepdaughter is resting for the moment at the bottom of your stairs.' He advanced on his hosts, huge, weather-beaten, clapping his hands.

'He might be scaring rooks,' muttered Louise Brachmann. 'Heaven help us, they're like a troop of farm-hands come up for the hiring fair.'

The Freiherr received the party with faultless courtesy, making a sign to Gottfried, who set about relighting the candles. Anton, at the end of the next phrase, stopped short, and folded his hands. Where was the Affianced? The elder guests murmured in pity and rank curiosity. She would be carried in, she was debilitated.

But Sophie, quietly followed by the Mandelsloh, came almost running across the room with her old impatience, pale, yes that's true, but eager and high-pitched as ever, transparently ready to enjoy herself. She was dressed in embroidered silk – Chinese silk, they thought – where would that have come from? Her hair was hidden under a white cap, quite appropriate for an Affianced. She wore a single white rose.

'Hardenburch!'

He was there.

'They said I must not come –'

Everyone had thought that this would be the end of young Anton's recital, but the Mandelsloh, who had decided on her tactics as soon as she entered the house, singled out the Freifrau and persuaded her that they must all of them hear it to the very end. The front rows of chairs emptied and shifted to make place for the newcomers. Anton nodded, and continued with a setting of some of Zinzendorf's hymns for the Brethren, passing on to the airs from two or three *Singspiele* and the, what was the piece that he played after that? – that very beautiful piece, I did not know it, could Anton have improvised it himself?

No-one admitted to knowing it, but all half-closed their eyes in pleasure.

He ended with Johann Sebastian Bach's *Capriccio on the Departure of His Brother*. Deeply the audience sighed.

Some of them at least, too, had expected at the supper to see an exchange of rings, after which the father of the future bridegroom, as host, might declare what he intended to give in the way of furniture, feather beds &c. &c., with, perhaps, a list of property. But the Hardenbergs did not do things in that way. The Freiherr only rose to his feet to halt the determined eating and drinking for a few moments, to announce his own happiness and that of his wife's, to welcome them all, and to ask them to join him in a short prayer.

It had also been thought that after the supper, on account of Fräulein Sophie's recent illness, there would be no dancing. But Sophie begged for the musicians.

The Mandelsloh reminded her that Dr Ebhard, perhaps relieved to have something definite to say, had forbidden dancing absolutely.

'I wish I had him here,' cried Sophie. 'I'd make him waltz till his brains boiled.'

She sat between her own mother and Hardenberg's mother, the Freifrau. Frau Rockenthien, as almost always, smiled. She wished Anton was still playing, particularly that piece, rather towards the end, whose name she had been sure she once knew, and she wished she had the baby with her. She was not embarrassed by her husband's loud voice – her first husband had also been very noisy, and neither of them had had any more effect on her than windy weather.

The Freifrau, meanwhile, struggled alone with the demon of timidity. The single glass of arrack which she had taken had not helped her at all. In her heart – although she was afraid this might be a sin of thought – she was terribly disappointed in her future daughter-in-law's appearance. Sophie had a certain touching, bright eagerness but it was a child's brightness. Perhaps because she had never been much to look at herself, Auguste attached great importance to dignity, to height, and to regal beauty. Perhaps Sophie might look better if she let her hair down. Fritz had told her that it was dark.

Since his Intended must not dance, Fritz brought forward the dignitaries of Weissenfels, one by one, to introduce them to her, and among them the younger ones, his own friends. 'I have the happiness to present you to Fraülein von Kühn, who has done me the honour . . . This is Sophie, this is my true Philosophy . . . This is Sophie, this is my spirit's guide in all things . . .'

'O, you must not mind him,' she replied to their congratulations. She was constraining herself not to tap her feet. The music seemed to pass into them and upwards through her whole body: she felt like a bottle of soda-water. A faint rose colour had come at last into her face.

'O, you must not mind him . . . when he says such things I laugh.' And she did laugh.

On the whole, Sophie impressed favourably. She was not at all the kind of wife they would have expected for a Hardenberg. But she was artless, and that pleased. Nature always pleases.

How much money would she bring with her? they asked each other.

George, nearly choked by his first high collar and frill, intended to join the dancing as soon as convenient, but did not feel that he had had quite enough to eat to keep his strength up. Downstairs in the half-darkened dining room, which had not yet been cleared, he came across a boy a couple of years younger than himself with the appearance (irritating to George) of an angel. George silently helped himself to cold pigeon-pie, doubling up his left fist in his pocket in case it came to a matter of best man wins, and it was necessary to give the angel a hacking. He said loudly, 'Don't you think my sister Sophie is pretty?'

'You are George von Kühn?' asked the angel.

'That's my business.'

'You are hungry?'

'At home we get more to eat than this . . . I asked you whether you think my sister, who is going to marry your brother Fritz, is pretty?'

'To that I can't give you an answer. I don't know whether she is pretty. I'm not old enough to judge of these things. But I think she is ill.'

George, cramming in more pastry, was disconcerted. 'Oh, there's always someone ill in every house.' The Bernhard said, 'Don't you think my brother Anton played the piano well?'

'The hymns?'

'They were not all hymns.'

'Yes, he played well,' George admitted. 'Where are you going?'

'I'm going out to walk by the river in the darkness. That is the effect the music has had on me.'

George drank off a glass of brandy, as nearly as possible in his stepfather's manner, and staggered upstairs to join the dancing.

The Mandelsloh, against all expectations, was an exquisite dancer, the best, in fact, in the room. But because her husband was not with her, and on account of Sophie, she would not dance that evening, not even with young George, to whom a year or so earlier, she had painfully taught the steps. 'Don't ask me!' she said to Erasmus, when he came trustingly up to her.

'I am not going to ask you to dance, I know I mustn't aspire to that honour, I am going to ask you to help me.'

'What do you want?'

Erasmus said, 'A lock of Sophie's hair.'

The Mandelsloh slowly turned her head and looked hard at him. 'You too!'

'A very small quantity, to put in my pocket book, close to my heart . . . You know, I did not understand her at first, but suddenly it came to me why my brother had the words "Sophie be my spirit's guide" engraved on his ring . . .'

She said again: 'You too!'

'A lock of hair, as a souvenir, is surely not so very much, not such a great thing . . . I had thought of asking Karoline Just to speak to Sophie, but you, of course, are the right person. Will you have a word with her?'

'No,' said the Mandelsloh. 'If that is what you want, you must ask her yourself.'

Erasmus chose his time carefully. Possibly our times are always chosen for us. The violins in the music room, where the dancing was, struck up a *Schottische*, and he had a curious sensation of not quite understanding what they were, or why they were playing. He seemed to himself to belong to two worlds, of which one was of no possible importance.

Now he was standing next to Sophie's chair, within a few inches of her delicate body, which smelled a little of sickness. She looked brightly up at him.

'You have hardly spoken to me all evening, Erasmus.'

'I have been making up my mind how to put what I wanted to say.' He stammered it out – of course he was only asking for one curl, one small quantity, not like the *Ringellocke* which Fritz had shown him in the early spring, and which he knew

179

was going to be plaited and set in a locket, or a watch-case. 'A watch-case,' he repeated, 'but of course, not at all like that . . .' Sophie laughed. She had been laughing, it was true, most of the evening, but not with such enjoyment as she did now.

Erasmus, retreating in humiliation, was confronted by the Mandelsloh. 'God in heaven, surely you did not ask her!'

'I don't understand you,' he said. 'You told me — I had thought of you as frank and open . . .'

'Did you expect her to take off her cap?'

He had not thought about it at all.

'Little by little it came away,' the Mandelsloh told him 'on account of the illness. For two months now, quite bald . . .'

She looked at him steadily, without a hint of forgiveness. 'You Hardenbergs shed tears easily,' she said. 'I have had occasion to notice this before.'

'But why did she laugh?' asked poor Erasmus.

45

She Must Go to Jena

Fritz knew that Sophie was bald, but was confident that her dark hair would return. He knew that Sophie could not die. 'What a man wills himself to do, he can do,' he told Coelestin Just, 'still more can a woman.' But they must not let time slip. Sophie needed better advice, indeed the best. She must go to Jena.

'They are coming to consult Stark. But with whom can they stay?' asked Friedrich Schlegel. 'Hardenberg used to have an aunt here in Jena, but she died, I think about a year ago. The Philosophy, I believe, will be in the charge of her sister, an officer's wife.'

'And Hardenberg's father, *der Alte*, may well, I suppose, be in and out,' said Caroline Schlegel. 'He will be anxious as to our beliefs and our moral life. Woe to the free, woe to the unprayed-over!'

The Jena circle, though not charitable, was hospitable. But the academic year was over, the town was beginning to swelter, the yellow clay soil would soon bake dry, the spire of the Staatskirche seemed to vibrate in the summer's heat. Soon they would all be on vacation, except for poor Ritter, who retreated to his attic and made himself invisible.

Sophie and the Mandelsloh, however, had already moved

into lodgings in the Schaufelgasse. The rooms were small, and there were three flights of stairs, but the house was recommended to them because the landlady, Frau Winkler, was used to invalid young ladies. It was clear, indeed, from the first that she had the temperament which is attracted to illness and everything to do with it. This was irritating, but meant that she would bring up jugs of hot water at any time, by night and by day. 'It's part of the attendance, gracious lady,' said Frau Winkler.

At least, the Mandelsloh had thought, reassuring herself, there will be no formality here – not that there was ever much at Grüningen – and poor Sophie can feel as though in her own dolls' house, with the patterned earthenware jugs waiting humbly on the crowded dresser. In truth, though, she was somewhat doubtful about her choice and had to summon up her courage to open her first letter from the Freiherr. She could not know that the Uncle Wilhelm, arriving uninvited at Weissenfels to give his advice, had declared that there were no lodgings in Jena (except perhaps the former palace, where Goethe usually stayed) which were in any way suitable for the Affianced of his eldest nephew.

'The rooms let out by the inhabitants are all at the top of the house, and are fit only for breeding pigeons. I know the town, better, in all probability, than any of you. This elder sister, take it from me, will have settled for a couple of garrets. Women are always satisfied with too little.'

The Freiherr immediately wrote to Frau Leutnant Mandelsloh that he hoped to come and see her as soon as possible, and that meantime he was entirely assured that she had chosen wisely.

46

Visitors

Friederike's Daybook, July 1796

Söphgen has been trying to keep up her diary, but she must not torment herself any longer to write in it. Let me be the recorder.

We are doing well enough here in our little rooms. Sophie's dinner I prepare myself, rather than sending out to the Rose, in order not to give offence to our landlady. But the Jena air does not suit me, and perhaps it suits no-one, since all the professors and literati seem to have some complaint against each other. Weather very hot. They are beginning to go away on their little outings and vacations. The streets where they live are empty.

Hardenberg's friend Friedrich Schlegel (I think he is not yet a professor) visited us yesterday evening. He too is on the point of some journey or other. I received him by myself. Sophie had gone out with Frau Winkler, to see a military parade. God knows I myself have seen my bellyful of them. But as soon as the pain goes away a little, my beloved little sister is ready to find everything amusing. She is then almost herself.

Well, Friedrich Schlegel. He is a philosopher and a historian. I was not at all put off by his melancholy gaze. He said to me, 'Frau Leutnant, your sister, Fräulein von Kühn, tries to make her mind work in the same way that Hardenberg's does, as one might try to teach a half-tame bird to sing like a human being. She won't succeed, and the ideas she had before, such as they were, are now in disarray and she hardly knows what to put in their place.'

I asked him, 'Have you ever met my sister, Herr Schlegel?'

He replied, 'Not as yet, but I believe she is an instance of a certain easily-recognisable type.'

I said, 'She is my sister.'

Later, Sophie returned in the care of Frau Winkler, who said, with a certain disappointment: 'I expected the young lady to faint, but she did not.'

Although Fritz now had his first official appointment as an Assistant Saline Inspector, and was allowed only short periods of leave, the Rockenthiens left Sophie's treatment entirely in his hands.

'No other system is so reliable as Brown's,' Fritz told Karoline Just, not for the first time. 'To some extent Brownismus is based on Locke's ideas of the nervous system.'

'We have to believe in someone,' said Karoline. 'Another one, I mean, besides ourselves, or life would be a poor thing.'

'I was talking of the exact sciences, Justen.'

Fritz had made a very early start from Tennstedt. There was some delay, however, when he reached Jena, in getting hold of Stark, who was at a professional conference in Dresden. But he was told that it would be possible to see the Professor's Deputy Assistant, Jacob Dietmahler.

'Ah, it's you, what good fortune,' cried Fritz. 'I sometimes think that at every turning point in my life —'

'My life, too, has had its turning-points,' said Dietmahler quietly.

Fritz was overwhelmed. 'Love has made me a monster.'

'Don't concern yourself, Hardenberg. I am happy to have obtained this appointment as a Deputy Assistant, and I have resigned myself to the long walk ahead of me.'

'I am truly sorry if —'

'We won't waste time on that. Why have you come here?'

'Dietmahler, Dr Ebhard will have written the Professor a letter of explanation. My Sophie is in pain.'

'In severe pain, I imagine. I can't, of course, offer any opinion until Professor Stark returns, but Ebhard mentions her complexion, which provides us with an important indication —'

'It is like a rose.'

'This letter says, yellowish.'

But Sophie wanted to go out. She had the remorseless perseverance of the truly pleasure-loving. There had been so little to do in Grüningen. What was more, she had never been serenaded. Here, at least, Dietmahler was able to be of immediate practical assistance. There were plenty of medical students left in Jena, penniless, and working through the vacation in the hope of getting their qualifications a little earlier, or of joining a regiment as a half-qualified bone-setter or wound-doctor. Could they play and sing? Naturally they could. How else can the needy pass their spare time, except with music? Outside the lodgings, in the warm dusk which filled the Schaufelgasse, they began with little airs, little popular songs, then a trio. When the Mandelsloh came down the three flight of stairs, with her purse in her hand, and asked them, 'For whom do you play?' they replied, 'For Philosophy.'

Friederike's Daybook

And now it seems that the great man is actually going
to call, that Goethe will actually be among us. We
didn't hear this from Hardenberg, but once again from
Erasmus, who after all, has not gone to Zillbach, but
has a room at the moment at a student's beer-house,
where he says he is sleeping on straw. That is emphatically his business, rather than mine. He tells me, also,
that it's well known that Goethe cannot endure the wearing of spectacles, and has said, 'What do I gain from
a man into whose eyes I cannot look while I am speaking, and the mirror of whose soul is veiled by glasses
that dazzle me? A feeling of disharmony comes over
me when a stranger approaches me with spectacles on
his nose.' I myself used never to wear glasses, but now
I do, for fine sewing and for reading, and since we
came to Jena I have worn them nearly all the time. On
occasion, though, one must ignore great men's fancies.

July 7, morning.

First we tidy our sitting room. With furnishings so
poor, there is not much that can be done: they are
intended for University assistant-teachers, who are
grateful for anything. The medicine bottles, the poultices, the syringes, beloved of Frau Winkler, go into
the bedroom; the sewing, the newspapers, under the
day-bed. On a day like this, dull and windy, the
windows must stay shut, but they do not fit properly.
There is a draught, we know that already, but I go
closer and confirm it, it is like a skewer. The great man
of letters will risk pneumonia, and that must always be
held against us.

Söphgen forgets that she is in pain, even that she is ill, in discussing the draught. The secret, says Frau Winkler, is to open the windows now, very wide, just for a time. If the air inside the room is the same temperature as the air outside, no draught can be felt. – But (I tell her) the room will be hellishly uncomfortable. – No matter, cries Söphgen, we'll shut everything tight when he approaches the house, and she collects what is left of her strength and before I can stop her throws the windows wide. Then she begins to cough. 'You should have left that to me. Now your cough pierces me like the nails on the cross. The draught couldn't have done it better.' – And Sophie laughs.

Goethe is coming up the Schaufelgasse. All to the window! He advances in a blue frock coat, and over that a summer dust-coat, a noble garment which almost touches the ground, and does touch the ankles of his splendid boots. He seems to have no servant with him: a private call.

I take off my spectacles and go down, Sophie too, she won't be left behind. She draws herself up, as though she felt no fear. Goethe introduces himself, and taking our hands quite frankly, asks us whether his servant can be accommodated in the kitchen: he *did* bring a man with him after all, but it seems that this man always walks a certain number of paces behind him, imitating, out of respect, his actions and gestures. Surely it would be of much more use if he went in front, and made sure they were going to the right house.

Upstairs, Goethe takes the hardest chair, saying, with much charm, that poets thrive on discomfort. However, in another moment he is pacing up and down the little room.

There is no bell, but I have arranged with Frau

187

Winkler to stamp on one of the loose boards, so that she will know when to bring refreshments. Goethe handily cuts the cake himself, and opens the bottle. He suggests sending down a glass of wine to the servant, which I agree to, although I can't see that he has done much to earn it. Meanwhile he talks a little about health and illness. Some maladies, he says, are nothing but stagnation, which a glass or two of mineral water would remove, but we must never let them linger: we must go straight to the attack, as in all things.

He must see that the case is quite otherwise with our poor little patient. It was clear that he wanted to draw her out. Unfortunately, he does not, as yet, know Hardenberg's poetry, indeed I suppose not much of it, so far, has appeared in print. Sophie, for whom the visit was perhaps too great an honour, could think of nothing to say. At last she ventured that Jena was a larger town than Grüningen. Goethe bowed slightly and replied that Weimar, also, was a larger town than Grüningen.

Sophie did not mention Hardenberg's story *The Blue Flower*. And Goethe, at least, made no reference to the draught.

Erasmus, who had found out exactly when the visit was to be, was waiting, or rather hovering, at the corner of the street.

'Excellency! Please, a word! I am Hardenberg's younger brother – that is, one of his younger brothers. I am a student of forestry – that is, not here . . .'

'I did not think it would be here,' said Goethe. 'There is no school of forestry in the University of Jena.'

'I have been studying at Hubertusberg. That is, I have just left Hubertusberg. May I walk a short distance with you?'

Goethe smiled, and said that there was no law against it.

'You have been calling on Fräulein Sophie von Kühn,' persevered Erasmus, 'and her elder sister, Frau Leutnant Mandelsloh.'

'Ah, she is the elder sister, is she? A woman of strength, I had not quite made out the relationship.' Since Erasmus, coughing, trotting by his side, could manage nothing more at the moment Goethe went on, 'I think I know what you wanted to ask me. You wonder whether Fräulein von Kühn, when she is restored to health, will be a true source of happiness to your brother. Probably you feel that there is not an equality of understanding between them. But rest assured, it is not her understanding that we love in a young girl. We love her beauty, her innocence, her trust in us, her airs and graces, her God knows what – but we don't love her for her understanding – nor, I am sure, does Hardenberg. He will be happy, at least for a certain number of years, with what she can offer him, and then he may have the incomparable blessing of children, while his poetry –'

Erasmus desperately caught the arm of the great man in mid-speech, spinning him round like flotsam in the tide. 'But that is not what I wanted to ask you!'

Goethe stopped and looked down at him. (The servant, twenty yards behind, stopped also, and stared into a barber's shop.)

'I was mistaken, then. You are not concerned about your brother's happiness?'

'Not about his!' cried Erasmus. 'About hers, about Sophie's, about hers!'

47

How Professor Stark Managed

When Professor Stark returned to Jena he made an examination, and said that an operation was necessary. He would insert tubes, to carry away the poison. There was no other way to drain the gracious Fräulein's tumour. Authorisation was needed from her stepfather in Grüningen. This arrived within twenty-four hours.

'It would be a pity if we were to miss the fireworks for the Elector's birthday,' said Sophie. This was her only objection.

'My stepfather and my mother leave all the details to me,' the Mandelsloh told young Dietmahler, one of whose more awkward duties was to deal with the patients' relatives. 'I shall have to send for my sister's betrothed. He has gone back to Tennstedt. But you, of course, know him well.'

'No, not well, but I have known him for what seems a long time,' said Dietmahler. 'I think his brother Erasmus is in Jena.'

'No, he left yesterday, I advised it. Staying here was helping neither him nor us. But Hardenberg, of course — Now, tell me the day and the hour when the Professor intends to operate. Write them down. Naturally I shan't forget them, but write them down here in my Daybook.'

But Professor Stark did not manage things in that way. It was his practice to give as little notice as possible, an hour at

190

most, of an operation. This was to spare the patient's nerves. Prevented, too, was the arrival of relatives long before they were wanted. Dietmahler, of course, had known this, but was not at liberty to say so. Now he had to go round once again to the Schaufelgasse with an explanation.

'The room reserved for the purpose must be kept ready at all times,' he went on doggedly. 'And there must be a good supply of old, clean sheets and old, clean undergarments of the finest linen.'

'Ready at all times, when we don't know when it will be wanted!' said the Mandelsloh. 'We have two rooms here, and only two. This is the sitting room, and my sister is asleep at the moment in the bedroom. You may leave the inspection to me.'

Dietmahler hesitated. 'And the other things?'

'Do you think we travelled here with piles of old, clean, cast-off undergarments of the finest linen? Wouldn't we do better to go back to Grüningen to fetch them?'

'No, the patient must not travel.'

'You mean that your Professor doesn't want to.'

'That is not what I said. How large is the bedroom?'

'The same size as this. One can scarcely move. Tell him he must bring no-one with him, except yourself.'

'Certainly, I can promise that. And your landlady. Would she be ready to be of use?'

'Only too ready.'

'Frau Leutnant, I don't wish us to be antagonists. Could we not look at things another way? I can assure you of the Professor's deepest sympathy and interest. Indeed, he has told me he intends to do the bandaging himself.'

She shook his hand, but it was no more than a truce.

Frau Winkler had discussed the expected visit of Professor Stark with all her neighbours within a certain radius, 'in order that there should be no misunderstanding, when screams and cries are heard. They might imagine some dispute . . .'

'A lodger, perhaps, strangling a landlady,' agreed the Mandelsloh. Frau Winkler, who by now obeyed her slavishly, had been able (since the Great Wash for the year was over) to borrow a quantity of clean old sheets. Strictly speaking, there was no such thing as worn-out sheets in Saxony, but some were thirty or forty years older than others. Holding the material against the broad summer sunshine, she demonstrated how delicately threadbare they were.

'Put them away, speak no more about them, bring me the weekly bill and some coffee,' said the Mandelsloh.

Sophie was out – out for a drive through the cornfields with the wife of the pastor whose sermons they attended on Sundays. They had started early, to avoid the sun, and had driven through roads shadowed with poplars.

'Thank you, Frau Pastor, you have been so very kind, you are so kind, you will be so kind I am sure as to excuse me for being tired so quickly.'

'I may perhaps be allowed to call for Fräulein Sophie next week?' said the pastor's wife, but the Mandelsloh intervened politely, saying that unfortunately they could not be sure of their arrangements.

'I wish George was here,' said Sophie.

'George!'

'I don't know why, we were not speaking of him, but I wish he was here.'

Hardenberg so far knew nothing about the operation. Possibly he did not even know that they were still in Jena. He himself, the Mandelsloh believed, was inspecting the Salines at Dürrenberg. But the Professor's instructions, which, in spite of her critical attitude, she took in a spirit of military obedience, were still, 'I will give you an hour's notice. That is best. Afterwards you may summon anyone you wish.'

192

It was Dietmahler, again, who brought this last message, and Dietmahler who appeared, bringing with him a hospital servant, on the morning of the 11th of July. 'The operation will take place at eleven o'clock. I will explain what has to be done.' The double bed was dragged to the middle of the room and made up with the ancient sheets, the front room sofa was piled with bandages, lint and sponges which the hospital servant had brought with him. Sophie seemed not to be disturbed.

Frau Winkler announced that a man was at the door. He was a messenger, with a note to say that the Professor found that he must postpone the operation until two in the afternoon.

'Just to remind us that he is a great man,' said the Mandelsloh.

'Frau Leutnant, that is unjust,' said Dietmahler.

He sent the hospital servant to an eating house, and walked the streets of Jena until a quarter to two. When he returned, Sophie was wearing an old wrapper, frail and yellowish, almost the same tone as her skin. She appeared smaller, perhaps shrunken. The Mandelsloh thought, 'What am I doing with what was entrusted to me?'

Two carriages, closed in spite of the high summer's day, turned into the Schaufelgasse. They drew up, the doors opened. 'There are four of you,' said the Mandelsloh, turning in bitter reproach on Dietmahler. 'You gave me your word . . .'

'Three of them are pupils,' said Dietmahler miserably. 'They are learning how these things are done.'

'I, too, am learning how these things are done,' said the Mandelsloh.

From the bottom of the stairs someone could be heard dismissing, or at least restraining, Frau Winkler. The Professor and his students made their appearance, correctly dressed in black. The students' frock-coats were absurdly too large. Doubtless they had been borrowed. The Professor bowed to the ladies. Sophie smiled faintly.

'We will administer the cordial.'

It was a mixture of wine and laudanum, to Dr Brown's prescription, which Sophie drank down without protest. Then to the bedroom, where all must skirt awkwardly round the bed in its unaccustomed place. The students, to be out of the way, stood with their backs to the wall, darting sharp looks, like young crows, each taking out the pen and inkwell from behind his lapel.

Sophie was helped onto the pile of borrowed mattresses. Then the Professor asked her, in tones of grave politeness – suitable, in fact, to a child on its dignity – whether she would like to cover her face with a piece of fine muslin. 'In that way you will be able to see something of what I do, but not too clearly . . . There now, you cannot see me now, can you?'

'I can see something glittering,' she said. Perhaps it was a game, after all. The students wrote a line in their notebooks.

Following the medical etiquette of Jena, the Professor motioned Dietmahler to his side, and asked him,

'Esteemed colleague, am I to make the incision? Is that what you advise?'

'Yes, Herr Professor, I advise it.'

'You would make two incisions, or one only?'

'Two, Herr Professor.'

'So?'

'So.'

Frau Winkler, waiting below on the bottom stair, had been able to hear nothing, but now her patience was rewarded.

48

To Schlöben

Between Artern and Jena, Langensalza and Jena, Dürrenberg and Jena, Fritz traversed the dusty summer roads, crowded now with migrants and soldiers. In his notebook he wrote –

I am like a gambler who has risked everything on one stake.
The wound I must not see.

Sophie underwent another operation to drain the abscess on the 8th of August, 1796. A third, towards the end of August, was necessary because the other two had been completely unsuccessful. Professor Stark spoke of things going as well as could be expected. The patient's forces were not declining, the pus was only moderate. The autumn, however, was always a dangerous time, particularly for young people.

Sophie to Fritz: 'Hardly, dear Hardenberg, can I write you a line but do me the kindness not to distress yourself – This asks heartily your Sophie.'

On each of the two fathers the third operation had profound effects. Rockenthien's noisiness, his persistent looking on the bright side, his dirty jokes, all vanished, not gradually but

overnight, as though a giant hand had closed over him, squeez-
ing him clear of hope. The Freiherr, on the other hand, for
the first time in his life, wavered – not in his religious faith,
but on the question of what to do next. Until the end of August,
he put off visiting Jena. Then he made up his mind to go,
taking as many as possible of his family with him, and staying
the night at Schlöben-bei-Jena. Even this was partly an attempt
to get rid of the Uncle Wilhelm, who was still a guest at
Weissenfels. 'I shall remain here, brother, until I can see that
my advice is no longer needed.'

'Very good,' said the Freiherr, 'then you will not be coming
to Schlöben.' He gave orders for only six or seven bedrooms
to be prepared.

For themselves and a week's provisions they would need both
the carriages, and four of the long-suffering horses. Fritz was
already in Jena, Anton was at military school in Schulpforta,
but Karl was at home – half the officers in his regiment had
been on leave since Saxony had withdrawn from the coalition
against the French – and Sidonie, and Erasmus. The Bernhard
had not much wanted to come, but neither did he want to be
left at Weissenfels with the baby, the servants and his Uncle.

The Freifrau, jolting along beside Erasmus, knew that it could
not be right, in the middle of the distress she felt for Sophie,
to recognise even a moment's happiness, and yet her heart beat
faster when they turned into the familiar valley and for the first
time in three years it was time to look out for the four great
chimney-stacks of Schlöben, and the tops of the poplars. She
had always loved the place. Perhaps because the house was
thickly surrounded with trees, it gave her an unfamiliar feeling
of safety. Anton had been born here, and a little girl, Benigna,
who had not survived. Her husband, she knew, even though
they came here nowadays so rarely, said on no account would
he ever part from Schlöben.

'The chimneys!' cried Sidonie, who was sitting up by the driver.

They passed the oak tree with the ropes of their old swings still hanging from a high branch and a lower one. To the right was the humpbacked bridge which crossed both the stream and the footpath and led to the farm buildings and the chapel.

The property was dark and damp, and in such bad repair that the top flight of the main staircase was no longer safe and the servants had to reach their bedrooms by way of ladders. The *Gutsverwalter*, too, had moved into the great house, simply for the sake of shelter, since his own place was in ruins. But there was none of the dignified wretchedness of Oberwieder-stadt, rather a diffused sense, in that misty valley, of relaxation, of perpetual forgiveness, of coming home after having done one's best.

Karl, sentimental like all military men, had tears in his eyes as they passed the remains of the swings, the old sledge-run down from the top of the valley, the pond, dry now until the autumn. He thought too of the months he had spent here not long ago, after his plans to marry money had ended in confusion, and he had had to take refuge from a furious and insulted woman.

'We used to put straw in our boots in winter,' said Sidonie.

'And take them off before we went indoors,' said Karl. 'How white your feet used to look, Sido, just like a fish, not like ours at all. Should you like to be a child again?'

'I should prefer us all to be children,' said Erasmus, 'then we should have a kingdom of our own.'

'That is not at all my experience,' said the Bernhard.

When he was very young the Bernhard had believed that the six-year gap between himself and Sidonie would gradually disappear and that just as he would come to be as tall as she was, or taller, so he would grow to be the same age as she was, or older. He had been disillusioned.

The warm twilight smelled of linden trees and chicken dung. 'Listen to the stream,' said Sidonie. 'We shall be able to hear it muttering away all night.'

The Bernhard replied that he preferred to live by a river.

While the luggage was being slowly unshipped, the house doors opened and the *Gutsverwalter*, Billerbeck, came out, followed by some flustered poultry, who evidently also considered the house as home. Everyone lived at the back. The front entrance was scarcely used. Through the pearly dusk which filled the main hall you could see the distant lighted kitchen at the end of a cavernous passageway.

Between the Freiherr and his *Gutsverwalter* there was scarcely any formality. Almost the same height as each other, they embraced warmly.

'We have suffered, we are suffering, Billerbeck. God is testing us.'

'I know it, Excellency.'

Four years ago, when he was last in Schlöben, Bernhard had been quite a small boy, sharing a four-poster with one of his brothers — he was almost sure it had been Erasmus — in a large room on the first floor. This room like most of the others on the north side had been seriously damaged since then by rain driving in through the broken windows. Any day now, Billerbeck repeated again and again, the repairs will be put in hand. Meanwhile, the Bernhard was lodged in a slip of a room on the second floor in a bed not much larger than a cot.

'My father and mother are already in bed and asleep,' said the Bernhard to himself. 'There is no wind, but from time to time the moon shines in and the room becomes bright. Somewhere, too, a clock is ticking.' And so it was, even though he could not see it. High up on the outer south side of Schlöben was an enormous and ancient gilded clock-face which set the time, even if not quite accurately, for the whole household; its works were in the thickness of the wall of the room where the Bernhard lay. 'I am lying restlessly in my bed,' he went on. 'Everyone else has heard what I did, and yet none of them give it serious attention.'

For some time now it had come to him that the opening chapter of Fritz's story was not difficult to understand. It had never been shown to him, or read to him. But there was nothing of any interest to him at Weissenfels that he had not had a good look at.

He had been struck – before he crammed the story back into Fritz's book-bag – by one thing in particular: the stranger who had spoken at the dinner table about the Blue Flower had been understood by one person and one only. This person must have been singled out as distinct from all the rest of his family. It was a matter of recognising your own fate and greeting it as familiar when it came.

49

At the Rose

They started for Jena next morning at five o'clock. The barely drinkable first coffee was served to them in the morning room. Outside, at the head of the valley, the sky was barred with long streaks of cloud which seemed to be waiting for the dawn to burn them into transparency. Schlöben itself, except for the glitter of the stream, was in shadow. 'You can hardly imagine the strange mood I'm in,' said Karl. 'I should like to sit at this window until the whole place grows bright.' 'We are enchanted here,' said Sidonie. 'Until we get started, we shan't be able to realise the depth of our unhappiness. We have come to see poor Fritz, and yet we're farther away from him than ever. I'm ashamed to feel such peace.'

'*Satt*!' cried Erasmus, banging down his coffee cup.

With an early start, they could return to Schlöben that evening, giving the horses eight hours' rest. At Jena, the Freiherr had reserved a large private room for them at the Rose. In spite of the family's difficulties he always went to the best inns, for he knew of no others.

'There is Fritz!' shouted Karl, who was driving the first carriage and turned well in front of the others into the yard of the Rose.

'No, that is not my brother!' cried Sidonie. First out, jumping down without waiting for the step to be fixed, she ran towards him. 'Fritzchen, I hardly knew your face.'

Such a large party, of course, could not arrive all at once at Frau Winkler's. The Freiherr would call there first, the others later.

'Should I not accompany you, Heinrich?' asked the Freifrau, summoning up all her reserve of courage. No, he would walk there with Fritz. They would start at once. The rest went into the Rose and upstairs to the handsome front room overlooking the square.

'There they go,' said Karl, lifting one of the white linen blinds. 'When did we last see the two of them walking together like that?'

After Fritz and the father were out of sight a group of prisoners, fettered by the leg, came to clean the street. Whenever the guard lost interest in them they laid down their brushes and held out their hands for charity. Sidonie threw out her purse.

'They will cut each others' throats for it,' said Karl.

'No, I am sure they have a system of distribution,' said Erasmus.

'Very probably the youngest will get least,' said the Bernhard.

'Coffee, coffee, for the respected ladies and gentlemen!' called the landlord, who had followed them up. A waiter in a striped apron asked if they desired wine.

'Not yet,' Erasmus told him.

'I want you to lie down,' said Sidonie to her mother. 'These sofas seem expressly designed not to be lain upon, but all the same, I want you to try.'

The Freifrau lay down. 'Poor Fritz, poor sick Söphgen. But it will cheer her to see our Angel.' She motioned to the Bernhard to come and sit beside her. The room was already growing warmer. The broad blinds hung without the slightest tremor.

The next arrival was Dietmahler, sent by Professor Stark to see if he could be of assistance. He hesitated in the doorway, looking from face to face in the shadowed room. He had come into the Rose and upstairs without being announced. They were all talking to each other, no-one looked round, and Dietmahler unwisely confided in the blond child who was standing close to him, examining the hydraulics of the coffee-urn.

'You are Bernhard, aren't you? I am a friend of your brother Friedrich, I have been to your house in Weissenfels. I don't know whether your sister Sidonie remembers me.'

'Very likely not,' said the Bernhard. 'However, I remember you.'

Sidonie, half hearing, came towards them, smiling. Naturally she remembered everything – the washday, the happiness of his visit, and, of course, he was –

'Of course,' said the Bernhard.

'I have now the honour to be the Deputy Assistant to Professor Stark,' said Dietmahler. 'You may have heard your brother mention me in his letters, in connection with the treatment of his Intended.' He took out his professional card.

That would bring his name to her mind, no doubt of it. But the few moments during which she had not been able to remember it confirmed Dietmahler in what, after all, he already knew, that he was nothing. What means something to us, that we can name. Sink, he told his hopes, with a kind of satisfaction, sink like a corpse dropped into the river. I am rejected, not for being unwelcome, not even for being ridiculous, but for being nothing.

'Dietmahler!' Erasmus called out. Now Sidonie did remember, and covered her face for a moment with her hands. 'Dietmahler, thank God you are here, you will tell us exactly what is happening. You haven't been practising long enough to know how to tell lies.'

'That is not very polite,' said Karl.

'Fräulein von Kühn is still feverish,' said Dietmahler. 'Long visits are out of the question; half an hour, perhaps. Unfortunately, her cough delays the healing of the incision. It splits open. The Professor believes now that if he was given permission to carry out one further operation we might hope for an immediate and complete recovery.'

'And what do you believe?' asked Erasmus.

'I don't question the Professor's prognosis.'

After this, Dietmahler excused himself. He had to think, he said, of his other duties.

'Of course you must,' cried Sidonie. 'And you must forgive us, but we are anxious. Even now we can't truly believe that you have any other patient but Fritz's Söphgen. People in distress are selfish beyond belief.'

'That is what your brother said to me.'

'Then he showed more sense than usual.'

She was trying to make amends, although she did not know what for. Then he was gone, and having nothing else to do, they stood at the window and watched him, in his turn, crossing the cobbled street to walk in the shade.

The Freifrau was sleeping uneasily. The landlord again asked if he should send up a few bottles of wine.

'If it will make you happy, yes,' said Karl.

'Wine from the district, Herr Leutnant?'

'Heaven forbid, bring Moselwein.'

As soon as the waiter had come and gone, Erasmus broke out violently. 'Father will soon be back, since he is allowed to visit for only half an hour. We have managed very badly. What will come of his visit? You know that whatever consent or permission he has given, he still considers the marriage quite unsuitable –'

'It is quite unsuitable,' the Bernhard interrupted him. 'It is our business to see the beauty of that.'

'You should not have come here, Angel in the House,' said Erasmus angrily.

'Nor, I think, should you,' said the Bernhard.

Turning to Karl, Erasmus went on, 'Why has the father been permitted to call so soon upon Söphgen, whose condition, poor soul, has had such an effect on Fritz that his own sister did not recognise him? What must he feel now? As a parent and a Christian he must pity her, but beyond that he can only think that his eldest son is to be tied for life to a sick girl, who may never be able to bear him children. He will have to withdraw his consent. No-one could expect him to do otherwise. And then it will be a matter for poor Fritz, the wretched Fritz, to break the cruel truth – to say: my dearest Philosophy, I regret that my father does not think you fit to share my bed –'

'My mother is waking up,' said Sidonie.

On the stairs there sounded a heavy tread which sent a tremor through the new sash-windows of the best room at the Rose. The Freiherr stood before them, with tears running down his face – to that they were accustomed at prayer-meeting, the tears of true repentance – but he was sobbing with grotesque intakes of air, with hiccoughs, as though choking over a gross mouthful.

'The poor child . . . ough! . . . the poor child . . . so ill . . . ough! . . . and she has nothing . . . '

He leaned – something none of them had ever seen before – against the frame of the door, grasping it with both hands.

'I shall give her Schlöben!'

50

A Dream

Karl pointed out that the father had no power to do anything of the kind. He had inherited Schlöben from his uncle, Friedrich August, in 1768, and it was entailed on Fritz, born four years later. But that did not take away in the least from the generosity of the sacrifice, inspired purely by human compassion, which the Freiherr had wished to make. – The Bernhard thought that it did take away from it a little.

At this time Fritz had a persistent image which hovered at the edge of his dreaming mind. Finally he stood aside to let it in. He was a student once again in Jena, listening to Fichte's lecture on the Self, and it came to him that he should not be doing this, that he was in the wrong place, because he had heard that his friend Hardenberg lived only two hours ride away, at Schlöben. His horse was not a good one, and he did not arrive until it was dark. He knocked at the door, which was opened by a young girl with dark hair. He thought that this might be his friend Hardenberg's wife, but did not like to ask. At Schlöben he lived as a welcome guest for two weeks. When the time came for him to leave, his host accepted his thanks, but told him he must not come again.

Fritz wrote down the incident as it had come to him, one

paragraph only. Since he had to go to Tennstedt, he asked Karoline Just whether he might read it to her.

'This is like past times,' he said, looking round, as though surprised, 'the parlour, the firelight, your uncle and aunt gone to bed, the reading.' Karoline thought, 'He never used to talk in this way. He might be one of the neighbours.' Fritz opened his notebook.

'I must tell you that this is the story of a dream.'

'In that case I can only listen to it on account of our long friendship,' said Karoline. 'You must know that people are only interested in their own dreams.'

'But I have dreamed it more than once.'

'Worse and worse.'

'Justen, you mustn't speak carelessly of dreams,' he told her. 'They are responsible for things such as have not appeared for seven years in philosophy's house of fools.'

While he read aloud she thought, 'Seven years ago I did not know him.'

'Is it worth going on with, Justen?'

'Let me read it through once to myself.' Then she asked, 'What did the young woman look like?'

'That doesn't matter. What matters is that she opened the door.'

The Freiherr's old friends and his colleagues at the Salines, even Coelestin Just, spoke of his gesture – the gift of Schlöben to Sophie von Kühn – as an absurd example of *Herrnhuterei*. About the legal position none of them were quite sure, but 'it is unheard of, uncalled for,' said old Heun. 'Our Lord himself did not do so much. Hardenberg's sons out-at-elbow, the Ober-wiederstadt estate penniless, this is not the time for excessive loving and giving.' Senf pointed out sharply that the Schlöben estate was also penniless.

These things, of course, were not said in the presence of

A Dream

Kreisamtmann Just, but he was well aware of them. Even in
his garden-house melancholy caught him by the sleeve. 'It is
only that you have been spoiled,' said Karoline. 'You have
myself and Rahel, who are fixed in our ways, so that it's hard
to imagine that we could ever change. And when your old
friend behaves in a certain way, so that he seems quite a different
person, you feel that old age itself is approaching 'with silent
step'.

'The truth is,' her uncle told her, 'the truth is, that old
Hardenberg has not changed. Give and take, he has always
been impossible to understand. I call this Hardenbergianismus.
But one must not complain, when a man is listening to messages
from God.' He looked more closely at his niece, and said, 'It
is absurd for you, Karolinchen, to call yourself fixed in your
ways.'

'But, fixed or not, I am always welcome here,' said Karoline,
smiling, 'you always tell me that, are you not going to say it
this time?'

'Tell me what I am to think, Erasmus, Karl, Sidonie,' the
Freifrau asked. 'I do not quite understand what has been proposed. Does Schlöben no longer belong to us?'

'Put your mind at rest,' Erasmus told her. 'Our poor Sophie
is interested only in going back to Grüningen.'

The Freifrau felt relief and at the same time a certain resentment, which only the Bernhard noticed, at what seemed almost
a criticism of Schlöben. Was it possible that the girl did not
want to live there? 'But if your father wishes it,' she said, 'she
must be made to.'

51

Autumn 1796

By September carts were beginning to make their way into Jena from the pine-woods with logs for the coming winter. Branches from the tops of their loads scraped against the windows in the side-streets, which were littered with twigs like a rookery. Manholes opened suddenly in the pavements, and gratefully received the thundering rush of wood. At the same time, pickling had begun, and enormous barrels of vinegar began to trundle down the rungs into the reeking darkness of the cellars. Each house stood prepared according to its capacity, secreting its treasure of vinegar and firewood. The students were back, 'and the whores', said the Mandelsloh. 'They have been trying their luck somewhere else during the vacation, Leipzig or Berlin.' They came back to Jena in modest wagonettes, though not to the streets near the Schaufelgasse. This was a disappointment to Sophie, who would have liked to have a sight of them. The *Fakultät*, also, returned to their houses and issued their announcements for the coming winter months. There were the free public lectures, many more private ones and some *privatissime*, the most expensive of all. Professor Stark was lecturing, *privatissime*, on female disorders.

Fritz, while he was still at Tennstedt, received a letter from the Schaufelgasse in a writing he did not know. From the signature he saw that it was from Leutnant Wilhelm Mandelsloh, the man himself, on leave from the Regiment of Prince Clemens zu Langensalza. His letter was undertaken, he said, at the command of his wife. Sophie herself could not sit comfortably for long at a writing table, and his wife made the excuse that she was busy with women's matters ('They want to give him something to do,' Fritz thought) so they had left it to him to give an account of the patient's health. – In spite of what he had said, Sophie managed to include a note, saying that she was very well, only unfortunately she was sometimes rather ill, and sending a thousand kisses.

At the end of November the Leutnant's leave was up, and he had to return, perhaps with some relief, to Langensalza. He may well have concluded that he was no longer of much importance to his wife's scheme of things.

The Schlegels and their hangers-on did not call at the Schaufelgasse, relying on Dietmahler to keep them posted. He could only say that Sophie's fever came and went, while the incision repeatedly healed up on the outside, then broke out once again and discharged on the inside. Stark prescribed an increased dose of laudanum, which Dietmahler brought round twice a week.

'I wish you good fortune in your future career,' said the Mandelsloh. They would be back in Grüningen by Christmas, and for Sophie's birthday, in March.

'Yes, she will be fifteen in the spring,' Dietmahler told Caroline Schlegel. 'Everything is still to be hoped for, both in mind and body.'

'That I can't see,' replied Caroline. 'Hardenberg can only hope that she will get older, which, it seems, she may well fail to do.'

Dietmahler thought to himself, 'There is no reason why I should stay in Jena, or with these people, or indeed in this country. All I need is a word from someone of importance to recommend me. I might perhaps go to England.' Although Dr Brown was dead, two of his sons, Dietmahler believed, were practising in London. 'As to my mother, I could see to it that she received money regularly, or she could come with me.'

52

Erasmus is of Service

'Fritz, best of brothers,' said Erasmus. 'Let me be of service to you. Until it's decided where my first appointment is to be, I am nothing but an encumberer of the ground. Let me escort your Sophie and the Mandelsloh back to Grüningen.'

It had to be soon, before the winter roads made the journey impossible for an invalid. Already, the Mandelsloh had thought of almost everything necessary. She had hired a closed carriage and seen to it that the horses were roughshod, in case of freezing weather, she had sent the heavy luggage on ahead, called on the wife of Professor Stark and presented her with a farewell present of silver-gilt asparagus knives, given the servants their tips, written a restrained note to the Schlegels and allowed Frau Winkler to weep for half an hour on her shoulder. All that Erasmus had to do was to ride alongside the carriage, a round-faced, unimpressive escort, and to be on duty at each stop. When they got within ten miles of Grüningen, he must press on ahead, to give notice of their arrival. This would be of some, if not very much, use to Sophie. His real motive was one of the strongest known to humanity, the need to torment himself.

The first day they started late, and covered only ten miles. At the Bear at Mellingen Sophie was taken straight up to her room. 'Already she is asleep,' said the Mandelsloh when Erasmus came into the inn parlour from seeing to the baggage. She had engaged the inn-keeper's niece to wait in Sophie's room and call her immediately if she was needed.

At rest for once, she was sitting, between the uneven light and shadow of the candles and the glowing stove above which, in a great arched recess, boots were propped up to dry and dishes were kept warm. The radiance fell across the left side of her serviceable face and turned it into gold, so that to Erasmus for the moment she looked not quite the Mandelsloh.

'The *Abendessen* is ready,' she said. He thought, she is a warrior saint, a strong angel of the battlefield.

'I have been to the kitchen,' she went on. 'Stewed pigs' trotters, plum conserve, bread soup.'

'I cannot eat,' said Erasmus.

'Come, we're Saxons. We can make a good dinner, even if our hearts are breaking.'

Erasmus sighed. 'So far, at least, the journey has not made her any worse.'

'No, not any worse.'

'But the pain –'

'I would bear it for her if I could,' said the Mandelsloh. 'People say that and hardly mean it. I, however, do mean it. But time given to wishing for what can't be is not only spent, but wasted, and for all that we waste we shall be accountable.'

'The years have taught you philosophy.'

To his amazement she smiled and said, 'How old do you think I am?'

He floundered. 'I don't know . . . I have never thought about it.'

'I am twenty-two.'

'But so am I,' he said in dismay.

53

A Visit to Magister Kegel

Hausherr von Rockenthien had not exactly been much loved in Grüningen, but his laugh was missed. Being a man without guile, he continued in the same manner as always, holding out his great arms, embracing his friends, whistling up the dogs to go shooting, but now, as though some mechanism had broken, without laughing.

It was not odd that he should go down into the town to see Magister Kegel. That had always been his way, he was too impatient to summon anyone up to the Schloss and wait until they arrived. What was unusual was that his wife should go with him. Even at this time of anxiety she remained as inactive or, to use a kinder word, as tranquil as ever. Still, the trap was brought round to the frosty front drive and both got in, the springs, on the Hausherr's side, rocking violently, as he took his seat.

'The weather was just like this,' he said, 'when Coelestin Just first brought Hardenberg to our house.'

'I rather think it was snowing,' said Frau Rockenthien.

Magister Kegel, since his retirement, had lived with his books in a small house near the subscription library. He congratulated Rockenthien on the return of his stepdaughters from Jena. Everyone in the district had missed Fräulein Sophie.

He hoped most earnestly that, God willing, her health was on the mend, but he was not at all anxious to come up to Schloss Grüningen.

'All the teaching you have required me to do at your house I have done. I have nothing to reproach myself with, but the results have been uniformly discouraging. Your two youngest have not, so far, been entrusted to me – but, in my view, poor Fräulein Sophie should on no account attempt to study, while she is ill, what was too difficult for her when she was well. I consider it quite inappropriate. It would be a pantomime.'

'It is what she wishes, however,' said Rockenthien.

'To what did she think of applying herself?'

'I think she would like to learn something rather showy,' said Rockenthien eagerly, 'or I had better say noteworthy, to astound her betrothed.'

'I am not the person from whom to acquire anything showy,' said the Magister, looking round at his modest possessions. 'And perhaps I may take the opportunity to say, that I think von Hardenberg has always been far too much indulged in your house.'

'All the young people in my house are indulged,' said Rockenthien miserably. He saw that Kegel was on the verge of refusing absolutely to come. Frau Rockenthien, who had so far said nothing, in fact said nothing now. It was possible that she was scarcely thinking at all. Kegel, however, looked intently at her as she rose from her chair, nodded slightly, and said that unless he heard to the contrary he would call at the Schloss the following Wednesday, 'but I should not wish to interrupt any medical treatment.'

'You need not fear that,' Rockenthien told him, 'Söphgen is now in the charge of Langermann, who prescribes for her nothing but goat's milk.'

Dr Langermann, who had taken over from Dr Ebhard, was a cosy, old-fashioned practitioner who was known to every family of good standing in Grüningen. It was his private opinion that they had been poisoning Fräulein Sophie in Jena. Recovery would come in the spring, when the goat's milk would be at its best.

54

Algebra, Like Laudanum, Deadens Pain

At Weissenfels they talked about the Neutrality Conference which had very nearly been held in the town but in the end, to the dismay of the tradespeople, hadn't been, about the Prussian disasters, about the death of the old whore of Babylon in St Petersburg, and about Hardenberg's Intended. But Fritz himself no longer saw his old friends, not the Brachmanns, not even Frederick Severin. 'You cannot expect him to be good company,' Sidonie told them. 'As soon as he has finished his office work for the day he goes up to his room. You can knock, and knock, but he doesn't answer. He has withdrawn to the kingdom of the mind.' Severin replied that the mind had many kingdoms. 'Fritz is studying algebra,' said Sidonie.

'Algebra, like laudanum, deadens pain,' Fritz wrote. 'But the study of algebra has confirmed for me that philosophy and mathematics, like mathematics and music, speak the same language. That, of course, is not enough. I shall see my way in time. Patience, the key will turn.

'We think we know the laws that govern our existence. We get glimpses, perhaps only once or twice in a lifetime, of a

totally different system at work behind them. One day when I
was reading between Rippach and Lützen, I felt the certainty
of immortality, like the touch of a hand. — When I first went
to the Justs' house in Tennstedt, the house seemed radiant to
me, even the green tablecloth, yes, even the bowl of sugar. —
When I first met Sophie, a quarter of an hour decided me. —
Rahel reproved me, Erasmus reproached me, but they were
wrong, both of them wrong. — In the churchyard at Weissenfels
I saw a boy, not quite grown into a man, standing with his
head bowed in meditation on a green space not yet dug up, a
consoling sight in the half darkness. These were the truly important moments of my life, even though it ends tomorrow.

'As things are, we are the enemies of the world, and
foreigners to this earth. Our grasp of it is a process of estrangement. Through estrangement itself I earn my living from day
to day. I say, this is animate, but that is inanimate. I am a Salt
Inspector, that is rock salt. I go further than this, much further,
and say this is waking, that is a dream, this belongs to the
body, that to the spirit, this belongs to space and distance, that
to time and duration. But space spills over into time, as the
body into the soul, so that the one cannot be measured without
the other. I want to exert myself to find a different kind of
measurement.

'I love Sophie more because she is ill. Illness, helplessness,
is in itself a claim on love. We could not feel love for God
Himself if he did not need our help. — But those who are well,
and have to stand by and do nothing, also need help, perhaps
even more than the sick.'

55

Magister Kegel's Lesson

Sophie's bedroom was crowded: the air was thick as wine.
Noisy, too, with the little ones competing on their highest pitch,
George's voice imitating someone – it was the voice he used
for imitations – the shrieking and rattling of the cage-birds,
witless barking.

'I cannot conduct a class among such disorder,' exclaimed
the Magister, as a servant showed him in. 'Kindly remove the
five dogs, at least, from the room. Where is Frau Leutnant
Mandelsloh?'

'My stepfather begged her to come down and put things
straight in his office,' said George.

'Ah, George. I have not seen you for some time.'

Sophie was lying among shawls on a little day-bed.

'Ach, dear Magister, George was giving – he was giving a
little –'

'He was giving an impersonation of myself. That I could
make out quite well as I approached.'

George, who had been left in charge, a grown boy on Christmas leave from his *Internat*, turned crimson. The cage-birds
sank into resentful twittering.

'Fräulein, I offer you my condolences on all you have gone
through, and must still go through,' said the old man, and

then, turning to the little ones, 'Don't you give a thought to your step-sister? Can't you see that she looks very different now from formerly?'

'We thought so at first,' said Mimi, 'but now we can't remember what she looked like before.'

They are fortunate, thought Kegel.

'Let them stay, they must stay,' Sophie cried. 'Ach, you don't know how dull we were, except just at first, in Jena. And now that I am back home —'

'You do not expect Hardenberg?'

'We can't tell about his coming and going,' said George. 'He is one of the family, he does not need to give us notice.'

The Magister signed to the nursemaid to take Mimi and Rudolf away. He himself put one of the shawls over the birds, still flustered and faintly muttering in their cages. Then he sat down in the chair at the foot of the day-bed, and took out a book.

'Ach, Magister, my old *Fibel*!' shrieked Sophie.

'No, this is for more advanced pupils,' he said. 'These are passages which tell us what the ancient Romans, or some of them, wrote on the subject of friendship.'

'It is so good of you to come . . .' Sophie managed to say. 'I want you to pardon me . . . I couldn't bear to hurt you . . . I am not laughing now, or not nearly so much.'

'My feelings do not matter in the slightest degree. If they did, I should not have become a teacher.'

The Mandelsloh was at the door. 'Did you not know that on no account must Sophie laugh or cry until the wound is healed completely?'

'I swear I did not know that,' cried George in great distress.

'I am sure you did not,' said the Magister.

'I am so foolish,' said Sophie suddenly. 'I am not of much use in this world.'

Rockenthien had blundered in after the Mandelsloh. 'I have

come to hear the lesson,' he called over her shoulder, adapting his voice, as he thought, to the sick room. 'I hope to benefit from it.'

'All who listen will benefit,' said Kegel. 'But half an hour will be sufficient for Fräulein Sophie.'

'That is what I have told them,' said Rockenthien.

'Of whom are you speaking?'

Of all of them, it seemed – everyone he had been able to gather together on the way up from his office – Mimi and Rudi once again, with their nursemaid, a young footman, two orphan girls who had been given work, for charity's sake, in the linen room and whose names nobody knew, the goats'-milk boy, who in ordinary circumstances never came into the house. Some hung back, but the Hausherr generously urged them on, telling them not to lose an opportunity which might come but once. 'I myself am not quite sure what Cicero said about friendship.' Sophie held out her arms to them all. In the racket her laughter and coughing could scarcely be heard. The little dogs, each desperate to be first, bounded back, with flattened ears, onto the bed to lick her face.

The Magister Kegel closed his book. 'After all, these people were born for joy,' he thought.

At the beginning of March 1797 Fritz had ten days official leave, which he spent at Grüningen. He asked Sophie: 'My dearest Philosophy, do you sleep well?'

'Oh, yes. They give me something.'

'The night is a dark power,' he said.

'Oh, I am not afraid of the night.'

On the evening of the 10th of March he said to the Mandelsloh, 'Should I stay here?'

'You must judge of that for yourself.'

'May I see her?'

'No, not now.'

'But later?'

The Mandelsloh, who appeared to have come to some sort of decision, said, 'At the moment, there is no healing. We were told yesterday to keep the wound open.'

'How?'

'With silk thread.'

'And for how long?'

'I don't know for how long.'

He asked once again:

'Should I stay here?' This time he got no answer and he cried out, 'Dear God, why does there have to be a bully like you, a lance-corporal masquerading as a woman, between me and my Söphgen?'

'You would not look at the wound,' said the Mandelsloh, 'but I don't hold that against you.'

'I don't want to hear about the things you don't hold against me. Am I to go or to stay?'

'We have talked about courage before,' the Mandelsloh reminded him.

'We agreed that it couldn't be measured absolutely,' Fritz said. 'The Bernhard was courageous when he ran away from us down to the river. The mother, in her way, was courageous when she met me in the garden –'

'What garden?'

'– Karl was under fire with his regiment at Mainz. And you, too, you were present at the three operations. And my Söphgen –'

'This is not a competition,' said the Mandelsloh. 'Anyway, it is of no use looking back. What can you do for her? That is all you have to ask yourself in this house.'

'If they would allow me to nurse her, although you may not believe me, I could do that,' said Fritz. 'Yes, about that I do know a little.'

'If you stayed here, you would not be wanted as a nurse,'

the Mandelsloh replied. 'You would be wanted as a liar.'

Fritz raised his heavy head.

'What then should I say?'

'God help us, from day to day you would have to say to her – "You look a little better this morning, Söphgen. Yes, I think a little better. Soon you will be able to go out into the garden. Nothing is needed but some warmer weather."'

She spoke the words as players do at a first rehearsal, without emotion. Fritz looked at her with horror.

'And if I could not say that, would you think of me as a coward?'

'My idea of cowardice is very simple,' said the Mandelsloh.

After a moment Fritz cried out, 'I could not lie to her, any more than I could lie to myself.'

'I don't know to what extent a poet lies to himself.'

'She is my spirit's guide. She knows that.'

The Mandelsloh did not answer.

'Shall I stay?'

Still she said nothing, and Fritz went abruptly out of the room. Where will he go? the Mandelsloh wondered. That is so much simpler for a man. If a woman has something that is not easy to decide, where can she go to be alone?

Sophie was disappointed when she heard that Hardenberg had gone back to Weissenfels, but not excessively. Quite often before he had had to leave at a time when she was not well enough to see him. If she was awake, she could listen for the sound of his horse being brought round from the stable-yard to the front of the house, although he no longer rode the Gaul, whose dragging steps she had always been able to recognise. Sometimes he would be on the point of leaving and then dismount and run back again across the hall, up the two staircases which were nothing to him, into her room to say to her once again, 'Sophie, you are my heart's heart.'

This evening that was not the case, and he did not come back.

Three hours and three quarters to Weissenfels, with a stop at Freyburg. Outside Weissenfels the vegetable plots lay bare, except for the stalks of the winter cabbage, in the moonlight. The town gates were shut. Fritz paid the fine which was collected from latecomers, and rode slowly down to his father's house.

It was the first week in Lent, and only a few lights shone in the windows of the Kloster Gasse. At the house, his father and mother were already in bed. Erasmus was the only one of the family still up.

'I could not stay –' Fritz told him.

'Best of brothers –'

Afterword

Sophie died at half-past ten in the morning on the 19th of March, two days after her fifteenth birthday. Fritz, at Weissenfels, got the news two days later. Karoline Just also received a letter from one of Sophie's elder sisters, which described how the poor girl, 'in her fantasy', had kept thinking she heard the sound of horses' hooves.

Fritz did not become well-known as a writer until after Sophie's death. In the February of 1798, he told his friends that in future he would write under an old family name, Novalis, meaning 'clearer of new land'. As Novalis he published his *Hymns to the Night* and worked on a number of projects, some finished, some left in fragments. The story of the Blue Flower, now called *Heinrich von Ofterdingen*, was never finished.

In December 1798, Fritz became engaged to Julie, the daughter of Councillor Johann Friedrich von Charpentier, Professor of Mathematics at the Mining Academy of Freiberg. She was twenty-two years old. He was now doing well in the Salt Mine Directorate and had been appointed Supernumerary Magistrate in the District of Thuringia. To Friedrich Schlegel he wrote that a very interesting life appeared to await him. 'Still,' he added, 'I would rather be dead.'

At the end of the 1790s the young Hardenbergs, in their turn, began to go down, almost without protest, with pulmonary tuberculosis. Erasmus, who had insisted that he coughed blood only because he laughed too much, died on Good Friday, 1797. Sidonie lasted until the age of twenty-two. At the beginning of 1801 Fritz, who had been showing the same symptoms, went back to his parents' house in Weissenfels. As he lay dying he asked Karl to play the piano for him. When Friedrich Schlegel arrived Fritz told him that he had entirely changed his plan for the story of the Blue Flower.

The Bernhard was drowned in the Saale on the 28th of November 1800.

George was killed as First Lieutenant at the Battle of Smolensk in 1812.

A year after Fritz's death, Karoline Just was married to her cousin, Carl August.

The Mandelsloh was divorced from her husband in 1800 and married a General von Bose. She lived to be seventy-five.

Fritz's gold ring with its inscription 'Sophie be my Guardian Spirit' is in the Municipal Museum at Weissenfels.